HESITANT HEROES

SHARON RENE

Cathy!
I hope you enjoy my book!
Sharon René

2 Corinthians 12:9

HESITANT HEROES

ANAIAH EPIC
An imprint of ANAIAH PRESS, LLC.
7780 49th ST N. #129
Pinellas Park, FL 33781

First Anaiah Epic eBook edition September 2021

Edited by Kara Leigh Miller

Books that Inspire!

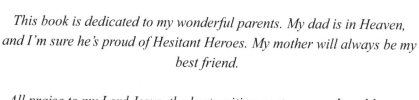

This book is dedicated to my wonderful parents. My dad is in Heaven, and I'm sure he's proud of Hesitant Heroes. My mother will always be my best friend.

All praise to my Lord Jesus, the best writing partner ever. I could never write a word without Him.

CHAPTER 1

*G*LOBAL COLLECTIVE UNIVERSITY
EUROPEAN COLLECTIVE — SEPTEMBER 13, 2062

JORDAN SCOTT PUSHED through the door of the centuries-old mudroom. She slammed her gear down and took a seat on one of the wooden benches lining the drab stone walls.

What a loser. I got killed in my first mock battle.

The rest of Team Seven streamed in behind her. A few claimed benches and started removing their boots, while others returned their power-play rifles to the gun rack.

She managed a tired smile as Matthew Taylor knelt beside her. He glanced around, then leaned close. "On the ride back from the mountains, Dorm Master Flynt told me Paul Hobbs left school. He's gone home to the Pacific Collective."

Jordan pressed her hand against her throbbing temples, trying to calm the tumble of thoughts bouncing in her brain.

Matthew blinked and brushed a strand of brown hair back from his forehead. Most of the time she enjoyed staring into his ocean-blue eyes

1

and dreaming that he was her boyfriend, but not now. Now, fear flickered in the blue depths.

Had Global Collective University discovered their secret Bible study group? Perhaps Paul had been sent home because he was their leader.

"Why would Paul leave GCU? He's the best computer master here. His grades are phenomenal." Jordan glanced around the windowless room. Did the other students know Paul had left?

Matthew drummed his fingers on his bent knee, his nails black with dirt. "This morning Mr. Flynt told the boys that Paul got sick in the middle of the night and went to the infirmary. They decided he was too sick to treat here, so they sent him home."

She chewed her bottom lip while sweat tickled its way down her back. The claustrophobic room enveloped her, the low ceiling hovering near like a thundercloud. Paul wasn't the first Christian student to abruptly leave Global Collective University over the last few months. This couldn't be a coincidence.

She grabbed Matthew's shoulder and leaned close enough to whisper, "Do you think we're in trouble because of...?"

Matthew's shoulder flinched beneath her grip. "We've been careful. Let's not panic yet."

Jordan's head ached with memories of being recruited to attend GCU, along with other gifted teens from each collective on the planet. She'd hated leaving Old Memphis and moving to the secular European Collective, but could anyone say no to the Global Collective Council? At GCU she'd been content to keep her faith to herself and worship in private until she met Paul Hobbs. *Oh, Paul, what happened to you?*

"You and me and Timberlyn need to talk," Matthew whispered in her ear, his breath warm against her neck. "Wait until the others head inside." He stood and rolled his shoulders, his head almost touching the ceiling crossbeam.

"It doesn't make sense. Why send Paul home?" Jordan brushed her cheek and dried mud crumbled between her fingers. "The medical technology here is a lot better than anything they have in Old Australia. I played cards with Paul last night, and he never complained about feeling bad. He wasn't his normally upbeat self, though."

Rafael Alvarado plopped down next to her. He stretched his long legs across the grey slate floor and used the arm of this T-shirt to wipe sweat from his tanned face.

"Sometimes people get sick fast. In the Latin Collective, deadly plagues would hit overnight." He massaged the long red streak on his pant leg and groaned. "Mercy. I can't believe those laser beams hurt so much."

Jordan ran her hand around her side, wincing at the pain spreading across her ribs. Dirt and crimson goo clung to her fingers. Leave it to this strange school, a mixture of classical studies and military training, to make pretend combat seem real. She'd been prepared for the oozing fake blood that spurted from their specially designed fatigues but not for the painful electrical shock that had brought her to her knees.

Her roommate, Hannie Jacobson, sat on the bench across from her. Getting out of her combat gear seemed to be her only concern.

"Hannie, I still can't believe you shot me." Jordan stuck out her tongue. "What kind of friend are you?"

"The best." Hannie grinned. "You got to sleep through the rest of the mock battle, didn't you?" Hannie kicked off one muddy boot and leveled a challenging stare at Rafael. "Of course, since I'm such an excellent soldier and never got shot, I wouldn't know how much it hurt. I'll have to take Rafael's word for it."

"Yeah, yeah, listen to the wannabe Israeli soldier sitting over there." Rafael reached over and pulled Jordan's ponytail. "Copper-top, you certainly made a pretty corpse stretched out on the battlefield."

She bowed her head, her face growing hot as she removed one heavy sock. There was nothing pretty about these auburn locks that frizzed at the threat of rain, or her tall, skinny body.

Rafael grabbed his jumbled backpack and headed to the opposite end of the narrow room where ten silver lockers stood against the wall. Dawson Montgomery and two other team members shoved their gear into the lockers.

Jordan popped open the clips on her camouflage vest, relishing this first touch of freedom. Loud voices sounded. She jumped and craned her neck. What now? She'd endured a rigorous mock battle, gotten shot, and learned that Paul Hobbs had left school. This day had been bad enough already.

Rafael knelt in front of a bottom locker. Dawson Montgomery slammed a top locker shut and stepped closer to Rafael.

"GCU is going to determine our destinies, and you think today's contest was only a game." Dawson flailed his arms. "I'll never win on a team with a computer geek who gets herself killed in the first five minutes, and Matthew, the North American super-jock who can't shoot straight."

Jordan blushed. Just like middle school. The last one picked for any team. Lousy at every sport.

Dawson's face blazed red. "The Israeli chick is the only one who knows how to fight."

Rafael stood. "What's wrong with you, *amigo*?" His Hispanic accent grew thicker with each word. "Calm down."

Jordan took a deep breath of dank air. The tension of the brewing battle filled the tight space. She broke free of her heavy vest and dropped it on the floor. Matthew pulled her up beside him, while Hannie jumped on the opposite bench and pressed herself against the wall.

Dawson waved his arm in front of Rafael's face, the Global Collective snow leopard tattoo jumping on his bicep. "And you—you're supposed to be an award-winning sharpshooter. You're nothing but a swaggering lover boy."

Rafael lifted his chin, an odd grin flickering against his swarthy complexion, then shoved Dawson across the room. Matthew jerked Jordan out of the way as Dawson landed beside them. Dawson grunted and jumped up, swinging at his opponent. Rafael dodged each blow then countered with a left hook to Dawson's jaw. Dawson swayed before recovering and throwing another punch. Rafael side-stepped and danced around like a professional boxer.

A loud thud shook the room as the door flew open, banging against one of the benches. Jordan spun around. The adult leaders, Cimarron and Mr. Flynt, stepped into the mudroom.

"Stop this fighting immediately," Cimarron ordered, her ever-present computer book in hand. She was old enough to be Jordan's mother, yet there didn't appear to be a maternal cell anywhere in Cimarron's perfectly sculpted body. The woman noted every move the students made and scored them accordingly. She probably graded them on how well they brushed their teeth.

Rafael clutched a handful of Dawson's shirt, his arm cocked back for another punch. Blood dripped from Dawson's lips and nose, but he hadn't yet landed a blow on his opponent. Mr. Flynt pushed past Matthew and Jordan then grabbed Rafael's fist.

"Stop this now." The man inserted his pudgy form between the battling boys. "Let go of him, Rafael."

Rafael clenched his jaw. He growled then let out a deep breath. He released Dawson's shirt, turned to Jordan, and winked.

That boy could flirt on his deathbed.

Dawson stepped around Mr. Flynt and lunged, shoving Rafael to his hands and knees. Rafael sprang to his feet, ready for more, but Mr. Flynt jumped between them. "No more fighting. It's over."

Dawson reached over Mr. Flynt's shoulder, grasping for Rafael. "Let me at him. I want to finish him off."

Mr. Flynt held him back. "Do you want to be expelled? Cimarron is reporting every move you make. GCU will not tolerate this behavior. No matter who your parents are."

Dawson's hostile gaze shifted from Rafael to Mr. Flynt. His posture relaxed, and he took a step back.

European Collective students believed GCU would launch them into important government careers. The rest of the students understood that after graduation they'd be sent back to their collectives to deal with the same poverty, violence, and disease they'd left behind, although they would become administrators, judges and enforcement officials, all stamped with the Global Council's seal of approval.

"I can understand Rafael behaving like a hoodlum," Mr. Flynt said. "But I thought you had more sense."

Dawson scuffed his boot against the dirty floor. "You're right. For a moment, I forgot who I am. A Montgomery and a scientist." Brushing his dark blond hair away from his face, Dawson stepped toward Cimarron. "I'm sorry for letting Rafael push me to the breaking point. It won't happen again."

"It better not." Cimarron snapped her computer book shut, the sound bouncing through the cavernous room. "My warning is for all of you."

She glared at each student. How could someone so beautiful look so menacing?

"I will not allow my team members to behave like wild animals. You're here to prove that you're worthy of representing the Global Collective Council all over the planet."

Matthew cleared his throat, and Rafael stared at the ceiling, while Jordan shifted from one foot to the other. Not even Hannie spoke out as Cimarron's usually icy composure melted. The woman took a deep breath and tugged on the golden chain around her neck.

"I'll have every one of you expelled and sent home in disgrace before I allow you to destroy my reputation, or damage me in front of the Global Council. I suggest that each one of you follow all rules and show proper decorum from this moment on."

Cimarron stalked back into the house with Mr. Flynt following. The rest of the students quietly headed inside. Matthew nodded at Jordan then grabbed Timberlyn's arm as she walked by.

The door closed behind the last student, and Matthew motioned to the benches. Timberlyn's brown eyes grew wide, and her full lips twisted into a frown. Her short, tight curls were held back with a decorative African headband that accentuated her chiseled face. They all plopped down on the metal benches.

Jordan had never met anyone like Timberlyn. She could pick up a wild rabbit and cuddle it. Last week, a lark lit on Timberlyn's shoulder. This ability to tame animals and heal with herbs was fascinating. At fifteen, the girl possessed uncanny knowledge.

Matthew folded his arms across his chest, causing his biceps to press against his sweaty T-shirt. Jordan's nerves sparked like static electricity, but Matthew's presence both soothed and excited her.

No matter what Hannie believed, Matthew was not her boyfriend. But she had a humongous crush on him. What girl wouldn't be attracted to six feet of lean muscle, brown wavy hair, blue eyes, and a crooked smile? They enjoyed spending time together and joked about their younger siblings. Matthew's voice had cracked when he told her that his mother died when he was twelve, leaving him with a drunken father and two kid sisters. Jordan had never felt this comfortable with any boy, but romantic relationships were forbidden at GCU.

Matthew cleared his throat and patted Timberlyn's shoulder. "Paul Hobbs was sent home last night. Mr. Flynt says he was sick."

"One of the girls told me." Timberlyn spoke barely above a whisper. "Do you think this has to do with our Bible study group?"

Jordan clasped her dirty hands together as her pulse raced. "I don't think Paul was sick enough to go home. Something strange is happening around here."

Matthew nodded. "Paul told me that six weeks ago, when the individual teams were being formed, the school's database of students crashed. Paul volunteered to help Mr. Price get it up and running. He discovered that each student's religious affiliation, if they had one, was listed by their names. That was how Paul knew the three of us were Christians."

"It's scary to think they list that type of information about us." Timberlyn's voice shook. "In the African Collective, I've seen religious people of all types beaten, starved, even killed. My grandmother had the healing gift. She taught me how to use nature's resources to help the sick and injured. We were needed in the village, so most people left us alone."

Jordan scooted back in her seat, her shoulder striking the solid wall. "Physical persecution is rare in the North American Collective. Religious people in general are discriminated against when it comes to jobs, salaries, and promotions though."

Her gaze traveled over the closed lockers to the solid floor beneath their feet. This mudroom had stood here watching year after year pass by. How many secrets did it hold?

Matthew shifted in his seat. "Yesterday, Paul told me he'd hacked into the GCU main computer system. He was worried that the school was classifying kids by religion." His voice cracked, and a muscle jumped in his tight, square jaw. "Paul didn't tell me what he found, but he said something odd was going on. And now he's been sent home. It's hard to believe this is a coincidence."

Jordan rubbed her eyes. Memories she'd tried to deny for the last two months attacked her. "When I lived in the North American section, before being put on Team Seven, I shared a room with a girl named Zoe. I've never told anyone about this, but..."

Matthew leaned forward and rested his elbows on his knees. "You can tell us. I think we've proven we can keep secrets over these last six weeks of undercover Bible study."

Warmth settled in Jordan's chest then spread to her toes. *How does he do this to me?*

"Late one night, I heard strange sounds in our room, like people arguing. I recognized Zoe's voice, but I didn't recognize the other voice. I tried to get up but couldn't lift my head. I must have been drugged." She stopped and swallowed the lump in her throat. "The next day, Zoe was gone. I asked our dorm master about Zoe. She said Zoe left because of a family emergency, and I must've had a bad dream."

"You didn't believe her?" Matthew asked.

"I guess I did, for a while, but it doesn't make sense. They barely let us communicate with the outside world. Why would GCU care about Zoe's family? And Zoe was a very vocal Christian like Paul." Her voice sharpened with each word. *Breathe in, breathe out, in and out.* The stale scent of sweat tickled her nose. "I'm frightened now that both Zoe and Paul have disappeared. We should do something, but I don't know what."

Matthew rubbed his forehead. "Let's look at this logically. Maybe Paul did get sick suddenly. It can happen. And Zoe may have gone home for family reasons."

"That's possible," Timberlyn said. "When I roomed in the African

Collective dorm, several students left during the first three months. Um, I don't think any of them were believers."

Jordan's mind raced. "A couple of girls from the North American Collective went home, and they weren't religious."

"Let's take it one step at a time, like climbing a mountain," Matthew said. "Why would this school, or any school, want to get rid of Christians? To quote what Cimarron has said many times, 'we're here to learn to work with all types of people, appreciate our cultural differences, and form a new society.' That doesn't sound sinister, does it?"

Jordan nodded and massaged the back of her neck. Matthew's words made sense. He reminded her of her dad, calm and levelheaded. She wanted to believe they were safe, but two of her friends had disappeared. That couldn't be a coincidence.

Jordan pulled her legs up and wrapped her arms around her knees. "We have to find out if something strange is going on around here and help Paul and Zoe if they're in danger."

"I agree." Matthew nodded. "Maybe Paul will manage to send an email and let us know he's okay back in Old Australia, but until he does... well, I'm going to do a little investigating. Maybe ask Dawson a few questions, since he was Paul's roommate." He glanced at the door leading to the house then stood. "I'm heading in. I really need a shower."

"Do you think it's safe to continue our Bible study every Sunday morning?" Jordan asked.

Matthew bowed his head and shuffled his feet, the soles of his sneakers squeaking on the surface. "We realized the Bible study was risky, even before Paul left. I think we should continue, but we need to be extra careful." He looked from Jordan to Timberlyn.

"Um, I want to continue the Bible study." Timberlyn tugged on a curl that had escaped from beneath her headband. "I feel close to my family in the African Collective because I know they're worshiping in secret, too."

Jordan nodded. Six weeks ago, she'd have voted to disband, but she needed this unique fellowship with her friends as they prayed and studied God's Word. Now more than ever.

Matthew nodded then headed inside. Timberlyn soon followed. Jordan jumped to her feet, but her shaky legs wouldn't support her. She tumbled back to the bench. *I'm more frightened than I thought.*

"Oh Lord, I have my nerve to ask You for anything when I'm hiding my belief in You," she whispered. "But, I'm not a super saint. I'm only sixteen, and I'm really scared. Jesus, please help us find out what happened to Paul and Zoe, and please don't let me lose another friend."

CHAPTER 2

The next morning, Jordan sat in the computer lab trying to concentrate on her latest project. As part of the innovative learning system at GCU each of the students taught their unique skills and talents to their team members. From Rafael's marksmanship to Matthew's mountain-climbing to martial arts and party planning, Team Seven had all the bases covered. Of course, no one partied in Old Memphis, and mountain-climbing was an impossibility in the delta.

Jordan loved the computer classes. The European Collective boasted the most advanced technology, and the computer classes were taught by the best adult computer masters on the planet.

Fear over Paul's disappearance shot darts at Jordan's brain, and she struggled over the simplest computer problem. Tension finally forced her to stand and stretch her achy shoulders. The other students had left. On the far wall, 11:40 A.M. flashed in red three-dimensional numbers. Plenty of time to grab a bite to eat and get to martial arts class by one.

As she grabbed her purse from the back of her chair, she spied Paul Hobbs's empty desk in the corner of the room. His computer was missing, but had they taken his computer book, too? Sometimes he left it in his desk drawer.

She scanned the room before creeping toward Paul's desk. Touching the drawer with one finger, she pulled it open. The small computer blinked at her, snuggled safely among papers and candy bar wrappers. Matthew said Paul hacked the mainframe and discovered some "odd information." Would Paul have transferred the information to his computer book?

Jordan reached for the computer and flipped it open then stopped. She couldn't do this. What would she say if the instructor walked in and found her? She was a terrible liar, and she couldn't think of an explanation that would satisfy Mr. Price.

She'd be expelled and sent home, her reputation ruined. No more computer-programming awards. Her family needed those cash gifts. She closed the computer and shoved it back in the drawer. She had to eat and get to karate class. She couldn't play detective now. She turned to leave, but her legs refused to carry her from the room. This device could hold a clue to Paul's abrupt departure. *I failed Zoe. I won't abandon Paul.*

She glanced around the room one more time, pulled out the desk chair, and took a seat. She grabbed the book, opened it, and stared at the blank screen. Paul had told her his password was *Lion of Judah.*

She whispered a silent prayer and keyed in Paul's code then waited while the computer screen flashed. She fingered the screen to pull up documents and started scrolling through the pages. Each student had been assigned individual projects, so most of the data didn't interest her. Tapping her foot on the floor, she continued to scroll, listening to the melodic hum of the mechanical brain. Suddenly, a strange list of names covered the screen.

The Chosen Ones for GCU Project SS:
Rachel Rivera, Latin Collective
Joseph Martinez, Latin Collective
Kathryn Garcia, Latin Collective
Omar Boxley, African Collective
Zoe Pirella, North American Collective

Zoe. Jordan tightened her grip on the computer book. Her buried fears about Zoe's mysterious departure blazed. The chosen ones? Chosen for what? This list didn't make any sense. She blinked, unable to focus on the next name because of the moisture flooding her eyes.

No! The silent scream filled her lungs, and she fell back against the padded chair. This couldn't be true. At the bottom of the list, she read the name that turned her stomach. Jordan Scott, North American Collective. A notation followed.

Jordan comes from a family of believers, which is problematic, but she's extremely gifted. I think it advisable to wait awhile before pulling her out. She's a naive girl, eager to please her teachers and follow all the rules, so she may not be a problem. Cimarron had signed the note.

Jordan's stomach clenched, and the room spun. She hit the button to shut down the contraption, shoved it back into the drawer, and jumped up. The chair wobbled before righting itself.

Pull her out? Was she destined to disappear along with Paul and Zoe? She wrapped her arms around her waist, struggling to keep her breakfast down. Her head pounded. She had to get back to the dorm and tell Matthew about this list. He'd know what to do. She rushed toward the door.

Footsteps sounded outside. Clip, clop, clip, clop drew closer and closer. Jordan glanced around. No way out.

Mr. Price's large antique desk claimed the far end of the room. She ran to it and crawled into the space underneath the mahogany structure. Voices entered the room as she pulled her legs up to her chin.

"Paul's desk is over here." A woman spoke in crisp, clipped syllables.

Cimarron? She was not a computer master. Why had she come to the computer lab the day after Paul Hobbs went missing? Jordan chewed her bottom lip, and her eyes watered. If only she could forget the words she'd read a few minutes ago, right before she had to scamper under the desk. Ominous words. Words indicating that Cimarron had engineered Paul's disappearance.

Paul's desk drawer squeaked, and Jordan cringed. "See, safe and sound," Cimarron said. "I told you we'd find his computer book."

A man cleared his throat. "You were right. Thankfully."

Jordan had sat through enough boring assemblies to recognize

Principal Reed's mundane voice. "I can't believe the guard didn't search Paul's desk."

I can't believe I'm hiding from my school principal and dorm master. She pinched her shaky knees tighter and pressed her sweaty forehead against her jeans.

"Do you think someone's been fooling around this desk?" The chair's legs scratched the floor, and Jordan's stomach rolled. She should have straightened the chair before dashing away from the desk. How could she be so stupid?

"Bentley, you have to stop this incessant worrying before your paranoia rubs off on me. Teenagers make a mess everywhere they go. I know. I share a house with ten of them."

"Maybe we should look around, just the same."

Jordan tried to squeeze herself into a tiny ball. She closed her eyes like a toddler who believed the adults couldn't see her if she couldn't see them.

"The kids probably charged out of here when class ended and knocked the chair askew. I don't think we need to be concerned." Cimarron spoke in a soothing tone. A tone she never used with her students.

"I can't help worrying. Paul could've caused a lot of trouble for us."

"Paul was too intelligent for his own good." The woman's voice rose an octave. "I doubt any of the other students would be capable of hacking the school's computer system."

"You're probably right. That boy is smart. He'll make a great addition to our little group."

Jordan stared at a fat wad of dust wrapped around the desk's wooden leg, every bit as trapped as she was. She willed her heartbeat to slow, but the rebellious organ wanted to jump from her chest.

"Everything will work as planned." Cimarron's husky voice purred the words. "The Global Council will be pleased."

Principal Reed cleared his throat again. "You're the most beautiful woman I've ever seen."

Jordan's jaw dropped. Principal Reed was a married man, even if his wife spent six months every year in Old Paris, officially GC Area 1, Sector 1. The campus gossips claimed that he'd gotten this cushy job here in the beautiful Alps because of his wife's political connections.

Groans, the sounds of shuffling feet and passionate kisses filled the classroom. Jordan took a deep breath of stale air and pressed her hands to her ears. *I might throw up.*

A fat spider crawled across the wooden floor, heading directly toward her. She clapped her hands over her mouth and fought back a scream. She scrunched back farther, bumping her head against the top of the desk, the thud echoing in her ears. Holding her breath, she waited for the adults to charge across the floor and drag her from her cramped hiding place.

Instead, Principal Reed moaned, and the kissing continued. Thankfully, they were too preoccupied to notice anything else. The hairy spider stopped and spun around. Jordan bit down on her fingers.

Get a hold of yourself, Jordan. That spider is the least of your worries. The creature paused then changed direction and scurried away. She released a silent sigh, rubbing her damp palms on her jeans.

Trapped in the dusty space, her thoughts drifted to the last major riot in Old Memphis. Mom had shoved her, TJ, and their baby sister into a tiny closet. Jordan had clutched baby Abby and prayed she wouldn't squeal. Her dad and three-year-old Kevin had been outside playing ball and got caught in the growing riot. She could still hear the blast and smell the smoke of the pipe bomb that stole the bottom half of Kevin's left leg.

That terrible day filled her nightmares. Now she was hiding again, but this time she was all alone. *Oh, God,* she prayed without sound. *You protected me years ago. Please protect me now.*

"That's enough, Bentley." Cimarron's voice broke through the passionate kissing sounds. "I have to get to martial arts class by one. We don't want anyone searching for the two of us."

Principal Reed grumbled but agreed. They kissed once more before the man's heavy steps mingled with Cimarron's clicking heels. The squeaky metal door banged shut, and Jordan jumped.

She placed her palms on the cold floor and pushed herself out from under the desk. What if they came back? She slid back into her hiding place, then watched the time click off on her wristwatch. After five agonizing minutes, she scampered out, shook her legs to restore the blood flow, then hurried out of the computer lab.

Folding her arms over her chest, she strode across campus, glancing over her shoulder every few minutes. Her stomach flinched at the aroma of vegetable soup and the medicinal smell of high-protein speed lunches when she passed the lunch stops.

A couple of younger girls wearing Baltic Collective sweaters trailed behind her, laughing and chattering. Several boys ran past her. Had they seen her leave the classroom? Were they rushing to report her to Principal Reed? Yesterday she wouldn't have noticed these kids; today they terrified her.

Paul, Zoe, and the other students on the list had not left campus willingly. She shivered in the afternoon chill. *The Chosen Ones for GCU Project SS.* What did that mean? The list haunted her. The list with her name on it.

CHAPTER 3

*J*ordan stepped into the crowded gym and searched for her teammates. The schedule glowed in green lights by the entrance and showed karate class on the opposite side of the gym. A group of students played basketball on this end, and the dribble of the ball and pounding of feet matched the pounding of her heart as she hurried past them.

So different from her school in Old Memphis. No cracks in the floor, bullet holes in the walls, or ragged equipment. TJ would hoot, holler, and run laps if he could see that basketball hoop and all of the fully inflated balls waiting to be slam-dunked.

She'd searched for Matthew during the walk from the computer lab, hoping to spot him at a lunch stop or the computer store. What would he say when she told him about the list? She'd love to run away, with or without him, but... escape in the middle of the European Collective would be impossible. He might say this was her problem—not his. She wouldn't blame him. Before she'd seen that list, she'd been excited about today's karate class. Now, she just wanted the minutes to scurry by so she could talk to Matthew.

"Jordan, over here." Hannie's demanding voice rang out over the hum of activity.

Jordan exhaled loudly. Matthew sat on the bleacher behind Hannie. Victor Petro, youth weight-lifting champion from the Baltic Collective, sat beside him. No one would ever consider Matthew small, but Team Seven's version of Goliath dwarfed him.

She wove her way through a small group of students doing push-ups and past a couple of boys entangled in a wrestling match, the smell of salty sweat stinging her nose and bringing tears to her eyes.

Hannie patted the bleacher. "Where've you been?" The girl virtually ignored the other members of Team Seven, and her abrasive personality intimidated most people, but Jordan liked her.

"We were getting worried about you," Matthew said. Timberlyn sat beside him and nodded.

Jordan glanced at her watch. "I'm not late, y'all. I'm right on time."

"Yes," Hannie said, "but for a goody-goody like you that's as good as late."

Jordan laughed despite her fears. "Very funny."

She glanced at the two lower bleachers occupied by the rest of Team Seven. In typical fashion, Dawson sat beside Laurel Connor. Romance might be a no-no around here, but those two pushed the limits. Her gaze traveled from Rafael on the other bleacher to the man who sat beside him. No! Not him.

Principal Reed sat talking with Team Seven's class clown. A typical cocky grin lit Rafael's face. Principal Reed ran his fingers through his rumpled gray hair and laughed at something Rafael said. The man had never joined them for a class before. Was he here to pull her out? Jordan's heart pounded her ribs. She couldn't disappear before she told Matthew about the list.

"Everyone, pay attention please." Cimarron stood in front of the bleachers, her plastic face and figure a stark contrast to the gym shorts and T-shirt she wore. She'd removed her high heels and replaced them with athletic shoes. She appeared calm and relaxed, but the tattoo of stars encircling her neck seemed almost wicked.

"Principal Reed decided to join us for martial arts class today." She motioned toward the unwanted guest. "He's very excited to see what Malese can do."

Cimarron sat, and Malese stood. She wore a black karate uniform tied with a striped black belt. Her waist-length raven hair was pulled back in a tight bun and bound with a red sash. She looked even smaller than usual draped in the heavy fabric, yet the uniform seemed to empower her. A basketball bounced behind her followed by a shouting boy, but Malese focused straight ahead. She didn't appear to notice the din of voices echoing around the gym or seem flustered by the principal's presence.

Jordan forced herself to watch Malese instead of staring at Principal Reed. This could be a coincidence. Perhaps he wanted to spend more time with Cimarron. They were a friendly pair after all. She blew her bangs off her forehead. Surely, if he knew she'd overheard him and Cimarron in the computer lab, he would have sent a guard after her by now.

"I'm going to perform an advanced kata," Malese said then began dancing through an intricate sequence of movements, her arms slicing the air like swords.

Jordan stared, unable to move her gaze from the lovely vision. She didn't know a lot about Malese, other than the fact that she came from a small island in the Pacific Collective. The girl's skill and strength amazed Jordan.

"Kiai!" Malese roared the karate yell. Jordan jumped, and Timberlyn squealed. What a powerful dance. When she shouted her final *kiai* and bowed, everyone clapped.

Hannie slapped her knee and whistled. "That was great."

Malese smiled. "Thank you."

"It was cool, but fighting is what I'm interested in." Rafael stood and stretched his back. "That's more like dancing. Not that I'm opposed to dancing." He glanced over his shoulder and flashed a flirty smile at Jordan.

Her cheeks burned. Last week in Laurel's dance class, Jordan had been paired with Rafael. Her insides had trembled, and her face heated when he held her. This reaction had shocked her since she never thought of Rafael in a romantic way. Had he noticed her reaction? Did he think she was interested in him?

Cimarron and Mr. Flynt rarely responded to Rafael's snarky comments, but Hannie could never resist the opportunity. "Why don't you keep your mouth shut, Rafael? She's the martial arts champ, not you."

"I don't think the champ needs you to fight her battles, *mi tigresa*," Rafael said then emitted a low growl.

Hannie started to rise, always ready for a scuffle, but Jordan put her hand on her arm. Hannie eyed her, relaxed, and settled back on the bleachers.

"I hate to agree with Rafael about anything," Dawson spoke through a busted lip, his face showing the bruises of yesterday's battle. "But really, Malese, what does that have to do with fighting?"

Jordan twirled one of her wayward curls around her finger. Shouldn't Dawson have had his fill of battle? Perhaps he wanted to learn about fighting from the champ. He could certainly use some lessons.

Malese nodded, her shoulders straight. "I'm about to show you what the kata has to do with fighting." She stepped on a thick blue pad stretched out on the gym floor. "Rafael, would you help me demonstrate?"

"Sure, baby doll, I'd be glad to." Rafael swaggered over to the pad.

"I'm going to explain the elements of the kata and how it's used in a fight. Rafael will be my opponent."

Malese bowed to Rafael. He returned the bow then turned to the audience and pumped his arm in the air like a victorious boxer. Jordan wished she could wipe that smug expression off his face, but she had a sneaking suspicion Malese was about to do just that.

"Attack me," Malese said.

Rafael pounced, but before he could reach the girl, she'd kicked and punched him halfway across the mat.

"Way to go, Malese!" Matthew clapped and jumped to his feet.

Rafael blushed and shook his head. He might be a champ in a fist fight, but apparently, he'd met a fighter he couldn't best.

"Those were movements from the kata," Malese explained. "Try to strangle me."

Rafael gripped the girl's delicate throat. In seconds, she'd broken his hold, stepped back, and kicked him in the stomach. He staggered back, clutching his gut, but the playful look on his face showed he wasn't injured.

"The katas are a way to practice fighting skills. They may look like a dance, but they're much deadlier."

"I like them because they do resemble a dance." Laurel brushed her hand through her perfectly smooth hair. "I bet I'll be good at them."

Spoken like an award-winning ballerina. A spark of jealousy flickered in Jordan's heart. Matthew smiled and blushed more when Laurel was around, and he always made a point to talk with the lovely blonde at breakfast.

Sorry, Lord, I know I shouldn't envy Laurel, but why does she have to be so perfect? Of course, a good deal of Laurel's perfection came from the European Collective beauty enhancers. *Bless her heart.*

"Yes, Laurel," Malese said. "I think you will be good at the katas. But that's only part of what I'll teach you in these classes."

Malese moved toward Rafael with measured steps. He jumped back, but in one swift move, she grabbed his arm and doubled him over. "Now, if I wanted to, I could break his arm."

"Do it," Dawson prodded.

"Of course, I don't want to hurt Rafael," Malese said without breaking her hold on her opponent.

Despite his helpless position, Rafael glared at Dawson. Malese released Rafael. Red-faced, he swayed on his feet.

"And, of course, you will all want to know how to throw someone over your back."

Rafael jumped back, holding his hands in front of him. "Haven't I been the victim long enough? Let someone else have some fun. Dawson, what about you? He deserves it more than I do."

Malese laughed. "You've been a good sport, Rafael. Now everyone on your feet, and I'll teach you a simple kata today. Next week, I'll teach you how to throw someone over your back."

They all jumped off the bleachers to join Malese, the clank of the metal blending with the dull gym roar.

Jordan grabbed Matthew's sleeve. "I need to talk to you. It's really important."

He opened his mouth but snapped it shut again, no doubt confused by the fear on her face, then took her arm and directed her toward the locker rooms.

"Jordan." Principal Reed's voice sounded from behind them, halting their getaway. "Could I speak with you?"

Jordan looked up at Matthew. She pressed her hand to her throat, the rapid pounding of her pulse slamming against her fingers. "I'll talk to you later at the dorm."

Matthew raised his brows. Could he hear the tremor in her voice? She had to face Principal Reed alone. She couldn't do anything to put Matthew in danger. He hesitated a moment, so she motioned to the students now forming a line behind Malese. Matthew glanced from Principal Reed to Jordan. She gave him a slight smile. He nodded and hurried to join the others.

Jordan turned around. Time to face the enemy.

Principal Reed walked toward her, and she stared at the floor. He wore sneakers with his suit. How silly that she'd focus on this small detail. Anything to keep her mind calm. She opened her eyes wide and clenched her fists.

Do not, do not, do not cry.

CHAPTER 4

*J*ordan lifted her chin and forced herself to stare into the principal's deep eyes hidden beneath bushy brows. He cleared his throat and smoothed his thinning hair.

Sweat trickled down her back. Was this a test? Was he hoping she'd break down and confess that she'd read that crazy list?

"What do you want to speak to me about, sir?"

"Cimarron is very impressed with your computer skills. You're the best student computer master at GCU, now that Paul Hobbs had to leave us." Principal Reed licked his lips and shuffled from one foot to the other.

Did his role in Paul's disappearance sting his conscience? Not likely. This man didn't care about Paul. From what she'd heard, he lived to please the Global Collective Council and Cimarron.

She pressed her hand against her chest and straightened her spine. "Thank you."

"The fact that you come from a second-rate collective makes your skills even more impressive. Cimarron and I have mentioned you to the Global Council."

The Global Council knows my name. Jordan trembled.

"We're very proud of your accomplishments. Students like you will show the world that the first semester of GCU's pilot program has been a great success."

Success? Dragging teens away from their homes and placing them in mind control camps didn't sound like success to her.

Shouts of *Kiai*, tinged with Baltic, Latin, and Israeli accents, filled the area as the students practiced the kata. How she wanted to join them. She struggled to make her face an unreadable mask as she stared at Principal Reed.

"If you continue to perform well at GCU, your computer skills will be put to great use for the Global Council in the future," Principal Reed continued. "Cimarron used to be a computer master when she was younger. Her father taught her all about computers, the same way your father taught you. Unfortunately, the chaos going on in the world at that time kept her from following her career dreams. I think she sees herself in you."

What a terrifying thought.

Jordan nodded. She couldn't speak. She could barely breathe. Principal Reed motioned in the direction of the others, dismissing her to go practice. He turned and walked away while she fought to keep down her last meal.

If only she could fight like Malese. Then she wouldn't be so afraid of Principal Reed and Cimarron. Of course, they were only part of the problem, the part she could see. The Global Collective Council posed the true threat.

Why hadn't she paid more attention in her boring history classes or listened to Mom and Dad discussing politics? She wished she understood the Global Council better—her powerful enemy. She did know that the Council was comprised of three representatives from each collective, except for the European Collective, which had fifteen. Being the most prosperous and least war-damaged collective on the planet had its perks.

Hunter Wallis, a military genius from Old France, established the European Collective by the time he was twenty-two and the Global

Collective ten years later. He ruled as the chairman of the Global Council. His sister, River Wallis, sat as vice-chair. Another one of those *go figure* situations. Jordan didn't understand all the geopolitical forces, but she knew that the Global Council wielded enormous power. No one —not even Malese—could fight them alone.

* * *

THAT EVENING, dinner seemed to last for hours while Jordan fought to tamp down her fears and keep from screaming. Matthew had returned from track practice right before dinner, so they hadn't yet been able to talk, but several times he looked across the table at her as if to say, 'what's wrong?'

When the meal finally ended, some of the students headed back to their rooms. A few gathered in the common area to talk and play games. Cimarron hurried off to Principal Reed's office to catch up on some work. What a joke. Jordan grabbed her jacket and tossed Matthew his; then they headed out to the patio.

"What's wrong with you?" Matthew asked. "You've been acting strange all night. Whatever you wanted to talk about earlier must be important."

"I hope no one else noticed." She walked to the far edge of the patio.

Matthew followed. He stepped in front of her and put his hands on her shoulders. "Jordan, what's wrong?"

"I searched the data on Paul's computer book. It was still at the lab."

He took a deep breath. "What did you find?"

"A list of names called 'The Chosen Ones for GCU Project SS,' and Zoe's name was on the list. And my name was on it, too, with a special notation typed by Cimarron. It said, 'Jordan is very skilled but comes from a family of believers. She's so talented we should give her more time. It may not be necessary to pull her out.'"

Matthew shuffled his feet. Even in the dim light, she saw the color drain from his face. "Pull you out. What could that mean?"

"I don't know, and that's what I'm afraid of." She gazed up at the inky sky. She'd always loved the stars, but tonight they were hidden cameras ready to reveal her secrets to Cimarron.

"Well, it probably means they'd send you home."

"No. It's much worse. Cimarron and Principal Reed came to get Paul's computer."

Matthew's jaw dropped.

Dear Lord, he's as frightened as I am.

"I hid under Mr. Price's desk. They were talking about Paul finding the list, about a guard taking him away, and about making him the ringleader."

"The ringleader? What does that mean?"

"I don't know." Jordan spoke too loudly. She glanced over her shoulder, expecting Mr. Flynt or one of the students to come running out the door. Why did Matthew keep asking these stupid questions?

Matthew's grip tightened on her shoulders. "Calm down, Jordan."

She shook free of his hold. "Don't tell me to calm down."

Now was not the time to remain calm. If ever there was a time to panic, this was it.

"All I know is that Zoe, a believer, was on that strange list. Cimarron knows I'm a believer. Now I've seen that list and seeing that list is what got Paul in trouble."

Matthew swallowed hard, his Adam's apple bobbing from the strain. "Cimarron knows you come from a family of believers, that's all, and she doesn't know you've seen the list. We have to find out what *Project SS* means. Do you remember anything distinctive about the names?"

"Not really. I couldn't think straight because I was so scared." Jordan brushed her hand through her hair, her fingers catching on the tangled knots. "Three of the students were from the Latin Collective, and one from the African Collective. Zoe comes from the North American Collective and Paul from the Pacific. Paul and Zoe are both Christians, but I don't know about the other names on the list. That doesn't give us much to go on."

He shook his head. "No, it doesn't. But we'll figure this out together. We won't stop until we find out what's going on around here."

Jordan sniffed and bit her bottom lip. "Why is God letting this happen to me? Is He mad at me? Punishing me?"

She'd never been that bad.

"Why did He let Zoe and Paul get kidnapped? They're good kids." A cool breeze touched her cheek like a delicate caress and brought a calming floral scent to her nose.

The wind lifted Matthew's hair from his brow. "For years I've wondered why God took my mother when I needed her and left my drunken father for me to take care of. I don't think we're supposed to know the answers. We have to let God be God."

"Oh, Matthew, I'm scared. I don't want to disappear."

He squeezed her arm. "You're not going to disappear."

She and Matthew had become good friends in such a short period of time. They talked about their families and their favorite books and hobbies. Attending Paul's Bible study had brought them closer to God and to each other.

"Don't worry. We'll figure this out." He pushed her hair away from her face and stroked her cheek.

Jordan's face burned. Matthew bent his head toward hers and brought his lips to her forehead. She stepped closer, seeking his warmth. He moved his mouth from her forehead to her eager lips—the kiss quick and tender. Jordan trembled, and he pulled her closer, wrapping her in his arms.

She snuggled her head against his chest, relishing the sound of his rapid heartbeat. It told her she wasn't the only one excited by the kiss or frightened by GCU. He held her in his strong arms, and for a moment, she was safe.

What a lousy time for a first kiss. *I've waited all my life for this moment, and it happens now when I'm scared to death and trapped in some mysterious drama.*

She looked up at Matthew's solemn face. "Cimarron wrote that I was naïve and eager to please. I follow all the rules, so I wouldn't be a problem. Am I really that stupid and spineless?"

He kissed the top of her head. "There's nothing spineless about a girl brave enough to search a missing friend's computer. And you're certainly not stupid."

She pressed her fingers to her lips, still savoring the warmth of his mouth on hers. How could a super-jock care about a not-so-pretty computer geek?

"I've never told you this," Matthew said. "But the main reason I joined the Bible study was to spend time with you."

Jordan huffed and tried to strike him with the glare of a disappointed schoolteacher, but his confession delighted her. Boys never sought her out. And they certainly didn't scheme to spend time with her. "I thought you were a good Christian boy, and you wanted to flirt with me."

"I am a good Christian boy, a better one since we started our Bible study." He grinned. "But I'm a seventeen-year-old male who can't resist your honey-colored hair and big green eyes. I think God will forgive me."

"I think He will, too." She laid her head on his shoulder again. Matthew cared about her. He wanted to get to know her better. How could the best thing ever and the very worst possible thing happen to her on the same day?

"We'll have to be extra careful now," he whispered. "We can stop the Bible study if it will make you feel safer."

She stepped back. "No, we can't do that. I won't let GCU take the Bible study away from us. If we do that, they win."

"I agree, but I don't want to put you in more danger."

"The Bible study puts all of us in danger. Not just me. We should tell Timberlyn about this and let her make her own decision."

Matthew nodded. "You're right. She deserves to know the risks. But I bet she'll make the same decision we did."

"God is going to get us through this, isn't He?" *Please, please, please say yes.*

"Of course, He is. He's brought us both through a lot of rough spots in the past." Matthew touched her chin. "He won't desert us. But right now, we need to go on with our daily routines like nothing ever happened."

Jordan shook her head. "I'm not sure I can do that. I'm not that good of an actress."

"You don't have a choice." He pulled her close, his voice firm but tender.

He was right. She couldn't drop out of school and catch the next plane to Old Memphis. Cimmaron would get suspicious if she suggested going home and that could put her family in danger. Her only choice was to remain at GCU and pray she didn't disappear.

Jordan stepped back and gazed up at Matthew. "We need to go in before the others wonder what we're up to out here."

Matthew cupped her chin in his hand and brought his lips to hers. This kiss was longer and more intense. Her heart fluttered, but she forced herself to break off the kiss and step away.

"This is something else we can get in trouble for. Romantic relationships are not allowed at GCU." She mimicked Cimarron's crisp voice.

The smoldering flash in Matthew's eyes told her he wasn't worried about getting in trouble.

"I'll risk it." He pulled her back into his arms.

Jordan clung to him, but a strange foreboding fell on her. Would they soon be forced to risk everything in order to survive another day at GCU?

"My, my, our little southern belle is out sparking with her beau."

Jordan spun around at the sound of Laurel Connor's voice behind her. Dawson stood at Laurel's side.

"The full moon brought out the lovebirds," Laurel said. A dark scowl covered Dawson's stony face.

Jordan's heart skipped a beat. How stupid. She'd let those two slip up on her. Of course, fear for her life and the thrill of her first kiss had undoubtedly dulled her senses.

Laurel posed before them, one hand on her hip, clingy yoga pants accentuating her long legs. The sweatshirt and light jacket she wore did little to disguise her elegance.

I look like a little girl fresh from the playground compared to this lovely ballerina.

Laurel tilted her head, her pale blonde hair tumbling over her shoulder. "Judging by your red faces, I'd say you two just got caught breaking the no-romance rule."

Jordan scurried away from Matthew, but he wrapped his arm around her shoulders and drew her back to his side. She started to push herself out of his grasp then froze. Here they were, alone in the dark, devising ways to discover GCU's dirty secrets. Not a story they could share with Laurel and Dawson.

Pretty smart, Matthew. I knew I liked you for more than just your looks. Let them believe she and Matthew were stealing kisses in the moonlight. That was preferable to the truth.

Matthew squeezed Jordan tighter and grinned at the intruders. "It seems like we're not the only ones with romance on our minds."

Dawson pushed out his chest. "Laurel and I are old friends."

Matthew laughed. "Yeah, we've all noticed how friendly the two of you are."

Laurel covered her mouth and lightly coughed while moving away from Dawson. Dawson's fanatical attraction to Laurel could never be denied or hidden. He'd almost come to blows with Rafael several times because he'd flirted with her, and he'd snapped at Matthew once or twice for talking to her. Jordan had wanted to snap, too, but she had controlled herself. As far as she could tell, Laurel didn't do anything to encourage Dawson's obsessive love. For a moment, sympathy for the all too perfect girl touched Jordan's heart.

Laurel pulled her green GCU jacket closed in front of her. "It's too cold for an evening walk. I'm going back in." She turned and strode toward the door.

Dawson opened his mouth to speak, then snapped his jaw shut and glared at Matthew. He stomped across the patio, heading for the garden, and disappeared into the romantic glow provided by the old-fashioned lanterns and European floodlights that painted the grounds. Apparently, Dawson was determined to take an evening stroll with or without company.

Jordan slipped from Matthew's grasp. "I'm going in, too." As much as she hated to leave Matthew, she'd had all the romance and intrigue she could handle for one night.

CHAPTER 5

*H*annie Jacobson rubbed her hands together to chase away the lingering cold as she walked down the narrow hall to her bedroom. Jordan had been acting strange the last few days. Strange even for the sweet southern belle. Hannie shook her head and wondered for the one hundredth time how she'd ever ended up sharing a room with a prissy girl from the North American Collective.

Of course, the roommate situation was probably for the best. Timberlyn and Malese seemed much too childish for her taste, and if she'd been paired with Laurel, she'd be incarcerated for homicide by now. Jordan could get along with anyone. Hannie was starting to like her. They might be opposites, but they had one thing in common. Jordan wanted to go home to her collective, and Hannie missed Israel every day.

Israel—the home that invaded her dreams every night. Unfortunately, the dreams were nightmares. Nightmares of her father's blood running in the street, her mother's frightened face, the baby's cries, and the searing fire that destroyed everything it touched.

She'd been six-years-old and scared to death when her adopted family of military officers and former spies found her. Over the last ten years, she'd enjoyed her unconventional lifestyle, until her battle skills and tactical mind brought her to the attention of GCU and trapped her in the school's far-reaching tentacles. Now here she was, courtesy of the European Collective, stuck in a mountain paradise surrounded by intelligent but foolish kids.

That morning at breakfast, Cimarron had announced that Sierra Stone, an important member of the Global Collective Council would speak at GCU next week. Since Team Seven was the highest-ranking team at GCU, they would sit in the front row and meet Councilor Stone after her speech. Cimarron acted as if they should be excited by this news. Dawson shouted that Ms. Stone was a traitor who had betrayed Hunter and River Wallis, and he had no desire to meet her. Cimarron agreed that Sierra Stone was a radical member of the Council, but her visit would bring acclaim to GCU.

Jordan's face had revealed her doubt. Jordan might be naïve, but she wasn't a fool. Hannie realized that she and Jordan both distrusted GCU.

Hannie knew a little about the infamous Sierra Stone, some exaggerated gossip no doubt. Her friends in Israel admired the former soldier turned councilor. Finally, someone on the Global Collective Council was speaking truth and promising change. Israel and most of the planet longed for change.

Radical member of the Council. Traitor. Cimarron and Dawson's words bounced in Hannie's brain. This Councilor Stone sounded like her kind of woman.

Voices sounded from the bedroom Hannie shared with Jordan. Who was Jordan talking to? They never invited the other students to their room, not that doing so was forbidden. GCU encouraged friendships among team members, but Matthew was Jordan's only close friend.

No way. Not goody-goody Jordan.

She'd never be reckless enough to invite Matthew to her bedroom because that might cause gossip and make Cimarron think she and Matthew had broken the rules. To Jordan, rules were as precious as an antique crystal egg. Hannie couldn't imagine Jordan breaking one. Curiosity bubbling, she pushed the bedroom door open.

Jordan sat at the sleek silver desk, the computer screen glowing before her. Matthew stood behind her, bending low to read over her shoulder. Malese was perched on Jordan's flowered bedspread, Timberlyn was cross-legged on the floor, and Victor sat at the foot of the other bed. So many people in such a tiny space. Body heat radiated through the room.

Hannie stepped inside and shut the door behind her. "So, roomie, are you having a party and forgot to invite me?"

Timberlyn jumped and squealed. Everyone, except Jordan, glared at Hannie as if she were an enemy agent invading a room full of patriots.

"Hannie, you're more than welcome to join us," Jordan said.

Matthew shot a warning look at Jordan. Distrust danced in Malese's dark eyes, and Victor chewed his thumbnail.

"I'm not sure everyone agrees." Hannie removed her jacket then tossed it onto her bed. The downy coat landed on Victor's lap. He picked it up with two fingers, examined it like it might explode, then placed it behind him.

"We can be honest with Hannie," Jordan told the stiff faces. "She doesn't trust GCU either."

Matthew's shoulders relaxed, and the tension fled the room.

"So, what're you guys up to?" Hannie exhaled softly, delighted by the group's acceptance.

I must be getting soft if I care about fitting in with this crew.

"We were all curious about Sierra Stone," Jordan said. "What kind of person would Cimarron consider a radical?"

"I've been wondering that myself." Hannie walked toward the bed where Victor sat staring at the floor. "Move over, big guy, and let me join you."

Victor blushed and moved so far that he tottered on the edge of the bed. Her leg brushed against him, and his face flamed brighter. Was he afraid of her in particular, or all girls?

"So, what have you found out?" she asked.

Jordan returned her attention to the computer screen. "She's forty years old and a member of the European Collective. She was born in EC Area 21, Sector 9. The country was called Ireland then. She lived through some violent times as the European Collective formed. About

34

two years ago, Sierra Stone became a member of the Global Collective Council."

Matthew squeezed the back of Jordan's chair and it creaked. "None of that sounds radical. Everyone her age lived through violence and chaos."

"There has to be more." Jordan pushed her auburn hair behind her ears. "Let me try typing in beliefs and doctrines of Sierra Stone." They all waited silently while the computer searched the web galaxy for more data.

Hannie glanced around the room, her gaze moving from one curious face to the next. Her fellow team members questioned GCU. This bunch had more chutzpa than she'd ever imagined.

"Councilor Stone advocates for more freedom of travel and social interaction between the collectives," Jordan read. "She stands against the Global Council's platform of uniformity in education and rejection of religious beliefs. She doesn't claim any religious affiliation, but believes that each person should have the freedom to worship, or not worship, a higher power no matter what collective they live in."

Matthew whistled low. "No wonder Cimarron called her a radical."

Jordan nodded. "It says that many religious groups support Ms. Stone, but a few groups don't trust her policy of religious freedom for all. They believe she's secretly working with Hunter and River Wallis to trap believers."

"Conspiracy theorists," Hannie said.

Jordan put her elbows on the desk and leaned closer to the screen. "It also says that Ms. Stone supported the formation of Global Collective University and believes the Council should go further in creating a world with more individualism and freedom."

Hannie slapped her denim covered knee. "She sounds like my kind of girl."

"Hey, look at this cool picture." Jordan pointed to the monitor. "She's a lot like you, Hannie. Come see."

Hannie moved to where she could see the picture of a young woman, dressed in fatigues, mud splotched on her face and a camouflage scarf wrapped around her head. An old-fashioned European rifle was slung over the woman's shoulder.

"Sierra Stone at age twenty, fighting against the Parisian faction," Jordan read, then looked up at Hannie. Her face grew pale. "That means she fought against Hunter and River Wallis."

"And now she's a member of the Global Council." Hannie straightened her back and bent from side to side to loosen her stiff muscles. "I never pictured Hunter and River Wallis as the forgiving kind."

Jordan nodded and scrolled to another story. "This article says that Ms. Stone is hated by many Global Council members. Despite very outspoken criticism, Sierra Stone's nomination to the Council was approved by a narrow margin due to her overwhelming support in Old Ireland, Old England, and Old Scotland. She's very popular with the common people, but in her two years on the Council she's made a lot of political enemies."

"That's not surprising," Malese said. "She's against almost everything the Global Council stands for."

Hannie walked to the window, pulled back the beige drape, and stared into the darkness. She'd love to open the window to let in a cooling breeze, but the conversation was much too dangerous. They would be in severe trouble should their words be carried on the wind to the wrong ears. Before she'd left Israel, her friends had warned her to be careful at GCU. Many believed GCU was more than a high school for gifted students. Too many powerful political forces surrounded it. Cimarron's reaction to Sierra Stone's politics tripled Hannie's doubts and fears.

"The Council has only been in existence for ten years, and now Sierra Stone wants to radically change it," she said as she stared out the window. "That makes powerful enemies."

"Remember those Global Collective formation classes we took our first three months here?" Matthew asked.

Hannie turned around. "The classes where they tried to brainwash us with the belief that the Global Collective Council was going to save the planet, and that we all owed unquestioning loyalty to Hunter and River Wallis."

"I hated those classes." Jordan stood and rolled her shoulders, grimacing at the effort. "They kept trying to convince us that if one all-powerful Council ruled the world, it would ensure equality and prosperity for all."

"After a while, it started to make sense." Victor spoke barely above a whisper. His blush had faded from blood red to light pink now that Hannie had moved away.

"That's what they're counting on." Matthew massaged Jordan's shoulders. Obviously, those two were growing closer. "They want to fill our young, pliable minds with their propaganda then send us back to our own collectives to spread the message."

Timberlyn tugged at the frayed fringe of the throw rug. "I'm surprised they're letting Sierra Stone speak at GCU."

"From what we've read, her popularity is growing with the common people, and she's a school supporter," Matthew said. "If she wanted to speak here, I guess it would be hard for them to say no."

Hannie's stomach churned. Her heartbeat intensified. Soon, she would come face-to-face with a woman who seemed to share her own rebel heart. She clapped her hands. "I'm looking forward to meeting Sierra Stone."

She stared intently at Jordan. Her own hope, concern, and doubt shone in her friend's green eyes. Did Sierra Stone truly want to lead the planet to a brighter future, or was she only another politician wrapped up in a crowd-pleasing package?

CHAPTER 6

riday afternoon, Jordan stood among a throng of noisy students all waiting to enter the GCU auditorium and hear Sierra Stone speak. Matthew stood beside her. The first rows were reserved for Team Seven and Team Four. Since Jordan and Matthew didn't have to worry about finding a good seat, they hung back from the crowd. The scents of sweat, perfume, and chewing gum tickled Jordan's nose, and she sneezed.

Five heavy cedar doors with intricately carved designs separated the crowd from the theater. The face of a snarling snow leopard covered the center door. Its deep eyes seemed to stare directly at Jordan, kicking her nerves into high gear.

She glanced at her digital watch. "Shouldn't they have opened the doors by now? The speech starts in fifteen minutes."

Matthew stepped back, bumping his head against the imposing portrait of Hunter and River Wallis hanging above him in an antique gold frame. He rubbed his head then took Jordan's arm and led her a little farther away from the picture of the Global Council leaders.

"I don't want to knock this thing off the wall and find myself facing a firing squad." He grinned.

"Don't joke about that." She slapped his shoulder. Her hand stung from the impact of solid muscle, but Matthew didn't flinch. "With all the weird stuff going on around here, it could happen."

Matthew's expression grew serious, and she thought he was going to wrap his arm around her, but he grabbed her elbow instead. Was it the no romance rule that made him hesitate? She'd hoped their kiss meant as much to him as it did to her. How foolish. Surely she hadn't been Matthew's first kiss. Probably one of many.

"I overheard Mr. Flynt telling one of the other teachers that Ms. Stone has received death threats since announcing her visit to GCU. They've upped the security around here," he whispered.

"Why would someone at GCU try to hurt Ms. Stone? She's a GCU supporter."

Matthew lifted his brows and squeezed her elbow. "But not everyone agrees with her politics. Remember Dawson and Cimarron's reaction to her visit?"

Disagreeing with political views and making death threats were two different things. Surely, Dawson wasn't capable of murder, but what about Cimarron? Her involvement in Paul's disappearance proved she was dangerous.

Who sent the death threats? The same people who wrote the list?

The theater doors swung open, and the excited students rushed by. Jordan and Matthew jumped back as a couple of younger boys sped past, shoving each other as they ran.

Just like my rowdy little brothers.

"River Wallis is so beautiful."

Jordan turned at the sound of a familiar voice. Courtney Moreau, from computer lab, stood beside a tall, thin girl with bright red hair. They both stared at the portrait. She'd seen the other girl before. What was her name? Jessica. That was it.

Courtney sighed. "I wish I could style my hair like River's, but my parents won't let me."

Why would anyone with thick blonde curls want to copy River's hairstyle? In the portrait, the Global Council Vice-Chair stood beside her brother, a solemn expression on her face. Did River Wallis even know how to smile? Jordan had only seen a handful of pictures of River, but she'd never seen a pleasant expression on the woman's face. Jordan's father and many of the older people claimed that River was insane. A chill settled over Jordan.

In this photo, River's silky black hair fell to her waist and parted on the side with one half dyed a bright silver. The garland of silver stars tattooed across her forehead accentuated her dark eyes.

Courtney blew a golden curl off her forehead. "My parents say we'd dishonor River if we copied her hairstyle since she's one of our great leaders."

Jessica nodded, her mouth agape, as she stared at the portrait. "My parents adore both of them. My dad fought in Hunter's regiment. He says that Hunter is stronger and more intelligent than any mere man."

The girl's voice reminded Jordan of Paul Hobbs's beautiful Australian lilt. Of course, Paul had a lot more sense.

"Hunter's wonderful." Courtney sighed again and ran her fingers along the frame's sparkling edge.

Jordan frowned. Hunter's dark hair skimmed his shoulders, and streaks of gray shone in his thick mane. He was handsome, for an older man, but Courtney acted like he was a possible prom date. She seemed a lot smarter in computer lab.

Jordan glanced at Matthew then slapped her hand over her mouth to suppress her giggles at his mystified expression.

Matthew shook his head. "Crazy," he mouthed.

She giggled and turned her attention back to the two girls.

"At least my parents let me get a tattoo like River's." Courtney patted her left shoulder. A raging river stretched from beneath her cotton top. A snow leopard sat beside it. "People say if you light candles and chant her name, River will grant your wishes."

Jessica grabbed Courtney's arm. "We better go find a seat."

Courtney nodded, then slowly turned away from the picture to follow her friend. "When I meditate, I chant River's name."

"Me too," Jessica said, deep reverence in her soft voice.

Jordan wanted to throw up, but instead, she silently followed

Matthew into the auditorium. Excited voices bounced from the cushioned chairs to the ornate rafters suspended across the high ceiling. GCU had a modern, state-of-the-art assembly area, but Sierra Stone would speak here in this classically beautiful auditorium, another relic of European aristocracy.

Jordan sat in the front row between Matthew and Hannie. With her stubby fingernails, she scratched the red crushed velvet covering the arm of her chair. Matthew wrapped his fingers around her wrist. She placed her other hand against her stomach, hoping to capture the butterflies that tormented her.

Why was she so nervous? Yes, she was excited about Sierra Stone's visit. Most of the students were. Eager chatter filled the room mixing with spurts of laughter and guarded whispers.

Jordan wanted to spew out her frustrations and fears. Ms. Stone's visit gave her a little hope. The woman was so different from Cimarron, Mr. Flynt, or Principal Reed. Sierra Stone seemed to share Jordan's beliefs and dreams for a better world, but unlike her, Councilor Stone was in a position to do something with these ideals. She held a place of power and could make a difference.

Could God be using the councilor to accomplish His will? The articles had said that Ms. Stone didn't claim any religious affiliation, yet she supported freedom of worship. In the Bible, God used pagan kings to fulfill His purposes, such as Cyrus and Artaxerxes. Could Sierra Stone be a modern-day official placed in the Global Council for such a time as this?

Principal Reed walked across the stage to stand behind the podium, his rigid posture accentuated by his crisp, dark suit. He was as plastic as Cimarron. Too many trips to the beauty enhancers, no doubt. He waved his arms to quiet the crowd.

"Faculty and students, I am honored to present our distinguished guest speaker. Councilor Sierra Stone has graciously taken time out of her busy schedule to tour GCU and speak to us today. Please join me in welcoming Councilor Stone."

Applause rose from the crowd as Principal Reed stepped back. Sierra

Stone appeared from behind the thick black curtains. Her green tweed skirt swayed against her calves as she crossed the stage then shook Principal Reed's hand. He presented her to the audience with a wave of his arm before taking a seat in one of the chairs positioned on stage behind the podium. Several adult team leaders occupied the other chairs. Not surprisingly, Cimarron sat beside Principal Reed, her short skirt revealing too much leg. Mr. Flynt obviously hadn't made the cut because he sat in the front row with the students.

Councilor Stone tilted her head and smiled warmly. "Thank you so much for this rousing welcome." She was thin, probably about 5'6" tall, yet her magnetic presence dominated the stage. "I'm thrilled to speak to all of you today."

She pushed an errant strand of chin-length hair behind her ear. The spotlights revealed red and gray highlights mixed with chestnut brown. Apparently, Ms. Stone did not frequent the beauty enhancers. She seemed real. Like Mom and Dad. So different from the falseness that permeated GCU.

"I supported the formation of GCU because it allows each of you to further develop your unique talents and to share these talents and abilities with your fellow students while interacting with people from every corner of the world." Councilor Stone clutched the sides of the podium. Was she nervous? *I'd be if I had gotten death threats.*

Jordan glanced around the large auditorium. A sniper could lurk in the empty balcony and any crazy with a gun could jump from behind the curtains and shoot Ms. Stone in the back.

"Your generation is our only hope for a brighter future. We have struggled greatly over the last thirty years, but I believe this planet can thrive again." The woman paused and took a sip of water from a bottle on the podium.

Jordan cringed. Poisoning the speaker's water would be a great way to kill her.

"I believe we can have peace and prosperity," the councilor continued. "But only if we allow individuals to use their skills to better themselves. We need to embrace the individuality of each person."

Cimarron folded her right leg over her left and jabbed the pointy toe of her black heel into the floor, a bleak frown replacing her usual plastic smile. Principal Reed cleared his throat loudly and tapped his foot. The red banner emblazoned with the European Collective snow leopard fluttered behind them. Had Ms. Stone's words upset the leopard, too?

For the next fifteen minutes, Councilor Stone expounded on her ideas and offered viable solutions to many problems shared by all collectives. If only Ms. Stone's dreams for the future could come true. They sounded great, but the Global Collective Council would surely do everything in their power to block these reforms.

Jordan glanced at Hannie, who sat on the other side of Matthew. She bent forward in her chair and nodded in agreement with the councilor. Jordan glanced around the room. A combination of awe, distrust, and boredom was painted on the young faces.

"If every citizen in each collective is allowed to dream their own dreams, believe as he or she sees fit, worship and live as they see fit, we'll have a better world." Ms. Stone took another drink.

"My mission can be summed up in one sentence." The councilor stared directly at Jordan. "I believe in the individual more than the collective. Individual over collective."

Jordan wanted to shout for joy that such a leader existed. She clapped, ready to spring to her feet, but Matthew grabbed her arm, shaking his head in warning. She scanned the audience again. This room held students from every collective on the planet. Most of them clapped politely, but these kids had suffered under politicians' slick lies all their lives. Mom and Dad were always slow to believe any popular figure who offered hope. The other students appeared to mistrust politicians, too. Very few of the European Collective students bothered to clap at all. Dawson kept his arms folded across his chest, and Laurel stared straight ahead.

Principal Reed stood. He walked to the podium, took Ms. Stone's hand, and thanked her for her time and much appreciated support of GCU. After dismissing the students, he asked the teams who had been chosen to meet the councilor to remain behind.

CHAPTER 7

*B*ouncing on her heels, Jordan waited in line to meet Councilor Stone. She took a deep breath and ran both of her hands through her hair. *There goes my hairstyle.*

How she wished she could talk to Ms. Stone alone and tell her about the strange disappearance of Christian students at GCU and the list of names she'd found on Paul's computer. Of course, the woman would think she was a delusional teenager and never believe her story without solid proof.

Her gaze traveled to Cimarron, who stood on the edge of the stage like a frozen statue. *If she ever finds out I saw that list, I'm dead.* Jordan swallowed hard and turned her gaze to the reception line.

Victor, head bowed, shook hands with Ms. Stone and mumbled a quick greeting. Timberlyn followed behind him. Principal Reed spoke Jordan's name, and she stepped up to meet Councilor Stone.

A proud expression covered Principal Reed's face. "Councilor, I'm delighted to introduce Jordan Scott, our top computer master."

Jordan's stomach clenched. He couldn't take credit for her skills. That credit belonged to her dad and grandfather. And she wouldn't be the number one computer master if Paul hadn't disappeared.

A delicate scent of lavender encircled Ms. Stone, calming Jordan's nerves and tickling her nose. "I'm honored to meet you, Councilor Stone."

"And I am honored to meet you." The Councilor smiled, revealing fine lines around the corners of her golden eyes, which brought a special warmth to her face. "I've heard a great deal about your excellent computer skills. A gift I admire, since I'm sorely lacking in that area. Ask my assistant, Grayson." She nodded toward the man who stood by her side, dressed in a dark suit and crimson tie. He held a computer book in his hand.

Another Cimarron. Grayson could be a poster boy for the Global Collective Council. Two bodyguards with wide shoulders and square jaws stood behind the Councilor. With death threats circulating, Ms. Stone had better keep them close.

Councilor Stone squeezed Jordan's hand. "I know that you will make a great contribution to the North American Collective and the rest of the planet with your excellent computer prowess."

"Thank you," Jordan whispered before stepping to the side to allow Matthew to greet the Councilor.

Matthew told Ms. Stone he had enjoyed her speech. She thanked him and patted his arm. Ms. Stone didn't seem to mind showing affection. Nothing like the adults running GCU.

Dawson and Laurel followed Matthew. Laurel blushed when Ms. Stone told her that she had attended one of her performances in Old Paris. She raved about Laurel's talent. Dawson shook Ms. Stone's hand but refused to speak. His narrowed eyes, and a deep frown broadcast his contempt.

As soon as Ms. Stone greeted the last team member, Grayson took her arm. "We're running behind schedule. We must leave now."

Most of the students had wandered away, but Jordan stood close by. She wanted to spend as much time as possible with this unique woman.

"Grayson is determined I stick to my schedule. I don't know what I'd do without him," Councilor Stone said. "But before I go, I must speak to Cimarron for a moment. She and I grew up together in Old Ireland." She turned and walked to where Cimarron stood at the edge of the stage. The bodyguards followed.

Grew up together. The words tumbled through Jordan's head like a rock barreling down a steep incline. Did Sierra Stone and Cimarron play together as children? They couldn't have been friends. She'd never met two women more opposite.

Jordan looked up at Matthew, confident that he shared her enthusiasm about the speech. "I think Ms. Stone is wonderful, so real."

Matthew's brow was wrinkled, and his mouth twisted into a frown.

"What's wrong? Don't you like Councilor Stone?"

He nodded. "I like her, and I think she gave a great speech, but I'm not ready to hail her as a savior yet."

"I'm not either," Jordan snapped. Did he think she was a naïve twit? Courtney Moreau's obsessive fascination with Hunter and River Wallis flooded her memory, and her cheeks burned.

She watched the remaining students grab their sweaters and bags and file out of the auditorium on their way to their next class. Hannie waved at her as she stepped through the heavy, gold embossed doors.

Matthew touched Jordan's shoulder and motioned toward the stage where Sierra Stone embraced Cimarron and patted her on the back. Cimarron stood, her body tight and a frown on her lips.

Ms. Stone's face was animated as she talked. Cimarron didn't respond. She tapped her foot on the floor and stared into space. Councilor Stone bowed her head and stepped back. She shook Principal Reed's hand then walked down the stage steps and headed out the side entrance. Jordan squinted in the flash of sunlight that rushed in when the auditorium door opened to release its honored guest.

What was up between the two women? Councilor Stone made it sound like they were old friends, but Cimarron seemed to hate Ms. Stone.

"I'm sorry I got so worked up about Ms. Stone," Jordan whispered, still too embarrassed to meet Matthew's gaze. "I'm not a fool, most of the time."

"I know you're not a fool. I think that with all the craziness going on at GCU, we need to be extra careful in what we say, believe, or do."

Matthew rubbed his chin. "I'm probably the stupid one here, but this terrible thought keeps racing through my mind."

Jordan turned to face him. She was the emotional, fear-ridden one while Matthew was the calm and logical one. Suddenly, their positions had changed, and she didn't like it.

"I keep remembering the list you found on Paul's computer." His voice was low, and she had to step closer to hear him. "*The Chosen Ones for Project SS. SS could mean Sierra Stone.*"

Jordan shivered. "No. She can't possibly have anything to do with the missing students. It has to be a coincidence."

"If it's a coincidence, it's a pretty big one."

"But Cimarron and Principal Reed hate Ms. Stone. Why would they be working with her?" She rubbed her hands against her throbbing temples, wishing she could wipe away Matthew's words. She'd finally met a politician worthy of her admiration, and she wasn't ready to give up that dream.

"I didn't say they were working with her. Ms. Stone might not know anything about Project SS. She might be a victim, too." He pulled Jordan close. "But until we find out what is going on around here, I don't think we should talk about Sierra Stone with anyone but each other. We don't want Cimarron to think we're overly impressed with the councilor."

"What about Hannie and Timberlyn and the others? They're interested in Ms. Stone, too. What should we say to them?"

Matthew hooked his thumb through his pant loop and stared at the floor for a moment. "We'll tell them we enjoyed the speech, and we think Councilor Stone is cool, then we won't talk about her anymore."

"I don't like being dishonest with them. Timberlyn is the only one we've told about Project SS, and the others deserve to know the truth."

He squeezed her arm. "The more we get them involved in this mess, the more danger we put them in. Right now, the less they know, the better."

She brushed her hair away from her face and rocked on her heels. Would life ever be simple again? What was she thinking? Life had never been simple, but she was used to small meals, family emergencies, limited resources, and periodic street violence. Her parents had always been there to protect her. She wasn't ready to be the responsible adult yet. Whom could she trust? She certainly knew whom to fear. She glanced back at the stage, empty now except for Principal Reed and Cimarron, the GC flag standing guard between them.

"You're right, Matthew. After all, we are nothing but a couple of teenagers too wrapped up in our own lives to concern ourselves with politics, right?"

He winked. "Sounds good to me." He sighed and glanced around the almost vacant auditorium. "Our youth gives us an advantage. They'll never suspect us of digging for GCU's secrets, or believe we're disloyal, as long as they think we're gullible teens."

Jordan nodded. *We are gullible teens in need of supernatural wisdom. Oh, God, please tell us what to do next and show us who to believe.*

CHAPTER 8

Sunday morning, Jordan and Timberlyn sat in the stone basement around a bushel of apples that they used as a table and waited for Matthew to arrive for Bible study. Jordan pulled her sweater closed and buttoned it to keep out the chill. She took a deep breath of musty air. This cellar was several hundred years old, and she could smell every decade, but this secluded place provided a safe meeting spot. Worshiping God and studying His Word brightened any spot, no matter how dreary.

A few minutes earlier, she had retrieved Paul's Bible, the only one they possessed, from its hiding place behind a loose brick in the corner of the basement. She hadn't touched it since Paul's disappearance. Her fingers trembled as they traveled over the worn leather cover.

She glanced at Timberlyn, who bobbed her head in encouragement. Jordan flipped through the pages, searching for the passage they planned to study today. The Bible parted at the thick page separating the Old and New Testaments. A string of numbers fluttered before her eyes.

"What in the world?"

Numbers, written in Paul's characteristic scrawl, spread across the page, but they weren't random. They formed a pattern.

Timberlyn leaned across the barrel and peered at the Bible. "What did you find?"

Jordan looked at Timberlyn. "These are computer codes."

Timberlyn's mouth popped open, and she twisted her hands in her lap.

Jordan's breath caught in her tight throat. Surely, oxygen would never find her lungs again. Paul must have left these codes for her. No one else would understand them, and he assumed she'd find them since she read the Bible on a regular basis.

"These must be the codes Paul used to hack the GCU mainframe," Jordan said.

"If Cimarron finds out we have those—"

"She won't find out." Jordan's voice shook, and her insides trembled like she was sitting on a powder keg. She wanted to tell Matthew about the codes, but why pull him deeper into this mess? "No one else can know about this. Just you and me. Agreed?"

"I'll never tell anyone." Timberlyn slapped her hand over her chest.

Jordan nodded. Timberlyn would keep their secret. Why would Paul leave these blasted codes for her to find? Perhaps he was afraid of getting caught, and he wanted someone else to be able to penetrate the GCU computer. A shiver vibrated across her flesh, and she hugged herself tightly. Her computer skills could never match Paul's, yet he'd gotten caught. He had disappeared. She would never be foolish enough to try to enter GCU's dark domain.

She clutched the page, ready to tear it out and burn it. The first ripping sound stopped her. She could almost hear Paul's voice. "C'mon, mate, you know what to do." The codes were too important to destroy. She smoothed the page with her palm, amazed it didn't ignite and burn beneath her skin."

"Good morning."

Jordan jumped at Matthew's greeting. She slammed the Bible shut and turned as Matthew stepped into the cellar, Victor by his side.

What else was going to happen this morning?

She rubbed her sweaty palms on her thighs. "Good morning."

She would pretend this was a chance encounter and that she and Timberlyn weren't waiting for Matthew to join them. *Sure.* How many impromptu meetings happened in a dirty basement? Perhaps Victor didn't know this was a Bible study. Jordan swallowed hard, afraid to say another word.

"I hope you don't mind if Victor joins us this morning." Matthew motioned for Victor to take a seat on a gray, wool blanket Jordan had tossed on the floor.

She had brought the blanket with her this morning in case they needed to bundle up. Matthew was smart to direct Victor to the floor. None of the boxes and barrels could support his weight. With his leg, Matthew scooted a crate of beans toward the apple barrel, then sat down.

"Of course, I don't mind if Victor joins us." Jordan exchanged a worried glance with Timberlyn while they both waited for Matthew to explain.

"Victor and I have been talking, and he's interested in learning about the Bible."

"Oh." Jordan's chin dropped. Their secret was out, and Matthew had been the one brave enough to reveal it. All this time, he'd been warning her to be cautious, and then he went and blabbed about being a believer. She shot a worried glance at Matthew, and he offered a reassuring nod.

"I didn't realize you were a Bible student, Victor." She might as well make the best of the situation and trust Matthew's judgment.

Victor chewed his thumbnail. "I'm not, but I'd like to learn. I want to know if there's something more to this life."

"Tell them about your experience as a child," Matthew said.

Victor blushed and bowed his head. Victor's difficultly with talking to girls was no secret. In the last three months, he'd barely uttered more than a few paragraphs, and when he did speak, it was always to Matthew or Rafael. He looked so young brushing his hand through his sandy blond hair.

"I lived in an orphanage when I was a child in the Baltic Collective. There was an old chapel on the grounds. It was in terrible shape, broken boards, and crumbling bricks, but for some reason, I was drawn to it."

His shoulders sagged as he clutched the edge of the blanket in his fist. How much had he suffered in his young life?

"I would sit and stare at this wooden cross dangling on one wall. When I was eight, I asked one of my teachers about the old building, and she said it was left from the days when people believed in God. She said it was silly superstition and no one in the Baltic Collective believed now. I still went there every chance I got."

Timberlyn pulled her chair a little closer to Victor. "Were you still going to the chapel when GCU recruited you?"

"No. I was three times as big as the other boys by the time I was ten. I started weight-lifting and wrestling in school tournaments. A wrestling troupe learned about me and recruited me for the team." Victor put his elbows on a barrel of beans and leaned forward. "After that, I lived and traveled with the wrestling team all over the Baltic Collective, breaking records for weight-lifting. I never saw that chapel again."

Unshed tears blurred Jordan's vision. How awful for a young boy to be forced into wrestling and grow up without a mother or any family.

"I never forgot about that chapel or cross. I always wanted to learn more about this God."

Jordan leaned across the dusty barrel and placed her hand on top of Victor's. "God brought you to us so you could learn about Him." She smiled at Victor and then at Matthew and Timberlyn.

Matthew put his hand on top of theirs. Timberlyn placed her hand on top of Matthew's.

"God sent his only son to die on the cross for you, Victor, and for me," Jordan said.

"God loved us too much to leave us lost in our sins." Matthew wrapped his arm around Victor's wide shoulders. "When Jesus hung on the cross, God took our sins and placed them on Him."

Victor shook his head, blond bangs falling across his brow. He took a deep breath, and tears filled his eyes.

"You can have a forever relationship with Jesus, if you believe," Jordan said, then waited for Victor's response.

"I do believe," Victor whispered. "Now I understand the perfect peace I experienced in that chapel. That peace was God."

Jordan loved Victor's child-like faith. The best kind of faith. They all bowed their heads, and Jordan led Victor in a prayer of salvation.

* * *

THE NEXT WEEK, Timberlyn invited Malese to join their Bible study group. Malese said she was not a believer but would listen with an open mind and keep the Bible study secret.

"The Pacific Collective has little use for God," Malese told them. "As a child, I learned that some of our ancestors used to adhere to primitive religions, but they laid these superstitions aside long ago. My people do not think they need a higher power in their lives."

"Perhaps your people could lay aside their gods because they weren't real," Jordan said. "Our God is different."

Malese continued to join them for the next several weeks and listened intently to the exciting Bible stories. If only Paul were here to see this. He was the fervent evangelist, and Jordan was the one afraid to even mention her faith.

Only cowards hid in a basement, but God proved that He could work anytime in any place. A tingle of fear touched her. Zoe had disappeared. Paul had been kidnapped. What would God ask them to do next?

CHAPTER 9

$\mathcal{T}$he calendar crawled by each day of the month until it reached November 7—Jordan's birthday and GCU visitation day.

I'm seventeen today. It's visitation day, and my family is thousands of miles away. Happy birthday to me. Jordan stared out the parlor window and rubbed her eyes to stop the threatening tears. This would be the first time she celebrated her birthday without her parents.

Mom won't be able to tell me about the day I was born, Dad won't call me his baby girl, and the kids won't beg for extra cake. Do they miss me as much as I miss them?

Jordan and Rafael stood at the large bay window watching students strolling by wrapped in a parent's embrace. European Collective parents had been arriving all day, bundled in luxurious fur coats and gloves. Travel between collectives was illegal, except for government workers, so Team Seven wouldn't receive many visitors. The friends stretched out in the parlor, sipping hot cocoa and playing computer games.

Matthew sat on the sofa between Timberlyn and Laurel. He plopped his feet up on the dark mahogany coffee table. "Where's Hannie?"

"She has a visitor." Jordan turned around. She'd had enough of the happy view outside the window. Why torture herself?

"How could she have a visitor?" Laurel placed her cup of cocoa on the table. Hannie and Laurel were as opposite as the sturdy mountain and the delicate flowers that graced it. They coexisted, but they certainly were not friends.

Jordan studied Laurel. A sad expression covered her pale face as she twisted her hands in her lap. Why had she joined them today, and where was her family? Her family could travel from Old Paris to GCU quickly. No doubt they'd show up later and make a dramatic entrance bearing tons of gifts for their lovely daughter.

"Israel is officially part of the European Collective," Jordan said. "Even if the EC treats them like step-children. So, visitors can legally travel here if they have the money to do it."

Rafael released the thick green drapes, letting them fall shut behind Jordan's back. "I didn't think Hannie had any family."

"Her parents were killed when she was young, and she spent most of her childhood on military bases," Jordan said. "When she was thirteen, she went to live in Jerusalem with an older woman who treated her like a granddaughter. Hannie even calls her *bubbe*; it's Yiddish for grandmother. She's visiting Hannie today."

"How nice for her." Laurel pulled her long legs up on the sofa and folded them underneath her. "Think how far that woman came to see Hannie. Maybe Hannie's never-ending bad mood will improve for a while."

Malese plunked down on a Persian rug in front of the sofa. "When will your parents get here?"

Laurel fastened her gaze on the fire blazing in the huge stone fireplace. It hissed and sizzled, bringing light to the dreary room. "My parents aren't coming to visit."

"Why not?" Timberlyn asked. "I mean… um, I hope they aren't sick or injured, or anything like that."

"They're fine. My sister, Lark, is a concert pianist. She's performing in Old London tonight." Laurel tossed her hair over her shoulder and continued to stare at the crackling fire. "They never miss her concerts."

Rafael joined the others. "GCU visiting day is only once a year. They can see her concerts anytime."

Jordan scooted across the hardwood floor, her socks slipping on the freshly polished surface. She wobbled but kept her balance, then sat on the arm of the sofa beside Matthew.

"You don't understand how much my parents love my sister," Laurel said. "Lark is beautiful and talented. She's always been their favorite."

Matthew touched Laurel's shoulder. "Well, you're pretty, too."

Jordan's stomach pinched. She took a deep breath and almost choked on the smoky air. She didn't blame Matthew for responding to Laurel's beauty. Laurel was perfect, after all, but why did he always rush to her rescue? Jordan had to face facts. A good-looking jock wouldn't want to tie himself to a computer nerd like her. A beautiful ballerina was more Matthew's style.

"Lark is naturally beautiful," Laurel said. "She didn't need to visit the beauty enhancers nearly as much as I did."

"I think we could all use a little help from the beauty enhancers." Jordan laughed then wrinkled her brow. *Why am I running to Laurel's rescue?*

"I needed a lot of help." Laurel sighed. "When I was eleven, my parents had my teeth straightened and bleached. At thirteen, my cheekbones were enhanced, and my jaw narrowed. My hair was streaked, and my skin permanently tanned at fourteen, my waist whittled at fifteen. Of course, the tattoo came after that." She gently fingered the white swan glistening on her shoulder. "Perfection is required in my family."

Jordan's heart ached with a shared lack of self-worth. All her life, she'd longed for her mother's beautiful blue eyes and dark hair, traits prevalent in the Hill family. Nana Hill had been a beauty contest winner back in the day before the planet self-destructed, and she was still lovely at sixty-five. Unfortunately, Jordan had inherited auburn locks and a pale complexion from her father. Not that there was anything wrong with her dad's appearance, but what girl wouldn't want to look like a beauty queen?

A couple of years ago, Jordan had won an award for writing an advanced computer program. One of the local newspapers sent a reporter to Old Memphis to interview and photograph her. She could still see the photographer sifting through the photos to pick the best one for the paper.

"Pretty face," the photographer said. "A little big, but pretty."

A little big. Those words were etched into her psyche. For months, the criticism had flashed in her brain like a neon sign. If she'd grown up with beauty enhancers at her disposal, would she have given into the desire to obtain perfection? She had no doubt that her parents would have forbidden her from having plastic surgery. They certainly wouldn't have encouraged her.

"You're a very talented ballerina," Malese said. "Your parents must be proud of that."

"They come to my performances, of course, when they don't clash with Lark's performances."

Jordan bristled at such blatant favoritism. TJ would loudly proclaim that she was their parents' favorite child, but in reality, Mom and Dad loved and cared for each child in a unique way.

Laurel covered herself with the patchwork quilt draped across the back of the sofa. "They were happy when Dawson took an interest in me. His family is very well connected and that pleased them. Dawson and his parents came to one of my performances in Old Paris, then came backstage to meet me. We dated a few times before we both got recruited by GCU, but we all know about the no-romance rule."

Laurel had never shared her thoughts and emotions with the team and suddenly, she was telling them the story of her life. Had homesickness hitched a ride on everyone's backs today?

"It's kind of odd that you and Dawson both ended up on Team Seven," Jordan said.

"Not really. I figured Dawson would make sure it happened. The Montgomery family gives a lot of money to GCU."

Matthew leaned forward and put his elbows on his knees. "Then you're happy to be on the same team with Dawson?"

Jordan chewed her bottom lip. Why was he so concerned with Laurel's happiness and desires? No doubt he'd be chasing after Laurel if Dawson wasn't around.

I'm his consolation prize. Her stomach rolled.

Laurel smoothed her glistening blonde hair. "Dawson and I can relate to each other because we both have demanding parents. Dawson's brother, Jonathan, died five years ago. He was the Montgomerys' favorite child, like Lark is my parents' favorite. Dawson told me his father has always fancied himself as some type of European nobility, and he used to say that, 'Jonathan was his perfect heir, but Dawson was all right for a spare.'" She swallowed hard. "That's awful, don't you think?"

Jordan refused to sympathize with the arrogant, conniving Dawson, but this explained his sick determination to succeed.

Rafael sat beside Malese on the floor and folded his legs in front of him. "Goes to show that parents aren't always right. My mother insisted I live in town with her and attend school when I wanted to stay in the mountains with my father and brother. They were freedom fighters in the Latin Collective."

Every head turned to gawk at Rafael. He'd never talked about his life before GCU, at least not with her. There had to be more to him beneath that brash, clown exterior. Freedom fighters. What else was Rafael hiding?

"I think your mother was very smart to make you go to school," Jordan said.

"When school was out, I spent a lot of time in the mountains. That's where I learned to fight and became an excellent marksman." Adrenaline seemed to rush through Rafael, and he rocked with excitement.

"Is your father still a freedom fighter?" Victor asked from the corner of the room, and Jordan jumped. She had forgotten about him. How could someone Victor's size so easily fade into the background?

Rafael hung his head. "He was killed a few years ago... but my brother, Hector, is still fighting in the mountains."

Jordan sniffed. The scent of this morning's cinnamon rolls still hung in the air, waking her hunger. Matthew bowed his head, and Timberlyn wiped tears from her eyes.

Laurel hugged her knees to her chest. "That's a shame about your father." Compassion danced in her pale green eyes, which were her most striking feature and apparently the one thing that hadn't been enhanced.

Rafael leaned back on his elbows. "He died the way he lived—fighting for a better life. Can't regret that."

"Your mother must've been proud when you were recruited by GCU," Jordan said.

"She was a lot happier than I was. Like most of us, I didn't want to leave my collective, friends, and family. Mom died three weeks before I left home." His voice sounded rough and full of unshed tears. "But at least she was proud of me when she died. She believed I had a great future ahead."

No one spoke as the computerized clock in the corner flashed each passing minute. Apparently, they'd all been captured by memories of home.

Jordan glanced from one silent face to the other. Victor had grown up an orphan without a parent's warmth, and Laurel had existed under the constant burden of never living up to her parents' expectations. Which damaged the most: to never know a parent's love or to be denied that love on a daily basis?

Rafael was an orphan, but his mother had loved him. Pride sparkled on his face when he mentioned his father. Matthew had been blessed with a mother who loved him and taught him about God before she died.

Parents were only human, so they couldn't possibly be perfect, but Mom and Dad came close. *Lord, thank You so much for my terrific parents.* Jordan missed them terribly, but the blessing of their love was well worth the pain.

Matthew jumped to his feet and rubbed his hands together. "Hey, let's brighten things up around here. We have something to celebrate today."

Malese and Timberlyn clambered to their feet, giggling, then scurried out of the room. Jordan studied the others, who all shook their heads in confusion. The two girls soon returned with Timberlyn balancing a lopsided chocolate cake on a wooden platter.

"Seventeen years ago today, the planet was blessed by Jordan's birth." Matthew grabbed Jordan's arms and pulled her to her feet. "Happy birthday!"

"We baked you a cake." Timberlyn and Malese squealed in unison; then Timberlyn placed the unexpected treat on the coffee table.

"How did you know?" She could barely push the words past the lump in her throat.

"You didn't think I'd forget something as important as your birthday, did you?" Matthew shuffled back and slapped his hand across his heart.

Jordan grinned. Remembering a girl's birthday was a pretty big deal. She'd mentioned her birthday to Matthew one time. She never dreamed he'd remember the date. He'd never asked her to be his *official* girlfriend, but maybe he thought of her as more than a consolation prize. Jordan wriggled her toes as they danced with excitement.

"Hannie told me you were sad because you wouldn't be able to spend your birthday with your family," Matthew said. "We wanted to cheer you up."

"Well, you did cheer me up and surprise me." She walked over to the two bakers and threw her arms around them, then hugged Matthew.

Rafael jumped to his feet, his arms spread wide. "Don't I get a hug, too?"

"Hugs for everyone." Jordan walked into Rafael's outstretched arms before hugging Victor, who blushed like an overgrown strawberry. She even hugged Laurel.

The smile that covered Jordan's lips almost hurt as she sat beside Laurel and considered the assorted group of friends surrounding her. Three months ago, she'd moved from the North American Collective dorms to this house and met this odd assortment of strangers. She'd been overwhelmed, and even intimidated by some of them, but now she loved each one.

A warm tear rolled down her cheek. "I'm spending my birthday with my family, after all."

"Enough mushy stuff for one day," Rafael said. "Let's eat that cake."

They all laughed but heartily agreed. Despite Malese and Timberlyn's dire warnings that this was the first cake they'd ever baked, they all devoured the sweet confection and declared it to be the best chocolate cake any of them had ever tasted. They spent the next few hours laughing, singing, and playing games.

"Thank you so much for doing this for me," Jordan whispered to Matthew as they stood in a secluded corner, watching Malese demonstrate a headlock using Rafael as her victim. "Today has meant the world to me."

"You're worth it." Matthew grinned, then placed a soft kiss on her lips.

Jordan's heart flipped from the kiss and the sudden fear that someone might see. Everyone knew she and Matthew were close, and she didn't believe that anyone in this room would tell on them. She even trusted Laurel to keep her secret, especially since she had a special relationship with Dawson. Why did fear cause her stomach to ache, and why wouldn't it release her from its overpowering grip? She'd fought it since childhood. Had there ever been a day in her life when fear took a vacation?

"Laurel!" A harsh male voice invaded the room. All laughter stopped. Everyone turned to face the menace at the door.

Dawson stood in the doorway, arms folded across his chest. "What're you doing wasting time with these people? You should be getting dressed for dinner with my parents."

If only Malese would hop up and put Dawson in a headlock.

Laurel jumped to her feet, scattering the cards she and Victor were playing with all over the hardwood floor. "I'm sorry, Dawson. I lost track of time. I'll change now." She walked to the door, ran her hand up and down Dawson's arm, obviously trying to soothe him, then led him away.

"As I said earlier." Rafael smoothed his rumpled hair. "Parents are not always right."

"She deserves better than that louse," Matthew said.

Don't give into jealousy, Jordan. Matthew likes you, not Laurel. He even remembered your birthday.

She rubbed her temple. If only she could get off this emotional roller coaster. Perhaps she should find a daisy and play the "he loves me, he loves me not" game.

"What've you kids been doing in here?" This time, Hannie stood in the doorway, her wild curls caressing her flushed face. "It looks like a bomb hit this place."

Playing cards lay scattered on the floor, the pillows from the sofa were still where they had landed during the impromptu pillow fight, and the furniture stood haphazardly against the wall where it had been moved to allow room for Malese's martial arts training.

Rafael threw a floral pillow at Hannie. "Who died and made you Cimarron?"

Hannie caught the pillow before it smacked her in the face but didn't offer a smart comeback. Her brows were drawn, and her normally bronzed complexion paled.

"Come join us," Matthew said. "There's a little cake left."

"No thanks. I'm heading upstairs." Hannie strode across the room. She stopped beside Jordan, clutched her arm, and whispered, "I need to talk to you, now. It's urgent."

Jordan's skin prickled from the pressure of Hannie's grip before the girl turned and left the room. Jordan swayed on her feet and pressed her hands against her rolling stomach. What had put that look of fear on Hannie's face? She shot a confused glance at Matthew before following Hannie up the stairs.

CHAPTER 10

"*Y*ou have to hack Cimarron's computer book as soon as possible," Hannie said after Jordan had entered their bedroom and closed the door behind her.

Jordan stared at Hannie and waited for her to grin or snicker. Funny joke. *Not so.* Hannie didn't blink.

"Have you lost your mind?" Jordan shoved her hand through her hair. "How can you ask me to hack Cimarron's computer as if this was the kind of stuff I do every day?"

Hannie moved away from the door and sat on the edge of her bed. She patted the place beside her. "You better sit down for this."

Jordan sat. Hannie scooted to the center of the bed and folded her legs in front of her. She held a strange metal object.

"What's that?" Jordan asked.

"I've used it to make sure our room isn't bugged."

"Bugged? Why would...? Where in the world did you get that thing?"

"My *bubbe* brought it to me. I've told you that my parents were killed when I was young, and I went to live with some soldiers for a while, and then with the mother of one of the soldiers."

63

Hannie had revealed the devastating details of her life one night as they were drifting off to sleep. She had lived a sad, unconventional life, but what did that have to do with hacking a computer? None of this made sense. Jordan tugged on some loose threads in the dark green quilt, certain that it was about to unravel like her torn emotions.

"This woman, your *bubbe*, visited you today, right?"

Hannie nodded. "I didn't tell you everything about these people. They weren't just soldiers. They were also former Mossad agents. Israeli secret service."

Did Hannie think she was so naïve that she needed a tutorial on the Mossad? "I know what the Mossad was. It was similar to the CIA in the United States."

"Well, the Mossad, the CIA, and a couple of other covert groups are not as dead as people think. They've gone underground and merged with each other. We now refer to the whole group as Marah. It means *bitter* in Hebrew. They communicate with each other, and they all spy on the Global Collective Council."

Jordan blinked. Her chin tickled, and her mouth dropped open. Her gaze lasered in on the silver bug detector. "I still don't understand what any of that has to do with me illegally accessing Cimarron's computer."

"We all know that GCU is the Global Council's pet project, and Principal Reed and Cimarron are closely tied to the Council."

Jordan pulled her legs up and hugged her knees. She rocked back and forth. Maybe she'd fallen asleep after eating too much cake, and this was all a bad dream. "A relative comes to visit you, and suddenly we're wrapped up in a web of espionage."

"She brought me a message from the Mossad—Marah. They're picking up chatter. Something big is in the works, and it involves GCU."

"Hannie, I'm not a secret agent, and I don't want to be." Jordan stood and fled across the room. She stared out the window, trying to get as far away from Hannie and her foolish talk as possible. *Picking up chatter.* What did that mean? And what did it have to do with her?

"I cannot believe the things I've done since coming to GCU, hiding under desks and in cellars, living in constant fear. My life used to be dull. I was sheltered by my parents and just studied computers." She rubbed her aching temples. "Sure, there were riots in the streets, and I knew some kids who got involved in bad things. But not me. I always followed the rules. And now you want me to break into Cimarron's computer. I won't do it."

"It involves Sierra Stone."

She spun around, speared by Hannie's words.

"There's a plot to kill Sierra Stone, and GCU is in the middle of it."

"That's crazy. How could GCU be involved in an assassination attempt?"

Hannie hopped off the bed and hurried to Jordan. Her fingers burned like icicles as they wrapped around Jordan's arms. "I don't know how, or even *if*, GCU is involved but we need to hack Cimarron's computer to find out. If GCU is involved, you can bet Cimarron is in the know."

"I'm not a computer hacker." That's what got Paul in trouble. That's why he disappeared.

"But you know how, don't you?"

"GCU has a very sophisticated computer system. Better than anything I've ever seen. Cimarron's computer book is bound to be heavily protected."

Paul had provided the codes in the Bible hidden in the cellar. If they worked on the mainframe, surely, she could tweak them enough to...

"I'm sure I could figure out how to hack it, but—"

"Good." Hannie released her pinching grip and stepped back. "We have to do this soon. Marah is hearing a lot of weird chatter about GCU, Project SS, missing students and—"

"Missing students?" The words escaped Jordan's throat with a cracking sound. She covered her pounding heart with her hand, amazed she could still breathe. Matthew was right. Project SS did stand for Sierra Stone. "All right, I'll do it."

What else could she do? She would never forget all the dark secrets she'd heard and read. Sierra Stone's life could be in danger, and she must help Paul and Zoe. She hadn't been able to help Zoe the night GCU took her away, but she wouldn't fail her friend again.

"Hannie, you know that if we get caught, you and I will disappear."

Hannie nodded and took a deep breath. "Then don't get caught."

* * *

GCU HAD PLANNED a grand winter banquet for the students. For the last week, the announcement had flashed across all the electronic billboards on campus. Supposedly, the banquet was GCU's way of rewarding the students with a night of fun and glamour, but in reality, it was another test.

Since arriving at GCU, the students had been learning to dine regally, dance divinely, and communicate with ease with government officials and dignitaries. At the banquet, each team could try out these skills and hopefully shine. Cimarron determined that Team Seven shine brighter than the snowcapped mountains surrounding GCU, and she stayed busy with banquet preparations. The fact that Mr. Flynt took more naps than any healthy human being Jordan had ever known now proved to be a blessing.

Jordan and Hannie told Matthew about their decision to hack Cimarron's computer. Who knew what they'd discover? Jordan couldn't face another life-shaking revelation without Matthew by her side. He might not be her official boyfriend, but she depended on him for strength and guidance.

He'd agreed that they were taking a huge risk, but what else could they do? They decided that Jordan would make her attempt to get inside Cimarron's computer book on the day of the winter banquet.

Now that day had arrived. Jordan fingered the trim on the green velvet gown hanging in her closet. As a little girl playing in the battle-scarred streets of Old Memphis, she never dreamed she'd wear such a gorgeous dress. Dresses like this only existed in old Hollywood movies, a young girl's dreams, or the European Collective.

The idea of a banquet had thrilled Jordan. She relished the chance to dress up like a seventeenth-century princess and spend the evening dancing with Matthew, her prince charming. Unfortunately, dancing and fancy dresses didn't matter much compared to the task before her tonight. She closed the closet door and turned to face her computer. It sat on the desk harmlessly flashing its red light, but to Jordan, it looked like a serpent poised to attack.

Hannie stood by the desk, her arms folded across her chest. "All right, girl, let's get this moving."

Jordan took a deep breath, walked to the desk, and sat down. She shook her sweaty palms before lifting the computer cover. The clock projected 4:15 p.m. on the wall. The banquet started at 7:00 p.m. That should give them plenty of time. Jordan placed the computer stick in the drive so it would be ready when the time came to download.

"Did you lock the door, Hannie?"

"Roger that," Hannie said. "Let's get moving."

"Oh, dear God, help me," Jordan prayed.

The world seemed to slow its rotation as she hit one key after the other. Minutes sped by as Hannie paced behind her, yet time no longer existed. Paul's codes didn't immediately unlock the prize, but after a mental challenge she secretly enjoyed, a list of documents appeared on the screen.

"We're in."

Hannie bent over her shoulder and stared at the screen.

Jordan wrinkled her nose and cocked one eyebrow. "Okay, so where is the file called GCU's evil secrets?" She scrolled through the pages in search of the magic file.

"Wait." Hannie pointed to the screen. "Project SS. I think we've found it. Start the download."

Jordan pushed more buttons, and data flashed across the screen. She held her breath and drummed her fingers on the desk while the computer whirred. Hannie whistled and clutched the back of Jordan's chair.

Rapid knocks pounded the bedroom door. Jordan squealed and jumped, turning to face the unknown menace.

"Girls, open the door, please." Cimarron's demanding voice poured through the heavy oak.

Jordan looked from the humming computer to Hannie's startled face and raised her hand to close the computer top.

"No." Hannie grabbed her arm. "She'll hear it running and get suspicious if it's closed."

"Hannie and Jordan, open this door right now."

Hannie hurried to the door and flung it open just before Cimarron's knuckles could pummel the wood again, leaving her fist suspended in midair. The light from the setting sun streaming in the window cast an eerie glow around the woman as she stepped into the room.

"What is going on in here, and why was your door locked?" Cimarron leveled a hard stare at Hannie and then Jordan. Those cold blue eyes chilled Jordan's blood. She wanted to confess and beg for mercy.

"Jordan was trying on some dresses for the banquet, and she's really shy," Hannie said.

Jordan studied her roommate. How could she lie so easily? *Thankfully, she's not a goody-goody like me.*

Cimarron stalked toward the closet. "I came up here to see if you girls were getting dressed for the banquet and find you playing on the computer."

Hannie shadowed the woman's every move, then stepped to the edge of the desk, using her body to block Cimarron's view of the computer screen.

"Why are the two of you wasting time when you should be dressing?"

Hannie shrugged. "You know how computer geeks are. It's like tearing them away from their favorite toy." Hopefully, Cimarron wouldn't notice the nervous tremor in Hannie's typically placid voice.

Cimarron raised her eyebrows and pursed her lips before peering into the closet.

"Jordan, I hope you're planning to wear the emerald gown. We provided you girls with many options, but I believe that gown would compliment your hair and complexion beautifully."

Jordan swallowed hard, the roar of the computer vibrating in her ears. Words rose to her lips but couldn't break free. Cimarron stared at her, waiting for a response.

"She did pick the green one," Hannie said. "And I picked a lovely one, too."

"Wonderful." Cimarron clapped. "Hannie, I will be happy as long as you don't wear camouflage."

Hannie laughed dryly. "No camouflage."

The woman gazed over Hannie's five-foot five form, her gaze searching the cluttered desk. Oh, why wasn't Victor the one standing there instead of Hannie? Data continued to flicker across the screen. Could the computer move any slower? When would Cimarron make out a blurry word and recognize her deepest, darkest secrets flashing before them?

"Help, please." Timberlyn dashed into the room, her thick mop of hair flying around her face. She ran to Cimarron. "I've been searching all over for you. You have to come with me and persuade Malese to wear that beautiful rose-colored dress. She's going to cut it up and make an island sarong as some political statement for the Pacific Collective."

"That's absurd." Cimarron dismissed the subject with a wave and directed her attention back to Jordan.

Timberlyn tugged on Cimarron's arm. "You have to come now. I've tried to talk her out of this crazy idea, but she won't listen, and I certainly can't fight her."

"Very well, I'm coming." The woman sighed and brushed an unruly strand of golden hair over her shoulder. "Get off that computer, girls, and get dressed. You have one hour before we leave."

Jordan nodded. Hannie clicked her heels together and threw her shoulders back in a soldier's attentive pose. They watched as Timberlyn led Cimarron to the door, stepped out, and pulled the door shut behind them.

"I'm going to throw up." Jordan clutched her aching stomach, threw her head back, and gulped air. She wiped sweat from her forehead as she stared at the spinning ceiling.

"What an adrenaline rush." Hannie bounced around the room. "I haven't had a rush like that in years."

She's crazy. Certifiable.

"I hope I never have a rush like that again. I'm going to be sick." Jordan's stomach lurched, and her head throbbed, but they'd completed their mission. She pulled the thin data stick from the computer. In her hand, she held the hidden truth about GCU.

CHAPTER 11

For months, Team Seven had spent most of their time hiking, running, swimming, and shooting guns while dressed in school uniforms, camouflage gear, and military boots. Tonight, Jordan stood in the familiar parlor, surrounded by freshly scrubbed teammates, and marveled at the transformation.

Rafael's appreciative gaze scanned Jordan, Hannie, Malese, and Timberlyn. "I've never been surrounded by so much beauty at one time."

"We all clean up pretty good." Hannie winked. "Even you grungy guys."

Rafael flipped his coattails and bowed. "Thank you, *mi tigresa*. And you look much better out of camouflage."

Hannie blushed. "But I feel ridiculous." She batted at the golden ruffles on her puffed sleeves. "The Global Council is supposed to be part of a modern new world, so why do they want to dress us up like ancient lords and ladies?"

"Supposedly, GCU wants to celebrate the grandeur of Old Europe." Matthew offered the pat explanation they all knew so well. "We boys got stuck in these monkey suits."

Hannie groaned and gave up her fight with the ruffles. "Another way of letting everyone know that the European Collective plans to rule the world."

"You have to admit the dresses are beautiful." Jordan twirled in place, laughing as the long skirt flew out around her, a swirling emerald cloud. "I never dreamed I'd wear something like this. Ever."

"I hoped I never would," Hannie said.

Dawson stood by the stone fireplace, at ease in his fancy suit, Laurel at his side. The musky scent of dying embers filled the room while the sparks battled the wood for their last glimmer of life. "You people prove the point that the European Collective is the only collective with class and sophistication." Dawson flashed a menacing glare at Hannie. "And the European Collective does rule the world."

Hannie bristled. "Only because they've lied to the world, pretended to be a friend, while stabbing the other collectives in the back."

Dawson crossed the room in several long strides. Hannie placed her hands on her hips and glowered at him.

Jordan patted Hannie's shoulder, hoping to soothe her bubbling rage. If only Cimarron would walk through the door and stop this coming battle.

Matthew stepped closer to Hannie, and Rafael stalked Dawson. The tension in the room brewed like a hurricane churning in the Gulf.

"You're the last one who should open her mouth." Dawson pointed his finger at Hannie. "You wouldn't even be at GCU if the European Collective hadn't included a few Israeli students for political correctness."

"And you wouldn't be at GCU if your father wasn't Malcolm Montgomery."

Dawson lunged for Hannie. Jordan screamed. Hannie should have known better than to antagonize Dawson. He'd always seemed a bit unstable. Matthew grabbed Hannie's arm and pulled her back behind him, while Rafael stepped in front of Dawson, his shoulder slamming against Dawson's chest. Dawson stumbled from the unexpected impact, falling against Matthew before righting himself. Dawson's face was blood red, his eyes wild. Hannie tried to move around Matthew and continue the fight, but he held her back.

Dawson looked from Matthew to Rafael, clearly weighing the odds. After a moment, he stepped back, turned on his heel, and stalked to the door. "We'll wait outside." He grabbed Laurel's arm

Laurel mouthed, "I'm sorry" as she followed Dawson out the door.

"That guy is loco," Rafael said.

Jordan frowned at Hannie. "You know better than to argue with Dawson."

I sound like Mom.

"I can handle Dawson Montgomery. By myself," Hannie said. "I don't need the two of you going all Sir Galahad on me." She pounded Matthew on the shoulder then pounced across the room. Her golden skirt swayed as she stumbled off her high heels.

"You are very welcome." Rafael executed a perfect bow, a playful grin lighting his face.

Before Hannie could respond, Cimarron walked into the room. For once, Jordan was happy to see the terrifying woman.

"Mercy." Rafael's jaw dropped.

Cimarron stood before them draped in a clingy satin creation that accentuated every curve of her perfect body. "I'm pleased to see that you all managed to arrive on time." She lightly touched the strand of pearls that fell from her neck to nestle in the ample cleavage below.

Mr. Flynt trailed behind her. He tugged at the collar buttoned tightly around his thick neck. "I hate these things. Hurry up, everyone." He waved his arm and stomped to the door. "Let's try to make the next transport."

The girls gathered their coats and capes from the closet then followed Mr. Flynt to the waiting transport ready to carry them to tonight's regal adventure.

The metallic structure wasn't a royal carriage, but it was good enough for a girl from Old Memphis who never dreamed she'd experience such grandeur. Matthew helped her board the sleek machine. Thick stars sparkled through the transport's clear roof as it glided up the mountain side toward the secluded banquet hall.

* * *

A CASTLE FORTRESS built in the Middle Ages hosted the winter gala. Only one tower, a courtyard, and the grand banquet hall remained of the vast structure. The GC snow leopard flag waved from the castle turret, bathed in a golden manufactured light that couldn't compete with the peaceful light of the full moon. A chill wind greeted Jordan, and she pulled her cape closed around her shoulders.

She clung to Matthew's hand as they walked through the courtyard and entered the elegant ballroom. The secrets of GCU, good or bad, rested on a computer stick back in her dorm room. She was anxious to discover the truth but happy to postpone the inevitable. This beautiful night begged to be enjoyed. Tonight, she wanted to be a typical teenage girl at a typical teenage dance. Of course, how many school dances were held at medieval castles? So much for typical.

Matthew squeezed her hand as they followed Cimarron and Mr. Flynt through the crowd of chattering students to a table at the front of the cavernous room. The smoky scent of oil lamps mixed with the smell of fresh flowers and baking bread. Cimarron motioned for them to sit at the table reserved for Team Seven, then took her place at a side table with Principal Reed and several other professors. Mr. Flynt sat at the head of the students' table. Jordan gave Hannie a nervous smile as she took a seat beside her. Even Hannie appeared awestruck by the splendor surrounding them.

Tables draped in deep purple linen and decorated with centerpieces of fruit and flowers were scattered across the room. Malese and Timberlyn sat opposite Jordan. Malese covered her ears to drown out the den of voices while over one-hundred-fifty students found their assigned tables. Timberlyn pointed overhead. Jordan looked up.

Good gravy! Her grandmother's favorite southern expression popped into her head at the awesome sight.

Directly above them, the high ceiling hollowed out into a dome where grand ladies and knights danced among colors of green, gold, blue, and purple. She glanced at Timberlyn and shook her head. "Amazing."

Timberlyn elbowed Malese and pointed upward. Malese's chin dropped when she spied the glorious images painted above.

At the head of the table, Mr. Flynt maintained his typical bored expression while nibbling on a hunk of freshly baked bread. Dawson sat close to Laurel, whispering in her ear, while she stared at the linen napkin folded in an intricate flower design. Neither she nor Dawson glanced up to admire the beautiful ceiling or seemed to hear as Victor and Rafael raved about the exotic fruits and rich salads. Apparently, European ballerinas and heirs from powerful families were hard to impress.

Jordan glanced around the room. The same scene was repeated at each table. The students from the European Collective appeared to be frozen figurines while the other students murmured and stared wide-eyed at the finery surrounding them.

How sad to be so young and uninspired. Perhaps there was some value in struggle. Adversity was a harsh teacher, but it taught its students to appreciate beauty.

After a superb feast of meats, cheese, vegetables, and exotic deserts, the band took their place, and the sound of strings and brass filled the room. The same elegant music had played in Laurel's dance classes when she'd taught them to dance to the classic tunes.

The first test had begun. Tonight, they wouldn't be tested on martial arts, sharp shooting, or bomb making. Tonight was the test of elegance. A showcase of gracious living but a test, nonetheless.

Matthew stood. "Would you like to dance?"

"I'd love to." She took Matthew's hand and followed him to the dance floor, the romantic chords of a waltz tantalizing her ears as they passed the bandstand.

"We're some of the first couples brave enough to venture into the intimidating world of *dance*." He waved his arm to take in the almost empty dance floor.

Jordan and Matthew enjoyed exclusive ownership of this area, but several other couples danced on the opposite side of the room. Matthew wrapped one arm around Jordan's back and pulled her close. Her dancing skills and inherent clumsiness had improved with Laurel's tutelage, and somehow, she managed to match her steps to Matthew's.

She glanced around the room, careful not to lose her balance. Surely, no one would be able to hear them over the strains of the orchestra. "Did you send Timberlyn to my room to get Cimarron this evening?"

"Well, I told her it was very important to keep Cimarron out of your room for a couple of hours."

She studied his calm face. "Did you tell her what we were doing?" She'd be devastated if he had dragged Timberlyn into their drama. Why put her life in danger, too?

"Of course not. I told her that you couldn't be disturbed for a while. I asked her to trust me, and she did."

"Thank goodness. I don't know what we would have done without her." Jordan rested her head on Matthew's shoulder, safe in his arms. If only they were regular kids at a regular school at an ordinary dance. She'd rather wear rags, safe at home than this beautiful dress in the heart of danger.

Jordan's shoe brushed Matthew's foot, but she managed not to step on him or stumble.

"I wonder what Cimarron thought when she went to Timberlyn's room and Malese wasn't cutting up her dress to make a sarong." Was Cimarron suspicious of them now?

"I wondered that myself." Matthew tightened his grip on her as they passed near another couple. Once they were out of earshot, he continued. "Timberlyn said that Malese was in the shower when they got to her room, and the dress was lying on the bed, so Timberlyn convinced Cimarron that Malese must have changed her mind."

"I can only imagine the evil eye Cimarron flashed at Timberlyn." Jordan closed her eyes as they spun around the room, trying to shut out the real world they'd soon have to confront. She clung to Matthew, hoping the dance would never end.

Unfortunately, the music refused to obey her wishes and stopped. She stepped out of Matthew's arms.

"Do me a favor and ask Hannie to dance. I want her to pass the culture test tonight, and I don't think anyone else is going to ask her."

Matthew chuckled. "You're right. No one will ask her because she's way too scary."

Jordan laughed. "So, you be a brave boy." She spun him around and pushed him toward the table.

Hannie accepted Matthew's offer, and his outstretched arm, without making any snide remarks. No doubt Hannie understood she had to pass all the tests, and at GCU, dancing seemed to be a required skill. Over the next half hour, more students gathered their courage and headed to the dance floor. Jordan grinned when a blushing Victor whispered to Malese and led the small girl out to dance. Another benefit of their weekly Bible study.

"Shall we dance, lovely lady?" Rafael spoke to Jordan from across the table.

Jordan's face burned at the memory of his arms around her when they'd waltzed in Laurel's dance class weeks ago. She didn't want to repeat those upsetting emotions. Not now when she and Matthew were growing closer.

"I'm a little tired right now, but I'm sure Timberlyn would like to dance." Jordan had determined that every girl on Team Seven pass the test tonight.

"How about it, Timberlyn?" Rafael gallantly shifted his attention to the quiet girl sitting beside him. "Are you willing to dance with a Latin lover like me?"

The light was dim, but Jordan saw Timberlyn's face redden. She nodded, and Rafael led her to the dance floor.

The modern young couples swayed to the classical music, each swirling skirt glimmering in the candlelight, as if a rainbow had dropped to earth. Jordan stared at the flickering candle in the middle of the table. Wax dripped down the candle's side and puddled in the holder. Tonight, she'd stumbled through a time portal to another century. If only she could stay here forever, lost in a simpler time and place.

Hannie laughed at something Matthew said, her dark curls bouncing across her shoulders. Matthew stood straight, his wide shoulders straining against his dark tuxedo. They looked like a bronze statue of the perfect couple magically brought to life.

Laurel and Dawson danced beside them. She wore a strapless velvet dress of royal blue. Her pale blonde hair was piled on top of her head, revealing the swan tattoo with its graceful wings stretching over her shoulder.

Jordan played with the trim on her emerald dress. This gown was fit for a princess. Jordan's lanky frame didn't do it justice. Hannie was striking, though not classically pretty, and Laurel was perfection. *I can't compare to either of them.*

A throaty laugh floated from the head table. Jordan turned to see the *fairest of them all* snuggling against Principal Reed's arm. The man stared helplessly at Cimarron, captivated by her beauty. Did Mrs. Reed know about her husband's extracurricular activities? The inconvenience of a wife didn't seem to bother Cimarron as she laid her head on the man's shoulder and whispered in his ear. How many secrets did this so-called school harbor?

For the rest of the evening, Jordan danced with Matthew, Victor, and several boys from other teams. Laurel danced with Victor. No doubt she wanted to dance with someone besides Dawson and considered Victor a safe bet. Not even Dawson would smart off to Team Seven's giant.

Jordan took a break from the dance floor to devour another cherry tart. Its tangy sweetness tickled her tongue. Number two or three? Her head swam as the sugar hit her system, so she took a sip of her fruit drink.

The adults indulged in a more potent brew. Cimarron wobbled on her high heels as her robust laughter carried across the room. *Looks like she's indulged a little too much, bless her heart. Of course, I've been as bad with sugar.*

Jordan pushed herself back from the table as Rafael appeared at her side.

"It's time for our dance now."

Matthew was dancing with Timberlyn, and Jordan had run out of reasons to say no to Rafael. She took a gulp of her drink for courage, set her cup on the table, and took his outstretched hand. Shivers traveled up her arm. When they reached the dance floor, Rafael pulled her close. Of course, he would choose a slow dance.

"I've wanted to dance with you all night," he said in that deep throaty tone he used all too well.

"Why me?" Jordan struggled to put some distance between their bodies.

"I always make it a point to dance with the most beautiful girl at any party."

"And Dawson wouldn't let you dance with Laurel, so you settled for me." She offered the only explanation she could think of.

A low chuckle reverberated from Rafael's chest. "Plastic dolls are not my preference. I prefer real women." His arms tightened around her.

"Then you should have asked Hannie to dance."

"I'm not that brave, or crazy enough to tangle with the little *tigresa*." He laughed.

Rafael could not think that she was prettier than Laurel. Not possible. Boys had never fallen at Jordan's feet.

"Surely you think Laurel is beautiful," Jordan said.

Matthew considered Laurel pretty, and Dawson idolized her. Rafael couldn't be immune to her charms.

"You're the one with true beauty because you're real." He expertly moved them across the floor as he spoke. Her cheeks warmed. Why did he have this irritating effect on her?

The melodious sounds of strings and brass combining with the scent of mingled perfumes relaxed her enough to enjoy the rest of the dance. By the time the music stopped, she and Rafael stood in a far corner of the room shielded by a tapestry-covered wall and an enormous ivy plant. How had that bad boy engineered this?

"I've never known a girl with hair this honey color." He twirled one of her curls around his finger. "And you have such beautiful cat-eyes and such creamy skin." His fingers moved to touch her cheek and brush the curve of her jaw.

She should ignore her fluttering heart and step away. Instead, she stared into Rafael's coal-like eyes while a shiver ran down her spine. Before she could process her incoherent thoughts, he bent his head, and his lips touched hers. The kiss was warm and soft. She pressed closer to him, as if drawn by an invisible rope, and he deepened the kiss.

What am I doing? Rafael Alvarado is not the boy who tugs at my heart. Matthew is. Jordan put her hands against Rafael's chest and shoved herself out of his embrace.

"We can't do this. It's against the rules," she whispered.

A puzzled expression claimed his much too handsome face. "Who cares about rules?"

He reached for her, but she dodged his grasp and stepped back. "I do. I'm in enough trouble already."

His forehead creased, and he lifted his brows, but she turned before he could ask for clarification and rushed back to the table.

"There you are," Matthew said as she approached. "It's time to board the transport and head back to the dorm." He held the thick shawl she'd draped over the back of her chair. "Are you all right?" Matthew wrapped the shawl around Jordan's shoulders, and a heavy cloak of guilt fell on her.

Rafael joined them. She avoided his gaze.

"I'm fine," she whispered. "A little nervous about what we may soon find out."

Hannie grabbed her arm. "We caught a break. Flynt said Cimarron is not coming back with us. It seems she has business to discuss with Principal Reed." Hannie motioned toward the head table where Cimarron practically sat in Principal Reed's lap.

Why am I not surprised? Jordan hung her head. Was she any less wanton than Cimarron?

Matthew wrapped his arm around her shoulders and smiled while her conscience burned.

Lord, please forgive me. How can I be so fickle?

CHAPTER 12

*W*hen they arrived back at the dorm, Mr. Flynt uttered his usual, "Keep out of trouble kids," and headed off to bed. The team said quick good nights and went to their rooms. By the time Jordan and Hannie had slipped into their flannel pajamas and robes and pulled up the stolen data file, Matthew joined them.

"Well, let's see what we've got." A slight tremor darkened his voice.

Jordan scrolled through the file while Hannie and Matthew peered over her shoulder.

Excerpts from an email from an unnamed Global Council official flashed onscreen. *"Sierra Stone to appear in Latin Collective in December to meet with local leaders and push her motto 'individual over collective.'"*

"That doesn't sound very ominous," Matthew said.

"Check out this email labeled SS." Hannie pointed to the screen.

Jordan touched the screen to open the file. "It's an email from Principal Reed to Cimarron," she said.

"We are on schedule to intercept Sierra Stone in Old Venezuela in Latin Collective. Keep up the good work with Team Seven. They will counterbalance the other students nicely in Old Venezuela."

"Team Seven." Jordan clutched her throat. "That's us. Are the other students the ones on the list?"

Jordan had told Hannie about the list she'd read on Paul's computer, and they'd emailed the information to Marah.

Matthew straightened, stretched his shoulders, then tugged at his shirt collar. "That doesn't sound good. Keep reading."

Jordan touched the screen to reveal the next email. She shook her head, then squinted and bent close to the computer. That signature couldn't be correct? "This message came from one of the new server types recently developed by the Global Council. It's almost impenetrable. I'm surprised I was able to pull it."

"Maybe that God of yours is watching out for us." Hannie patted her on the shoulder.

"He's your God, too." Jordan grinned, happy to hear Hannie acknowledging God's help, even if it was in a joking manner.

Hannie gave a one shoulder shrug. "So you keep telling me. Chosen people and all that stuff. Now, what does the email say?"

"Stone cannot be allowed to continue this radical trend. She must be permanently stopped in December. Orders from River."

Jordan's heart pounded her ribs. Sweat broke out on her forehead. "Orders from River Wallis—second in command?" She gaped up at Matthew and Hannie. "This plot goes all the way to the top of the Global Council. What have we gotten ourselves into?"

"Read the next message." Matthew's voice sounded hoarse. Hannie's face was pale.

Jordan read the next communication to Cimarron from an unnamed account.

"Are you confident the profiles for the chosen students are complete in the selected collectives? Are they secure at the holding camp now? They are vitally important to the success of this mission. I will forward your response to our contact at the Council."

Jordan scrolled to the next message. "Here's Cimarron's reply. *Everything is going as planned. They have been returned to the compound and are secure. They will be ready for transport at the appropriate time."*

Jordan's breath caught in her throat, and her stomach churned.

Matthew stepped back and sat on the edge of Hannie's bed, his skin as white as old milk. "Well, you were right, Jordan. Zoe and Paul were kidnapped by GCU."

Jordan rubbed her forehead, trying to drive away her blossoming headache. "At least we know they're alive."

"Who is Zoe?" Hannie asked.

Jordan quickly told Hannie about her missing roommate. Of course, Hannie knew Paul was a Christian. Jordan explained that Zoe was also an outspoken Christian.

"That makes sense." Hannie stretched her arms and cracked her knuckles. "The Council hates Christians, almost as much as they hate Jews or anyone who dares to worship anything other than the government."

Matthew pounded his fist against his leg. "It sounds like they're planning to use the missing students in an assassination plot against Sierra Stone. But how?"

As the old-fashioned clock on Jordan's bedside table struck the minutes away, they continued to read the numerous communications between Cimarron and Principal Reed, some ominous, some sickeningly sensual. Principal Reed would be in big trouble if Mrs. Reed could see these.

"I could've lived a lifetime without knowing how close Cimarron and Principal Reed are." Matthew's face was tinged with pink.

"Definitely too much information," Hannie agreed.

Jordan grinned at Hannie's blush. *Maybe she's not so worldly after all.*

Jordan should have told them about Cimarron and Principal Reed's affair, but she'd been trying to erase the memories from her mind. She didn't want to relive them now.

She quickly moved onto another message. *"The Council is pleased with the additional plan involving Rafael's brother, Hector Alvarado."*

"Rafael's brother is a freedom fighter," Jordan explained to Hannie, since she'd been absent when Rafael shared this news. "This could be the reason they recruited Rafael in the first place."

Hannie nodded. "This plot is well-developed and long range. Marah suspected something big was in the works."

Matthew stood and shoved his hands in his pockets. "I'd call an assassination plot big. We gotta get this information to Marah soon. We can't handle this alone."

"Hannie's *bubbe* gave her a communicator that allows us to send encrypted messages to Marah in Israel. We'll let them know what we found."

He nodded, and his shoulders relaxed a bit. Jordan wished she could run home and ask Mom and Dad what to do. They always had the right answer. Hopefully, once Marah got the information, they'd handle everything, but right now, Jordan and Team Seven had to help their missing friends.

"We need to find this hidden camp and help the students." The words slipped through her lips before fear could stop them. Bravery was not her thing. She never took risks or craved adventure, but she'd never been in a situation like this one. Paul and Zoe were in danger, and they needed her help.

For the next half-hour, she scoured the data trying to find the camp's location. Matthew paced, and Hannie repeatedly punched her pillow. Jordan squealed when she finally discovered a folder with some unnamed coordinates and an odd map.

"Can you make sense of this?" She stood and let Matthew take her seat so he could examine the map. He was the cross-country runner, mountain-climbing expert after all, so he must know something about maps. She covered her mouth and yawned, amazed she was sleepy when so much adrenaline flowed through her system.

"Yeah, I think I could find this. I'll download it to my portable computer." Matthew pulled the small device out of his pocket and started the download process. "I'll study this in my room and see if I can pinpoint a location."

"What then?" Jordan asked as he put the device back in his pocket and stood.

"I'll make the trek out there tomorrow and see if this place really exists, and if our friends are being held there."

Zoe had been missing for four months. She must be living in constant fear. Jordan prayed she was safe and unharmed.

"I'll go with you," she said.

"You're not coming with me," Matthew blared, much like a commanding father. "This is not some stroll in the park. It's too dangerous."

Jordan put her hands on her hips. "I'm not a helpless little girl. I might not be the warriors that Malese and Hannie are, but I'm not a total wimp."

"I know you're not a helpless little girl." Matthew ran his hand up and down her arm as if that would soothe her temper. "But there is no way I'm letting you go up into those mountains."

Letting me?

Jordan shook her arm free, her blood surging through her veins. "My father is in Old Memphis, and *you* can't tell me what to do."

Matthew had never tried to boss her before, and she didn't like it now and wouldn't put up with it.

"You're the computer master, the only one we've got, and we can't possibly do any of this without you." His voice sounded calm, and his words made sense, but she wasn't in the mood for logic.

She opened her mouth, ready to release the barbs stinging her tongue, but Hannie punched her shoulder.

"Matthew's right. We need you for your brains, not your brawn."

Matthew reached for her arm again and gave it a tender squeeze. "You're indispensable to our mission."

What if Matthew was captured in the mountains and locked away with the rest of the students? She might never see his baby blue eyes again or laugh at his corny jokes or enjoy his kisses.

"You're indispensable to me," she said. *How did those words fly out of my mouth? He'll think I'm in love with him, and I am not. Crazy about him, yes—in love with him, no.*

She backed away from Matthew and pressed her hands to her face to cover her burning cheeks "I mean you... you are... indispensable to this mission, too. If it's that dangerous, you can't go alone."

"I'll take Rafael with me." Matthew folded his arms across his chest as if that settled the matter and no further discussion was needed.

Hannie grabbed Matthew's checkered shirt sleeve. "You can't tell Rafael about this. This can't go any further than the three of us."

"I have to tell Rafael. His brother is Plan B, remember?" He pulled his shirt from Hannie's grasp. "Rafael may be a scapegoat for GCU. He deserves to know about this mess."

Jordan took a deep breath of the chilly air. They'd need to crank up the heat before going to bed. Of course, she didn't expect to get much sleep tonight.

"Matthew's right. Rafael's brother could be in danger. Rafael could be in danger. We have to tell him."

Hannie paced across the floor several times, her camouflage slippers pounding the surface. Where did she ever find camo slippers? Hannie stopped and stretched her back. "All right, you can tell Rafael. But no one else. The more people who know, the more danger we're in."

Jordan hated keeping this information from Victor, Timberlyn, and Malese. They were believers now, or at least seekers, and this new information proved that Christians were in danger at GCU. They had a right to know the truth, but Hannie was right about the risk. Secrets had a funny way of escaping their boundaries.

Matthew nodded. "This information stays between the four of us, for now." He fixed Jordan with a hard stare, took her hands in his, and squeezed them tightly. Was he trying to give strength or receive it? Maybe both. "Once we make contact with Hannie's friends in Israel, and have more information, we might be able to tell the others."

Jordan stared out the window over Matthew's shoulder, her view total darkness. She was drowning in darkness. A cloak of secrets, fear, and deceit.

86

She squeezed Matthew's hands. "Agreed."

Hannie stepped closer. "If those coordinates lead you to a mystery prison camp, everything is going to change. And it's going to change fast."

Matthew and Jordan stared at one another. She'd never seen such intensity on his face before. None of them had lived an easy life. The Bible said adversity strengthened people. If that were true, they should all be pretty strong. The Bible was full of ordinary people doing extraordinary things. She prayed that God's miracles were not limited to the pages of Scripture.

Matthew tugged one of Jordan's curls, then turned and left the room. Guilt over this evening's kiss pummeled Jordan's heart.

"Hannie, can I talk to you?"

Hannie plopped down on her bed and folded her legs beneath her. "Sure, what's the problem?"

"What makes you think it's a problem?"

"We are surrounded by problems right now. And that stricken expression on your face gives you away. Who'd you kill?"

Jordan collapsed on her bed, rolled onto her back, and stared up at the feather cracks in the ceiling. "I feel so guilty, and then I feel guilty for feeling guilty at a time like this. This isn't about me. We have much bigger things to worry about, but the guilt is killing me."

"People from Old Memphis must speak a different language because I don't have any idea what you're talking about. One thing's for sure, I've never met anyone as hard on themselves as you are." She waved her hands in front of her. "You're not pretty enough. You can't break the rules. So, tell me, what did you do this time?"

"I kissed Rafael at the banquet," Jordan confessed with a squeal, then rolled over to her stomach to watch Hannie's reaction. "Well, actually he kissed me, but I let him do it, and for a split second, I think I enjoyed it." She bowed her head and pounded her feet against the firm mattress.

"Of course, you enjoyed it. I can't stand the guy, but even I'll admit he's scorching hot. Why torture yourself with guilt?"

Should she reveal her secret relationship with Matthew? She could trust Hannie. Besides, if Cimarron found out they'd hacked her computer, she'd probably kill them, so breaking the no-romance rule was no longer an issue.

"Because, because… I've kissed Matthew, too," she whispered. "Several times, and I really enjoyed it."

Hannie's face revealed little emotion.

Here I am kissing boys left and right, and Hannie doesn't look the least bit shocked. "You must think I'm horrible."

"Do you want to know what I think?"

Blunt and forthright, Hannie never pulled punches. Jordan paused. Did she want to experience the full brunt of her condemnation?

"Yes, I want to know what you think." She'd been beating herself up long enough. Let someone else sling the stones.

"I think you're a seventeen-year-old girl who has two extremely hot guys falling for her. I think you're physically attracted to both of them, but emotionally attracted to Matthew only."

Jordan breathed in every word as if Hannie held a master's degree in psychology.

"I think it's normal for a seventeen-year-old girl to be confused about boys and romance, and you're not engaged to Matthew, so there's no need to wallow in guilt over a kiss." Hannie grabbed her feather pillow and pulled it onto her lap.

"You don't think I should feel guilty?"

"Not at all." Hannie stressed each word, then threw the pillow at Jordan. It struck her in the face. She'd never been good at catch.

Jordan grabbed the giant marshmallow-like object and rolled to a sitting position. "I'm so glad we're friends, Hannie. I needed someone to talk to."

"Don't get used to it. I don't have friends, at least not girlfriends." Hannie winked.

"You're not as hard as you pretend to be, Hannie Jacobson. We're all becoming friends here. Most of us anyway."

"Are you telling me you're going to kiss Dawson next?"

Jordan groaned and threw the pillow at Hannie, aiming for the girl's smarty face. It fell harmlessly into Hannie's lap. She'd never been good at toss either.

"You know what I'm talking about. I'm enjoying getting to know Malese and Timberlyn. Victor is like a little brother." She laughed. "Maybe *little* isn't the right word. Even Laurel is not the person I thought she was at first."

"I can tolerate the other three, but I'll never find anything good in that plastic doll." Hannie snorted.

Jordan stood and walked over to Hannie's bed, then flopped down beside her. "There's more to Laurel than shows on the surface."

"I'm certainly not interested in digging deeper into her privileged life or beneath her surface. But I have seen a couple of guys on Team Four that I wouldn't mind getting to know a little better. Maybe I'll check them out and see if I can kiss more guys than you can." Hannie grinned.

Jordan shoved her shoulder, pushing her down on the mattress. Laughing, Hannie propped herself up on her elbows. She stared at Jordan, and her smile vanished.

"One thing's for sure... if Matthew and Rafael find that camp and GCU is involved in an assassination scheme like we suspect, worrying about which boy to kiss will be the least of your problems."

CHAPTER 13

a thick darkness hung above the mountains as Matthew and Rafael snuck out of the dorm in search of the lost students. Using the coordinates Jordan had found on Cimarron's computer, Matthew plotted a course on the sketchy map. The camp appeared to be in the vicinity of the old castle where they'd dined and danced the night before. The computer had provided them with enough information to locate the prison camp—if it really existed.

Hopefully, those weird emails had a very innocent meaning and the camp was only a figment of their overactive imaginations. The sun rising above the tree line warmed him, but his jacket would come in handy later as they climbed the peaks to higher altitudes and the temperature dropped. They should reach the camp in two hours.

Since this was Saturday, and the students were given some measure of freedom, Jordan and Hannie would be able to cover for their absences if anyone asked. If they were lucky, Cimarron would be too preoccupied with her love affair and recovering from a hangover to notice they weren't around.

"I don't know about you, *amigo*, but I could use a rest break and something to eat," Rafael said after they climbed over the latest mountain ridge. He wound up the rope to secure it for the next climb, then wiped the sweat from his face and took a deep breath.

Matthew glanced at his watch. His stomach growled. "We have time for a short break. I could eat something myself."

Last night, Matthew told Rafael everything he and the girls had discovered about GCU, the missing students, the assassination plan in Venezuela, and Rafael's brother. Rafael had been surprised, but he didn't have any trouble believing the accusations. His brother, Hector, had been fighting the Global Council's control in the Latin Collective for years, so Rafael was more than happy to join Matthew on this search for the suspected prison camp.

Rafael sat on a wide boulder and took a few deep breaths. "You've got me beat when it comes to mountain-climbing, Mr. Super Jock." He reached into his backpack, pulled out a couple of energy bars, and tossed one to Matthew.

Matthew laughed. Rafael was in excellent shape, but the strain of today's adventure showed on his face. Sweat dampened his cheeks, and dark circles nestled beneath his eyes. The mountains could take a lot out of a man with the crisp winds and thin air.

Matthew sat on the ground, crossed his legs, and tore open the protein bar wrapper. "Well, as an expert marksman, you can outshoot me. That's what makes us a good pair." He took a big bite of the bar, the honey flavor exciting his taste buds.

"Maybe GCU is right about this team building stuff, huh?" Rafael grinned. "I guess they can't be wrong about everything."

"Yeah, we do have a very talented team. I've enjoyed learning from our teammates."

Rafael nodded between bites. "I'm enjoying getting to know our team members. One more than all the others." He fixed Matthew with a curious stare. "So, tell me, what's going on between you and Jordan?"

Matthew almost choked on his last bite. He coughed several times then stared questioningly at Rafael. Was he serious? The playful glint that usually danced in his eyes had disappeared.

Matthew opened his mouth then snapped it shut again. That stupid no-romance rule. He couldn't say anything to get Jordan into trouble. "Jordan and I are very good friends."

Over the last few months, Matthew had learned to see past Rafael's cockiness and discovered they had a lot in common. They both kept a photo of their mothers in a picture frame by their beds, and Matthew had spotted tears in his roommate's eyes several times. Rafael's grief was fresh and raw.

Grief ached worse than any physical pain. Like an acid melting your insides. Matthew had little time to grieve when his mother had died five years ago since he had to take care of his sisters, Chloe and Maeve, while his father sought solace at the bottom of a whiskey bottle. Hopefully, Maeve was happy with the boy she'd married to escape the family's vagabond lifestyle.

Matthew had told Rafael that he and Chloe and Dad moved into a war-ravaged mansion that once belonged to a famous movie star in Old Hollywood. Rafael loved the classic Hollywood movies, and he'd been very impressed. Matthew had been equally intrigued by Rafael's descriptions of the jungles, mountains, and waterfalls in Old Venezuela.

Rafael was okay for a buddy, but Jordan captured his thoughts and sometimes made an appearance in his dreams. He'd been attracted to her from the first day they met, but the attraction had become something more. He took a long drink from his canteen, hoping the cool water would put out the fire burning in the pit of his stomach.

Rafael clapped away the crumbs from the power bar. "Just friends. Great. Then you won't mind if I take a shot at her."

"Jordan is not your type." Matthew's voice dropped an octave or two. He stood and stretched his achy shoulders as a circling condor screeched and dove over the adjoining ridge to secure its prey. "Find another girl to pursue."

"A very passionate reaction to have over *just a friend*." Rafael ground the dirt under the toe of one boot and leveled a hard stare at him.

"You know the rules. Romantic relationships are forbidden at GCU."

Rafael laughed. "Unlike you, I never let rules stand in my way."

Matthew squinted in the sun's blinding glare as the cold breeze stung his cheeks. "Jordan always follows the rules. One of the many ways the two of you are different. She's not your type."

Suddenly, he had a competitor for Jordan's love. And, of all people, it had to be 'every girl's dream come true,' Rafael Alvarado.

Rafael oozed charm and knew all the flirty things to do and say. Matthew had never asked Jordan to be his steady girlfriend or pledged his love in any way, and most girls liked to hear that kind of stuff.

Rafael jumped to his feet, his lean body taut. "You don't think I'm good enough for her, do you?" The wind whistling over the ridge ruffled Rafael's dark hair, and he brushed it back from his stern face.

"No one is good enough for Jordan," Matthew said. "She's loving, intelligent, and innocent. Not your type at all."

Rafael stepped toward Matthew. His boots connected with several small rocks, sending them scattering out of the way. "I guess you think only a North American Collective jock is good enough for her."

Don't do it, Matthew. He's playing mindgames like athletes before a big match. Now was not the time to fight.

Rafael flashed a cheeky grin. "She didn't seem so innocent when I danced with her last night. I think she enjoyed being held in my arms, judging by the way she snuggled close and pressed herself—"

"Don't talk that way about Jordan!" Matthew yelled.

"I'm not saying anything bad about her. I think she's beautiful. Any guy would want to hold her in his arms. She's not an innocent little girl."

If Rafael didn't shut his smart mouth, Matthew would shut it for him. No one could disrespect Jordan in front of him. He threw a punch at Rafael, but Rafael ducked out of the way, and the blow glanced off his shoulder.

Rafael stood in a boxer's pose, his fists in front of his face. Rafael was fast and clever. He'd whipped Dawson without breaking a sweat, but Matthew had more bulk and strength than either Dawson or Rafael. *I can't out-shoot Rafael, but I can out-fight him.*

The old saying about pride coming before a fall bounced through Matthew's brain as Rafael landed a stinging punch on his jaw. He stumbled from the impact but managed to wrap his arms around his opponent's waist. He must have surprised Rafael because the expert boxer lost his balance, and they both tumbled to the ground. The screech of hawks and alpine swifts taking to flight surrounded them as they hit the hard dirt. Dust enveloped them. Matthew sat up and wiped the rancid grit out of his mouth.

Rafael rose to his knees, his hands balled into fists. He struggled to catch his breath in the thin mountain air. Matthew could make his move on the weakened boy and finish the fight, but common sense took over.

"What's wrong with us? We're acting like little boys on the playground," Matthew said. "That camp is a few miles away. This area could be crawling with GC Council thugs."

Rafael climbed to his feet and brushed dirt from his shirt and pants. "You're right. I'd hate to be captured by GC soldiers because I was fighting over a girl."

"Well, that would be kind of embarrassing." Matthew managed a slight grin despite his sore jaw. "Why don't we finish this discussion when we get back to GCU?"

"Sounds good to me." Rafael stretched out his hand. Matthew grabbed it, and Rafael tugged him to his feet.

Matthew rubbed his jaw and spat blood on the ground. Rafael brushed the dirt from his palms, retrieved his backpack, then grabbed the canteen he'd left sitting on the boulder.

"By the way, I know Jordan's not my type. She's too good for a bad boy like me. But who is my type?" Rafael tilted the canteen and took a long drink.

The question was rhetorical, but Matthew answered anyway. There was one girl on their team who was more than a match for Rafael.

"Hannie is your type."

"Hannie?" Rafael sputtered, water running down his chin. He slapped his thigh and laughed. "We'd kill each other in a week."

"Maybe," Matthew agreed. "But I bet it would be an exciting week."

Rafael chuckled and gathered his gear. Matthew's heart pounded much too fast, and it wasn't due to altitude or the fight. What if Rafael did act on his feelings for Jordan? Matthew wasn't stupid. He'd seen girls ogle Rafael, the dark Latin lover, and Jordan blushed when Rafael put his arm around her shoulder or teased her.

Jordan did dance with Rafael last night, and she'd acted strangely afterward. He'd believed she was afraid of what they'd find on Cimarron's computer book, but maybe that wasn't the only reason for her odd behavior.

Matthew's face burned as a buried memory pushed to the surface, bringing the pain of rejection with it. Why couldn't he forget the past? Jordan was nothing like Kim—the girl who broke his heart. It had been two years, but he could still hear Kim explaining that she liked his best friend better than him. In one day, he lost his girl and his buddy. After being dumped, trust didn't come easy.

"Come on, *amigo*." Rafael motioned to Matthew. "Let's get moving and see if we can find that mystery camp."

Rafael's voice shook Matthew and brought him back to the present. Right now, they had more important things to worry about. If they discovered the missing students and found out GCU was as dangerous as they suspected, there wouldn't be much time left for romance.

Matthew would fight for Jordan if he had to, yet he still believed it wouldn't come to that. He and Jordan shared a special bond. Matthew grabbed his gear and followed Rafael. With every step, he prayed he was right about Jordan's heart.

* * *

AFTER ANOTHER HALF-HOUR of hard climbing, they reached a jutting rocky ledge. Sharp ridges warned nosy climbers to stay away. Wind whistled over the top, bringing light showers of snow with it. In another month, this area would be blanketed in snow.

Matthew shivered and made certain every button on his jacket was fastened. His boots would cling to the sides and help him climb, but it wouldn't be easy.

"If my calculations are correct, the camp should be over that rise and in the valley below." He gulped in deep breaths, trying to slow his rapid heartbeat.

With a groan, Rafael pulled out the grappling hook and rope. Fear twisted Rafael's face, and the same fear waged war in Matthew's heart. He wasn't anxious to climb that last crest and face whatever waited on the other side.

"Rafael, if we find a prison camp, what're we going to do then?" he asked, hoping Rafael didn't notice his voice crack. "The girls and I didn't come up with a plan. I think we're all hoping this map leads to a harmless GCU classroom."

Rafael studied the ground and kicked a couple of snow dusted rocks. "I grew up around politics and intrigue, but this doesn't seem real, not even to me. GCU is a school, not a military base."

"So, what do we do if we find a prison camp?"

Rafael shrugged. "Improvise."

Improvise. Great. I feel a lot better now.

As quietly as possible, while straining with exertion, they threw the hook into the cliff's sheer wall and hauled themselves up over the edge. Staying low, they crawled east. Raw bushes powdered with snow lined the side of the ledge, providing a protective barrier between them and whatever lay below.

Matthew pressed his finger to his lips and motioned for Rafael to follow him closer to the ledge. He peered through the bushes' spidery arms and scanned the valley below. A large log cabin sat nestled between glistening fir trees. A campfire burned brightly, and several people covered in heavy coats stood by the fire, holding a long stick over the flames as if they were roasting marshmallows. Could they be the missing students?

Matthew glanced at Rafael. Rafael shook his head. The camp appeared harmless enough. Maybe they had stumbled upon an innocent camping trip.

Rafael slapped Matthew on the shoulder and motioned for him to look in the other direction. A man walked from behind the building, a Global Collective power-rifle slung across his shoulder, the Global

Collective snow leopard etched on his jacket. So much for family fun. Sweat bathed Matthew's chest beneath his flannel vest as reality struck him. GCU was actually holding students prisoner on a mountain top. He trembled.

"I've never seen anything like this," Rafael whispered as he stared through a pair of binoculars. "No barbed wire, no fence. What keeps the students from running away?"

"The guards and the firepower, I guess."

A second guard walked over to the first one and handed him a cigarette.

"We need to get closer so we can figure out how many students are being held here." Rafael started belly-crawling through the thick shrubs.

Please give me wisdom, Jesus. Matthew silently prayed as he followed closely behind Rafael. Thankfully, his jacket protected him from the sharp spikes protruding from the bushes.

As they inched ever closer to the camp, a tall, thin boy emerged from the cabin and joined the others standing around the fire. Matthew stopped abruptly and lifted his head higher to get a better view.

"Paul," he whispered.

Rafael glared at him and raised his eyebrows.

Matthew acknowledged his warning then turned his attention back to Paul, alive and seemingly unharmed. Rafael crawled a little farther along the sheer ledge. Matthew followed. The cabin's tinted windows revealed several human silhouettes. He couldn't tell if they were male or female, but there were three distinct shapes.

If they could manage to get a little closer, he might be able to get Paul's attention without alerting the guards, since both men stood on the other side of the cabin. If Paul spotted him, he would know Matthew hadn't forgotten him and give him hope of a rescue. Matthew crept along the ledge above the campfire, the smoke tickling his nose.

He reached the edge of the cliff, and his foot collided with a large rock. It tumbled down the side and charged toward the camp. He held his breath as the rock gained speed and barreled down the cliff. Once that thing plowed into the camp, the guards would start looking for them. The rock continued its descent, one bounce after another until it collided with an invisible surface and bounced back. Sparks flashed. The stone came to a stop several feet away.

Rafael's grip bit into Matthew's shoulder as he yanked him back. "It's a force field."

The guards ran toward the disturbance. The two burly men eyed the students standing by the fire while the students stared up into the mountains. The men walked to the edge of the camp and scanned the horizon. Matthew pressed his body into the hard earth. If only the ground would open and let him sink into its depths.

CHAPTER 14

*M*atthew peered through the bushes, his body still pressed firmly against the ground.

"Just a little rockslide," one of the guards said. "Probably a wild hare. No problems here." The man turned and walked back toward the fire and shouted for the students to get back inside the cabin.

The second guard moved to where the rock had impacted the force field and glanced up and down the perimeter. Shielding his eyes, he studied the mountain range. Matthew's breath danced in cold puffs in front of him as he waited for the man to finish his inspection.

Just my luck to get a guard who takes his job seriously. Without a doubt, the man would spot them soon due to his apparent determination.

We're going to prison. No need to get Jordan and Hannie in trouble. He'd convince the police that Paul had told him about the students' disappearance, and he and Rafael had been investigating.

Suddenly, the guard started waving his arm in front of his face. He ducked and stumbled back as if dodging a blow from an invisible enemy. A swarm of insects had targeted the man.

"Ow," the guard shouted, slapping his neck. He backed up, waving his arms around like a wild man. He spun around then retreated to the other side of the camp.

Thank you, God. Even nature does Your bidding.

Matthew slithered away from the ledge. Rafael followed. Once they reached the clearing, they grabbed their gear and bolted to the cliff's edge. They tied the ropes around their waists, pulled out their climbing hooks, and repelled down the steep surface. Matthew's legs banged against the rocks as he hurried down. Bitter winter twigs tore at his face, but he and Rafael refused to slow their pace until they put plenty of miles between them and the camp. Exhausted, they silently trudged back to GCU.

* * *

JORDAN SHUT and locked her bedroom door after Mathew and Rafael entered the room. A large bruise marred Matthew's scratched face.

"What happened to your jaw?" She touched his chin.

He flinched and caught her wrist. "It's nothing." He shot a quick glance at Rafael.

What happened between the two of them in those mountains? Jordan's stomach flipped. Surely, Rafael didn't tell Matthew about their kiss?

Matthew squeezed her wrist tenderly before releasing it. "Trudging through the mountains can be hazardous. That's why I wouldn't let you come with me. Your face is much too pretty to get damaged."

"Ugh." Hannie punched Matthew on the shoulder. "Now that we're all completely sick, tell us what you found."

All playfulness vanished from Matthew's eyes. "The camp is real. We found it by using the coordinates in the computer."

"Did you see Zoe or Paul?" Jordan pushed the words past the lump rapidly forming in her throat.

Matthew sat on the foot of her bed. He pulled her down beside him. Hannie plopped down on the other bed.

"We saw several students." Matthew's tense jaw and wrinkled brow broadcast his fear. "I don't know if Zoe was one of them, but I did see

Paul." He massaged the knee of his pants, probably trying to soothe an aching muscle.

"How did they look?" Hannie asked. "Could you tell if they've been mistreated or starved?"

"From a distance, they looked healthy." Rafael sat on the desk then propped his long legs up on a chair. "We didn't get very close."

"The place they're holding them looks like a regular campground, no barbed wire or fences to spark any suspicion," Matthew said.

Jordan brushed her hair back from her face. This couldn't be real. Had she fallen into a bad Hollywood movie?

"Why couldn't you get close to them or help them?" She stood and paced around the small room. They'd finally found the missing students, and then left them behind.

"There were a couple of armed guards watching the students." Rafael appeared hurt that she would doubt their commitment. "And a force field surrounding the entire area."

Hannie whistled. "My buddies at Marah knew the European Collective was working on force field technology. This proves they've achieved it."

Jordan forced herself to listen as the boys explained the details to Hannie. They described the configuration of the camp, and Rafael raved about the immense fire power of the newly crafted rifles the guards carried. As far as they could tell, only five or six students were being held there. She didn't care about force fields or diagrams. Zoe, Paul, and the other students were her only concern. Real people with real lives.

"We have to rescue them." She slammed her fist against her opposite palm, ready to storm the mountain singlehandedly, but common sense told her she couldn't fight the Global Council's powerful cronies alone.

"That's impossible." Rafael stood. The difficulty of the mountain trek showed in his tired eyes and the thin worry lines on his brow. She wasn't the only one caught in this grasping quicksand.

She took a few deep breaths, hoping for calm. No luck. Her nerves fired like electric impulses. "We have to do something before GCU kills them." Tears slipped down her cheeks. Jordan cried whether she was angry, fearful, or sad. Why couldn't she be a rock like Hannie?

"It's been almost two months since Paul disappeared, and longer for Zoe," Matthew said. "If they were going to kill them, they would've done it by now."

"Matthew's right," Hannie agreed. "They're keeping them alive for some reason, and that's what we have to find out."

"It has to be tied up with the plot to kill Sierra Stone." Rafael stretched his back and groaned. "We know they plan to involve my brother in the assassination, and from what you read on Cimarron's computer, the students are an important part of their scheme."

Matthew put his elbows on his knees and rested his head in his hands. "Why use a bunch of teenagers in an assassination plot, and why pick these particular students?"

"These people are crazy," Rafael said. "Who can guess why they do anything?"

Hannie scooted back on the bed and stretched her legs out in front of her. "What do we know about these missing students? There has to be a common factor."

"We know that Zoe and Paul are both Christians, outspoken Christians." Jordan brushed the tears from her cheeks.

"But what does that have to do with Rafael's brother?" Hannie questioned. "He's not a Christian."

"Watch your mouth." Rafael's voice deepened. "Hector and I both grew up going to mass at the Catholic church every time our mother could drag us there."

"We've suspected Christianity was the connection all along, and it's starting to make more sense." Matthew stood. "The Latin Collective has historically been very Catholic, and they are still the most religious collective on the planet."

"Marah is going to be very interested in all of this." Hannie twisted a knot into the worn quilt draped over her legs. "I've been involved in dangerous stuff most of my life, but I've never dealt with anything like this." Her face flushed, and her mouth twisted.

A shiver ran up Jordan's spine. "We have to tell Victor and the girls about all of this."

"No way!" Hannie jumped off the bed, flinging the quilt to the floor. "We can't tell anyone else right now. Too many people know already." She flashed a contemptuous look at Rafael.

Jordan sighed. Hannie didn't like Rafael, but why did she distrust him? His brother was in danger, too.

Jordan turned to Matthew for support. "We now have solid proof that Christians are in danger at GCU. We have to warn the others at our next Bible study."

Hannie's nails bit into Jordan's bicep. "You have a Bible study?"

"Ouch." She shook free of Hannie's grasp. "Matthew, Timberlyn, Victor, Malese, and I meet every Sunday morning."

Hannie's brown eyes sparked, but Jordan didn't cringe or blink.

"You do like to live dangerously. You have to stop this Bible study immediately."

"No," Jordan and Matthew declared at the same time.

She reached for Matthew's hand. His strong, callused fingers intertwined with hers.

"We're not stopping the Bible study." Matthew's voice sounded firm. "But we won't tell the others anything right now. We've already warned them to be careful and not to advertise their religious interest around here. We don't need to tell them anything else—yet."

Surely, Hannie would not agree with Matthew's ruling. Jordan didn't agree and opened her mouth, eager to argue that they shouldn't keep secrets from the others, but the fatigue and determination in Matthew's eyes silenced her.

Hannie nodded, dark curls bouncing over her shoulders. "If that's the best I can get from the two of you, I'll take it."

"Can I join you guys at the next Bible study?" Rafael asked.

Jordan flinched. Did Rafael say *Bible study*? Of course not. She must be crazed with fear. The kiss they'd shared at the banquet haunted her, and she bit her bottom lip. She couldn't include Rafael in their study group. That was probably very un-Christian of her, but right now, she didn't care. What if he wanted to use the Bible study as a way to get close to her?

Could I be more conceited?

Matthew had admitted that she was the reason he joined the group. If a nice boy like Matthew could harbor ulterior motives, she shuddered to think what Rafael might have in mind.

"Of course, you can join us," Matthew said, and Jordan cringed. "If you can get out of bed at five o'clock in the morning."

Her shoulders immediately relaxed. What were the odds that Rafael would drag himself out of bed before the crack of dawn?

"You can join us, too, Hannie," Jordan said.

"No thanks. I'm not completely insane—yet." Hannie sighed. "Do me a favor and say a prayer for this crazy mission, and don't get caught. This is too big a mess for me to clean up all by myself."

CHAPTER 15

The next morning, Jordan sat in the cellar on a three-legged stool beside a wooden crate. Victor sat on the basement floor, Malese perched on a crate of lima beans, and Timberlyn occupied a rickety rocking chair that had been relegated to the basement depths.

Where was Matthew? She glanced at her watch. Surely, he wasn't waiting on Rafael. The cellar door creaked. Matthew walked down the stairs with Rafael by his side. Victor's eyes grew wide, and Timberlyn squealed. Jordan's mouth dropped.

"Wow, what a welcome." Rafael grinned. "I grew up Catholic. My mother dragged me to church all my life."

Victor eyed Jordan. Timberlyn and Malese both stared at her as if asking *what do we do now?*

Throw him out, Jordan's mind shouted, but instead, she motioned for Matthew and Rafael to join them. What choice did she have? Matthew pulled up a wobbly stool, and Rafael sat down beside Victor.

Jordan's hands trembled as she searched for her place in the Bible. Rafael's presence should not cause her to tremble. She started reading the text they planned to discuss today. Matthew's intense stare practically set her on fire. What was wrong with him? He appeared to be jealous, or angry, or both.

I am going to strangle Rafael if he told Matthew about that stupid kiss.

She stumbled over the scripture verses. Matthew's stare, Rafael's presence, and the mountain prison camp overwhelmed her. She couldn't live with all these secrets. She stopped and put the Bible on the crate. "I can't do this. We have to tell everybody about the danger."

Matthew leaned close and squeezed her shoulder. "We promised Hannie."

"Hannie is wrong. They have a right to know, and we're going to need everyone's help if we have any hope of winning this battle with GCU."

"What is she talking about?" Victor asked Matthew, open trust displayed on his baby face.

Rafael buttoned his heavy sweater, as the chill filling the basement seemed to grow like a raging blizzard. "I've joined the group, and she doesn't think I can keep a secret."

"It's more than that, isn't it, Matthew?" Victor asked.

Matthew gulped in a deep breath. "We've always kept these Bible studies secret because we suspected we'd be in big trouble with GCU if they found out what we're doing."

Jordan could tell he was weighing his words carefully. Victor, Malese, and Timberlyn were only fifteen. Matthew was almost eighteen. He'd practically raised his little sisters, and Jordan understood his protective, take-charge personality all too well.

She had to help him out. "We now have solid proof that if GCU finds out we're believers, they'll lock us up."

"Do you mean we'll be arrested?" Malese asked.

Jordan tugged a strand of her rumpled hair. The silky touch of the curl helped steady her nerves. Once Matthew had told her he liked the way her hair looked a little wild and messy on Sunday mornings. Silly thing to think about now.

She took a deep breath. "Not arrested, exactly. Matthew and Rafael discovered a makeshift prison camp in the mountains, and Christian students are being held there."

"Umm, do you mean these students are being held against their will?" Timberlyn's voice squeaked from the strain of the words.

Rafael stood and plopped his foot on a barrel of apples, then leaned forward, resting his arms on his knee. "If the armed guards and force field are any indication, I'd say yes."

Jordan glared at him. How could he be so flippant?

"But why?" Timberlyn tugged on her brown sweater and frowned.

Jordan ruffled her fingers through the Bible's crisp pages. "We think it involves an assassination attempt on Sierra Stone."

Timberlyn shrieked.

Victor stood and paced across the small room. He bent in certain areas to keep the ceiling from knocking him in the head. "None of this makes sense. This is a school."

"Apparently, it's much more than that," Jordan said.

Timberlyn inhaled deeply. She rocked back and forth, then winced at the loud creak produced by the old rocker. She came to an abrupt stop. "This sounds a lot like my collective. Nothing is ever what it appears to be on the surface."

"What're we supposed to do about all of this?" Victor asked. "We're just a bunch of kids."

"Hannie has some friends in Israel who are former Mossad agents," Jordan said. She'd been shocked when Hannie told her about Marah and the covert world. These three must be reeling. "We've managed to send them an encrypted message with all the information we discovered. We hope they're going to write back soon and tell us what to do next. I'm sorry about the way I threw this at the three of you, but y'all have a right to know what's going on around here."

Timberlyn folded her arms across her chest. Victor still paced, chewing on his fingernails. Malese stared off into space, her dark eyes hollow. Hannie had been right after all. Telling them had been a huge mistake.

Malese's bronze complexion paled, and her lips quivered. She looked like a corpse making a futile effort to breathe. "I must tell you something." She spoke barely above a whisper and stared directly at

Jordan. "For many weeks now, I've been meeting with Cimarron after our Bible study to tell her about Jordan's activities."

"Mercy!" Rafael hit one of the wooden rafters with his fist. "Everyone thought I couldn't be trusted."

Jordan grabbed Matthew's hand, digging her nails into his flesh. Were they all destined to join the missing students in the mountain prison camp?

"How could you do that to us?" Victor's voice trembled.

"I'm so sorry." Malese twisted her fingers in her lap. "Cimarron promised me she'd have my brother brought to GCU. My father was a great martial arts champion before he was killed in a battle between rival factions in our local government. Kana is now a champion, and I haven't seen him in many years."

Jordan sunk low in her chair, as if Malese's words were pulling her into a swirling quicksand. Malese betrayed them, but Malese had lost her family. Jordan glanced around the room. Everyone here had suffered, but they didn't join up with the enemy.

Matthew pried Jordan's fingers away from his hand then wrapped his arm around her shoulders and pulled her close. "Exactly what have you told Cimarron?" he asked Malese, stressing every word.

"I never thought she'd do anything to harm Jordan, and I had no idea about missing students and assassinations." Tears rolled down Malese's blazing cheeks as her gaze darted from one startled face to the other. Her gaze stopped and lingered on Jordan. "I haven't told Cimarron anything important."

"What information have you given her?" Matthew continued his interrogation.

Malese rubbed her forehead. "I'm trying to think. I told her we were having a Bible study, but I made it sound like it wasn't serious and mostly we partied."

"What did Cimarron say about the Bible study?" Matthew gritted his teeth. He probably wanted to grab Malese and choke her. Jordan certainly wanted to.

"She didn't seem to care, especially since we weren't taking the Bible part seriously. She's been disappointed with my information, so I told her you and Jordan were dating to make it more interesting."

"I'm surprised she hasn't hauled me off to that prison camp already," Jordan whispered.

"Cimarron said she didn't care if you romanced every boy at GCU. She's only concerned about what you think of Sierra Stone, and if you're suspicious about Paul leaving." Malese narrowed her eyes and shook her head slightly. "It's strange really. It's like she's trying to prove that you are *not* a traitor, rather than prove you are one. She says you're a very gifted computer master, and she'd hate to lose you."

"We should wait before we pull her out," Jordan repeated the typed message from Cimarron. The one she'd read on Paul's computer the day her life became a living nightmare.

Matthew ran his fingers through his hair and sighed. "It doesn't sound like you've caused us any harm."

"I'll go to her now and tell her that I can't do this anymore. I love my brother, but I can't be a part of kidnapping and murder. Kana wouldn't want it that way." Malese stood and headed toward the stairs.

"No," Matthew said as Rafael blocked Malese's path.

Jordan almost laughed. Did Rafael really think he could stop Malese from leaving?

Malese turned to Matthew, her face twisted in sorrow and confusion.

"You can't go to Cimarron and quit. She'd figure out that you've told us the truth. You have to continue to play along." Matthew rubbed his chin. "We might be able to use this to our advantage."

"Good thinking, *amigo*." Rafael walked toward them. "We can feed Cimarron exactly what we want her to know. Maybe Malese can get some useful information out of the ice queen."

"I'll do my best to get information, but I'll probably have to beat it out of her." Malese's voice was low but sincere.

Jordan tugged on a long curl falling against her cheek. *That sounds like a good idea to me.*

Matthew laughed. "Well, we don't need to go to those extremes—yet. For now, keep convincing Cimarron that we're only a bunch of teens too preoccupied with our flirtations and romances to worry about world politics."

Malese moved to stand in front of Jordan. She brushed tears from her round cheeks. "I'm so sorry, Jordan. I've been acting like Judas."

Jordan stood. Her legs wobbled beneath her. At least Malese had learned something in the Bible study. "It's not that bad. You confessed before any real damage was done. You've proven you're a friend."

Funny how much easier forgiveness flowed now that she wasn't in eminent danger. She reached for Malese and pulled her close. Timberlyn stepped up and joined them in the hug.

With a sniff, Jordan stepped out of Malese and Timberlyn's embrace. "Now that y'all know the truth about GCU's plans, we'll understand if you want to stop the Bible study."

The thick walls of the cellar pushed in on the small group, unable to contain the growing tension. Victor's heavy breathing filled the room, broken only by the sound of Rafael's foot tapping against the stone floor.

"I don't see any reason to stop the Bible study." Timberlyn broke the silence. "We already knew this was dangerous, and we're used to being careful."

"I agree," Malese spoke in a firm voice. "And we don't want to make Cimarron suspicious."

"As long as there's a Bible study, you can count me in." Victor studied the floor. He hadn't interacted with Malese since her confession. Would their developing relationship survive? Malese moved to Victor's side. She reached out and touched his arm. He shook free and stepped away. Malese stared at her hand as if it had been burned then placed it over her heart.

"You're all so very brave." Jordan battled back the tears.

"None of us will ever be controlled by GCU or the Global Council." Rafael sat on a wine vat and stretched his legs out in front of him.

Matthew stepped close to Jordan and glanced around the room. "Hannie was wrong. This mission takes more than a few people. It takes a team. It takes strength." He nodded at Victor. "Bravado." Rafael acknowledged his comment with a salute. "Loyalty and tenderness."

Timberlyn and Malese grinned. "It takes a strategic brain like Hannie, and a computer master like Jordan, and even a dreamer like me."

"They put us together." Rafael jumped to his feet, raising his arm in a triumphant gesture. "They handcrafted Team Seven, and now Team Seven will be their downfall."

"I think a Higher Power created Team Seven." Matthew wrapped his arm around Jordan's waist.

Jordan picked up the Bible and held it against her chest. "This reminds me of one of my favorite Bible stories. The one about Queen Esther. God placed her in a pagan kingdom to perform a special mission and save many people in the process. Maybe He placed each one of us at GCU to save Sierra Stone and the missing students."

"Let's pray we can accomplish His will." Matthew held Jordan with one arm and grabbed Timberlyn's hand.

Jordan took Malese's hand. Malese reached for Victor, but he stepped away and grabbed Rafael's hand instead. Rafael's eyes reflected sympathy as he reached for Malese. With the circle complete, they bowed their heads and prayed for strength, wisdom, and protection.

When the prayer ended and the others had left, Jordan turned to Matthew and Rafael. "You know what scares me?"

"What?" Matthew asked.

"I have to go tell Hannie that I blabbed and told the whole team our secrets."

"*Vaya con Dios.*" Rafael shook his head and chuckled.

"That's right. Go with God." Matthew grinned. "I'll be glad to go with you if you want a bodyguard."

"No, thanks." Jordan shook her head. "I decided to blab, so I have to face the consequences alone."

CHAPTER 16

*A*s Jordan suspected, Hannie wanted to strangle her when she told her that she'd blabbed to the Bible study group. Once Hannie calmed down, Jordan consoled her with the fact that she now had more recruits to boss around.

"Great," Hannie had said. "If they don't obey orders any better than you do, we're sunk."

Several tense days passed as Jordan and Hannie waited for a return communication from Marah. Had their message gone through at all, or worse, had it been intercepted by GCU?

Matthew and Hannie both assured Jordan that if GCU had found the email the three of them would've joined the other students in the prison camp by now. Those two could definitely use some lessons on offering encouragement.

Jordan sat on the low brick wall encircling the ornamental garden, her computer book in her lap. The sun's warmth kissed her face and soothed her nerves. She shivered and pulled her sweater closed against the December chill. The tweet-tweet of a snowbird singing in the treetops broke through the gloom and dread in her heart.

"I wish you could deliver our message to Israel," she whispered to the trilling bird. "You'd probably be quicker."

The bird continued its song, blissfully unaware of the danger at GCU. No wonder King David had written in the Psalms, 'Oh that I had wings like a dove, for then would I fly away, and be at rest.'

I can relate.

At the sound of approaching footsteps, she glanced up from her computer book. Victor rushed toward her. A deep frown marred his baby face.

Her heart flipped. "What's wrong, Victor?"

His massive form blocked the sun as he towered over her.

"Everything's all right." He took a few anxious deep breaths. "I didn't mean to frighten you, but something happened between Laurel and me, and I don't know what to do."

"Tell me." Jordan patted the wall for him to take a seat. Her tight shoulders ached with stress and craning her neck to see his face didn't help at all.

Victor settled himself beside her. "Laurel told me she'd noticed that I've changed a lot. She said I was happier and more confident, that I didn't seem sad any longer. She wanted to know why I'd changed."

Jordan's pulse quickened. "What did you tell her?"

"I probably should've kept my mouth shut, but God had been calling me to come to Him since I was a child, and He might be calling Laurel, too. I silently prayed and asked God what to do."

"And?" Jordan had prayed for guidance many times. Sometimes the answer was clear, but more often it came veiled in a cloudy mist.

"I felt like God wanted me to tell the truth," Victor said. "I told her I'd recently given my life to Jesus."

His answer was no surprise. Of course, God would want him to share his faith. That was a no-brainer. Laurel had missed out on her parents' love. She needed to know God loved her.

The wind lifted Jordan's hair from her shoulders, and she trembled. Wrapping her arms around her body, she rocked back and forth. "What did she say?"

She probably tossed her silky blonde hair over her shoulder and called him a religious nut. Victor's wrinkled brow and tight lips indicated

SHARON RENE

that Laurel's reaction had been anything but good. Had the danger escalated?

"She said that if Jesus made me this happy, she wanted to know Him, too. That's when I got scared and told her I'd talk to her later." Victor chewed his thumbnail. "What should I do? Do you think we can trust her?"

Jordan looked from Victor to the tree where the bird still sang, as if the creature could carry their conversation to predatory ears. Where was Matthew when she needed him? He would know the right thing to do. He always did. She started to tell Victor to find Matthew but bit her tongue before the words could escape.

Months ago, Jordan had inadvertently mentioned God in front of Laurel. Laurel had stiffened, tossed her hair over her shoulder, and scurried away. Now, she knew Victor was a believer, but she didn't know the truth about Matthew and the others. Jordan couldn't involve Matthew in this and put him in more danger.

Could they trust Laurel? The timing was suspicious. Perhaps, Cimarron doubted Malese's version of the Bible study and was using Laurel to test them. Laurel was the darling of the European Collective and would no doubt do anything to win Cimarron's approval. Jordan whispered a silent prayer.

"Go ask her to come talk with me now." She drummed her fingers on her computer book. "I'd rather take the risk of being caught if Laurel is tricking us than refusing to share salvation with her if she's seriously seeking God. I wouldn't be able to live with myself."

Victor sprang to his feet, a smile on his round face.

"I'll find her."

Jordan grabbed his wrist. "But this is between you and me and Laurel. We can't let her know that the others are Christians. They're in enough danger already."

"Agreed." Victor shook his head, then went in search of Laurel.

Oh, Lord, please let Laurel be sincere, and even if she isn't, please protect us from any harm she could cause.

Victor and Laurel soon returned, and for the next half hour, the three sat on the brick wall discussing God's word.

"Ever since the first day I met you, Victor." Laurel shaded her eyes and gazed at Victor. "I believed we were kindred spirits. I could see a special kind of loneliness in you." A tremor shook her voice. "The longing for a parent's love. Knowing that you never measure up. But now that I've talked with the two of you, I understand why you've changed so much." Laurel grabbed one of Victor's giant hands and squeezed it between her two delicate ones.

"Jordan, you once said something about living for eternal value, but I was too afraid to listen. I've had European Collective doctrine pushed at me my entire life. I was taught to be independent and be my own god." A deep intensity of emotion flamed in the girl's leaf green eyes. "It's hard to believe that God loves me just the way I am, flaws and all, but it's the best thing ever."

"Jesus died on the cross so that each one of us could be forgiven for our sins," Jordan said. "It's a free gift, but like any gift, we have to accept Jesus's sacrifice. It's a lifeline in a stormy ocean. It only saves the people who cling to it. Jesus saves us when we cling to Him."

Tears streamed down Laurel's perfect cheeks.

"Do you believe what I've told you?" Jordan asked.

"I do believe," Laurel whispered. "I want Jesus to be my Lord and Savior more than I've ever wanted anything. No one else ever loved me enough to die for me. If someone loves you that much, you'd be stupid not to trust Him and love Him in return." She smiled then bowed her head to pray.

"Wait," Jordan said. "Before you do this, you must understand the danger. GCU doesn't approve of Christians, so you can't tell anyone about this decision, especially not Dawson."

"I'd never tell Dawson." Laurel's eyes opened wide. "He'd laugh at me and say I was acting stupid."

"It's more than being made fun of," Victor said. "Religion is dangerous around here."

Laurel had no idea how dangerous. Jordan believed Laurel's

conversion was sincere, but she wasn't foolish enough to trust the girl with the whole truth. Like the Apostle Paul in the Bible, Laurel would have to prove her trustworthiness.

"Victor's right," Jordan said. "You can't tell anyone that we're believers."

Laurel squeezed Jordan's hand. "I know the Global Collective despises believers. I'm one of the in-crowd, remember? But I'm not changing my mind, and I'll never tell anyone about you and Victor. You can trust me."

Jordan nodded as a strange peace fell on her. She'd gained a sister. Victor stood and positioned his massive body between the girls and the dorm. Hopefully, he would keep nosy onlookers from getting a peek at them. Beneath the snow-touched tree limbs, with the bird's song for accompaniment, Laurel and Jordan bowed their heads and prayed.

CHAPTER 17

*J*ordan woke to the sound of a low buzzing, her drowsy brain unable to make sense of the noise. She rolled to her side and stared at the time reflected on the wall. 3:15 A.M.

"Ugh." She pulled the covers over her head.

The Marah communicator.

She pushed herself up, throwing the blanket to the floor, jumped out of bed, then clapped twice to turn on the lights.

"Hannie, wake up." Jordan wobbled over to the desk, opened the drawer, and yanked the noisy communication device from its shelter. "Hannie, wake up!"

Hannie groaned and sat up. Yawning, she rubbed her eyes with her fists.

"Get over here quick and read this message. It's in Hebrew. Talk about double encryption."

English was the official language of the Global Collective and the Global Council, due to its prevalence on the planet before the wars, famines, and disasters changed everything. Of course, each collective still had their own languages. Jordan had mastered Spanish and French, but she'd never studied Hebrew. The strange lettering danced in her blurry vision.

"Okay, okay," Hannie moaned, staggering across the room. Her big toe caught in the torn edge of the rug, almost throwing her to the floor. "Ow. You're such a whiz kid, Jordan, you should be able to read Hebrew. Honestly!"

Jordan pushed Hannie down in the desk chair. "Sit here and read this."

Hannie eyed the contraption and yawned.

Jordan twisted one of her wild curls around her finger. "What does it say?"

"Assassination attempt on SS to occur Old Venezuela, Latin Collective during her speech in December. Will coincide with a large gathering of Christians in the Latin Collective. Freedom fighter HA to rally supporters at the same time. GCU involvement is certain but details unclear. Attempting to contact HA and obtain boots on the ground information. Update soon."

"That's it?" Jordan grabbed the communicator from Hannie's outstretched hand. "We knew most of that already. They didn't tell us what we should do next." Her stomach soured and tossed like the muddy Mississippi River.

Hannie headed back to bed. "Information gathering doesn't happen overnight. They'll update us soon, probably once they get more info from Hector Alvarado."

"What do we do until then?" Jordan asked.

"I'm going back to sleep." Hannie climbed into bed and pulled the blankets over her face. "Did you see what time it is?" She clapped her hands, leaving Jordan in the dark.

Jordan paced the floor for the rest of the night, listening to Hannie's even breathing. *How can she sleep when I'm on the verge of a nervous breakdown?*

Oh, Lord, I was not made to be a spy. I hated those old spy movies. Hannie grew up in Israel with Mossad members, so she can sleep in the middle of chaos. I grew up the over-protected daughter of a college professor. Why did You put me here? Was all this some big cosmic mistake?

She sat on the edge of her bed, hugged her knees to her chest, and swallowed back tears. Somehow, her mother's familiar voice penetrated her fear and self-pity. Every time she'd complained about her face, her hair, her personality, Mom would confidently say, "God doesn't make mistakes."

* * *

THE NEXT MORNING, Jordan scrunched down in the well-worn auditorium seat and released a giant yawn. If her anxiety level wasn't at the nuclear point, she'd fall asleep in this chair. Principal Reed had convened a special student assembly today. What was GCU up to now? Another loud yawn bellowed from within her. Matthew frowned.

"I didn't sleep well last night, so I'm really tired," she explained to Laurel, Dawson, Hannie, and Mr. Flynt, all of whom had turned around to gawk at her. *Sheesh, didn't people ever yawn in the European Collective?*

"Tired? Not sleeping well? You could be getting sick," Laurel said. "Maybe you should visit the infirmary."

"I feel fine." Jordan glanced at Hannie then bowed her head to escape Hannie's harsh glare.

Over the last week, Laurel had sought Jordan out, eager to spend time with her new friend. This worried Hannie, but Jordan assured her that harmless girl talk was not dangerous. She'd explained to Hannie that Laurel had asked Jesus into her heart and was not the same selfish girl she used to be. Hannie had laughed and warned Jordan to be careful around the "European Collective angel."

Mr. Flynt grunted from his seat in front of Matthew. He tugged on his shirt collar before releasing the top button. "No one can get sick now. It would push Cimarron over the edge."

Before anyone could question him, Principal Reed walked to the podium, which was draped in a snow leopard banner and decorated with an abundance of small red GC flags. Cimarron stood by his side, wearing a tailored suit with a sparkly red blouse that accentuated the tiny star tattoos around her neck. As usual, she carried her computer book in one hand.

Principal Reed squinted in the overly bright spotlight. He raised his arms and waited for the students to hush. "We've called this unscheduled assembly to make a very exciting announcement."

Now wide awake, Jordan sat straight up in her chair and grabbed Matthew's hand. A GCU announcement was seldom good and always terrifying, especially one that required a special assembly with banners and theatrical lighting.

"As some of you may have heard, Councilor Sierra Stone will be making a special visit to the Latin Collective this month on a diplomatic mission. Ms. Stone will be representing the Global Council at several banquets and political gatherings."

Matthew tightened his grip on her damp hand. Jordan hadn't yet told him about the early morning message from Marah, but he seemed to share her nervousness.

"GCU has been given the great honor of participating in this momentous occasion. The two highest ranking teams will accompany Ms. Stone on her visit."

A low murmur filled the room, and a chill settled on Jordan.

"I'm proud to announce that Team Four, led by Mr. White and Ms. Dunlap" —Principal Reed motioned to the athletic Mr. White and perky blonde Ms. Dunlap sitting in the front row— "and Team Seven, led by Mr. Flynt and Cimarron, uh, Ms. Butler, will be traveling to Latin Collective Area 4, Sector 8, the former Venezuela, in two weeks. Congratulations to all of you." He grabbed a GC flag from the podium and waved it.

The audience jumped to their feet, clapping and cheering. Jordan pressed her hands against her ears while her head swam, and her vision blurred. This must be a dream. A bad nightmare.

In front of her, Dawson stood, grabbed Laurel, and swallowed her in a bear hug. The members of Team Four slapped each other on the backs, whistled and squealed. Matthew stood, pulled Jordan to her feet, and wrapped his arms around her.

"Have to play along," he whispered.

Victor embraced Timberlyn. Even Hannie and Rafael hugged. Team Seven had suddenly become more entangled in this spider web called Global Collective University. Now, instead of being tucked away, somewhat safely, in the European Collective trying to get information to Marah, they'd be in the Latin Collective in the middle of the assassination attempt.

The room spun while people shouted, stomped, and clapped. The woodsy scent of Matthew's cologne tickled her nose, and she breathed deeply, thankful his arms were wrapped securely around her. If he let go, she'd surely faint. Over Matthew's shoulder, she spied Principal Reed and Cimarron whispering to each other, large smiles masking their faces.

I think I'm going to barf.

As soon as they returned to the dorm, the girls messaged Marah, letting them know this latest revelation. Jordan collapsed onto her bed, spread her arms wide across the downy comforter, and stared at the ceiling.

"I can't do this anymore, Hannie."

"Okay, if you're tired, stay here and take a nap. I'll go let the rest of the team know about the message we received this morning." Hannie ran a brush through her wild curls, pulled them back, and secured them with a khaki ribbon.

Jordan covered her face with her hands. She was more than tired. She needed a blood transfusion or a courage implant. What would happen next? Would Marah expect them to do more than gather intel once they arrived in Old Venezuela? In Hannie's return message to Marah, she'd practically committed them to singlehandedly stopping the assassination and rescuing the missing students, as if they were teenaged superheroes. Surely, Marah wouldn't take Hannie's offer seriously. But—what if they did?

The messages on Cimarron's computer stomped through Jordan's mind. *Orders from River.* Team Seven couldn't confront River Wallis and survive. If they were caught passing information, they'd be thrown in prison, or worse. Right now, she wished she'd never found the list of missing students or hacked Cimarron's computer. She and Matthew and Hannie were already trapped in this mess, but how could she ask the others to sacrifice their lives?

She sat up and faced Hannie. "A nap won't help this kind of tired. I can't play secret agent any longer. I'm done."

"Done?" Hannie tilted her head to one side, eyeing Jordan like she'd turned purple. "Are you trying to say you're quitting?"

"That's exactly what I'm saying."

"Well, you can't quit. That's all there is to it." Hannie stomped across the room.

If those brown eyes were laser beams, I'd be dead now.

"You're the only computer master we have, and we'll need you in Old Venezuela. What are you planning to do anyway? Sit in your hotel room while the rest of us have all the fun and save Councilor Stone?"

Jordan pounded the mattress, the soft texture yielding to her blows. "This is not a game, and we're not capable of stopping an assassination by ourselves." Why must she point out the obvious? Had Hannie completely lost all sense of reality?

"We won't be alone. Hector Alvarado has a small army," Hannie insisted, as if Hector was some kind of military genius.

"We don't know if Hector will agree to help us. You're the one who doesn't trust him. You don't even trust Rafael."

"This is a fine time for you to start listening to me." Hannie plopped down on the bed, the mattress bouncing from the impact. "Even if Hector refuses to help us, Marah will get people into Venezuela, but it'll take all of us to stop the assassination."

"I won't be much help. I'm a lousy fighter. I couldn't live through a pretend battle, remember?" Jordan grabbed the hem of the flowered quilt. The cotton futilely tried to resist her vicious twist. "I'm in way over my head, and I'm scared to death. I'm so afraid that I'll do the wrong thing and make all of this worse. I'm not strong like you. Y'all will be better off without me."

Hannie folded her arms and wrinkled her brow. "Jordan, you're the heartbeat of Team Seven. The unofficial leader. You can't quit now."

"You can be the leader. I don't want the job." She started to stand, but Hannie jerked her back down.

"No one will follow me." Hannie's fingers bore into Jordan's upper arm. "They don't like me, but everyone loves you. You're the reason they were willing to get into this mess in the first place. They follow you."

Jordan shook herself free of Hannie's grip and took several deep breaths to clear her mind. She was not the heartbeat of Team Seven. She certainly didn't want to be.

"I think God had something to do with their decisions. They all want to serve Him, not just follow me."

Hannie jumped up and yanked Jordan to her feet. "God put you here, didn't He? Even He knows you're a born leader."

"I'm not so sure about that." She hung her head and shifted from foot to foot. Could Hannie be right? Had God placed her at GCU for such a time as this?

Hannie sighed, her breath heavy with the scent of spearmint gum. "Jordan, you're the Queen Esther of Team Seven. So, wash your face, brush your hair, and let's go have a planning meeting with our squadron."

Jordan grasped Hannie's arms. Why would Hannie mention Queen Esther? She never talked about God. Jordan wasn't even sure Hannie believed in God. She'd never been to one of their Bible studies, and she didn't know that Esther was one of Jordan's favorite Bible stories.

Are you trying to tell me something, God?

Jordan squared her shoulders and met Hannie's steady gaze, the truth of her words revealed in those cocoa depths. She'd just made an irrevocable choice.

I want to follow You, Lord and do Your will, but I can't do this on my own. Jesus, please give me strength.

CHAPTER 18

Twenty minutes later, Team Seven gathered in the garden. Malese and Timberlyn occupied a stone bench nestled beneath an overhanging arbor. Jordan, Matthew, and Hannie sat at a white trestle table surrounded by bare rose bushes, while Rafael and Victor strolled up and down the shrub-lined path, all trying to look like an innocent gathering of kids enjoying the sunny day.

"I believe it's God's will that we're going to Venezuela. He must want us to stop the assassination," Matthew said.

Jordan's jaw dropped. Had Matthew lost his mind? All this time, Jordan thought he was the sensible one.

"Look at us, Matthew." She motioned to her companions. "We're not soldiers. We're a bunch of kids."

"Sierra Stone wasn't much older than us when she was leading a band of rebels," Hannie said.

"That was a different time, a crazy time, and a lot of people died. The world population was cut in half during those years." Jordan would never make Hannie see reason, but her words might make an impression on Matthew.

"I'm not saying we can storm in there and rescue Ms. Stone," Matthew said. "But I believe God is sending us there so we can help

Marah by gathering intel. We'll have a front row seat at every event, so to speak."

Jordan sighed. "That's true. I agree that God may be sending us there, but I want all of you to understand the danger." She glanced at Malese and Timberlyn on the bench, then back at Hannie and Matthew. "Right now, Hannie and I are the only two who could be convicted of passing information to Marah. I suppose Matthew and Rafael would be in trouble too, but the rest of you are not involved. Yet. If you get caught helping us in any way in the Latin Collective, you'll be going to prison along with the rest of us."

Matthew nodded. "Jordan's right." He stared up at Victor as the boy paused in front of the table. "This might be the time for the three of you to get out of this mess."

"I'd be in big trouble if Cimarron knew I was a double-agent," Malese said. "What've I got to lose?"

"I'm not backing out now." Timberlyn's voice was soft but firm. "I'm willing to do anything I can to help Ms. Stone and the missing students."

"Me too," Victor mumbled then continued to pace.

"My brother is there." Rafael walked to the table. "He'll know what to do."

"We're not positive Hector will be willing to help us." Hannie drummed her fingers on the table. "He may head back to his mountain hideout and leave us on our own."

"Hector will not abandon us!" Rafael shouted.

Jordan cringed and craned her neck to look down the secluded path leading to the house. A squirrel scampered up a tree, but it seemed to be the only witness to Rafael's outburst.

"I never said he'd abandon us." Hannie pushed the words through gritted teeth. "But Hector leads a group of freedom fighters, and he has to do what's best for his soldiers and their ultimate mission."

Dealing with Rafael and Hannie was like playing with downed power lines.

"Rafael, your brother doesn't know you're going to be in Venezuela,"

Jordan said. "Hopefully, Hannie's contacts will be able to get that information to him soon."

"We can count on Hector." Rafael's muscles tensed, and he clenched his jaw. "He'll help us, and we'll be able to stop the assassination."

Hannie tossed her hair over one shoulder and glared at Rafael. "If you're finished pretending to be some wild rebel commando, we need to plan our next move."

"What makes you think you're in charge of this team?" Rafael spoke in hard, biting words. "You act like you know so much, but you don't know any more than the rest of us." He planted his hands on the table and leaned forward, frowning at Hannie.

"I grew up surrounded by fighting and covert plots. I know a lot more than you do." Hannie kept her voice low, but the sparks in her eyes were as loud as firecrackers. Didn't they have enough real enemies to worry about without Rafael and Hannie attacking one another?

"Have you forgotten who my father was?" Rafael countered. "Who my brother is? I know something about battle, too. You're a little girl pretending she's tough."

"And you're a conceited boy bragging about his big brother." Hannie slapped her palm down on the table. "You're no more qualified to lead this team than I am."

Matthew groaned. A chilly breeze blew brown leaves down the path as Jordan patted Hannie's shoulder. If only the breeze could cool off the childish combatants.

"You're not a Mossad agent," Rafael said. "You're a bossy, know-it-all."

Hannie jumped up. "And you're not Hector Alvarado."

Matthew came to his feet, hands balled into fists at his side. "This is not some Hollywood spy movie, and we don't need the two of you arguing over top billing. We're all in this together. So, sit down and shut up. Both of you."

Jordan rocked back and forth in her chair, not sure who would throw the first punch, Rafael or Hannie. Hannie swallowed several times, pushed her hair behind her ears, and sat down. Rafael bowed his head and shifted from one foot to the other before pulling out a chair and taking a seat.

Jordan wanted to laugh with relief. Victor now stood by the table, and Malese and Timberlyn leaned forward on the bench.

"Okay," Matthew said. "Does anyone have any ideas how we can get more information about this diplomatic mission in Old Venezuela? It'd be nice to know what to expect once we get there."

"Assuming I have permission to speak." Hannie leveled a deadly stare at Matthew.

Matthew responded by nodding and rolling his eyes.

"Jordan, since you and Laurel have become best buddies lately, try to find out everything she knows about this trip."

"What makes you think she'll know any more than we do?" Jordan asked.

"Dawson has connections to the Global Council through his parents. She has a connection to Dawson, enough said."

Jordan hated to spy on Laurel, but it did make sense. Life would be much easier if only Hannie would accept her new friendship with Laurel.

Why do I keep getting stuck in the middle of everything and everybody?

"Be very careful what you say to her," Hannie warned.

"I'm not stupid," Jordan snapped. Hannie's superior attitude was hard to stomach. She understood Rafael's impatience with her. "Laurel is not a Global Council spy, and she's not dangerous."

"She's Cimarron's favorite and Dawson's girlfriend. Either way you look at it, she's in the enemy camp." Hannie flopped back in her seat. "We can't trust her."

Jordan opened her mouth, but Matthew spoke first. "Hannie's right. As sweet and innocent as Laurel may seem, we can't trust her yet."

Sweet and innocent. Did Matthew always have to brag on Laurel? Thankfully, he wasn't the one being sent on this mission. He'd probably reveal all of their secrets the first time he stared into Laurel's hypnotic eyes.

White fluffy clouds floated over the garden, and soft snowflakes touched the table before instantly vanishing on the white surface. Jordan inhaled the milky air as an idea flitted in the back of her mind.

"Malese." She turned to face the bench where the girls sat. "If I can manage to slip a data puller out of computer lab tomorrow, do you think you could insert it in Cimarron's computer book the next time the two of you meet?"

Malese nodded, her long black hair swaying against her waist. "I'll find a way to do it. You can count on me."

Rafael brushed snow from the shoulder of his jacket. "What's a data puller?"

"It's a new European Collective invention. Tiny, but powerful. It will pull data from any computer in a matter of seconds."

"So, it's called a data puller?" Hannie raised one dark brow and smirked. "How creative."

"It has a fancy, technical name." Jordan grinned. "But it's commonly called a data puller. It won't get emails, but it'll pull pictures and video."

"That could be helpful." Matthew glanced up at the sky, which was quickly growing dark with the weight of increasing snowflakes. "We should break this meeting up before Cimarron or Flynt get suspicious, or we turn to ice."

"Sounds good. I'm freezing." Timberlyn stood. "Malese, let's go make some hot chocolate."

"That sounds delicious." Malese followed Timberlyn but paused at Victor's side. Shoving her hands in her jacket pockets, she stared up at him. "Do you want some hot chocolate?"

"No, thank you," Victor mumbled, then turned his back to Malese and stepped away.

Malese glanced at Jordan, a frown marring her valentine-shaped face, her brown eyes wet with tears. What did Victor want from Malese? *We've all forgiven her. Why won't he?* Timberlyn wrapped her arm around the sad girl's shoulders and led her away.

Rafael stood and cleared his throat. "Big guy, it's a good thing you're perfect, so you'll never need forgiveness from anybody."

Victor spun around and took a giant step toward Rafael. Rafael's body tensed, and a flicker of fear crossed his face. Suddenly, Victor stopped. He turned to Jordan, his cheeks pink and eyes wet.

"Jesus forgives me every day."

"Yes, He does," Jordan said. Victor might resemble a giant, but he was a boy, no different from her little brothers.

He let out a deep breath then headed toward the house. "I need some hot chocolate," he shouted over his shoulder. His plodding footsteps soon turned into a gallop.

Jordan laughed, snowflakes falling on her face and lips. She stuck her tongue out to taste the moisture. Snow was rare in Old Memphis, so she enjoyed every mountain snowfall at GCU. She softly hummed one of her favorite hymns. Sin was a lot like the dirt buried beneath today's snowfall. And like the snow, God's love and forgiveness made everything beautiful.

* * *

SEVERAL DAYS LATER, in the middle of the night, Marah reported that they had contacted Hector Alvarado. He had agreed to act as their ally on the ground. The girls would be given instructions about how to locate the rebel leader once they arrived in Old Venezuela.

Rafael would be thrilled with the news about his brother, so the next morning Jordan asked him to take a walk with her.

"I told you we could count on Hector." Rafael's smile touched his eyes, relief and pride reflected in those dark depths.

They stood beneath a canopy of snow-kissed sweet chestnut trees. The recent snow had covered the earth in a luxurious white blanket, and the sunlight sparkling on the icy trees reminded Jordan of classic gemstones she'd only seen in magazines.

"You're going to see your brother soon. You must be excited."

"Yes, I am. It's been two years. Most people think of Hector as a rebel, tough and bloodthirsty, but I know the real Hector, my brother. He fights for what he believes in, for freedom. I know he'll do all he can to protect Ms. Stone."

"I feel a little better knowing he'll be there with us." How odd that she was overjoyed to team up with a notorious Latin rebel. "Marah is trying to get some people into Old Venezuela," she added.

"Good. We'll need all the help we can get to stop the Global Council. If they can be stopped at all."

Rafael's ominous words mingling with the brisk morning air caused her to shudder. She clasped her gloved hands in front of her and shuffled her feet to stay warm. Rafael pulled her close, wrapping his arms around her. She snuggled against him, happy for the warmth and strength he provided.

What are you doing, girl? Push him away.

The shrill cry of the morning birds singing in the trees taunted her. Warmth flooded her body as she tilted her head and gazed up at Rafael. Her heart raced. Rafael's dark hair fell over one eyebrow, and his tanned skin added to his appeal.

As Hannie said, he was smoking hot, but something was missing. She would never turn to Rafael for advice or guidance. She didn't trust his wisdom or his heart like she trusted Matthew's, and she much preferred to be wrapped in Matthew's arms. She was only seventeen, and she had a right to be confused. She couldn't have everything figured out at this age. Right?

"I wish we lived a normal life," Rafael whispered, his warm breath dancing on the frigid air. "I could hold you forever, not worrying about spies and assassinations."

"I wish we lived a normal life, too." If she had a normal life, she wouldn't want to spend it with Rafael. She didn't want to be held in his arms now or forever. Sure, she cared about Rafael, but when she imagined forever, he was not a part of it. His fingers tangled in her hair as he lowered his head. Before his lips reached hers, she stepped back and pushed him away.

"We can't do this." She could blame her hesitancy on her fear of GCU, and the forbidden romance rule, but Rafael deserved to know the truth.

"I'm afraid I've been leading you on." She stared at the ground to avoid his magnetic eyes. "You're very good looking, and it's flattering to have a guy like you interested in me, but…" She ground the toe of her shoe into the frozen earth, watching the ice crack beneath the pressure, just as she was cracking a little every day. "Well, we're in the middle of a world catastrophe." She forced herself to look up at Rafael, knowing she must face him to truly break free of his hold on her. "And, and we, well…"

"And you're crazy about Matthew." Rafael finished her sentence, released a deep breath, and stepped back.

"Yes, I'm crazy about Matthew," she admitted. "It's funny, while you're kissing me, I tingle all over, and when Matthew kisses me, I tingle all over, but with Matthew, the tingles never go away." Hopefully, her words made sense to Rafael. They finally made sense to her. At last, she understood her heart.

"There you are."

Jordan jumped at the sound of Matthew's deep voice behind her.

"I've been looking all over for you." Matthew stopped a few feet away from them.

Oh no! What had he seen? What had he heard?

CHAPTER 19

*J*ordan held her breath as Matthew strode toward them. A large snowflake slapped her in the face, telling her to speak, but instead, she stared up at the hazy sky, trying to avoid Matthew's eyes.

"Rafael and I were taking a walk so I could tell him that Hector is going to help us." Jordan hated the nervous tremor tainting her voice. She backed away from Rafael and went to stand by Matthew. Surely, he could see the guilt on her face.

"Why were you looking for us?" Rafael asked, his tone relaxed as usual.

"I think you and I should make another trek to the prison camp and see if anything has changed since the announcement about the trip to Old Venezuela."

"That makes sense." Rafael nodded and stepped from under the tree. "I promised Flynt I'd straighten up the mess in my room. Cimarron looked in there yesterday and flipped out. I'll ask him about our schedule for the week and figure out a good time for us to get away." Rafael winked at Jordan.

Jordan's cheeks burned despite the cold temperature. Her temples throbbed as Rafael walked toward them. He was certainly bold enough to blab everything to Matthew. Would he say she'd led him on, call her a tease, or blame her for breaking his heart?

If guilt could kill, I'd drop dead this minute. Jordan glanced from Matthew to Rafael. *I've crushed them both.*

Rafael punched Matthew on the shoulder. "She's all yours, *amigo*. No contest." He flashed her a smile, then sauntered away, his heart very much in one piece.

She'd been nothing more than a challenge to him, one of many girls falling prey to his Latin charm.

I am such a conceited fool.

Thankfully, Rafael wasn't heartbroken, and they could still be friends, but good gravy, he should have been a little disappointed. Would Matthew have reacted the same way if she'd chosen Rafael instead of him?

She forced herself to face Matthew. "Did you hear any of our conversation?"

"Something about tingles." His eyes were cloudy and his jaw set. "And the fact that you kissed Rafael."

A knot formed in Jordan's stomach. "I only kissed him one time. It was at the dance and really, he kissed me."

"Is that supposed to make me feel better?"

She flinched at the tone of his voice. "I wish you hadn't found out this way."

A shadow fell across Matthew's face as a thick cloud hid the sun. "Me too. You should have told me."

She bowed her head as a shiver rocked her. "I couldn't face you. I felt too guilty."

"Glad to know you have a conscience."

Jordan's head popped up, and she met his hostile stare with one of her own. Sarcasm was not called for. She shouldn't have kissed Rafael, but it wasn't like they rode off into the sunset together.

"You don't have any right to get this angry about a silly kiss. You're always drooling over Laurel."

Matthew's brow crinkled, and his eyes opened wide. She almost laughed at the look of confusion splayed across his face.

"You think I want Laurel?" He sounded innocent. *Ha!*

"You're always complimenting her."

Matthew shifted from one foot to the other as the lightly falling snow intensified. "She doesn't have any self-confidence. I'm trying to help."

Jordan's cheeks stung in the cold wind, and she brushed her unruly hair out of her face. She wasn't backing down yet. She'd wasted too much time and energy being jealous of Laurel to give up so easily. "But you do think she's beautiful."

"Yes, she's beautiful. But not as beautiful as you."

Jordan rolled her eyes and groaned. "I'm not the most self-confident person on the planet. It hurts me every time you praise Laurel. Rafael complimented me at the party, and it sounded good."

"I never thought you were that shallow."

"I'm not shallow." She lifted her chin and folded her arms over her chest. "I don't want a relationship with Rafael. I just told him so. Can't we put this stupid kiss behind us?"

Matthew shoved his hands in his pockets. "I want to, Jordan. I really do. It's just... well, when I was younger, a girl dumped me. I trusted Kim, but she used me." He shuffled his feet in the snow. "Now, well... I just need to think."

Mixed feelings soared through Jordan. How dare some girl break Matthew's heart, but that wasn't her fault. Why should she pay for another girl's mistake?

"I understand that you're hurt and you need time. But remember, I'm not Kim, and it's not fair for you to act like I am."

He opened his mouth and stepped closer.

She raised her hand. "There's a lot going on right now. Our romantic problems don't matter much."

"They do matter," Matthew said. "They matter to me. I just need to think."

Jordan stuck out her hand and captured the falling snowflakes. "Take all the time you need. Once we set foot in Old Venezuela, our lives are going to change drastically. And not for the better."

* * *

SATURDAY MORNING, Mathew and Rafael left before dawn and headed up the mountain to the prison camp. Jordan had given Malese the data puller before her regularly scheduled meeting with Cimarron. Malese guaranteed she'd soon return with more evidence.

Jordan jumped at the sound of the soft taps on her bedroom door. She opened the door and ushered Malese and Timberlyn inside, locking the door behind them. Hannie sat cross-legged at the top of her bed with Jordan's computer balanced on her knees. The girls clambered up on the mattress.

"Mission accomplished." Malese handed the data puller to Hannie, a proud smile on her face.

"Did Cimarron suspect anything?" Jordan asked.

"No. She was too busy screaming and running out of her room." Malese convulsed in giggles, fell back on the mattress, and kicked her legs in the air.

"What's she talking about?" Jordan grabbed Timberlyn's shoulder. Timberlyn lost her balance and fell against Jordan. "What did Malese do to Cimarron?"

Had Malese beaten Cimarron as she'd threatened? Would European Collective police soon break down their door and drag them all to jail?

"Cimarron's fine," Timberlyn said. "Now."

Jordan's heartbeats pounded in her ears as she waited for someone to explain. She glanced at Hannie, who shrugged.

Malese popped upright, pulling her knees to her chest. "Do you remember that family of mice that have been living in the cellar?"

Lord, give me the strength not to choke her. Why is she talking about mice at a time like this?

"Well, it seems that Cimarron doesn't care for mice. Timberlyn secretly deposited the little family in Cimarron's bedroom right before my meeting. When Cimarron saw them, she screamed and ran out of the room, leaving her computer book behind."

"That was pretty clever." Hannie eyed the data puller.

"We each have our own talents." Malese tossed her silky locks over her shoulder. "Since my talent is beating people up, and Timberlyn's talent is animal taming, we chose to use her talent in this case."

Jordan glanced from one smiling face to the other. "You two are amazing." She let out a deep breath. "Timberlyn, did you get the mice out of Cimarron's room?"

"Of course. I wouldn't make those helpless creatures share a room with Cimarron. They've been safely returned to the cellar."

A giggle burst from Jordan's throat. She slapped her hand over her mouth, but the giggles refused to leave. Jordan clutched her shaking stomach as she laughed.

Timberlyn threw her head back and laughed. Malese's grin morphed into a chuckle. Even Hannie let out a giggle or two.

"Okay, ladies, enough of this foolishness," Hannie said, twisting her face to stop the laughter. "Let's see what this thing holds."

Jordan squared her shoulders as Hannie placed the small doughy device on the computer. It attached itself to the side of the machine with a whooshing sound, and video flashed on the screen. The picture flickered a few times before clearing enough to reveal a large group of people standing around the old Washington Monument.

"That's in D.C., the capital of the Old United States," Jordan whispered. She'd never been there, but she'd seen pictures. "This doesn't make any sense."

Hannie motioned to the screen with her head. "Listen to what they're saying."

A girl shouted to the crowd. "Sierra Stone must be stopped. She wants to destroy religious liberty." The girl's light brown hair concealed her face, but a tingle of recognition flooded through Jordan. The girl spun around, waving a sign, her hair flying in the wind.

"Zoe." Jordan's eyes filled with tears, and the screen blurred. Same hair, same brown eyes, same freckles dotting her nose, but it couldn't be Zoe. "She looks vicious, confused. What have they done to her?"

"Drugs can change personality." Timberlyn wrapped her arm around Jordan's shoulders. "Even some herbs and plants are powerful enough to make a person delusional. Judging by that wild look in her eyes, I'd say she's taking some type of drug."

The crowd grew larger, and Zoe continued to shout. The camera panned to a reporter.

"This is the latest gathering of radical Christians led by former GCU students." The microphone shook, and the young man rubbed his forehead. "I suppose we should be grateful this demonstration hasn't turned violent like the one in the Latin Collective last week."

Hannie shifted, and the computer on her lap swayed. "If they didn't keep us so isolated here, we'd have seen these earlier."

Jordan buried her face in her hands. "I can't watch this anymore. They've destroyed Zoe."

"The time stamp on the video says October 18." Hannie pointed to the screen. "That was before the boys found the prison camp in the mountains. At least we know Zoe was alive in October, and from the number of students at the camp, she's probably still alive. That's a good thing, so calm down."

Jordan uncrossed her legs and bounced on her knees. "We are surrounded by monsters. How can I be calm?"

"It's Paul." Timberlyn grabbed Jordan's arm so roughly Jordan fell over, her backside slamming against the mattress.

She stared down at the screen, directly into Paul's face. He held a sign that read *Sierra Stone supports the brainwashing of Christian students at GCU.* The swoosh of water lapping against the shore sounded in the distance. A giant structure reminiscent of shell-like waves stood behind Paul.

"That's the Sydney Opera House," Malese said. "It's one of the most famous buildings in the Pacific Collective that's still intact."

The strong sunlight hid Paul's eyes, but his limp posture alarmed Jordan. Words traveled the bottom of the screen indicating that fighting had taken place, arrests had been made, and one police officer had been killed.

"That's not the Paul we all know," Jordan said. "He'd never willingly participate in a violent protest."

Tears rolled down Timberlyn's cheeks. "Paul is the best Christian I've ever known. He looks so frail. What have they done to him?"

Malese punched a pillow. "I don't understand why Cimarron would keep this stuff in her computer book."

"Maybe she's going to show it to her superiors," Hannie guessed. "Or use it as evidence after the assassination in Venezuela."

Jordan chewed her bottom lip. "Every police force on the planet will be searching for Zoe, Paul, and the other kids."

"Not if we stop the assassination and expose these lies," Hannie said.

"We have to do it." Jordan squared her shoulders. She sniffed and roughly brushed the tears from her face. "We may not be soldiers or professional spies, but we cannot let Cimarron and GCU win."

A knock sounded on the door. Timberlyn squealed, Jordan jumped, and Hannie came to her feet. "It's me." Matthew's voice poured through the wooden door.

Jordan tensed. She hadn't seen Matthew since their breakup. Was she ready for the awkwardness?

Grow up, Jordan. Her friends had been kidnapped, and Sierra Stone might die. This was not the time to act like a silly schoolgirl.

Hannie rushed to the door and let Matthew and Rafael in. Strain shown on Matthew's face as he removed his outer jacket and shook it. Leaves, twigs and melted snowflakes danced in the sunlight pouring in through the windows.

"Hey," Hannie said. "You're getting our floor all wet."

"Sorry," Matthew said.

Rafael puffed out his cheeks and blew on his hands. His dark skin was tinged pink, and his expression was solemn.

Jordan climbed to her knees on the bed. The mattress sank beneath each kneecap. "Any change at the camp?"

"There was a lot of activity when we first got to the camp." Matthew spoke after a long pause. "They were loading the students on a transport vehicle."

Timberlyn gasped, and Jordan clutched her churning stomach.

"They must be sending them to Venezuela ahead of us." Hannie's steady voice penetrated Jordan's fear.

Matthew took a deep breath. "That makes sense. If they plan to use them in the assassination plot."

"That is definitely their plan," Hannie said. "There's some interesting video on the data puller."

Matthew and Rafael exchanged worried glances. Surely, the horror in Jordan's heart was displayed on her face. Her voice cracked when she described Zoe and Paul's drugged appearance. Matthew put his hand on her shoulder. A flicker of hope teased Jordan, but Matthew dropped his hand and took a step back.

"One more thing." Rafael rocked back on his heels. "They dismantled the camp. They don't plan on bringing the students back from Venezuela."

Zoe's heart-shaped face filled Jordan's thoughts. Were they going to kill Zoe and the others after the assassination, or were they going to turn them over to the authorities? Life in a GC prison would be worse than death.

"We couldn't save them from their mountain prison," Jordan said. "We have to save them in Old Venezuela. That's the last chance we're going to get."

CHAPTER 20

$\mathcal{L}$ ATIN COLLECTIVE
DECEMBER 7, 2062

THE SEARING DAMP heat smacked Jordan in the face as she stepped off the plane in Old Venezuela. *I feel like I'm back in Old Memphis.*

Six months in the seductive mountain climate at GCU had softened her. She'd been used to heat and humidity at home. Old Memphis touted hot summers and cold winters with little to cool the days or bring warmth to the winter nights. At GCU, efficient heating warmed the nights, and air-conditioning cooled the few hot days. December in the Alps had not prepared her for December in Old Venezuela.

"Is it always this hot?" Jordan asked Rafael as she slapped a mosquito making a feast of her arm.

"It'll be cooler outside," Rafael promised as the team walked through the war-mangled airport. Mortar, brick, and wood filled the perimeter of the airport, and sunlight filtered through the various holes and tears in the roof.

A couple small planes stood on the runway, and debris littered the grass and dirt paths. This airport should be condemned, yet they had landed here, and another plane waited for the signal to take off.

"The mountains are cooler and beautiful." Pride and excitement mingled in Rafael's voice as he waved his arm toward the soaring mountains.

Of course, Rafael was happy to be home. She'd be overjoyed to see Old Memphis again. That day couldn't come too soon. Jordan stumbled over a hunk of cement, and Rafael put out his hand to steady her. A damp breeze ruffled her hair and wet her cheeks.

Perfect weather for my hair. I'll be a frizz-ball soon.

Momentarily blinded by the sun's harsh glare, Jordan shielded her eyes. Lush green mountains surrounded the city, bringing needed beauty to the devastation below them. Shacks with tin roofs filled the side of the mountains, stacked on top of each other like a staircase. How could people live in such conditions?

A modern European Collective plane capable of traveling seven hundred miles an hour had brought them to Old Venezuela, but a muddy bus marred with bullet holes and patched, dangling side mirrors waited to transport them to their hotel.

The bus wound slowly through the crowded streets, coming far too close to the people crossing the avenue or standing nearby. Cimarron wrinkled her nose at the sharp smell of gasoline fumes, trash, and roadside food stands.

Dirty little children followed well-dressed adults, tiny hands open wide, crying for whatever food or money they could spare. Beggars dressed in tattered clothes surrounded the bus when it stopped at a gas station.

The bus driver yelled several unsavory words, and the people scattered. Sometimes, Jordan wished she wasn't fluent in Spanish. Old Memphis hadn't prepared her for this ravaged place. Poverty was common in the North American Collective, but Old Memphis had fared better than most cities during the wars and plagues.

"It's very bad here," Rafael explained, as if he could read her mind.

"The hotel is in a much nicer part of the city, a little higher up in the mountains."

"There isn't anything nice about any part of the Latin Collective." Dawson spoke loudly from the back row.

Rafael started to rise from his seat, but Jordan wagged her head and whispered, "He's not worth it."

Rafael relaxed back into his seat and turned his attention to Courtney Moreau, who sat beside him. The blonde from Team Four giggled at one of Rafael's jokes and tossed her hair over her shoulder.

Jordan sat back. Rafael would be preoccupied with Courtney for the rest of the journey, so Jordan could relax. None of them could afford to waste a moment confronting Dawson's childish nature. Cimarron and Principal Reed sat in the two front seats, their heads close together as they talked. Team Seven had much bigger enemies to battle.

Matthew had claimed the seat beside Jordan when they boarded the bus. Did he really want to sit beside her or was he trying to keep Rafael away? She wanted to believe that Matthew still cared about her, but she would not become a toy tugged back and forth between Matthew and Rafael.

The scenery improved as they neared the hotel. The streets became less crowded and a little cleaner.

Jordan squirmed in her seat. During the bus ride, she and Matthew talked about the scenery and the weather. Both safe topics. Should she say anything about the state of their relationship? No. She'd already apologized for kissing Rafael. What else could she do? She certainly wasn't going to beg.

Thick humidity still clung to Jordan's skin when the bus stopped in front of a large hotel, but the air smelled fresher. The building was probably built in the 1990s and stood eight stories high, a combination of brick and stucco. It had been recently refurbished, but Jordan spotted bullet holes and other wounds in the structure as they entered the open-air lobby.

Huge ceiling fans spun above their heads, and a cool mountain breeze blew across the polished marble floor. A balcony encircled the lobby, the wrought iron railing providing beauty and protection. The hotel paled miserably by European standards, but after hours on the airplane and bouncing around on the tattered bus, Jordan was grateful to have a solid roof above her head. They'd been told the hotel was one of the few with decent computer service. That was why Councilor Stone had chosen it. Jordan clutched the cloth bag that held her computer and the Marah communicator, her lifelines to her allies. The hotel's décor didn't matter. The promised computer service was the only necessity.

After they checked into their rooms, Laurel insisted on introducing Team Seven to Dawson's family. The Montgomerys had flown to Old Venezuela to hear Ms. Stone's speech and mingle with their friends from the Global Collective Council. The Montgomerys didn't support Councilor Stone's politics. Why were they here? Were they involved in the assassination attempt? If so, Team Seven could add a couple more names to their enemies list.

Dawson retreated to the Montgomerys' penthouse, and the rest of the team, minus Hannie, decided to check out a festival promoting religious freedom. Rafael had bragged that the Latin Collective wouldn't give up religion without a fight. Laurel told Cimarron they wanted to interact with the local culture to enhance their scholarly growth. The woman bought it. Jordan assumed Cimarron was too preoccupied with Principal Reed and the upcoming murder to care about Team Seven's activities. Hannie remained behind to contact Marah.

* * *

AFTER A COUPLE OF HOT, sticky hours, Jordan, Matthew, and Rafael returned to the hotel room Jordan shared with Hannie.

"Did you learn anything helpful at this religious gathering?" Hannie questioned after ushering the group into the room.

"We met some very nice people." Jordan dug a brush out of her luggage then tugged it through her windblown hair. Her pale skin glowed pink from the heat, but she trusted that the sunblock she'd slathered on had protected her from burning.

Hannie flopped across one of the twin beds. "We got a return email from my friends at Marah. The Global Council is planning to frame these very nice people, along with our missing GCU students, for Sierra Stone's assassination."

"But Ms. Stone is very popular with this group and with most Christians." Matthew plopped down in a wicker chair sitting beside a small vanity. "She's supportive of religious freedom. She's pushing individual above collective. I'm not sure the Global Council can convince the world that Christians are behind her assassination."

Hannie adjusted her khaki headband. "People are gullible and easily swayed by what the government tells them."

Jordan placed her hairbrush on the vanity then joined Hannie on the bed. Rafael leaned against the small desk in the corner of the room, his long legs stretched out in front of him.

"The assassination is scheduled for Saturday, during Ms. Stone's speech," Hannie continued. "They're planting false evidence among the leaders of today's religious gathering. Something tying them to our missing students. They're also planting evidence in Ms. Stone's files to make it look like she's been getting reoccurring death threats from the group. Once she's dead, they'll tell the world that the Christians are to blame and can't be trusted. This will make the Christians public enemy number one."

"How can they get false evidence planted in Sierra Stone's own files?" Jordan asked. She might be a computer geek, but this spy stuff was way over her head.

"They have a mole inside Ms. Stone's administration." Hannie supplied the answer no one wanted to hear. They had plenty of enemies they could see. Now they must fight an unknown enemy, too.

"We can't even trust the people surrounding Ms. Stone." Jordan's voice shook. "How are we going to warn her?"

"Are they sure about this mole?" Matthew asked.

"Yes," Hannie said. "There may be more than one. They're trying to get a name, but so far no luck."

"What about my brother?" Rafael pushed away from the desk and moved to the center of the room. "Have they arranged a time and place for us to meet?"

"Yes. Tomorrow at 12:30. We're to wait for him in the park by Rivera's fruit stand at *Avenida de Mayo*," Hannie answered. "No more than two of us should go to the meeting because it's going to be hard to slip away unnoticed."

"Well, I'm definitely going," Rafael stated with a tone that left no room for argument.

"Of course, you have to go." Matthew stood. "I'll cover for your absence if Flynt asks. Jordan, I think you should go, too, so you and Hector can come up with a way for us to communicate."

Hannie nodded. "That's a good idea. I can cover for Jordan's absence."

Jordan's heartbeat increased, and she eyed Hannie. "Are any of your spy buddies coming to Venezuela?" Jordan wanted Marah to come in and take over this mission. A group of teens couldn't fight the government alone.

Hannie shook her head. "Security is extra tight right now since Councilor Stone arrives tomorrow. They haven't managed to slip anyone in yet, but they're still trying. For now, it's Team Seven and Hector Alvarado."

CHAPTER 21

The next day, Jordan and Rafael stood by the farmer's fruit stand near the park, waiting for Hector to arrive. Rafael purchased a couple of bananas and handed one to Jordan. Scents of papaya, watermelon, and mango blended with the stink of unwashed bodies and a hint of marijuana.

Jordan glanced at Rafael. He was uncharacteristically quiet, and he stared straight ahead.

I wish I was about to be reunited with my family. What joy he must be experiencing. Of course, her family members didn't include a notorious rebel leader. She brushed a fly away from her face and shivered.

Rafael glanced at his watch. "It's 12:28. Where is he?"

"He'll be here soon." Jordan tried to sound confident as she shifted her weight from one foot to the other and tossed her banana peel onto an overflowing basket beside her. The local flies swarmed on the new treat she'd added to the pile.

She glanced around, searching for a familiar face, a member of Team Four, one of the adult leaders, anything that would indicate they were being followed. Hannie had scanned the hotel room for bugging devices, and she didn't think the computer transmissions had been compromised, but Jordan had been living in a constant state of fear for weeks, and it was taking a toll on her emotions.

A mud encrusted black truck parked by the curb. It backfired, and a dark cloud spewed from the exhaust pipe. The door opened, swinging loosely on its hinges, and a squat, muscular man stepped out. He headed in their direction.

Jordan's heart pounded against her ribs. The man wore dark jeans and a black T-shirt. Tattoos covered his thick neck. He drew closer, and the confused look on Rafael's face told her that this was not Hector Alvarado.

The man stopped and stared at them with cold, emotionless eyes. "*Ven conmigo.*"

He wants us to come with him.

Jordan held her breath to stifle a scream. A jagged scar ran from the bottom of the man's left ear down across his cheek and over to his chin. What could cause a scar like that? She grabbed Rafael's arm and stepped closer to him. She didn't want to go anywhere with this fiend. What if GCU had found out about their meeting with Hector and this man had been sent to kill them?

"How do I know my brother sent you?" Rafael asked. "We're not going anywhere with you without proof."

Hurrah! If he wants to kill us, make him do it right here in front of witnesses.

Something close to a painful grin covered the man's face. "Hector said you were a smart kid."

Jordan swallowed hard to clear the lump in her throat and waited for the man to continue. One glance at his hard face and hollow eyes told her she was out of her league.

"Hector said to remind you that when you were a baby your mama would rock you and sing old hymns. She always teased you that hymns were the only songs that made you stop crying."

Rafael's posture relaxed. He released a deep breath. "Let's go," he said.

Jordan glanced around, weighing her options, then followed Rafael to the pickup truck while her heart did somersaults in her chest.

Oh, God, please don't let this be a trap.

The sweaty rebel opened the door. She climbed in then slid across the torn seat. Rafael slid in beside her.

"My name is Carlos," the man said after he got in the driver's seat.

Jordan sat between Carlos and Rafael and silently prayed. How had a computer geek from Old Memphis ended up trapped in a net of espionage on her way to visit a notorious rebel leader? Thankfully, her parents believed she was safely tucked away at GCU, studying government propaganda. Her mother would have a heart attack if she could see her now.

The truck bounced over bumpy roads and swerved to avoid giant potholes. They passed the city dump, and Jordan's stomach roiled from the stench. People swarmed the trash heaps like ants searching for their next meal. Even toddlers wandered through the piles, shooing away persistent birds. The banana in Jordan's belly flipped, and she feared she might lose her stomach contents if the journey didn't end soon.

About fifteen minutes later, the truck parked in a dirty back alley.

"Get out," Carlos ordered.

"I don't want to play anymore. I'll wait right here." Jordan spoke to Rafael's back as he slid out of the truck. Let Rafael have his family reunion without her.

"Come on, Jordan." Rafael held the door open. "I can't do this alone. I need my computer geek."

She sighed and slid across the seat, the torn vinyl sticking to her jeans. She stepped from the truck, and the stink in the alley nearly knocked her to the ground. She had to give Hector credit. This was a great meeting place. Not even a rat would come back here. No way a fancy GCU lackey would step foot in this filth.

Crumbling buildings made of tin, brick, and wood lined the narrow alley. A seeping heap of trash stood at the end of the alley. Jordan covered her nose and mouth as the man led them closer to the trash pile. Her foot struck a broken board, and she stumbled. Rafael caught her before she hit the ground.

They continued to a grey stucco building stained with green mold. Carlos opened the door and ushered them inside. Jordan strained to see her surroundings while her eyes adjusted to the dim light.

I was wrong about the rats. A rodent the size of a small cat scurried across the floor in front of them.

"I never thought I'd see my baby brother again." The voice came from the shadows, deep and strong. Jordan turned to see a young man walking toward them.

"Rafael, *mi hermano.*" The man grabbed Rafael by the shoulders. "You're a grown man now. I can't believe my eyes." He spoke with a gravelly voice, as if the words were being pushed through an aching throat. A wide rope burn wound its way around his tattooed neck.

"Hector." With a few tears running down his face, Rafael wrapped the man in a bear hug.

"I'm so sorry I couldn't come to Mama's funeral." Hector's voice cracked.

"I understand." Rafael broke the embrace and stared hard at his brother. "There were GC soldiers at the funeral, and you would've been caught if you'd been stupid enough to show up."

Jordan shifted from one foot to the other as the two brothers slapped each other on the back, laughed and cried. What a privilege to share this part of Rafael's life. She'd never think of him as a foolish playboy again.

Rafael touched her arm. "Hector, this is my friend, Jordan."

The rebel flashed the same flirtatious grin she'd seen Rafael use a dozen times. It must be a family trait. "They told me Jordan was a computer geek, but I've never seen such a pretty computer geek." Jordan's fingers ached in Hector's grip. He was Rafael's brother all right.

"Thank you," she said.

Hector stood about an inch taller than Rafael, and his body was solid muscle. The same look of bravado shone in his ebony eyes, but there was no playfulness in their depths. Rafael was all show, an excellent shot, and great in a fist fight, but Hector was the real thing. No wonder Rafael's mother had been happy to send him to GCU and get him away from this hard life.

Hector released Jordan's hand. "Now we must get down to business." He wrapped his tattoo covered arm around Rafael's shoulder and led him toward a small table. Jordan followed.

"Our sources think the students are being held in this area." Hector touched the map spread across the wooden surface. The table wobbled on its three legs.

"I'm familiar with that part of the city," Rafael said. "It's a big area to search."

"It is," Hector agreed. "We're making good progress. But we need you and your *amigos* to let us know if you hear anything helpful."

"How can we contact you?" Jordan found her voice at last.

"We were hoping you might have some high-tech equipment we could use to communicate with you," Rafael said.

Hector slapped Rafael on the back. "We aren't the CIA or the Mossad, bro. But even they aren't really themselves anymore."

Rafael blushed at his brother's patronizing comment. No doubt Rafael wanted his brother to see him as a man and not think of him as a naïve boy.

"But I do have a very useful high-tech gadget here." Hector opened a dirty jewelry box and pulled out a golden chain with a gem hanging on the end. "This will allow us to communicate. I think it will be best for the lovely lady to wear this." He placed the necklace over Jordan's head. The chain caught in her ponytail holder before falling around her neck.

Hector turned to Rafael. "I have a simple wallet communicator for you. Carlos will explain to Jordan how the jewel works while I get to know my little brother again." Hector wound his arm around Rafael's shoulder, pulling him close.

"Carlos?" Jordan questioned as the scarred rebel walked toward her.

"Carlos is our computer geek," Hector answered.

"Carlos?" Rafael cocked one brow.

"Carlos," Hector repeated. "Now you know why I was so surprised at the beauty of your computer geek."

The men all laughed, and Jordan's damp face grew even hotter. *Lord, are You sure You know what You're doing? I'm in way over my head.*

CHAPTER 22

*J*ordan and Rafael returned to the hotel, both covered in sweat and grime. Jordan wiped dirt from her cheeks and moaned. "I need a shower fast." Hopefully, the soothing water would calm her nerves as well as clean her body.

When they entered the lobby, Laurel greeted them. A big grin covered her delicate face. She wore dark blue shorts and a ruffled peasant top. How did she look so fresh and sweat-free in this oppressive humidity? Thankfully, she didn't ask them where they'd been or comment on their grungy appearances. She seemed anxious to share some big news. Rafael excused himself and headed upstairs. No doubt he'd give Hannie and Matthew a report on the meeting.

"Okay, Laurel, tell me, what has gotten you so excited?" As much as she wanted to cut this conversation short, Jordan giggled at Laurel's enthusiasm.

Laurel clutched Jordan's arm and bounced up and down. For a moment, Jordan got caught up in the pure teenage excitement. She touched the red jewel that dangled from her neck and reality pounced. Would she ever be a simple teenager again?

"Sierra Stone is coming to the Montgomerys' suite for dinner this evening, and I've been invited." Laurel squealed.

That was big news. *If only we could trust Laurel with the truth, she might be able to warn Ms. Stone.* Jordan licked her dry lips while her emotions see-sawed. Laurel was deeply involved with Dawson and entrenched in the European Collective. She didn't have much practice at thinking for herself, bless her heart, so she did whatever her parents, teachers, or friends told her. Laurel could not be trusted with the team's secrets yet.

"That's very exciting," Jordan said. "You're a lucky girl to dine with Councilor Stone."

"But it gets better." Laurel twirled in front of her. Obviously, that was what ballerinas did when they were excited.

"Mr. Montgomery asked me to bring a friend tonight. So, will you come to dinner with me?"

Jordan blinked and stepped back. Her knees hit the leather sofa in the center of the lobby and buckled. She dropped onto the cushions. The expression on Laurel's face told her that this was not a joke.

"Of course, I'll come with you." Giggles bubbled from Jordan. This was too good to be true. "But are you sure you understood Mr. Montgomery correctly?"

Laurel nodded, her silky hair sliding over her bare shoulders. "He wants Ms. Stone to see examples of GCU training up close and personal. That's us." She patted her chest and flopped down beside Jordan.

"But I didn't think the Montgomerys were supporters of Councilor Stone," Jordan said. This dinner would make more sense if Ms. Stone was going to be assassinated by poison rather than bullet. Of course, they didn't know how the councilor would be assassinated or when.

"The Montgomerys disagree with her on a lot of issues, but they all want GCU to succeed. Mr. Montgomery told Dawson that we need to reach out to our rivals and learn to work with them, especially someone as popular as Sierra Stone."

Jordan nodded and blew a sweat drenched curl off her forehead. "Thank you so much for inviting me. I'm really looking forward to it." She couldn't wait to tell Hannie and the others.

"Mr. Montgomery wanted Dawson to bring a friend, too, but Dawson doesn't have any friends," Laurel stated as a matter of unquestioned fact. "Hey, why don't you bring Matthew with you?" She clapped and grinned. "He can be a friend for Dawson."

Jordan rubbed her nose. *Lord, could this get any better?*

A blush settled on Laurel's cheeks. "I'm sorry. You may not want to bring Matthew. I've noticed... I mean, it seems like you and Matthew aren't as close as you used to be."

Jordan tugged on the bottom of her sweaty T-shirt. Surely, all of Team Seven had noticed the abrupt change in her relationship with Matthew. She'd confided in Hannie since Hannie knew about the kiss, but she hadn't mentioned anything to the others. How embarrassing.

Broken romance or not, Jordan knew Matthew wouldn't give up this opportunity to visit with Ms. Stone. Their mission was more important than teenage angst, and truth be known, Jordan wanted Matthew by her side tonight. Why face the enemy alone if she didn't have to?

"I'd love to bring Matthew, but Dawson doesn't really like him, or me, for that matter."

Laurel frowned and wrinkled her brow. "True. But out of all our team members, he dislikes you and Matthew the least."

Jordan smiled at the simple logic and nodded in agreement.

"I'll meet you both in the lobby at seven to take you to the Montgomery suite." Laurel stood. "By the way." She paused and glanced down at Jordan. "Did you know that Team Four and Team Seven aren't the only GCU students in Old Venezuela?"

Jordan's stomach tossed. If she hadn't been sitting down, she would've passed out. "Uh, why, why do you think that?"

"I overheard Mr. Montgomery talking on the phone, and he said, 'make sure the other students are secure until we're ready for them.' I wonder what that means?"

Jordan dropped her gaze and studied the wrought iron coffee table in front of her. She didn't trust her voice to cooperate if she tried to speak. She now had proof that the Montgomerys were involved in this plot. Did

Dawson know about the kidnapped students? He'd shared a room with Paul. Surely, he wasn't involved in Paul's disappearance.

"I started to ask Mr. Montgomery about the other students," Laurel continued, "but decided I better not. I didn't want him to think I was eavesdropping."

Jordan sprang to her feet. "Don't dare ask him about it," she shouted.

Laurel's eyes went wide. Jordan glanced around the lobby. The young man working at the front desk stared at her curiously. She licked her lips and swayed from side to side.

"What I mean is, well, since we haven't been told about these other students, GCU must be planning some type of surprise. You wouldn't want Mr. Montgomery to know you found out about it." Amazingly, her voice sounded steady. Steadier than her frayed nerves.

"You're probably right," Laurel said. "You're the smart one. I just have the looks."

The smart one? *Lucky me.* Knowledge was a very dangerous thing. *If only I could forget all the terrible secrets I know about GCU.*

THAT EVENING, Jordan's stomach churned as she and Matthew stepped into the Montgomery suite, Laurel by their side. Dawson hugged Laurel, greeted Jordan and Matthew with a curt nod, then followed his father into the penthouse office. Mrs. Montgomery greeted them sweetly and directed them to take a seat in the living room before she grabbed Laurel and started burying the girl in compliments. The woman declared that "Laurel's beauty made any dinner party a success." No wonder Laurel spent her whole life believing she was nothing more than a pretty object.

While Mrs. Montgomery and Laurel scurried around giving orders to the servants and ensuring every detail was taken care of, Matthew and Jordan sat side by side on the cushioned sofa and studied the opulent suite. The large living area held a crushed velvet sofa, three overstuffed chairs, and a wicker rocking chair. An oblong rug stretched across the floor, bathing the room with pale blue, green, and rose colors.

"Reminds me of the movie star mansions in Hollywood, without the bullet holes and decay," Matthew whispered.

"I've seen the ruins of grand hotels in Old Memphis. This must've been what they looked like back in the day." Jordan's gaze traveled from the rich blue drapery to the marble floor shining beneath the pale light of the crystal chandelier. An archway separated the parlor from the dining area where a solid mahogany table sat like a queen decked out in her jewels. Laurel had said the suite held a kitchen, office, and two bedrooms. Absent divine intervention, they'd never be able to talk to Ms. Stone privately tonight.

A shudder climbed Jordan's spine. How had two teenagers from a second-rate collective ended up at a dinner party with the rich and powerful? They didn't belong here, but God must know what He was doing. She'd love to tell Ms. Stone about the kidnapped students and warn her that she was on GCU's hit list. Not possible without solid proof.

Earlier today, Jordan had accessed Ms. Stone's computer, but a security code was required to enter further or send messages. This had prevented her from implanting the incriminating emails between Cimarron and Principal Reed. Hopefully, they'd get the chance to reveal GCU's secrets to Ms. Stone soon. Dining with her tonight should show the woman that Jordan and Matthew were stable, well-rounded students, not loons who believed in conspiracy theories.

At 7:30 p.m., Councilor Stone and her assistant, Grayson King, arrived at the Montgomery suite. Two burly bodyguards stationed themselves at the suite entrance while Ms. Stone and Grayson joined the others for dinner. The guards would intimidate most people, but she doubted they frightened Cimarron or Principal Reed. With River Wallis on their side, they didn't need to fear a thing.

Not surprisingly, Cimarron and Principal Reed had also been invited to attend tonight's festivities. As Jordan glanced around the dining table, she was reminded of the vultures that filled the trees in Old Venezuela. Thankfully, Matthew sat beside her. His presence gave her strength even if they weren't a couple any longer.

Dark circles underlined Ms. Stone's golden eyes, and tension lines creased her forehead. *I'm not the only one feeling the strain of this gathering.*

Cimarron's famous fake smile covered her lips as she raved about the success of GCU. Mrs. Montgomery bragged about Dawson and Laurel's accomplishments and even mentioned Matthew's athleticism and Jordan's keen computer skills. Mr. Montgomery remained stoic throughout dinner, commenting only on the fresh flavor of the fish and the beautiful Venezuela mountains.

Why was Mr. Montgomery hosting this dinner? He wasn't a member of the Global Collective Council, although he had many friends who were. Many councilmembers were arriving tomorrow in time to attend the grand banquet and hear Ms. Stone's speech the following day. The duty to entertain Councilor Stone must have fallen to Mr. Montgomery by default. Politics was a strange business. Was the opponent always wined and dined before their assassination?

"Jordan, have you enjoyed your time at GCU?" Ms. Stone asked.

Jordan glanced across the table at Cimarron. Her low-cut, red dress contrasted with Ms. Stone's black and white, conservative blouse. Principal Reed sat by Cimarron's side, looking as dopey as ever.

Jordan took a sip of water as her mind struggled for the words that would please Cimarron but not choke her as she said them. "It's been wonderful to meet so many people from around the planet. Growing up in Old Memphis, I never dreamed I'd make friends from across the globe or travel to the Latin Collective."

"That's the great value of GCU." Genuine interest shone on Ms. Stone's face. "We can all learn and grow by knowing people from different areas and backgrounds. The individuality of each collective is what makes them special."

"As you know, Councilor Stone is a big supporter of the individual," Grayson announced between bites of peacock bass.

"Individual over collective," Matthew said. "Your speech at GCU was very interesting."

"Certainly, individualism is important," Mr. Montgomery spoke from the head of the table. "But I think we can all agree that we must have a strong governing body. Look at the chaos that has reigned in all the individual collectives over the last twenty-five years." He folded his linen napkin and placed it beside his plate. "The Latin and African collectives have a primitive belief in some type of god, and violence and poverty dominate their culture. Since the establishment of the Global Collective Council ten years ago, peace and progress are growing. Surely you don't advocate the destruction of the Global Collective Council. Do you, Councilor Stone?"

Ms. Stone leveled a hard gaze at the stern man. She swallowed hard and seemed to be weighing her words before speaking. "Of course, I don't want to see the Global Council dissolved, as I'm a member of it myself." She flashed a faint smile. "I would like to see the power more evenly distributed among the other councilors and collectives. So much European Collective power can't be good for anyone."

Mr. Montgomery retrieved his napkin and patted his lips, muffling his words as he spoke. "It's very good for the European Collective."

Cimarron leaned forward in her chair, placing her water glass on the table. It clinked on the wood, and the ice cubes bounced like rubber balls. "Sierra and I both grew up in Old Ireland and have known one another for years. Sierra's always had radical ideas and has never given Hunter Wallis the respect he deserves as leader of the Global Council."

Mrs. Montgomery bowed her head, and Principal Reed cleared his throat. Dawson pushed his chair back, the legs scraping on the marble floor.

"Very well said, Cimarron," Dawson said.

"I show Hunter Wallis every proper respect." Ms. Stone's voice dropped an octave. The picture of rebel leader Sierra Stone brandishing a rifle against the Parisian faction flashed through Jordan's mind.

"I simply refuse to worship him," she continued, "as many people are now doing. Hunter Wallis is only a man, after all. Not a deity."

"You would know a lot more about him being a man than I do." Cimarron spat the words. Then twisted her mouth into a harsh frown.

Laurel gasped, Dawson smirked, and Grayson shifted in his chair.

Ms. Stone closed her eyes and took a deep breath before reaching for her glass. Her hand trembled as she lifted the crystal goblet to her lips.

Hunter Wallis and Sierra Stone, an item? Jordan couldn't believe that a strong, progressive woman like Ms. Stone had ever been involved with a tyrant. Whatever kind of relationship existed between the councilor and Hunter Wallis must have ended years ago; otherwise, the gossip would have spread across every collective.

The councilor's composure returned as she squared her shoulders and smoothed her short hair with one hand, but her face told the whole story. *I may be young and inexperienced, but I know the look of lost love in a woman's eyes when I see it.*

Mr. Montgomery stood. "Your desire to spread the power around won't win you any friends." He looked so much like Dawson with his heavy lids and bushy eyebrows, but his eyes were cold and voice flat.

"I have many friends." Ms. Stone placed her elbows on the table and tented her fingers. "In many collectives."

No wonder Mr. Montgomery and the Collective Council wanted Sierra Stone dead. She was advocating an end to their way of life, and she refused to worship at the throne of Hunter Wallis. Jordan wanted to jump up and warn Ms. Stone of the evil in this man's heart. If she did, would they drag her from the room and lock her away in a mental hospital?

"Let's move into the parlor for drinks." Mrs. Montgomery broke the strained silence and brought Jordan back to her senses before she could make a fool of herself or get arrested.

Everyone stood and made their way to the living area. Mr. Montgomery settled himself in the recliner and lit a cigar. Cimarron, Principal Reed, and Dawson sat on the sofa. Ms. Stone, Grayson, Mrs. Montgomery, and Laurel stood by the decorative fireplace. Jordan and Matthew stood near the wall, eavesdropping on the other conversations. Jordan hoped they could blend into the floral wallpaper.

"Laurel will be performing at the banquet tomorrow night." Mrs. Montgomery grabbed Laurel's arm and presented her to Ms. Stone like a diamond in a black velvet box. "Isn't she lovely?"

Laurel blushed and bowed her head. Mrs. Montgomery seemed to be as enamored of Laurel as her son was.

Ms. Stone patted Laurel's shoulder. "You're very lovely, and talented. I'm looking forward to your performance tomorrow night. I know it will be wonderful."

"Thank you." Laurel beamed.

Jordan and Matthew hovered nearby, trying to stay out of everybody's way. The sickeningly sweet smell of Mr. Montgomery's cigar turned Jordan's stomach.

Ms. Stone stepped closer to Jordan. "I hope to have the opportunity to talk more with you while we're in Old Venezuela. I'm fascinated by your computer skills. I'd love to have such an intelligent young woman on my team someday."

Jordan's checks burned beneath Ms. Stone's stare. She pressed her hand to her stomach. "I'd be honored to work with you, Councilor Stone."

Once again, she fell under the spell of Sierra Stone. Unlike Ms. Montgomery and Cimarron, Ms. Stone hadn't visited the beauty enhancers, and the lines around her eyes crinkled when she smiled. The naturalness of her movements and imperfections on her face reminded Jordan of her mother and grandmother.

"I'd be happy to take a look at your computer book now, and see if I can make any enhancements," Jordan offered.

If she could examine this treasure, she might be able to find the code she needed to penetrate the firewall. Ms. Stone reached for the small computer book dangling from her belt, but Grayson stopped her before she could pass it to Jordan.

"That would not be keeping with proper protocol. Jordan isn't an official member of your staff, Councilor Stone."

"What would I do without Grayson to keep me straight?" Ms. Stone hooked the computer book back on her belt. "I'm afraid I'm not as adroit at politics as he is." She laughed.

"I understand," Jordan said. *So close and so far away!* "But if I can ever be of any help, please let me know."

Councilor Stone was just what the Global Collective Council needed. Perhaps there had been something between Ms. Stone and Hunter Wallis years ago, but who hadn't made a few mistakes in their youth? Her past didn't matter. She was a woman now, and she'd obviously learned a lot in life.

Oh, Lord, we can't let her die. Please show us the best way to protect her.

CHAPTER 23

The next night, bedecked in a golden gown that fell below her knees, Jordan walked into the hotel's grand banquet room with Matthew by her side. He tugged at the tie around his neck, and she giggled. His attire might not be comfortable, but he'd never looked more handsome.

Sadness pinched Jordan's heart. It appeared that Matthew had decided to be her friend and nothing more. She had plenty of friends. She and Matthew belonged together. Why had she messed everything up? She clenched her hands at her sides. She couldn't fret over a broken relationship when they were trapped in a web of danger.

Cimarron sat at the end of the long table prepared for Team Seven. She leaned against Principal Reed's shoulder, laughing and sipping champagne. How could she be so callous when her old friend would be executed tomorrow? Jordan shivered.

Rafael stepped up behind Jordan. "She outdid herself tonight." He eyed Cimarron and wagged his eyebrows. "Dressing up for the big shots, I guess."

Cimarron glowed, bathed in candlelight and the sparkle of the crystal chandeliers. She wore a silver dress that clung to every curve. Her blonde hair was fashioned into a bun with pink tendrils falling to her shoulders. A sparkling band encircled her head, and her skin shimmered due to a special body spray that was the rage in the European Collective. Obviously, she didn't want to fade into the crowd tonight. Had there ever been a time that Cimarron didn't want to stand out?

Thankfully, the guest rooms and banquet room were air conditioned. Jordan couldn't imagine wearing a fancy dress in this humid heat. She'd be covered in sweat in minutes, and plastic Cimarron would probably melt.

Hannie sat at the Team Seven table, rubbing her hands up and down her thighs in a very unladylike fashion.

"Another night of dressing up like a clown," she said as Jordan approached the table. "This thing makes me itch."

Hannie wore a satin skirt that flowed to her calves in sea-blue waves. Her mahogany curls were pulled back from her face and anchored in place with a silver headband. She might label herself a clown, but she looked beautiful.

Matthew glanced around the room before pulling out a chair for Jordan. Always a gentleman. He sat between her and Hannie. "Where's Team Four tonight?" he asked.

"Their table is on the opposite side of the room." Rafael motioned in that general direction. "They're displaying us separately, so everyone has a chance to eye a genuine GCU specimen up close and personal."

Hannie tugged on her modest blouse, practically pulling it to her chin. "I see you didn't have any trouble locating Team Four. Is your blonde buddy keeping you updated on their whereabouts?"

"There are five lovely ladies on Team Four." Rafael flashed a wolfish grin. "When the band starts, I'll be heading that way."

Hannie groaned. Rafael sprawled into a chair beside Victor and greeted the boy with a punch on the shoulder. Malese sat beside Victor, and Timberlyn sat across from Malese. The girls glistened like polished stones in a majestic crown.

Mr. Flynt sat at the end of the table, Dawson beside him. Dawson was almost handsome decked out in his dark suit and red tie. If only his personality weren't so objectionable. Laurel deserved a whole lot better than Dawson Montgomery.

Jordan took a deep breath, soothed by the scents of the tropical flowers decorating the room. Around her, people chattered and laughed, completely unaware of the seething tide of evil in this room. She twisted her linen napkin. Soon, everything would change. Either for the better or the worse. But nothing would ever be the same.

Matthew had told her to 'keep up her faith.' He still believed they could rescue the students and stop the assassination. But time was their enemy. Her faith took a hit with every passing hour, and doubt tormented her. Why didn't she share Matthew's confident faith? She was such a weak Christian.

If they were successful, Ms. Stone would gain greater power in the Global Council. Mr. Montgomery, Cimarron, and Principal Reed would go to prison, and Laurel would be free of Dawson. But now they must continue to play their parts, endure this banquet, and pray that Hector finds the missing students tonight.

The only bright spot of the evening was the fact that Laurel would perform. Earlier today, Jordan had prayed with Laurel, asking God to calm her nerves and use her talent for His glory. Laurel said she had no desire to run to the bathroom and throw up as she typically did before a performance. God was making a huge difference in her new friend's life.

The male members of Team Seven, including Mr. Flynt, didn't appear to be impressed with the gala, but they were very interested in the various trays of appetizers covering the table. Rafael kept glancing toward the Team Four table, and he winked every time one of the girls acknowledged him.

Matthew offered Jordan a shrimp cocktail. She shook her head and wrinkled her nose. The shrimp looked delicious, but with the raging sea in her stomach, she'd probably barf. What would they do if Hector didn't find the missing students tonight? They couldn't possibly save both Ms. Stone and the students tomorrow. Could they? She prayed they wouldn't be forced to sacrifice one for the other.

The room quickly filled with local officials, global council members, and other important people. Security guards patrolled the area, and personal bodyguards sat beside high-ranking members of the Global Council. Once all the guests arrived, Principal Reed headed to the stage, pausing to greet various councilors on his way.

Tonight, the audience would see the best and brightest that Global Collective University could offer. Principal Reed read the names of each member of Team Four and Team Seven, motioning for them to stand as he praised their unique abilities. Marksmanship, martial arts, swimming, gymnastics, science, and technology, these two teams had it all covered.

Jordan stood on shaking legs when Principal Reed called her name.

I feel like a prize horse at auction.

She tried to look like she was enjoying the applause, but inwardly, she cringed. Matthew winked at her. Timberlyn flashed a fake smile to rival Cimarron's, and Malese stood with her head bowed. Victor blushed as red as the roses decorating the table, and Hannie kept the same hostile look on her face she always presented. Once everyone had been given sufficient time to gawk at the wonder students, Principal Reed introduced the night's first performer.

Kayden, a Team Four boy from the Pacific Collective blasted a romantic ballad in a rich baritone. His voice was clear and strong, grasping each note with skill and releasing a perfection of sound. No wonder GCU wanted to brag about him. Of course, GCU didn't have anything to do with Kayden's exceptional talent. His voice was a gift from God, but as usual, GCU had no desire to share the credit with anyone, especially not the Almighty. Applause erupted when the boy finished his song and left the stage.

Moments later, the lights dimmed, and a spotlight hit the center of the stage, revealing an ethereal presence. Laurel posed in a short skirt of white feathers, her blonde hair fashioned in a bun encircled by a feather crown. The strains from a classic ballet sounded, and Laurel danced across the stage. From the point of her toe, curve of her arms, and lift of her delicate chin, she no longer appeared human. Jordan almost believed the swan tattoo on Laurel's shoulder had come to life and transformed her into the dying swan.

Jordan glanced away from the stage to check out her friend's reactions. Timberlyn and Malese stared wide-eyed, and Rafael's usually playful eyes followed every move Laurel made. The music built to its dramatic climax, and Laurel performed the dance of death to perfection. A tense silence hovered as she bowed her head and died.

People jumped to their feet, clapping and cheering. Even a few whistles bounced around the room. Ms. Stone stood in front of the stage, clapping heartily. The councilor had requested Laurel perform the dance of death because it was her favorite scene in this ballet. How ironic. A chill fell over Jordan. If they failed to warn Ms. Stone in time, tomorrow afternoon this audience would watch a death scene play out on that stage —and it wouldn't be fake.

Dawson stood, clapping and shouting. His eyes reflected a possessive love. Would a boy raised by Malcolm Montgomery, a boy labeled the 'spare heir' ever know the true meaning of love?

After changing in her dressing room, Laurel joined them for dinner. They all praised her performance. Even Hannie graced her with, "Good job, blondie."

Hotel waiters in crisp white aprons served plates of mahi-mahi, chopped pork, and chicken with vegetables. Jordan took a few bites, hoping that feeding the butterflies in her stomach would give her some peace. It didn't work.

Hector had told Rafael he'd notify him through his communicator as soon as he located the missing students. Jordan made eye contact with Rafael and raised her brows in question. Rafael shook his head as the sound of a drumroll floated to the table followed by a catchy dance tune. He shrugged and stood, then patted her on the back before heading to the Team Four table to collect his first dance partner.

Ladies in silk and taffeta and men in tuxedos flowed onto the dance floor. The beautiful music captivated Jordan, and she almost forgot the danger soaring around them. Principal Reed and Cimarron joined the dancers. Cimarron molded herself against the man's body as they swayed to the sultry music. Obviously, his marriage vows didn't mean anything here, and the couple didn't care if everyone found out about their affair.

Everything would change tomorrow, and they seemed confident they'd win. When River Wallis learned of their successful mission, they'd probably receive powerful jobs in the Global Collective or spend the rest of their lives at a tropical island retreat.

Hannie took a big bite of *bienmesabe*, a coconut flavored sponge cake. "If Rafael keeps dancing around like a fool, we'll be lucky if he even notices a message from Hector."

"Give him a break, Hannie," Matthew said. "Rafael is more dependable than you think."

Hannie grunted between bites.

Matthew stood and pushed his chair under the table. "I think we should follow his example. Jordan, may I have this dance?"

She took his outstretched hand, her cold fingers relishing the warmth of his grip.

"I'm not sure we should waste our time dancing." Her legs shook when she stood. Did they shake from fear or because Matthew wanted to dance? She couldn't get her hopes up. Surely, he only wanted to dance to keep up their cover.

"There's nothing we can do until we hear from Hector," Matthew said. "And Cimarron will get suspicious if we all sit here like duds. Look how much fun Team Four is having."

Every member of Team Four danced with Global Collective councilors or one another. Matthew was right. They couldn't do anything to cause suspicion. "Victor, Malese, join us," Jordan said.

Victor looked at Malese, who quickly nodded, and they followed Jordan and Matthew to the crowded dance floor. Soon, every member of Team Seven was twirling across the floor, except for Hannie. Jordan glanced over Matthew's shoulder as Hannie plunged her fork into another piece of cake.

Jordan and Matthew reached the dancefloor as the orchestra began playing a soft classic tune. She stood still and waited for Matthew to make the first move. He wrapped his arms around her and pulled her close. She snuggled against him, a perfect fit in his arms as they moved with the rhythm of the music.

What am I doing? This is probably the way his old girlfriend acted. Forward and flirty.

Jordan stepped back to put a little space between them. "Sorry if I got too carried away with the dance. I know it's just an act."

Matthew missed a step, and they almost tumbled to the floor. He jerked to attention slamming her against his chest.

Jordan giggled over the strains of a violin. "I'm the klutz. Not you."

Matthew brought them to a stop. "Jordan, I need to talk to you. Let's head over there." He motioned to the far corner of the room, then took her arm and directed her through the dancing couples.

Jordan's heart pounded almost as loudly as the orchestra drums. Matthew's serious expression unnerved her. Whatever he wanted to say must be important.

CHAPTER 24

*H*annie watched the dancers until her eyes glassed over. Unless something happened soon, she'd fall asleep. Out of the corner of her eye, she spotted Rafael moving toward their table after what must have been his twentieth dance. Her pulse quickened. He must have news from Hector.

He plopped down in a chair beside her, grabbed the crystal water pitcher, and poured himself a drink. His lazy expression told her Hector hadn't contacted him yet.

She yawned. "I see you decided to grace us with your presence once again." Her harsh voice surprised her. *Why does he aggravate me so much?* She could easily ignore most people, but Rafael irritated her like a fungus under the skin.

"I'm happy to know you missed me, *mi tigresa*," he responded in his usual glib manner.

The once delicious coconut cake had morphed into an over-inflated balloon bouncing around inside her stomach. Tomorrow was D-day for Sierra Stone, and they hadn't made any progress on stopping the assassination or finding the missing students. Matthew and Jordan danced, Victor and Malese danced, Rafael danced with anything in a skirt. Was she the only one who had sense enough to worry?

"I didn't miss you. I've actually enjoyed watching you make a fool of yourself with every female in the room."

"I've been attempting to gather information from the council member's wives and the girls on Team Four."

A very unlikely story. "Have you had any luck?"

"Unfortunately, no. Even Mrs. Montgomery seems to be in the dark."

"It was so brave of you to sacrifice yourself for our cause," Hannie snapped.

Rafael opened his mouth to speak, but Timberlyn interrupted from across the table. "Hannie, you haven't danced tonight. You should dance now, with Rafael."

Hannie wanted to slap the girl's round, innocent face. "Why don't you mind your own business? You aren't the belle of the ball either. How many guys have you danced with?"

"I've danced with one boy from Team Four, Victor, Matthew, a councilor from the Baltic Collective, a Coun—"

"I don't need details." Hannie slapped the table instead of slapping Timberlyn.

Timberlyn jumped.

"What you need is a kick in the pants." Rafael's voice sounded low and menacing. He leaned closer to her. "But let's dance instead." He jumped up, grabbed her arm, and pulled her to her feet.

Her eyes widened, and her knees shook, but she could never be afraid of Rafael. No doubt, she could best him in any match.

"I'm not going to dance with you." She yanked her arm from Rafael's grasp, but he refused to let her step away, and he didn't retreat.

"Cimarron is watching." He brought his lips close to her ear and whispered, "Don't make a scene."

Hannie twisted her head so she could see Cimarron sitting at the end of the table. Sure enough, the woman had them locked in a deadly gaze. She was probably terrified that two of her well-trained zombies were about to come to blows. She'd love to deck Rafael and watch Cimarron have a meltdown. As much fun as that would be she refused to give into this childish whim. They had a mission to accomplish. They didn't need Cimarron locking them in their rooms.

"Fine." Hannie grabbed Rafael's arm and pulled him toward the swirling crowd. "Let's dance."

As soon as they reached the dance floor, the music changed from an upbeat rhumba to a slow melodious tune. Hannie gritted her teeth.

Just my luck.

Rafael pulled her close, probably afraid she'd turn and run. Wrapped in his arms, she struggled to match his steps.

"This would be a lot easier if you would let me lead," he whispered.

His breath tickled her ear, tangling her thoughts. "Sorry," she mumbled and stopped fighting him. *I am so out of my comfort zone here.* Dancing got a lot easier when she allowed Rafael to lead.

Several women nodded at them as they danced by on the arms of their overweight husbands. Even Mrs. Montgomery waved at Rafael when she twirled by with a grim-faced Mr. Montgomery. Hannie rolled her eyes at the ridiculous women, obviously as smitten as the silly females on Team Four.

Matthew and Jordan floated by. Jordan did a double-take when she spotted Hannie in Rafael's arms. Hannie glared at her, but Jordan flashed her a wide smile. *My word, they were only dancing.* They weren't headed for the altar. Heaven forbid!

Rafael was an expert dancer. Of course, he should be with all the practice he got. Hannie missed several steps, her feet tangled with his, and she tilted to the side, certain she'd hit the hard floor any minute. Rafael grinned and tightened his grip to keep her aright. The music blended with muffled voices and light laughter while the scents of sweet perfume and spicy aftershave stung her nose. Rafael moved them from one end of the room to the other, and for a moment, she almost enjoyed their trek across the crowded dance floor.

She'd attended a few festivals with dancing and drinking while growing up in Israel, and she'd danced with Matthew at the winter banquet at GCU, but her heart hadn't pounded against her chest. What was wrong with her tonight? She longed for the dance to end yet hoped it would never stop.

Rafael had one arm wrapped securely around her waist as they glided under the wide stone archway separating the banquet hall from the hotel lobby. The band played the last note, and their dance ended. Hannie stepped out of Rafael's arms. They stood in an alcove behind a banner draped column, the menacing Global Collective snow leopard waving above their heads.

Rafael stared at her as if he'd made a great scientific discovery. "You're a very pretty young woman."

"Don't start that stuff with me." She stepped back, the cold satin skirt cooling her fists. "I'm immune to your charms."

He flashed a killer smile and winked. "No, you're not." He grabbed her wrists and yanked her toward him. "And you are beautiful. I've just been too afraid of you to notice it before."

Hannie pulled her wrists from his grasp and punched him in the arm, her fingers tingling with the impact. Yes, she could be a scary character. She wore the tough girl mask beautifully. But what girl wanted a guy to say he was afraid of her? More importantly, why had Rafael suddenly lost his fear? She certainly hadn't done anything to encourage him. They'd only shared one dance. What was wrong with the male species?

Rafael stared at her. He opened his mouth then snapped it shut, seemingly as confused as she was.

"What's going to happen when this is all over?" Hannie asked the question that had been torturing her all night, and immediately wanted to kick herself. She sounded like a silly girl worrying about the future instead of focusing on their current mission. Yet, she couldn't stop her fears or her words. She stepped closer to him and lowered her voice.

"Let's say we save Councilor Stone from assassination and expose GCU as evil puppets of the Global Council. Are we heroes? Does Ms. Stone soar to the top of the political world, taking us with her, or does GCU and the Council twist all of this and make us enemies of the collective good?"

Rafael released a deep breath. "I don't know. It could go either way. We could soar, or we could crash."

The band must have taken a break. No music, no dancing feet, only mingled voices and the sound of the waiters' feet pounding the floor. Hannie and Rafael stood behind the thick marble pillar, lost in temporary seclusion.

"Will we end up back at GCU?" Hannie blabbered. "Or will we be stuck in a Venezuelan prison? Will we ever get to go home?"

Have I lost my mind? Here I am sharing my fears with Rafael, of all people.

"I don't know about the rest of you." Rafael's jaw was set in a determined line. "But I'm not going back to GCU, no matter what happens. I'm staying here with my brother. I'll join his rebel band and live in the mountains. Now that I've found Hector, I won't be leaving."

"I understand. I'd love to return to my rebel friends in Israel."

Rafael took a step toward her and ran his hands up and down her arms. "Maybe Matthew was right about you and me."

"In what way?" She fought the urge to put some distance between them, flustered by the sparks shooting up her arms.

"Matthew said we'd make a good couple. We're a lot alike."

"And what did you say to him?" she snapped. How dare Matthew play matchmaker.

Rafael grinned. "I said we'd kill each other in a week."

"You were right." She turned to go back to their table.

He grabbed her arm and spun her around. "But it would be a great week."

He pulled her close, wrapping her tightly in his arms. Her head rested against his chest, the erratic thump of his heart pounding in her ears, but it didn't beat for her. Rafael was interested in a new girl every day.

She raised her head to tell him what she thought of him, but he brought his lips to hers before she could speak. He pressed his right hand against the back of her head, pulling her closer and deepening the kiss while he wound his other arm around her waist. She shivered at his touch and the warmth of his lips on hers. If only she could remain locked in his arms forever. She hated acting like a romantic girlie girl, but his kiss captivated her.

Why is Rafael kissing me, Hannie Jacobson, tough girl? Because I'm handy.

Hannie broke off the kiss and shoved Rafael away. She stepped back to regain her composure as she swiped the back of her hand across her mouth.

"A few weeks ago, you were chasing after Jordan at GCU." Her emotional voice frightened her. Why was she letting Rafael push her to the breaking point? She didn't care about him anyway. "Tonight, you've danced and flirted with every girl on Team Four. So, don't bother wasting your charms on me. Go back to your harem."

Rafael jerked his head back. Soon, the lover-boy grin recaptured his lips.

"Whatever makes you happy." He turned and walked away, leaving her alone with her roaring emotions.

Nothing makes me happy.

Happiness ended when a six-year-old girl watched her entire family die in one day. Hannie longed for Rafael to hold her, but she couldn't allow herself the luxury of such weakness. Rafael didn't care about her. He couldn't be her strength, her knight in shining armor. Knights didn't exist.

CHAPTER 25

*J*ordan and Matthew stood near the wall and watched the elegant couples glide across the dancefloor. A table, overflowing with desserts, was nearby, and several young people stood beside it laughing and drinking punch. Jordan turned to face Matthew. His tight jaw and tense posture told her he had a lot on his mind.

"I've been thinking about you and me," he said. He stepped back closer to the wall as a spinning couple came a little too close. He glanced over his shoulder then tugged Jordan around the corner.

They now stood in a small empty hallway. Matthew smiled. "Maybe we won't get run over out here."

Jordan nodded, glad that Matthew had obviously come to some sort of decision. They'd only been at odds for about a week, but she hated every moment of this drama. Their lives were in danger and that was drama enough.

"What have you been thinking, Matthew?"

He cleared his throat. "It hurt a lot when I found out you kissed Rafael."

"I told you it wasn't much of a kiss. I was confused and—"

Matthew pressed his finger against her lips. "Let me finish."

Jordan nodded, still not sure she wanted to hear what he had to say, but glad this mess would soon be settled one way or the other.

"You and Kim are very different. She was immature and shallow. She used me to get to my best friend. You kissed Rafael, but you didn't run after him."

"Definitely not." Her voice rose, and she winced. Thankfully, the orchestra was loud enough to hide her words from anyone who might be around. "Rafael ran after me."

"Life is crazy right now. We may not get out of Venezuela alive." Matthew reached out and caught her hand in his. "I don't want to waste my chance for a great relationship with you because I'm afraid I may get dumped again."

She rested her hand in Matthew's familiar grip. "That's a very mature decision."

He grinned. "Life is forcing us to grow up real fast." Squeezing her hand tighter, he looked away for a moment. "I'm sorry for misjudging you. Are you willing to give me another try?"

His jaw tightened, and he refused to meet her gaze. How could he possibly doubt her answer?

"Let me think a minute." She glanced at her watch. He deserved to sweat for a moment or two. "Okay, I thought about it. The answer is yes."

"Whoo hoo," Matthew yelled, then lifted her off her feet and spun her around. "You've made me very happy."

"Put me down, Matthew," Jordan said between her laughter.

Matthew set her on her feet. He kissed the top of her head, then his lips slowly descended to meet hers.

Jordan's heartbeat throbbed in her ears and those familiar tingles covered her. She belonged in Matthew's arms. They were a perfect fit. The trumpets in the orchestra blasted a rowdy song, and Jordan reluctantly stepped out of Matthew's embrace.

"We should get back to the table. Hopefully, Hector has some news about the students."

"You're right," Matthew said. "Duty calls."

"Let's get one thing clear before we go." Jordan grabbed Matthew's hand. "I have never dumped any boy, and I don't intend to start with you, Mister. You're stuck with me."

* * *

HANNIE WATCHED Rafael slip into the noisy crowd. She rubbed away the unshed tears. Next month, she'd be seventeen. Not a child afraid of the dark anymore. She was strong and completely capable of taking care of herself. Rafael would be running through the mountains with his rebel brother. She'd be on her own again without Rafael complicating her life.

Hannie stepped around the pillar, ready to return to her table and forget all about this dance. She touched her lips. Just her luck she'd get her first kiss from a boy she didn't even like. Could he tell she was completely inexperienced? Had he been disappointed? No doubt, he'd kissed countless girls and knew what a kiss should be like. Oh, why did she even care? She hadn't wanted to kiss him anyway. Rafael didn't mean a thing to her.

"Hannie, are you all right?" Jordan's voice struck her from behind, and she spun around. "You look upset."

"I'm fine." Hannie brushed imaginary wrinkles from her skirt.

"Where did Rafael go?" Jordan glanced around.

Hannie waved her arm in the general direction of the Team Four table. "He went back to his adoring fans."

"I'd be glad to listen if you want to talk," Jordan offered in a gentle voice. "Goodness knows you've listened to my dramas, plenty of times." She grinned and tugged on Hannie's arm. "Matthew and I are back together."

Hannie pulled her arm free of Jordan's excited hold and attempted to smile. "I knew it would happen eventually. Happy for you."

"Maybe you and Rafael can dance again tonight and—"

Hannie waved her hands in front of her face. "No way and no drama here." Hopefully, Jordan would take the hint and leave her alone. Jordan was her only real friend, but right now she'd like to slap that look of pity off her face.

"All right. But remember that I'm always here for you and ready to listen."

Hannie nodded. *No, Jordan, you will not always be here. One way or the other, everything will change tomorrow.*

The sound of high heels clicking across the floor interrupted their conversation. Laurel rushed toward them.

"Jordan, I need to talk to you. It's very important." Laurel pushed the words through broken breaths. She glanced anxiously around the room, as if someone was following her.

"What's wrong?" Jordan asked.

Laurel glanced at Hannie and grabbed Jordan's arm. "We have to talk in private. Come to my dressing room." Wisps of blonde hair swirled aimlessly around her flushed face. Hannie had never seen the normally perfect girl look so unkempt.

Jordan's brows lifted in confusion. Hannie shrugged.

"I'll see you later," Jordan said as Laurel pulled her across the dance floor.

Hannie shook her head. Blondie was one of the looniest females she'd ever met. She'd probably broken a fingernail and it needed immediate attention.

What am I doing with these people?

She was too rational for Laurel, too independent for Rafael, and even Jordan could get on her last nerve. She belonged in Israel with her true friends, fighting insurgents and gathering intel. No matter what happened tomorrow, she wasn't going to stay with this group. She was going back to Israel, even if she had to swim the ocean to get there.

CHAPTER 26

"*L*aurel, what has you so upset?" Jordan asked as she stepped into the small dressing room, and Laurel shut the door behind them.

"I'm not sure what's happening." Laurel tugged on the pearls draped around her neck. "But Dawson left to go meet with some students and make sure they're transferred to the correct location for tomorrow's speech. Those were Mr. Montgomery's words."

"It's starting then." Jordan dropped onto the round vanity chair sitting in front of the makeup table, her legs suddenly too weak to hold her.

"What is starting?" Laurel asked. "No one will tell me anything. I was in the penthouse. Dawson told his father that he wouldn't let him down. He said he'd kill anyone that got in his way. I know that's only an expression, but he sounded so serious."

Laurel was not a fool. She'd figured out that Dawson and his father were dangerous, and she'd come to Jordan for help. She wasn't involved in this plot. Her boyfriend might be a monster, but this fragile girl couldn't hurt anyone.

"I don't have time to give you details, but there's a plot to kill Sierra Stone. Mr. Montgomery and Dawson are involved."

"I knew they hated her." Laurel's voice sounded flat and emotionless.

"I heard Mr. Montgomery and his Global Council friends talking this evening. None of them are fans of the councilor."

Jordan jumped to her feet and paced across the Persian rug stretching from the makeup table to the small closet. "I need to know where Dawson went."

"Someone emailed the location to Dawson," Laurel said. "I thought something strange was going on, so I slipped Dawson's computer book out of his pocket before he left."

Laurel opened the top drawer of the makeup table, retrieved the small computer, and punched a few buttons. She passed the device to Jordan so she could read the address.

Could this be true? After all these months and Hector's intense search, she now knew the students' location.

"You're wonderful!" Jordan threw her arms around Laurel and squeezed her tightly.

"People tend to underestimate me," Laurel said when Jordan released her. "The dumb blonde. But it comes in handy because they say things in front of me, and they never suspect me of anything."

Jordan laughed. "You're anything but dumb." She pulled the ruby red jewel from its hiding place under her gown.

Laurel stared wide-eyed as Jordan performed the necessary manipulations that effectively turned the jewel into a communicator then relayed the location to Hector. Hector responded that a couple of his men would meet them outside the hotel.

"Laurel, you've been a godsend. Literally."

When will I ever learn to stop doubting God?

"I'm so glad." Tears sparkled in Laurel's eyes. "I so want to do His work."

"Believe me, you have tonight." She kissed Laurel's cheek then turned toward the door. Suddenly, she stopped as she realized Laurel could do much more.

"Search that computer book while you have it and see if you can find a code for sending emails to Ms. Stone. She has a protected email address. Mr. Montgomery might have access to it since he's so connected to the Global Council," Jordan explained. "But be careful. These people are very dangerous."

Laurel nodded, dropped into the cushioned chair, and began her search. A search that could save Sierra Stone's life.

* * *

JORDAN BOUNCED in the jeep beside Hannie as it sped through the city. She stared into the thick darkness. Matthew, Victor, and Timberlyn followed closely behind them, piled in the bed of a pick-up truck. Jordan had sent Malese to guard Laurel after giving her instructions for sending the incriminating emails if Laurel found the passcode on Dawson's computer book.

Jordan pressed her hand over her heart. A cement vest seemingly covered her chest. Could a human heart actually burst? She'd been praying for this moment—the chance to rescue the missing students, yet her faith had been weak, and she never truly believed rescue was possible. The hot wind whipping her hair across her face shouted that the moment had come, and the danger was all too real.

"This would happen when we're dressed like party dolls and wearing these blasted high heels," Hannie complained.

"This tie is no fun either." Rafael sat up front by the driver. He removed his tie and tossed it out the window.

Jordan's southern manners were slipping. She didn't even know the driver's name. Here she sat, speeding into the unknown with a stranger behind the wheel. *I guess introductions aren't necessary in the middle of a last chance rescue mission.*

"At least you can toss your tie and jacket." Hannie tore a row of ruffles from her shoulder. "I'm stuck in this oppressive get-up and torture shoes."

"A lot of whining from a girl who pretends to be so tough." Rafael slipped his arms out of his dark jacket and let it fly into the night.

Hannie grabbed the back of the seat and leaned forward. "I can outfight you whether I'm in combat gear or ruffles."

Jordan laughed. A small giggle that turned into a guffaw. She slapped her hands over her mouth but couldn't hold back the hysterical laughter. Hannie stared at her and pushed back in her seat as if trying to distance herself from a mad woman. Rafael turned around, his forehead wrinkled, and confusion carved on his face. Even the nameless driver eyed her with suspicion through the dangling rearview mirror.

They probably think I've gone over the edge. Maybe I have. Oh well, I made them shut up.

She straightened her shoulders, the laughter gradually subsiding. Clutching her stomach, she took several deep breaths. If she breathed in too much of this humid air, she'd drown.

What would they face when this jeep stopped? Whoever held Paul, Zoe, and the others wouldn't release them without a fight. Hopefully, Hector had devised a rescue plan because she didn't have any idea what to do next, and she doubted any member of Team Seven had a clue. No matter how much Hannie and Rafael bragged, they were just kids in way over their heads. The jeep swung around a curve, throwing her against Hannie. Darkness surrounded them. Jordan silently prayed that God would provide the victory tonight.

The jeep came to an abrupt stop at the end of a long alley. Hector, Carlos, and three other men stood by a dented sports car. Music blasted from the radio, and each man held a can of beer. They appeared to be typical youth with nothing better to do than drink and party. How clever. Team Seven joined Hector by the car.

"Juan scaled the roofs and managed to get a view of the target." Hector motioned to the seemingly endless row of stucco houses. A rippling wave of roofs framed the alley leading to the house where the students were held.

Hector nodded at the young man beside him. "Juan's heat sensor picked up fourteen bodies. The sensor hasn't been very dependable lately. Can only count on it picking up a range of eighty to one hundred degrees Fahrenheit, so if there's a bunch of zombies inside, we're in trouble."

Rafael frowned. "We're going to be facing at least seven hostiles."

Jordan turned to Juan. "Did you see any vehicles that would indicate a plan to transfer the students?"

The swarthy young man tightened the bandana around his forehead. "There's a jeep, a car, and a covered pickup truck."

"Then we have to move fast." Rafael rocked back and forth on his heels. "Let's go."

"Wait, little brother." Hector grabbed his arm. "Juan will scale the roofs and come in through the back of the house. Me and Carlos will lead the rest of you down the alley. There's some kind of tunnel leading into the house. My supply of modern weapons is low. Hopefully, I can stock up on some new stuff during this raid. I have three twentieth century rifles. Who can use them?"

"You know I can," Rafael said, right before his brother handed him a weapon. Matthew and Hannie claimed the remaining rifles.

Hector hooked a small pistol onto his belt. "This is an EC power pistol. Doesn't make a sound when it's fired, but I only have three bullets. I'll use it when we first enter the house. Two of my men will wait here to get us out when we return. We'll take the students to a safe house."

Jordan sighed. Thank God, Hector had crafted a plan. A plan that included rifles and power pistols. She examined her friends' stoic faces. Did they share her crippling fear?

Hector stepped back and kicked one of the worn whitewall tires. "I don't like getting you kids involved in this rescue. My men are spread out all over Old Venezuela. They haven't had time to get here since Marah contacted me, so—"

"This is our mission." Hannie inspected her rifle as she spoke. "You can't cut us out of it."

Rafael put his hand on his brother's shoulder. "Hector, you've been fighting since you were twelve, so you can't say we're too young."

"I was trained by the best." Hector's admiration for his father sounded in his raspy voice.

Matthew slung his rifle over his shoulder. "We're better trained than you realize. We might surprise you."

Doubt washed over Hector's face as he turned to Jordan. "You three without weapons keep to the rear and wait until we give the all-clear." He touched her arm. "When we find the students, I'll need you to convince them to trust me and my men. We don't exactly look like choir boys." Laughter tinged his voice. She nodded.

"All right, let's move," Hector ordered. "*Andale, Andale.*"

"Wait," Jordan said.

They all stopped and stared at her.

"Dear Lord," she began, barely above a whisper. "Please guide us and protect us now. We need You to help us rescue Your children tonight. In Jesus's name, amen."

"Amen," echoed Matthew, Timberlyn, and Victor. Hector shook his head and motioned for them to fall in line.

Jordan followed Matthew down the dark alley lit only by a few functioning streetlights and the glow of a full moon. Victor stayed close behind her. The homes they passed were bigger and more modern than most of the houses she'd seen in Old Venezuela. A stench of garbage wafted through the air, but it didn't smell as bad as the alley where she and Rafael had met Hector.

With each step, they drew closer to their target. A stone fence topped with broken bottles and twisted barbed wire surrounded a large house, and a metal gate blocked the driveway. Hector raised his arm to halt their progress.

They couldn't possibly climb that fence without being cut to shreds, and ramming the gate would alert the guards. A circular metal structure about three feet tall jutted out from the house, partially hidden by overgrown vines, blooming flowers, and grasping trees. Was that the entrance to the tunnel Hector had mentioned?

Hector motioned for Rafael and Carlos to follow him. Jordan stood frozen, hoping to dissolve into the blackness of the night. Her insides trembled. She didn't want to enter that ominous structure, but Zoe and Paul were inside that house, and she'd do whatever necessary to reach them.

Rafael and Hector bent down to remove the cover. Wouldn't the inevitable screeching sound of metal rubbing metal alert the neighbors? Jordan bit her lip and waited. Silence. Something was wrong.

Hector motioned for Hannie to come stand guard. Carlos now grabbed the barrier along with Rafael and Hector. The men tried once again to remove the cover. Their groans and grunts floated through the air, but the barrier refused to budge.

Victor elbowed Jordan. "Three men will never be able to get in the proper position to move that thing. It's a one-man job." He sighed and headed toward the men.

Jordan clung to Timberlyn. Matthew offered them a hopeful smile.

Victor nudged Hector, Carlos, and Rafael out of his way. The men stepped back slowly. Hector shook his head, but Rafael slapped Victor on the back. Victor bent his knees and assumed a weightlifting position. He took a deep breath and grabbed the structure.

Squeaks, screeches, and snaps filled the night. That thing needed to be oiled. *Lord, please don't let the guards hear.* The screeching gave way to a loud pop, and Victor lifted the metal cover and placed it on the ground.

"Mercy," Hector said and shook hands with Victor.

Jordan wanted to applaud but settled by silently clapping. "Thank You, Lord," she whispered then she, Timberlyn, and Matthew ran to join the others.

Carlos volunteered to enter the structure first. A chill ran down Jordan's back as the man lowered himself into the ground. He gave the all clear, and the rest of the team followed. They carefully wound their way through the long tunnel.

Memories of huddling in the closet in Old Memphis, clutching baby Abby assaulted Jordan. Sweat slid down her spine, but she forced herself to follow Matthew and forget the past. She had a mission. Fear would not stop her.

Overhead lights dimly lit the tunnel, which was wide and tall enough for a truck to pass through. Uneven blacktop with gaping cracks stretched beneath their feet. Half the team followed Carlos down one side, and the other half followed Hector on the opposite side. Jordan's silk top clung to her skin. She stumbled and fell off her high heels, slamming against Matthew's back.

"Okay?" he mouthed.

She nodded, too afraid to speak. Did guards patrol this tunnel? Was a hidden camera revealing their every move? *Am I the only one scared to death?*

Hannie and Timberlyn had both exited their shoes and traversed the tunnel in bare feet. She was tempted to do the same but feared stepping on broken glass or a nail, or worse. No telling what kind of creepy, crawly things inhabited this structure.

The tunnel made a sharp turn to the right. Deep growling sounds filled the space. They all stopped. Hector raised his arm. "No one move," he ordered, then walked slowly around the curve.

Jordan grabbed Matthew's arm and pulled Timberlyn close to her side. Hector disappeared from their view. The growls sounded louder and stronger. Hector ran from the shadows, stumbled, but righted himself before hitting the ground.

"Dogs," he said. "Four of them, big and mad."

CHAPTER 27

*C*arlos pointed his rifle in the direction of the growls. "We can shoot the dogs."

"No," Timberlyn protested, squeezing Jordan's arm.

Hector shook his head. "We can't shoot them without alerting the guards, unless we use my power pistol. I don't want to waste these bullets." He patted the pistol hanging at his side.

The growling sounds drew closer, but the dogs were still hidden in the shadows. Hector motioned for everyone to back up.

"We can't retreat now." Hannie sounded as menacing as the dogs but obediently stepped back.

The dim light revealed several pairs of red eyes and four large shapes. Dogs, the size of wolves, filled the tunnel, blocking their path. Jordan huddled closer to Matthew and Timberlyn as the dogs stalked toward them. If they turned and ran, would the dogs chase them or allow them to flee? Jordan took in ragged breaths. She clutched Matthew's sweaty shirt sleeve and held Timberlyn's hand.

Hector had joked about facing zombies, but obviously, he hadn't considered dogs and their higher body temperature.

Hector kept his rifle pointed at the animals even though he'd said they couldn't shoot. They might not have a choice. Jordan loved animals, but not enough to offer herself up as the dogs' midnight feast.

"Victor, do you have any talent for wrestling wild animals?" Hector asked.

"Let me try." Timberlyn stepped away from Jordan and walked slowly toward the creatures.

Hector jumped in front of the petite girl. "I was joking. You'll get killed."

Matthew raised his arm. "Let her try. She has a way with animals."

Hector looked from Matthew to the snarling dogs then back at Timberlyn. He seemed to be stumped in his leadership role. Obviously, he wanted to keep them safe, and no one could believe Timberlyn's gift until they'd experienced it. They were out of options, so Hector moved to the side.

Timberlyn stepped softly toward the growling beasts, her gentle voice filling the dark tunnel. The soothing African words sounded like a love song. The four dogs stared at her as she approached, their growls still deep and deadly. One lunged, and Jordan squealed, but it abruptly stopped before reaching Timberlyn. It shook its head, trying to decide if this human was a friend or enemy. Timberlyn continued to coo and whisper.

You've gifted her with taming wild animals, Jordan silently reminded the Lord. *Please protect her now.*

Timberlyn inched ever closer to the creatures. The growling stopped, but the dogs didn't retreat. A spotted hound whimpered and stretched out on his belly. A drooling mutt circled her legs then lay down beside her. Timberlyn reached out her hand. The snarling dog who had lunged a moment before hadn't yet made up his mind about the mysterious girl. He sniffed Timberlyn's fingers, then opened his mouth. A slimy tongue extended through jagged teeth and licked her palm. The massive German shepherd lingering in the rear came and joined his buddies at Timberlyn's feet.

"Great God in Heaven." Hector made the sign of the cross.

"That's exactly right," Jordan said as Timberlyn fell to her knees, petting and cuddling the once vicious beasts.

"You'd better get to the house now," Timberlyn said. "I'll follow once all of you are safely away."

The team didn't hesitate. They stepped carefully around the four dogs then scurried through the tunnel.

Jordan followed behind Matthew, silently thanking God for protecting them and for providing Victor and Timberlyn. They wouldn't have made it this far without them. Before she could catch her next breath, Hector raised his arm for them to stop. What now? How many more obstacles would they encounter before they entered the house?

"Juan says there's a heat signature up ahead," Hector whispered, his hand pressing against the earpiece he wore. He motioned to Carlos, and the two of them inched forward, disappearing around another curve.

Jordan grabbed Matthew's arm. She glanced at Hannie and Victor. Hannie stood at the ready, and Victor chewed his nails. Carlos soon returned and motioned for them to follow. A burly man lay on the ground, unconscious and bleeding. Jordan's heart flipped as she walked past the man. How foolish she'd been to believe that no one would die tonight. The guards were not going to throw open the doors and release the students without a fight.

Hector spoke to Juan once again to coordinate their entrance, then mounted the steps and opened the hatch. Once inside, he gave the signal that it was safe for the others to join him.

They all stood, shoulder-to-shoulder, in a massive storage closet. Canned goods, cleaning utensils, linens, and paper products filled the shelves and spilled onto the floor. Timberlyn popped up from the tunnel, and Jordan pulled her close.

"Juan says we'll encounter two guards in the hallway," Hector said. "Rafael, Jordan, and animal tamer, you're with me. We'll head to the right. The rest of you follow Carlos, left."

Jordan nodded, but icy fingers of fear tugged at her. Could she take another step if Matthew wasn't at her side?

Matthew must have seen the dread in her eyes. "God is with us," he whispered, his breath tickling her ear.

Maybe this was for the best. During the mock battle at GCU, she'd burned with jealousy when Matthew sacrificed himself to protect Laurel. Matthew would do anything to protect Jordan now. This battle was real, and the bullets were not harmless laser beams. She'd never forgive herself if Matthew got injured trying to protect her instead of himself.

Hector opened the pantry door and crept into the hall, his silent pistol at the ready. A grunt sounded, quickly followed by a loud thud. Rafael tensed and dashed into the hallway.

Jordan couldn't breathe. Hector couldn't be dead. They'd never survive without him.

Rafael glanced around then gave a thumbs-up. Jordan grabbed Timberlyn's trembling hand and fled the pantry. Timberlyn gasped, and Jordan stifled a scream, then stepped around a man lying on the floor, blood covering his plump belly.

Carlos and his team ran in the opposite direction. Jordan glanced back at Matthew. She sighed when he vanished around the corner. *Get it together, girl.* Matthew would be okay. She had to concentrate on what waited at the end of the hall.

Hector led his team toward a bright red door. "The heat sensors show there are students inside," he whispered.

How many guards waited on the other side? Guards who were surely aware of their presence by now. *Oh, Lord, please don't let them kill the prisoners.*

Hector kicked the door open and burst inside, followed by Rafael. A spray of bullets pounded the broken door.

Jordan and Timberlyn flattened themselves against the wall. Jordan took a deep breath, then coughed from the gun smoke. Her fingers clawed at the wall behind her. She had to move. Had to find Zoe. She dropped to her knees and crawled to the bedroom entrance.

Three girls huddled together in the far corner beside three twin beds on a vivid orange and purple rug. Two armed men positioned themselves between the prisoners and the door, guns drawn. Bullets struck the wall beside Hector, sending wood chips flying across the room.

Time stopped. Reality ceased. Smoke filled the air. Voices shouted. If not for the stone floor scratching her knees and her skirt bunching between her legs, Jordan would've thought she was watching an old movie. A girl with long brown hair knelt by one of the beds. She lifted her head, and her eyes met Jordan's. Zoe. Thank God, Zoe was alive. So far.

Hector and Rafael returned the gunfire. Hector's bullet struck a young guard, and blood gushed from his shoulder. An older guard took cover behind a chair and called for reinforcements. No doubt, he had access to an endless number of GC police. They wouldn't stand a chance if reinforcements arrived.

A high-pitched screech filled the air as Juan crashed through a large window, shards of glass flying across the room. Juan shot the guard hiding behind the chair. Hector finished off the injured man.

"Get the girls," Hector ordered while he and Rafael stood guard at the door.

Despite her shaky knees, Jordan scrambled to her feet and ran to the girls cowering in the corner. Timberlyn followed close behind.

"Zoe!" Jordan pulled her former roommate into her arms.

Zoe's tangled hair stuck out in all directions. Drops of blood mingled with her freckles. "Jordan, I never thought I'd see you again. I never thought I'd see anyone again."

Jordan grabbed Zoe and held her close while the girl sobbed. Her ribs poked against Jordan's chest. "We're going to get all of you to safety," she told each gaunt, sallow face.

"This is Rachel and Kathryn." Zoe's voice sounded a bit calmer now. Kathryn's shirt was splattered with blood, and Rachel's blouse was streaked red around the shoulder.

"Were you shot?" Jordan asked as Timberlyn reached for Rachel's bleeding arm.

"I don't think so," Rachel spoke through trembling lips.

Timberlyn quickly examined the three girls. "Rachel was cut by flying glass. They all have a few cuts, but nothing looks serious. Most of the blood is splatter."

"Juan, Rafael, get everyone out of here before reinforcements come," Hector said. "I'm going to help Carlos and the others."

Jordan gathered Zoe in her arms, and Timberlyn pulled Rachel and Kathryn to her side. Juan led them down the hall, Rafael bringing up the rear. They wound their way through the house, stopping at every corner to make certain no guard lay in wait. At least they wouldn't need to sneak out through the tunnel.

They stepped on the porch. One of Hector's men waited beside a covered pickup truck. Jordan herded the girls toward the truck but kept glancing back at the house. Where were Matthew, Hannie, and Victor? She trembled and clung to Zoe. She'd never been more frightened. *Oh, Lord, my friends are still inside. Please keep them safe.*

CHAPTER 28

*M*atthew followed Carlos toward a room at the end of a small, dark passageway that branched off from the main hall. He assumed Juan had told both Hector and Carlos where the students were located.

A loud bang sounded. Matthew grabbed his shoulder. It stung like a family of hornets had attacked him. He jumped to the side, while Hannie dropped to her knees, and Victor slammed himself against the wall. Matthew reached through his torn dinner jacket trying to find the wound. His raw skin tingled. Drops of blood tinged his fingers, but he couldn't find a hole in his flesh.

"How bad is it?" Hannie whispered.

"Not bad. The bullet just grazed me, thank God."

A volley of bullets filled the hallway. Matthew's eardrums ached, and smoke stung his nose. Carlos managed to hit the guard targeting them.

Carlos ran to the end of the hall then threw himself against the closed door. It flew open with a thud. Matthew glanced at Hannie. What now? Hannie's eyes were wide, her mouth open. She straightened her shoulders, jumped to her feet, and ran after Carlos. Carlos was a one-man army, but he needed their help, so Matthew nodded at Victor then followed Hannie down the hall.

Carlos stood on the other side of the broken door. A guard lay at his feet, his chest covered with blood. An African boy sat on a bed, and a tall Hispanic boy stood by a small sofa, guarded by two armed men.

Hannie dashed into the room and dove for cover behind a table the size of a tree trunk. "Get down!" she shouted at the frightened boys, then fired her rifle at one of the guards. Her bullet found the man's shoulder, slamming him back. His skull banged against the wall and knocked him out. He sunk to the floor.

The remaining guard fired at Carlos, striking him in the thigh. Carlos groaned and dropped to his knees, still firing his rifle. The guard crumpled and fell in front of the doorway where Matthew and Victor stood. Blood spewed from the man's chest. Sweat ran down Matthew's face, and his knees shook. He gaped at Hannie. She wasn't all talk after all. The girl could fight.

Hannie climbed to her feet and headed toward the frightened boys. The injured guard raised his pistol and leveled it at her back. Without thinking, Matthew pointed his rifle and fired. The man's gun flew across the room, his hand torn apart by the impact of the bullet. If the man somehow survived his gaping chest wound, he'd never use that hand again.

Hannie spun around. Her gaze traveled from the smoking rifle to the groaning man on the floor. "Thanks."

The two students jumped to their feet, fear and confusion distorting their features. Matthew didn't recognize either one. Where was Paul? He glanced from the twin beds to the unconscious guard and back to Carlos. Where was Dawson? Laurel had said Dawson was coming to move the students, but every guard here was Latin. Matthew's stomach churned. Had they already killed Paul?

Hector ran into the room and quickly surveyed the scene.

"Good work," he said.

Matthew wasn't sure *good* was the right word. The room smelled of smoke, sweat, and blood. His legs wobbled, and the room seemed to tilt. The man on the floor would probably bleed to death. Even though his death would be from Carlos's bullet, Matthew had added to the man's agony. The guard's cries attacked his conscience.

His gaze traveled from the man to Hannie. If he'd hesitated a split-second, she could be dead. He'd done what he had to do, and he didn't regret his decision. A vicious thug would die, but Hannie was alive. God would forgive him for this violent act.

I hope I can forgive myself.

"They called for reinforcements, so let's move." Hector motioned for them to follow.

"Wait." Matthew stepped in front of the students. "Where's Paul?"

"They took him," the Hispanic boy said, pushing his glasses up with one finger. "That boy called Dawson and a couple of guards took Paul away about an hour ago."

Matthew's stomach churned. "Did they say where they were taking him?"

"No, but a guard said, 'you'd better be glad we didn't pick you,'" the African boy said. "'This one won't live to go to prison with the rest of you.'"

Hannie shifted the rifle slung across her shoulder and waved for the boys to follow her. "That confirms the students are going to be framed for the assassination, like we suspected," she said.

Matthew couldn't move. Dawson must be a monster if he could kill Paul—his former roommate.

"Let's move!" Hector yelled.

Matthew jerked, then hurried out the door. He could barely put one foot in front of the other. After all these months of worrying about Paul, they'd been one hour too late to save him.

Christians were about to be framed for a heinous assassination, Ms. Stone was going to die tomorrow, and tonight, he was running from a bunch of Venezuelan thugs.

As he stepped out the door, he cast a glance at the guard's lifeless body surrounded by a large red pool of blood. "Please Lord, help this man."

Matthew wanted to cry at the sight, but not now. He'd cry later. Now, he'd escape.

CHAPTER 29

*J*ordan hugged Zoe goodbye as Rachel and Kathryn climbed into the back of the waiting pickup.

"Thank you so much, Jordan." Zoe squeezed her so tightly she could barely breathe. "We've spent all these months not knowing what they were going to do to us. They've taken pictures and videos and had us sign some blank documents. We've been praying and trying to trust God, but it's been so long."

"Did they mistreat you? Not feed you? You're so thin," Jordan asked, not certain she wanted to hear the answer.

"They never physically hurt us, and they fed us well enough." Zoe wrapped her arms around herself. "They kept us drugged a lot. Sometimes I'd go to sleep in one collective and wake up in another one and not remember what I'd done the day before. Why have they done this to us?"

Juan cleared his throat. His arms were covered with cuts and bruises, and blood dotted his shirt.

"We don't have time to explain now," Jordan told Zoe. "God led us to you, but we're not finished yet. We still have a lot to do."

Juan scanned the perimeter and entry gate. "We need to get out of here fast."

Zoe bit her bottom lip, fear etched on her tired face. Juan wasn't much older than Jordan, but a chain of tattoos covered his neck. A stocky man stood at the front of the pickup. A bandanna encircled his head, partially concealing his long greasy hair. These girls had been held hostage for months, and now she was sending them away with men who looked like prison escapees.

"You're safe now," Jordan said. "You can trust these men. Go with them and do what they say."

Zoe nodded then climbed into the back of the pick-up truck. Juan pulled the cover down over the girls, then he and the other man jumped into the cab and headed for the gate.

The iron monstrosity swung on its hinges and opened for the approaching vehicle, while the golden Venezuela dawn crept close. Soon, the pickup disappeared from view.

Jordan stood with Timberlyn, Rafael, and two of Hector's men, surrounded by silence, and waited for her friends to emerge from the house. Her heart tried to pound its way out of her chest. She couldn't swallow or speak.

At last, Hector appeared on the front porch. He ran down the stairs, two at a time, Hannie and two boys right behind him. Where was Matthew? Seconds crawled by. She clutched her throat. The porchlights revealed Matthew and Victor. Jordan shouted. Carlos limped behind them, his pant leg streaked with blood. Matthew was safe. They were all safe.

She ran toward Matthew. She'd almost reached him when a flash of headlights temporarily blinded her. Two large sedans pulled into the drive, bullets flying from the windows, tires squealing as they approached the house. Hector's men took shelter behind their jeep and returned fire. Rafael pulled Timberlyn behind a massive tree, firing his rifle at this new enemy. Jordan fell to her knees.

Five men, armed with modern rifles, jumped from each vehicle. Carlos and Hannie had retreated inside. Hector crouched behind the porch column, shooting at the enemies. Jordan's gaze drifted from the sedans to the shrubbery and back to the porch. Nowhere to hide.

I should have been shot by now. Gun smoke clung to the humid air, the sound of firepower deafening. She had to reach Matthew. Together, they could fight their way out of this mess.

Matthew still stood on the porch steps. Victor hunched behind some overgrown bushes by the side of the porch.

Jordan jumped up and ran toward the house. "Matthew!"

The smoke filled her nostrils, rumbles like thunder pounded in her ears. Matthew turned to her and held out his hand. She reached for it, but Victor jumped from the bushes and knocked her to the ground. They both groaned as their bodies pounded the hard earth.

She twisted her head as an unknown man crumpled and fell from the impact of Hector's bullets. The world spun while she lay cradled beneath Victor's heavy form. Matthew fired his rifle several times, and groans of pain mixed with Spanish curses filled the air. Carlos and Hannie sprang from the other side of the house and blasted the last two attackers.

The ear-piercing sounds stopped. The smoke lifted. Hector yelled, "All clear!"

Jordan struggled to roll away from Victor. Somehow, she managed to slip out from under his limp body. A warm, sticky substance covered her blouse. She ran her hand across her chest. No bullet holes.

This isn't my blood. "Oh, Lord, no. Victor, you've been shot."

Matthew was beside them now, helping Victor struggle to his knees. Blood soaked through the left side of his shirt.

"Get him up," Hector yelled, grabbing Victor under one arm. "We've got to get out of here before the local police show up. We'll never be able to explain this."

Hector and Matthew hoisted Victor to his feet while Carlos and Hannie ran inside to retrieve the boys still hiding in the house.

"But Victor is hurt," Jordan said. "We can't drag him around."

"He can walk, that's good enough," Hector said, despite Victor's groans.

A man pulled a truck into the driveway, blood pouring down the side of his face. Carlos pulled the tailgate down and dragged himself into the cargo bed. Matthew and Hector helped Victor climb into the back of the pick-up.

Jordan's head swam at the sight of Victor's wound. "We have to get him to a hospital."

"Are you crazy?" Hector's gravelly voice spit out the words, and his mouth twisted in a brutal scowl. "They'll be looking for us at every hospital in the area."

"I'll be all right, Jordan." Victor's face was ghostly, but his breathing sounded steadier. "I'm not hurt that bad." He flinched. He reminded her of her little brother. Kevin had been so brave the day he was injured by the pipe bomb, and he'd never complained about his disability.

She grabbed Victor's hand. "I could shake you for taking that bullet meant for me. I'm not worth it."

"Jordan, you and Matthew gave me the greatest gift ever." Jordan's knuckles ached from the pressure of his hand grasping hers. "You led me to the Lord. I'd do anything for you."

"Let me check him." Timberlyn climbed into the back of the pickup, tore Victor's shirt, and started examining the oozing wound. Victor and Carlos's blood mingled on the floor of the truck bed.

Jordan's stomach rolled. She was definitely not doctor material. She stepped back to let the two male students climb into the truck. Enveloped in worry for Victor, she'd paid little attention to these boys. They sat slumped against the sides of the truck. One boy chewed his nails, and another played with his glasses. Where was Paul? Yet another problem to face. Right now, Victor was her only concern.

Matthew wrapped his arm around her. Hector yelled for his men to gather the weapons from the dead and wounded. Muffled groans floated through space accompanied by the trill of early rising birds. Jordan stepped closer to Matthew. There had never been a time when she needed him more.

"The bullet lodged in a muscle." Timberlyn let out a deep breath. "Not surprising since Victor is all muscle. I can remove it and treat him. He should be okay." She pulled the wide satin belt from her waist, wrapped it around Victor's wound, and instructed the boy seated next to him to keep pressure on it. She then started examining Carlos's leg.

"Thank God Victor is going to live." Jordan swiped at her tears. Her hands were splattered with blood, but none of it was her own.

The distant sound of police sirens grew louder. "Marco, take Victor, Timberlyn, and the boys to the safe house," Hector ordered. "I've got to get you kids back to the hotel before daybreak."

The pick-up lurched, backfired a couple of times, then headed down the drive. Jordan didn't appreciate the truck's dramatics. She'd heard enough gunshot sounds tonight. She waved goodbye to Timberlyn and Victor, hating to be separated from them. They were a team. But what choice did she have? They couldn't parade a bleeding Victor through the hotel lobby, and Timberlyn was the only one who could help him. Poor Timberlyn was going to be a busy girl treating the injuries sustained by Victor, the girls, and Hector's men. Jordan had to let them go and trust that God and Hector would take care of them.

Jordan and her friends slipped back into the hotel as the sun rose over the mountain, ready to reign over another blazing day. A front desk clerk sat half-asleep behind the desk in the deserted lobby, while a couple of maids gaped at the filthy group of foreigners. They must look like they'd come from the wildest party on the planet. Jordan pulled Matthew's dinner jacket closed around her. It fell to her knees and managed to cover her blood-soaked dress.

She kissed Matthew good night after Rafael promised he'd retrieve Timberlyn's medical kit and treat Matthew's wound. She couldn't process everything that had happened tonight. Like a computer struggling with information overload, her brain whirred, and her thoughts tossed. She could have lost Victor. In one frantic moment, any one of them could have died.

Hannie's satin skirt was split in half, revealing way too much of her muscular legs, and her bare feet were covered in dirt. How could they ever explain their damaged outfits to Cimarron? Jordan giggled. *I guess that doesn't matter anymore.*

Wobbling, Jordan reached for the doorknob. She had lost the heel off one of her shoes. She opened the door and stepped inside.

"Thank God, you're all right." Laurel jumped off the bed. "We've been worried to death."

"What are you doing in our room?" Hannie scowled and pushed past Laurel and Malese.

"Waiting and praying for you to return safely," Malese said.

Hannie didn't comment. She unbuttoned her dress and let it fall to the ground before flopping onto her bed.

"Did Timberlyn go to our room?" Malese glanced around, alarm showing in her brown eyes.

"Hector took Timberlyn and Victor to a safe house." Jordan quickly told the girls about the rescue of the students and how close they'd all come to dying. Malese turned pale when Jordan told her Victor had been shot.

"Timberlyn's sure he's going to be okay," she added. "She'll take good care of him."

"I know she will." Malese lifted her chin, a tremor in her voice.

Malese and Victor shared a special relationship. Jordan would be devastated if Matthew had been injured and taken off to some unknown destination. Malese raked her fingers through her long dark hair. Her obvious concern for Victor marred her face.

"I found the security code in Dawson's computer book and managed to send the emails to Ms. Stone," Laurel said.

Hannie popped up, then leaned back on her elbows. "Great. Now let's hope she reads them soon."

"And let's pray she believes them." Jordan glanced at the time reflected on the wall. "We have to be at breakfast in three hours, and we all need to make ourselves presentable." She looked down at the edge of her tattered dress, then back to Laurel and Malese still clothed in ball gowns. They were lovely but not appropriately dressed for breakfast.

Laurel wrapped her arm around Malese's shoulders. "We'll get your clothes from your room, then you come and stay with me, so you won't have to be alone."

Malese nodded. Her lips puckered.

"Hey, blondie," Hannie said. "That boyfriend of yours is in the thick of this mess. If you see him, try to get us some more information."

Laurel nodded. "You can count on me."

"But be careful," Jordan said right before the door closed behind the girls.

Jordan glanced at Hannie, spread-eagle across the bed, then headed to the bathroom. She peeled off her ball gown, covered with dirt and blood, then turned on the shower. Steam soon filled the small room. She pulled back the curtain and stepped into the spray. The water pounded her aching muscles. She rubbed the bar of soap over her skin, washing away sweat, dirt, and Victor's blood.

"Dear God, thank You for letting us rescue the students. Thank You that we're all alive." Tears poured down her face, mingling with the shower's spray. "Please heal Victor and Carlos and save Sierra Stone." She stuttered over the words and crumpled to her knees.

Red-tinged water flowed across the tile floor before running down the drain. She covered her face and cried.

"Oh God, we can't do this alone. Help us please. I want my mama. I want my daddy." The hot water hammered her shoulders as she sobbed.

* * *

Down the hall, Matthew sat on the bed, the humid air bathing him with thick guilt. He removed his shoes. His fingers shook as he untied each string.

Rafael brushed dirt and muck from his hair. "Go clean up so I can bandage your wound. I promised Jordan."

Matthew couldn't move. "Rafael, we know Hector and his rebels killed men tonight. With all the bullets we shot, I'm afraid you or I may have killed, too."

Rafael set the brush on the vanity table. "I know." He spoke in a solemn voice, his usual bravado unrecognizable.

"So, what does that make us?"

Rafael took a deep breath. "We rescued the students, so I guess that makes us heroes."

"A bunch of hesitant heroes," Matthew whispered.

In those old Hollywood movies, bodies crumpled, red goo covered the ground, and the hero received the glory.

I don't feel like a hero. The movies were wrong. If death and destruction formed a hero, he didn't think he wanted the job.

CHAPTER 30

*J*ordan sat in the crowded hotel dining room, nibbling on a
wheat roll. Matthew and Rafael ate scrambled eggs with
peppers and beans. She pressed her hands against her rolling
stomach. *How can they eat at a time like this?*

Malese told anyone who asked that Timberlyn was suffering from a
sick stomach and staying in bed today. The boys concocted a story about
Victor going to lift weights at one of those newfangled gyms. As usual,
Mr. Flynt was oblivious to everything except the mountain of food piled
on his plate.

Thankfully, Cimarron was too preoccupied with Principal Reed to
concern herself with the students. She now stood at the buffet table
chatting with a Global Council leader. She'd apparently relinquished all
her GCU chaperone duties once they arrived in Old Venezuela. A shiver
ran up Jordan's spine. She'd never dreamed Cimarron was capable of
kidnapping and murder. The woman radiated beauty, but her heart was as
dead as an Egyptian mummy. Plastic perfection on the outside—a soiled
corpse within.

Jordan glanced up and down the table. As they all expected, Dawson
hadn't joined them for breakfast. Where had he taken Paul, and what
part did he play in today's assassination attempt? Laurel, looking as

fresh as if she'd slept eight hours, pulled out a chair and sat beside Jordan.

"I spoke to Dawson briefly this morning," Laurel whispered. "He gave me the key to his parents' suite and told me to go there and wait for him after Ms. Stone's speech."

"Why would he give you a key?" Jordan questioned. "Won't Mr. and Mrs. Montgomery be there?"

"They're leaving this morning. It seems Mr. Montgomery has been called back to Paris on a business emergency." Laurel raised her eyebrows. "They want to be far from the scene of the crime, if you ask me."

"So, it's still going down today," Jordan said.

The students had been rescued, and a big part of the Global Council's scheme had unraveled. She'd hoped that the rest of the enemies' plans had been derailed. Obviously not.

Matthew scooted his chair closer to Jordan. Hannie and Rafael sat directly across from them. Rafael's elbow bumped the butter dish as he stretched across the table, trying to hear the conversation.

Courtney Moreau and a boy from Team Four walked past their table. Courtney giggled and waved at Rafael. He returned the wave and winked. Hannie rolled her eyes and groaned.

Laurel grabbed several grapes and popped one in her mouth. "Dawson told me to sit near the back of the auditorium so I could get out easier once the speech was over."

"He's expecting mass chaos after the assassination," Hannie said.

Matthew turned to Malese. "Are you sure the emails went through to Ms. Stone?"

"They went through." Malese stood and moved to stand behind Jordan's chair. "But it was three a.m. Maybe she hasn't seen them yet."

Jordan drummed her fingers on the table. "I have to talk to Ms. Stone. She may think the emails are a hoax, but I can convince her they're real."

Matthew squeezed her shoulder. "We have to find out where Dawson is, and what he's planning to do with Paul."

Jordan took a deep breath, the scent of strong coffee invigorating her.

She grabbed the silver coffee pot and poured herself a cup of the rich brew. Did Matthew think she'd forgotten about Paul? Zoe and Paul had been her driving purpose for months.

"We need to find out where the assassin will be located, and what time he will strike." Rafael pushed several half-full juice glasses out of his way and leaned closer.

"We don't know much of anything." Hannie threw her napkin across the table. "The best we can hope for is that Councilor Stone will read those emails and cancel her speech."

"But we still have to rescue Paul." Determination was etched on Matthew's tired face.

Even if Ms. Stone canceled her speech, Paul was still in danger. They couldn't abandon him, but how could they find out where Dawson had taken him? Jordan wanted to scream, but instead, she silently prayed.

Lord, now would be a good time to give us some answers and point us in the right direction.

She turned to Laurel. "You don't still have Dawson's computer book, do you?"

"No. I was afraid Dawson would suspect me of spying on him, so I hid it where he could find it and think he'd misplaced it."

Disappointment hammered her heart, even though getting rid of the computer book had been the smart thing to do.

"But I do have the key to the Montgomerys' suite." A mischievous look covered Laurel's face. She pulled the key card from her pocket. "They're leaving in twenty minutes. You guys could search their suite and maybe find some information."

"Blondie, you are definitely smarter than you look," Hannie spoke with true admiration as she reached for the key.

Laurel grinned. "I may be able to arrange a meeting between Jordan and Councilor Stone."

Jordan clutched Laurel's arm. "How could you possibly do that?"

"I have an idea." Laurel pursed her lips. "What if I tell Ms. Stone's staff that I have an important message from Mr. Montgomery? I could say it involves computer lingo that I don't understand, so I brought you along to explain it. It might not work, but it's worth a try." She shrugged. "What've we got to lose?"

Nothing. We have nothing to lose. Jordan had prayed for guidance. If this was an answer from God, they'd be foolish to ignore it.

* * *

MATTHEW, Hannie, Malese, and Rafael stepped into the Montgomery penthouse, and an eerie dread fell over Matthew. They were wasting time here and playing with Paul's life. Mr. Montgomery had dined casually with Ms. Stone, a woman he planned to kill. A man that cold and clever wouldn't be stupid enough to leave evidence lying around. Matthew let out a deep breath. Long shot or not, they had to look anyway. As his father used to say, occasionally the 90-to-1 horse paid off big.

"I'll check the bedroom." Hannie stood by the door leading into the master suite. "You guys see what you can find out here while Malese searches the office."

Malese nodded and headed toward the office at the opposite end of the penthouse. Rafael offered Hannie one of his trademark salutes. She shook her head and disappeared into the bedroom. Matthew examined the recliner where Mr. Montgomery had stretched out after dinner the other night. He pulled the lever that lifted the foot of the chair then glanced underneath. What did he expect to find? A cryptic note to the assassin, the identity of the mole in Ms. Stone's camp? His gut told him that he'd only find crumbs.

Rafael sat on the back of the sofa, staring at the bedroom entrance where Hannie had stood moments before.

"I love the way her eyes light up when she's in the middle of an adventure."

Matthew straightened, ran his hand along the top of the soft leather chair, and waited for Rafael's next smart remark. His words had sounded like a compliment, but since when did Rafael compliment Hannie? Matthew raised his brows.

"Are you talking about Hannie?"

"Yeah, crazy huh?"

Matthew stepped closer to the couch. "Well, I saw the two of you dancing last night, but everything went wild after that." He squinted in the sunlight that poured through the sliding glass door and streaked the floor with jagged light. Was this sudden change in Rafael real?

"We did more than dance." Rafael slapped him on the back. "We kissed."

Did Rafael kiss every girl he danced with? If so, he'd better not take a spin across the dance floor with Malese. He wasn't sure if the flirty boy would be in more danger from Victor's jealousy or Malese's swift kicks.

"So, why isn't Hannie acting like a woman in love?" Matthew asked.

"She shot me down." A tinge of regret sounded in Rafael's voice. His furrowed brow and sincere eyes implored Matthew to say something.

Matthew hooked his thumbs in his belt loops and searched for the right words. This was definitely not the Rafael he'd come to know and tolerate.

"Sorry, buddy. Hannie is not the type to give her heart away with a kiss."

"That's for sure." Rafael stood. "She's a real handful, but that's what intrigues me. She's a pretty good kisser, too." He flashed a wicked grin.

"Well, Rafael Alvarado doesn't give up without a fight. I know that better than most." Matthew rubbed his chin and grinned at the memory of their tussle over Jordan. "Why don't you take another shot at her?"

Rafael stretched his back. He glanced toward the bedroom before returning his gaze to Matthew. "That's a good idea. If we're still alive tomorrow, I might do it."

"Hey guys, come look at this," Hannie yelled from the other room.

Matthew and Rafael found her on her knees in a large walk-in closet. She held the lid of a trap door, torn red carpet encircling her legs.

"I noticed that the carpet looked strange here, so I pulled it up and found this." She came to her feet, still holding onto the lid. "It appears to be a secret way out of here."

"This hotel was built in the 1990s." Rafael leaned against the doorframe. "I guess this suite is the one reserved for terrorists and drug runners. How often would a common tourist need to make a secret getaway?"

"Cool find." Matthew brushed his hand across his pounding head. Lack of sleep and constant worry was about to do him in. "But this doesn't help us find Paul or stop the assassination."

"But this might help a little." Malese appeared beside him.

Matthew jumped. He'd never get used to her cat-like stealth.

She handed him a crinkled piece of paper. "I was digging through the office trash and found this."

He read the note. *"Flight 681 to Paris—depart 10:30 a.m."* Followed by some doodling junk. He scrunched the paper and started to throw it across the room. "I don't see how this helps."

Malese snatched the paper from his fist. "Look at this." She pointed to some scribbled words at the bottom of the page. *"Off the radar by 1:45 p.m."*

Matthew shook his head and exchanged a confused glance with Rafael.

Malese smirked at them, rocking back and forth on her heels. "I'm not a military genius like Hannie, but it seems to me that Mr. Montgomery wants to be far away from Venezuela by 1:45 p.m. I wonder why?"

Hannie slapped her hands together. "The assassination will probably happen around 1:45 today. You're brilliant, Malese."

"It might not mean anything, but it's the best we've got right now. I'll let Hector know." Rafael pulled out his billfold communicator and sent a quick message to his brother.

Matthew took a deep breath. This musty closet could use a good airing out. Wire hangers hung on the rod and several lay tangled on the floor. Very similar to the twisted mess his life had become. Would this crazy nightmare ever end?

Something creaked in the parlor.

"Shh, did you hear that?" Hannie whispered.

Female voices drifted into the room, combining with the hum of a catchy tune. Apparently, the housekeepers had come to clean the

Montgomery suite. Matthew's shoulders tensed, and he pulled the closet door closed behind them. Hopefully, they wouldn't look inside the closet. It didn't look like it got cleaned very often.

Hannie glanced at the trap door. "Let's see where this thing leads."

"I'll go first." Rafael stepped toward Hannie and grasped the lid.

Matthew more than understood Rafael's protective instincts toward a girl he was falling for, but he didn't think Hannie would appreciate the gesture.

"What's wrong with you?" Hannie placed her palm on Rafael's chest. "I don't need a protector." She stepped closer to the trap door as a shrill laugh penetrated the closet.

"Somebody go, now," Malese whispered, glancing back at the door.

Matthew nodded. They'd never be able to explain why they were hiding in the Montgomerys' closet. This would all be reported to Cimarron, and he shuddered to think of what would happen next.

"You go last." Hannie pointed her finger at Rafael. "If those women open the closet door, at least you'll be able to speak their language."

Rafael stepped back while Hannie lowered herself down into the dark hole.

The housekeepers' Spanish words and giggles grew louder. Sweat beaded on Matthew's brow as he waited for Hannie to let them know it was safe to follow. Once she gave the all clear, he stepped through the trap door and landed on a solid wooden platform overlooking a thick steel ladder. An eerie blue light encased Hannie as she scurried down the ladder.

They were eight floors up, and he couldn't see the bottom. The strange light helped him maneuver down the ladder in this mystical tunnel to nowhere. Hopefully, this tunnel didn't hold the same dangers they'd encountered last night. Malese came through the trap door above him, followed by Rafael.

They traveled slowly down the steep ladder. Matthew had won ribbons for mountain-climbing, but he didn't trust this tight dark space built by men decades ago. He preferred God's creation. His foot slipped on a weakened piece of steel, but the ladder proved sturdy. He brushed his forehead against his shoulder to wipe away the sweat. *Am I the only one afraid of the unknown? What if this ladder leads to a trap?* The memory of old movies where vats of boiling oil and snake pits waited for the heroes taunted him.

With a thud, Hannie jumped off the last rung. Matthew followed. His feet hit solid ground, and his heart resumed its normal rhythm. *Old Hollywood has made a wimp out of me.*

"This looks like another closet," Malese whispered.

It was smaller than the penthouse closet, and the four of them stood shoulder to shoulder in the tiny space lit only by a weak lightbulb. Suddenly, Hannie grunted and punched into the dim light. A white object fell to the ground, landing at Rafael's feet.

Rafael retrieved it and held it in front of his face. "Congratulations. You've successfully neutralized a ballet tutu."

"We're in the performers' dressing room." Matthew let out a deep breath, and relief washed over him like a peaceful ocean wave. "Laurel used this closet last night."

Hannie pressed her ear against the door. "I don't hear anything."

Matthew cracked the door and peered out at a vanity table, trunk, and chair. All clear. They were safe. *Thank You, Lord.* Without a word, they dashed out of the closet and headed to the bustling hotel lobby.

CHAPTER 31

A sign stood outside Counselor Stone's conference room. *Authorized Personnel Only.* Jordan's heart plummeted, but Laurel had no problem convincing the young man sitting at the door to allow them to speak with Councilor Stone. Poor guy didn't have a chance when confronted with Laurel's devastating charm. Jordan used to be so jealous of Laurel's beauty, but it could be a real asset. She grinned as the blushing man ushered them into the large conference room containing a desk, sofa, and several chairs.

"Make yourselves comfortable," he mumbled before leaving.

Comfortable was out of the question. Laurel took a seat on the floral couch. Jordan paced, wrung her hands, and silently rehearsed what she would say to Ms. Stone. She had to convince the woman to cancel her speech. A speech that nearly one hundred dignitaries had flown thousands of miles to hear.

Good luck, Jordan.

Laurel patted the sofa, and Jordan took a seat beside her. The large bouquet of flowers sitting on the antique desk released a calming, rosy scent while she watched the desk clock count down the minutes.

Before long, the large oak door creaked, then flew open. Jordan and Laurel both jumped to their feet when Councilor Stone walked into the room. Her complexion was ashen, and her strained face revealed every line. As usual, Grayson stood by her side. The two bodyguards from dinner last night followed close behind.

"Councilor Stone, did you read the emails I sent you?" Jordan blurted out the question that gnawed on her insides.

"Yes, Ms. Stone read the emails," Grayson said before the Councilor could speak. "We're very upset that you sent them."

Grayson had always exuded power, but today he appeared to be in charge, and Ms. Stone was his cringing lackey.

"I know they're upsetting and surprising, but we had to warn you." Jordan's words sounded shrill and shaky. Why were they mad at her? She hadn't done anything wrong. They should be upset with Cimarron and Principal Reed.

Ms. Stone stared at the glass coffee table in the middle of the room and refused to make eye contact with Jordan.

Jordan glanced at Laurel, who tilted her head to the side and pursed her lips.

Grayson took Ms. Stone's arm and walked toward them. "Team Seven's meddling, and the unbelievable rescue of the students last night, has forced us to rethink our plans." The man's voice held a deadly edge.

Rethink our plans. How did he know that Team Seven had engineered the rescue? Jordan's lips quivered, and her stomach churned. He was talking like one of the bad guys, but he was Councilor Stone's assistant, her right-hand man. Ms. Stone finally looked at Jordan. Her eyes sparkled with unshed tears and her jaw clenched. Suddenly, Jordan understood. Marah had warned about a traitor in Ms. Stone's organization. Jordan stared at Grayson. This was the face of betrayal.

The bodyguards stood behind Ms. Stone, their muscles straining against their black jackets, pistols hanging at their sides. More traitors in the ranks.

Ms. Stone straightened her shoulders and lifted her chin. "Oh girls, I wish the two of you weren't mixed up in this. I hate to see you suffer for me."

"Now that you know the truth, you can cancel your speech." Laurel clutched Jordan's arm.

Grayson laughed, a harsh sound that pierced through the tension. "Obviously, brains are not among your many assets." The man's gaze roamed over Laurel's body; then he shared a suggestive smile with the bodyguards. "Ms. Stone will not be canceling today's important speech. And the two of you will have an up-close and personal backstage view of everything, complete with blood and guts."

Why was Ms. Stone subdued and fearful? The picture of the young, mud-stained rebel flashed in Jordan's memory. Where was that woman now?

Grayson motioned to the sofa behind them. "Have a seat, girls."

Laurel and Jordan sat as Grayson took Ms. Stone by the arm and propelled her to a chair at the end of the sofa. Jordan bristled when he roughly shoved the woman into the chair.

Laurel huddled close to Jordan. One of the bodyguards drew his gun and positioned himself at one end of the sofa, the barrel pointed directly at them. Did he really think they were going to jump up and charge across the room, throwing him and his muscular cohort to the floor on their way out the door? Malese might give it a try, but she and Laurel weren't capable of such feats.

"I'll say one thing for you kids, you really made us scramble." Grayson straightened his striped tie. "We've had your friend Zoe Pirella and a couple of the others for five months. We've been able to plant their pictures and names in phony terrorist databases all over the planet. They now look like fanatical Christians out to change the world by killing Sierra Stone."

Jordan shifted on the couch, and the small communicator hidden beneath her blouse bounced against her chest. The necklace. Their salvation? Slowly, she ran her fingers along the golden chain, hoping the guards wouldn't notice. If she could activate the device, it would transmit their conversation for fifteen minutes before cutting off. Hector would hear every word as if he were sitting beside them. If only he was.

"You kids really surprised us with that midnight raid." Grayson stared at Jordan. His face twisted with icy malice. "Of course, we didn't know you'd teamed up with Hector Alvarado. We had a mole in Hector's organization, but he dropped dead of a heart attack a couple of months ago. And you kids managed to turn Cimarron's mole, the karate chick, and use her to your advantage. You've had a string of good luck."

Luck had nothing to do with it. God worked in mysterious ways. The smooth necklace chain slipped through Jordan's fingers and flopped against her neck.

The office door opened, scratching across the floor. Cimarron stepped into the room. Dressed in a red dress with her hair piled on top of her head and a string of pearls around her neck, she looked beautiful and almost professional. No one would imagine that the woman's heart was warped. She strode across the floor, her jaw clenched and face flushed. She cast a sideways glance at Jordan and Laurel before moving to stand beside Grayson.

"I see you have everything under control here." She spoke in those crisp, clipped tones Jordan knew so well. The same tone she'd heard months ago when she'd hid under Mr. Price's desk in computer lab. Had that really only been months ago?

Grayson took a step toward Cimarron. "I told you we were taking care of the problem," he said, his voice rough with impatience. "What're you doing here?"

Cimarron narrowed her eyes. The tension between the two churned. Apparently, Grayson wasn't ready to start answering to another female.

"Bentley's incessant worrying was driving me crazy." Cimarron tapped her foot on the marble floor. "So, I told him I'd check on the situation. He's such a spineless wimp."

Laurel squeezed Jordan's arm and gasped. This was definitely too much information.

Ms. Stone came to her feet like a frozen warrior who had suddenly thawed.

"Cimarron, you have to help these girls." The councilor clasped her trembling hands in front of her. "I know you don't care what happens to me, but you've shared a home with Laurel and Jordan for months. You must care about them. Please don't destroy their lives."

"The way you destroyed my life?" Cimarron's face blazed red, her voice rose and cracked. The Ice Queen's composure had finally slipped.

"I've apologized to you many times." Ms. Stone's voice dropped an octave. "I'm sorry I got you involved in my drama all those years ago. But this is different. These girls are so young."

"I was young, too. That's why I followed you on your impossible quest." Cimarron turned to Jordan and Laurel. "Girls, I'm very sorry you have to suffer for Sierra. I had big plans for you, Jordan. I was so much like you when I was a girl. I thought of you as the daughter I never had."

Jordan trembled as a shiver climbed her spine. *I'll never be anything like you.* She wanted to shout the words but now was not the time to irritate Cimarron. But she would not cower to the woman. She lifted her chin and stared into Cimarron's frosty blue eyes.

"Oh, Jordan, you could have climbed to the top," Cimarron continued. "I'll be amply rewarded for ridding the world of Sierra Stone and will most likely become a Councilor in the Global Council. I would've hired you as my personal assistant." She sighed. "That dream is over now."

Straightening her shoulders, she turned away, obviously not having any difficulty dismissing Jordan from her life. "I'll go tell Bentley that everything is under control." With a curt nod at Grayson, she started toward the door.

"Oh, by the way, Sierra." Cimarron paused, glanced over her shoulder, and stared directly at Ms. Stone. "River says to tell you goodbye." She let out a harsh laugh, then opened the door and left.

Orders from River. That was the email they'd read when they first stumbled onto this sinister plan. Cimarron's hatred for Ms. Stone was personal. Was River acting on a private vendetta as well?

Grayson cleared his throat and smoothed the front of his dark grey jacket. "Well, Jordan, it looks like you're one of the few people to break Cimarron's heart."

"She'd need to have a heart for it to break," Laurel spoke barely above a whisper.

Grayson laughed. "You're right about that, blondie. That woman is as cold as ice. But she wasn't always cold and manipulative, was she, Councilor?"

Ms. Stone sank down into the chair and took a deep breath. She squeezed the arms of the plush chair until her knuckles turned white.

"You see, girls," Grayson said. "Councilor Stone hasn't lived the life of a saint." He put his hand on the back of Ms. Stone's chair. "This lady has left a lot of damage in her wake."

"Yes, I have." Ms. Stone's voice cracked, but she continued. "I imagine your parents have told you how chaotic the world was before you girls were born. The entire planet was basically embroiled in one big civil war. Half of our population died from war, disease, and hunger."

Jordan's parents had shared stories detailing the horrors of the past, but they'd left out most of the gory details. The schools now taught what the Global Collective told them to, so she'd never had a clear vision of the past.

Ms. Stone sat up straight and licked her lips. "Cimarron never wanted to join the battle against the Parisian Brigade. She was content to sit back and let everyone else fight it out. I was determined to fight for freedom. Cimarron's father was killed. So, she joined my band of freedom-fighters and traveled across the country fighting beside me."

The councilor flopped back in the chair and stared blankly ahead as if she'd traveled to another place and time. Her shoulders slumped, and her skin paled.

"I still don't understand why Cimarron hates you so much," Jordan said. "She had to know it was going to change her life when she joined you and your rebels. It was her decision, wasn't it?"

"Now that is a very interesting story." Grayson looked from Jordan to Ms. Stone. He was obviously enjoying this history lesson. "Why don't you enlighten them, Sierra? Considering all the trouble they've gone through for you, I think they have the right to know the truth."

Grayson's phone vibrated in his suit pocket. He retrieved it and walked over to the desk cloistered in the corner of the room.

Ms. Stone took a deep breath. "I knew Cimarron didn't consider me a friend any longer, but I never thought she hated me enough to kill me."

Jordan waited, but Ms. Stone looked away as if the conversation had ended. What truth was Grayson talking about? He was right about one thing—she and Laurel deserved answers.

"When you gave your speech at GCU, you said that you and Cimarron grew up together in Old Ireland." Jordan continued to run her fingers up and down the golden chain as she talked. The priceless gem had tangled in a thread beneath her blouse, and she tugged it gently, trying to set it free. "Were the two of you close friends?"

"We were the best of friends. That day at your school, I tried to talk to Cimarron. I wanted to tell her how happy I was that she'd worked her way up to an important position at GCU, but she didn't want to hear any of it. She hasn't forgiven me for the past."

"Why would Cimarron need to forgive you?" Laurel asked. "After knowing the two of you, I'd think Cimarron would be the one who needed forgiveness."

Ms. Stone sighed. "It's a long story, too much to go into now. I was always a rebel. Cimarron was a computer master."

Ms. Stone's voice dropped lower, so Jordan bent forward to hear better.

"I needed a computer master on my team. I convinced Cimarron to join my rebels and work for us covertly before her father died. I was fighting for Ireland, Scotland, and England. We didn't want to be consumed by Hunter and River Wallis. I was full of fury and didn't care who got hurt. I wanted to win." The woman bowed her head, the auburn streaks in her hair blazing in the light from the chandelier.

"I know a girl who's a lot like that," Jordan said, picturing Hannie's confident face full of hope and big ideas. "It's not a bad thing to be idealistic and want to make a better world."

"It's a bad thing when those ideals hurt other people." Ms. Stone raised her head, tears sparkling in her golden eyes. "Parisian operatives killed my parents. They killed Cimarron's father, too, because she was working with me. He was the only family she had."

"That's terrible." Laurel sniffed and shifted on the sofa, pulling her legs up beside her.

"Cimarron was crushed when her father died. She'd been able to live at home, attend school, and work as my computer master in relative safety, but after her father died, she had to run away with me. Later, my fighters were devastated in a battle with Hunter's Parisian band. I still have nightmares about the death and horror. Cimarron was burned badly. Her back terribly scarred."

Cimarron wore backless dresses at GCU. She didn't have any scars. *I guess that explains Cimarron's addiction to the beauty enhancers.* Jordan bit her lip. She couldn't waste her time pitying Cimarron. She had to focus on surviving this day.

"Hunter Wallis took pity on us." Ms. Stone's expression softened when she said Hunter's name.

"He realized our fighters had been decimated so we weren't much of a threat. He kept us prisoner for months. During that time, he arranged for Cimarron to have plastic surgery on her back. The Parisian forces were easily taking control of Europe. Soon, Ireland, England, and Scotland were swallowed up by the newly founded European Collective. River wanted to execute me, but Hunter didn't think I could cause any more trouble, so he helped us escape."

Grayson walked toward them, clapping like he'd been watching a play. "See, girls, Hunter Wallis was the hero, as usual."

"But Hunter has changed." Ms. Stone leveled a hard stare at Grayson. "He's listened to River one too many times, and she's convinced him that he's a demi-god."

Everything always came back to River. Did Hunter even know about the assassination plot?

Lord, please help me activate this communicator. It's our only hope.

Perhaps if she kept Grayson talking, he'd be too distracted to notice her fidgeting with her necklace. "Now that we've rescued the missing students, who are you planning to blame for the assassination?" Jordan asked.

"You and your friends, of course." He raised his brows and smiled smugly. His perfect teeth gleamed. How many visits to the beauty enhancers had he made? "We're busy shifting all the evidence over to the talented Team Seven, as we speak."

Jordan tugged on the chain and managed to pull the necklace up over her collar. It now dangled freely over her chest.

Grayson folded his arms and rocked back and forth on his heels. "Rafael Alvarado got you poor kids mixed up with his brother Hector and that crazy Venezuelan Christian group. Next thing you know, you're involved in the assassination of Sierra Stone." Grayson made the announcement like a news anchor.

Mom and Dad would hear that announcement on the ten o'clock news. Of course, they'd never believe these lies. But the rest of the planet would believe and hate Team Seven. They'd think all Christians were violent radicals.

Jordan turned to Ms. Stone. "How can you let them do this?"

Ms. Stone rubbed the arm of the chair and nibbled her bottom lip. A fleeting spark of rebellion flamed in her eyes then flickered out just as quickly. What was allowing Grayson to control her? She'd been a rebel most of her life. She wouldn't be easily controlled by guns and fear. There had to be something more.

"You can reveal their plan when you give your speech," Jordan said. "You can't stand there meekly and let them kill you and frame us."

The councilor blinked and swallowed hard. "I don't have a choice."

"Of course, you have a choice!" Laurel's voice sounded high and sharp. "You'll be surrounded by TV cameras. This is your chance to tell the world the truth about these people."

"I wish I could," Ms. Stone mumbled, refusing to look at them.

"I don't understand why you're willing to go out on that stage, pretend all is well, and wait to be shot." Jordan shoved her fist against her palm.

Grayson stood beside Ms. Stone's chair. The balding guard stood near the door, and the younger one still had his gun leveled at them. This nightmare didn't make any sense. Why wouldn't the woman fight back?

Ms. Stone crossed her legs and placed her folded hands on her knees. "I have to do as they say and die if necessary. They'll kill my sister if I don't."

CHAPTER 32

*S*ister.

Sweat dampened Jordan's brow. That explained it. She would give her life for Abby in a flash. Now Jordan completely understood. Ms. Stone was willing to sacrifice her life to save someone she loved.

Jordan took a calming breath. The scent of Grayson's strong aftershave mingled with the smell of roses and lilies. "I didn't know you had a sister."

"That sister of hers is a mental wreck." Grayson sneered. He read something on his computer book then walked back to the desk. "In politics, you don't advertise the fact that the candidate has a crazy sister."

"Brianna is not crazy!" Ms. Stone pounded the arm of the chair.

Jordan glanced at Laurel, then down at the dangling jewel. A couple of strokes with her thumb and the communicator would start transmitting their conversation.

Surely, Grayson wouldn't expect her to be wearing a transmitter even though she was working with Hector Alvarado. Grayson's European Collective pride should prevent him from believing a Latin rebel possessed such modern technology. Hopefully, the guards would think she was playing with her necklace. She definitely had good reason to be nervous.

"Brianna suffered a lot during the battles in old Ireland when she was young," Ms. Stone explained. "She was with my parents the day they were killed. It was a miracle she survived at all."

Laurel reached over the arm of the sofa and grabbed Ms. Stone's hand, diverting the guards' attention. Jordan quickly made the necessary strokes on the transmitter. Hector would now be able to hear their conversation.

Don't let me down, Hector. Please have your earpiece in, and please pay attention.

"Brianna was twelve years old, and she's never been the same since that night." Ms. Stone's voice caught in her throat. "She changed a lot."

Grayson laughed. "Changed? She lost her mind."

Jordan glared at the man. How could anyone be so heartless? "Are you sure they really have your sister?" Jordan asked.

"Yes, we really have her sister, little girl," Grayson shouted from across the room. "We're not a bunch of teenagers playing spy games."

"I spoke to her on the phone," Ms. Stone said. "Brianna has suffered so much in her lifetime. Recently, she's been improving. She's taking medication that's helping. I can't let them kill her."

"After they've assassinated you, what's going to stop them from killing her anyway?" Laurel asked the question in a gentle voice, but Ms. Stone jerked and drew in a sharp breath.

"I hope the chaos started by my assassination will protect Brianna. That the enemy won't need more ugly publicity." Was she trying to convince them or convince herself? "But you're right. I don't have any guarantee. But I don't have any choice either."

"Do you have any idea where they're holding her?" Jordan asked. If she expected Hector to do the impossible and rescue an unknown woman from an undisclosed location, she had to get him more information. Assuming that Hector was even listening.

"You're asking too many questions, girlie." Grayson stood and walked toward them, the heels of his freshly polished shoes slapping the floor.

"Why do you care if I ask questions? What can I possibly do?" Jordan shrugged. "I'm just a teenager, remember?"

"A very brave teenager," Ms. Stone spoke up before Grayson could respond. "You both risked your lives to save me. I'm so sorry you ended up here in this mess with me."

"It's not over yet," Jordan said. "If Brianna was safe, you could expose Grayson and his cohorts in your speech."

"But she's not safe." Apparently, Ms. Stone had resigned herself to her fate. "I brought her to Venezuela because I have many enemies in Old Paris. I put her in a home here with people I trusted. I wanted her safe with me, and instead, I put her in danger."

"You did your best." Laurel patted Ms. Stone's arm. "That's all any of us can do."

"I hate to break up this therapy session, but it's almost show time." Grayson typed something into his computer book then motioned for them to stand.

Ms. Stone stood and ran her hands across her dark skirt as if trying to remove some imaginary wrinkles. Jordan came to her feet, grabbed Laurel, and reached out to Ms. Stone.

"We should pray." *Did that voice belong to me?* A few months ago, she wouldn't even admit she was a believer. Now, she wanted to pray while men pointed guns at her.

Ms. Stone nodded. Jordan didn't know if the Councilor was a true believer, but she wasn't anti-religion. They grasped each other's trembling hands and bowed their heads.

"Dear Lord, You know the trouble we're in," Jordan spoke loudly, hoping Hector could hear each word. "Ms. Stone is being forced to give this speech and sacrifice her life to save her sister. Her sister is being held prisoner in a home here, owned by people she trusts, and Laurel and I are going to be framed for this assassination. Please, Lord, intervene for us. We know You can do it and trust that You will."

"Shut up, little girl, no one can help you now," Grayson said in a deep, brutal voice.

"In Jesus's name, Amen."

Grayson shook his head and motioned for them to head toward the door. He leveled a quizzical stare at Jordan. "You really are a religious nut. At least that part won't be a lie when we print it in the paper."

Jordan wrapped her arm around Laurel's shoulders and followed Grayson and Ms. Stone out of the conference room then down the dimly lit hall leading to the backstage area. They climbed a few stairs to reach the platform where a heavy black curtain separated them from the stage.

Laurel grabbed Ms. Stone's arm. "You can't let them shoot you." Her voice cracked. "Go out there and tell the truth. They may not kill Brianna. They'll be too busy trying to escape."

"Shut up, blondie." Grayson grabbed Laurel's hair, yanking her head back. Laurel squealed and grasped the man's wrist.

"Councilor, I guarantee that Brianna will die painfully, and my friends will dump her broken body outside your hotel suite." Grayson tugged Laurel's hair. She gasped, and tears ran down her face. "These two will die the minute the truth passes your lips. So, I suggest you play your part, then make the grand sacrifice."

"Let go of Laurel." Ms. Stone's eyes flashed with the fire of a long-ago warrior. "I told you I'd go through with this speech, and I will."

"You always were a smart woman," Grayson said. "It's a shame your politics are so Twentieth Century."

He motioned for Ms. Stone to step on stage. As soon as she was out of hearing range, he turned to the guards. "Don't let these two out of your sight. Once Sierra is dead, take them to the arranged place and kill them." With a shove, he flung Laurel toward Jordan.

Jordan grabbed her and held her close.

"You didn't really think we'd let you live, did you?" Grayson stared at them with dead eyes. "Your friends and Hector Alvarado will take the rap for the assassination. Blondie is connected to the Montgomery family and that means some news reporter might believe her when she protests her innocence. Why take a chance?" Grayson laughed, straightened his tie, and smoothed his hand over his hair.

He might be as ugly as sin on the inside, but he was well put-together on the outside.

"I hope that God of yours has promised you a big reward in Heaven, because you're about to lose everything here on earth." He brushed the curtain back, then paused and glared at Jordan and Laurel one more time. "Don't look so sad, girls. It will all be over in two hours and forty minutes. Then you two can soar to the pearly gates." He chuckled before stepping on stage. The thick curtain closed, separating Jordan and Laurel from the rest of the world and sealing their fates.

Jordan had read today's agenda. After lunch, the mayor would speak, then Principal Reed would introduce Ms. Stone. She shuddered. Her callous principal was going to present the councilor for an execution he had helped to orchestrate.

The two guards laughed. Low, throaty rumbles that sent chills up Jordan's back. Jordan glanced at her watch. 11:05 a.m. If Hector couldn't rescue Brianna, Ms. Stone would die at 1:45 p.m. She and Laurel would die soon after.

CHAPTER 33

$\mathcal{H}$annie stood in one corner of the banquet room, Matthew beside her. All the dinner tables had been moved from the room, and metal chairs stood in neat rows covering the hardwood floor. The elegance of last night had been replaced by the realities of politics.

She scanned the crowd, searching for Jordan and Laurel. What had those two girls gotten themselves into? She never should have allowed them to confront Sierra Stone alone.

Matthew leaned against the wall and kept his security guard hat pulled down low to cover his face, his brown hair and blue eyes a contrast to the darker Venezuelan guards. Earlier today, Hector and Malese had subdued a few security guards and taken their outfits.

"Something bad must've happened to Jordan and Laurel," he said for the hundredth time.

He had a right to be worried but repeating the obvious didn't help.

A burly man with a cigar hanging from his lips pushed past them and began setting up a tripod and television camera in the corner. The room was packed with excited news media. How often did so many dignitaries gather in one place? These press hounds would be drooling if they had any idea of the bloody scene their cameras might record today.

Hannie and Matthew strolled slowly toward the back wall where dozens of reporters stood beneath red and black flowing banners. Cigar smoke engulfed the small space. Hannie wanted to hurl at the sight of the snarling snow leopard on each flag.

"I can't believe my eyes." A familiar male voice rose above the din of the crowd. "My little cousin."

A man touched her arm and pulled her close. She balled her hand into a fist, ready to fight. Her jaw dropped.

"David," she whispered.

The man wore a cap and sunglasses, and a camera case dangled from his shoulder. She threw her arms around his neck and clung to him.

Memories assaulted her. His was the first face she remembered seeing after her family was killed. Only a teenager, he'd been her savior. He sat by her bed at night and held her when she woke up screaming from nightmares. He taught her to fight and shoot and scolded her when she misbehaved.

She must be seeing things. The scent of his aftershave and warmth of his arms told her this wasn't a dream. David was here, and he would know what to do. He would make everything right.

"David. Thank God you're here."

"We have to talk," he whispered in her ear. "Alone." He stepped back and pulled her toward the banquet doors.

Hannie motioned for Matthew to follow. "Matthew can be trusted."

Two desk clerks dressed in clean, crisp uniforms manned the front desk, craning their necks to watch the people swarming into the banquet room.

David led Hannie and Matthew to an empty spot in the back of the lobby.

Hannie squeezed David's arm. "Matthew, this is one of my dearest friends in the world, my brother, David Jacobson."

Mathew frowned. Curiosity and fear mingled on his face. "David is with Marah," she added.

Matthew took a deep breath and shook David's hand. "I'm very glad to meet you. We need all the help we can get right now."

David removed his sunglasses. "Marah found out that Sierra Stone's sister is being held hostage."

Hannie frowned. "Sierra Stone has a sister?"

"Yes, and she's being used as a pawn in this assassination attempt."

"I'm very sorry about Ms. Stone's sister," Matthew interrupted. "But right now, I'm more concerned about my friends, Jordan and Laurel."

David raised his brows. "What makes you think they're in danger?"

"They went to speak with Ms. Stone earlier today. We haven't seen them since." Matthew tugged at several buttons on his shirt.

Hannie slipped her arm around David's waist. She'd never met a better soldier. David would be able to find Jordan and Laurel.

"You have to help us," she said.

"We have to stop the assassination first," David said. "That is top priority."

"Then we have different priorities." Matthew's jaw was set in a rock-hard line. "We want to stop the assassination, too, but Jordan and Laurel are our top priority." He gripped Hannie's shoulder as if to gain her support.

How could Matthew ever doubt her loyalty?

"I want to protect your friends, too." David's voice held compassion. "I believe their survival depends on Councilor Stone's survival."

Hannie's legs buckled. She sank down onto the arm of the sofa and stared at David's chiseled face, dark eyes, and sturdy jaw. She reached for his hand, anxious for the strength he always provided.

"My disguise as a reporter has allowed me free access around the hotel today," he said. "And I have a couple of sources here. The mole in Councilor Stone's organization has taken over. He's holding Brianna Stone hostage so the councilor will allow herself to be assassinated."

"If Jordan and Laurel are still with Ms. Stone..." Matthew choked out the words, unable to finish his sentence.

"I think they'll be safe as long as Ms. Stone is alive," David said.

Hannie pressed her fingers to her forehead, hoping to stop the swirl around her. Ms. Stone, her sister, Jordan, and Laurel all in danger. This mess had exploded. Could they possibly save everyone?

Her gaze traveled across the lobby, and she spied Hector rushing toward them with long determined strides. He stopped behind Matthew and clamped his hand down on his shoulder. "Security, get back to your post."

David tensed and reached for the camera case by his side. Hannie jumped to her feet and stepped between David and Hector.

"David, this is Hector Alvarado." She motioned to Hector. "David is with Marah. We can trust him."

Hector nodded, and David visibly relaxed, then shook Hector's hand. "We've communicated remotely several times before, since Marah and your rebels play in the same circles. Good to finally meet you in person."

Hector cleared his throat and shifted from one foot to the other. "Jordan just got a message to me. We have to rescue Sierra Stone's sister and bring her to the hotel before Ms. Stone is assassinated."

"How did Jordan sound?" Matthew's eyes were wide, his face pale. "Is she safe?"

"The girls are safe now," Hector said. "But not for long, unless we can rescue the sister."

David stepped closer to Hector. "Did she say where they're holding Brianna?"

Hector shook his head. "Not really. Jordan indicated the sister was being held at the home of one of Ms. Stone's trusted friends."

David straightened his shoulders and twirled the sunshades he held. "It must be Salvador Juarez. He's a Venezuelan representative on the Global Council. Ms. Stone has always considered him a friend. He and his family left this morning with the Montgomerys."

"The rats are running from the crime scene," Hector ground out the words, his raspy voice even deeper than normal.

Hannie's head ached, unable to process these new events. What if the creeps killed Ms. Stone's sister before leaving town? Would they be able to stop the assassination and save Jordan and Laurel without Brianna? Probably not.

"I know where Juarez lives," David said. "We should be able to pull off the rescue with a small team."

"We need to rescue Jordan and Laurel first," Matthew stated in a firm voice, taking a step toward David.

"Rescuing Brianna is the best shot we have at saving your friends," David said.

"David's right," Hannie said. "This place is crawling with GC cops. Even if we knew where Jordan and Laurel were, we couldn't shoot our way in and rescue them."

Hector slapped Matthew on the back. "I could tell from Jordan's message that she wants us to rescue the sister. Once we have Brianna, Ms. Stone can tell the world the truth."

"Once the truth is revealed, we'll be able to rescue the girls without much difficulty," David said.

Matthew shoved his hands in his pockets and stared at the ceiling. "Well, I guess that does make sense."

David readjusted the camera case on his shoulder. "Hector, Matthew, you're with me."

Hannie tugged David's sleeve. "Don't forget me."

"We don't have a weapon for you, Hannie." Hector scratched his stubble-covered chin, long past the five o'clock shadow stage.

"I'm going with you anyway." She wouldn't be pushed aside like a helpless child.

"You stay here," David ordered. "Someone has to coordinate things at the hotel. We still need to locate that assassin, and you might be able to find out where they're holding the girls."

She started to protest, but Matthew raised his hand. "Jordan needs you, Hannie. Stay here and make sure she's safe. I know you'll do all you can to protect her."

Hannie closed her eyes and nodded. Jordan was her best friend, and she needed her. What if David and the others couldn't rescue Brianna Stone in time? Hannie would stay behind and search for Jordan and Laurel. She might be their only hope.

Hector passed her his earpiece and communicator. "With this you can communicate with Rafael and the rest of the team. You'll be able to hear Jordan, too, if she's able to send any more messages."

Hannie placed the earpiece in her ear, then covered it with her hair. She pinned the communicator to her collar.

"You're in charge now, *amiga*," Hector said.

"She'll do great." David wrapped his arm around her shoulders and pulled her close. "We trained her well."

She swallowed hard, trying to dislodge the lump stuck in her dry throat. Her knees shook, and her heart wanted to fly from her chest, but she'd never admit that to David.

David put on his sunglasses. "Let's get this moving."

"Where's Malese?" Hector glanced around.

Matthew readjusted his cap to cover even more of his North American face. "She went outside to watch the people entering the hotel."

"Good. We can grab her on the way out." Hector slapped Matthew on the back as they headed toward the exit.

"Does she have a weapon?" David asked.

"Malese is a weapon," Matthew said.

Hannie wiped sweat from her brow as David and the others passed under the archway strewn with colorful orchids and the distinctive scarlet rose of Venezuela. The front door was propped open, and the stifling air assaulted the lobby. People shoved past one another, rushing toward the banquet hall.

Hannie headed for the grand staircase leading to the balcony where Rafael was stationed in a small alcove that contained a computer for the hotel guests to use. He'd joked that the claustrophobic room resembled a Catholic confessional, but the one strategically placed window provided a great view of the banquet room below.

Rafael was armed with a European Collective Trans-shooter that Hector had covertly acquired a year ago but hadn't had the need to use. The unique weapon shot a miniature transmitter instead of a bullet. If it entered the human body at the base of the brain, it rendered the individual unconscious and implanted a special tracker which could be used to monitor the victim's movements for the rest of his life. If the transmitter struck any other part of the body, it reacted like an ordinary bullet and killed or maimed. Rafael was the only one with the skill needed to make the coveted shot.

Once she updated Rafael on the newest developments, Hannie planned to search the hotel from one end to the other. She looked at her watch. 11:15 a.m. If the assassination was scheduled for 1:45 p.m., as they suspected, she didn't have long to locate Jordan and Laurel.

She had great faith in David's abilities and was confident the group would rescue Brianna. But what if they failed and didn't make it back in time to stop the assassination? Jordan and Laurel would die. She couldn't take that risk. Hannie wasn't going to wring her hands and wait for a rescue that might never come. She must act.

CHAPTER 34

*T*he hot wind slapped Matthew in the face as the battered jeep bounced down the street. Hector drove while David gave him directions to the Juarez house. Matthew prayed that David's suspicions about Mr. Juarez were correct. If he was wrong, they'd never be able to find Brianna in time to save Ms. Stone. Jordan and Laurel would be at the mercy of the Global Council, and the snow leopard was not a merciful creature.

Malese sat beside him. He gave her a slight smile, hoping it reflected a little confidence. Confidence he didn't possess.

Oh, Lord, please help me hold it together. We must save Brianna, and we can't do this alone. We need You.

Hector and David sat straight and tall and didn't appear to share his anxiety. The two men were young, about twenty-five, but well-trained and experienced.

David craned his neck to look back at Matthew. "I heard about the bad fire-fight you kids went through last night. It shouldn't be that bad today. I expect more electronic security and fewer armed guards."

"How're we going to get past the electronic stuff?" Matthew asked. Last night's bloody fight had been terrible, but effective. Electronics could shut them down completely. Especially since their computer master wasn't here to help.

David patted the case slung over his shoulder. "Let's just say this camera case has many hidden talents."

Matthew took a deep breath. He may have killed someone last night. Would he have to kill today? He didn't want to, but he'd do anything to save Jordan and his friends.

"Do you think they could be holding Paul with Brianna?" he asked.

"It's possible," David said. "It could be part of their plan."

"Or he could be dead." Hector slowed the speeding jeep to take a sharp curve.

Matthew hung his head as the jeep swerved then bounced over a deep pothole. Why did Hector have to be so harsh? Didn't he have any emotions? Of course, Hector was right. Considering the type of people they were dealing with, Paul's body could turn up in a stinking Venezuelan alley any day now.

Matthew pounded his fists on his knees. Would four people be able to pull off this rescue? Not if they were met with the kind of firepower they faced last night. The Biblical story of Gideon flashed through his mind. Gideon's forces were outnumbered by the enemy, but God told Gideon to whittle his forces down even more. In the end, three hundred men stood against thousands, but they won because God was on their side.

And God is with us, too.

Hector slowed as they drove past the Juarez mansion. It didn't look like a prison, but the surveillance equipment rivaled a maximum-security penitentiary. Huge concrete walls encircled the expansive home. A wrought iron gate blocked the driveway. Cameras peered down from every angle, and a brick guard house sat outside the gate.

According to David, Mr. Juarez's personal bodyguards traveled with him, so the odds were in their favor. None of this soothed Matthew's churning stomach. He swallowed hard, wishing they only had bullets and explosives to deal with. How could they slip past dozens of electronic eyes?

Hector parked the jeep in an alley about a block away from the house.

"I should be able to open the gate and short circuit the security cameras," David said. "Hector, you'll have to neutralize the guard in the gatehouse."

Hector nodded, his fingers encircling the large knife that hung on his belt.

"Once the cameras go down"—David continued—"we can expect the remaining guards to come in search of the problem."

"You and I can handle that." Hector flashed a wicked smile at David.

Matthew's stomach sickened at the dark pleasure reflected in the rebel leader's eyes.

"I have an experimental DNA sensor that Marah lifted from the European Collective. We've loaded it with a sample of Sierra Stone's DNA. Something else we covertly acquired from the Global Council." David sounded like an encyclopedia, but Matthew forced himself to listen. "The sensor will lead us to the closest DNA match in the house. So, you two follow me. Malese, stay close to Matthew since you're unarmed."

Malese bobbed her head, her long ponytail bouncing against her back, and her hands pressed against her stomach. She may be able to fight with the skill of an Amazon warrior, but she was probably every bit as terrified as Matthew.

David climbed out of the front seat of the jeep. "All right then, let's get this moving."

Matthew and Malese moved swiftly but silently behind the two men. Hector's wild impulsive style frightened Matthew, but he couldn't possibly pull this off without Hector and David. Hector was Rafael's brother, after all, and he was risking his life to help them.

David emanated confidence and strength. No wonder Hannie was such a capable soldier. She'd been trained by men like this. He now understood the look of relief that covered Hannie's face when she recognized David at the hotel.

The man stood over six feet tall with a strong spine and wide shoulders that never slumped. Matthew pictured the daring heroes in the

Old Testament. Caleb, Joshua, Gideon, and this man's namesake, King David. This David had obviously inherited the skills of his ancestors. When they reached the mansion, David raised his arm to stop them. He waved for Matthew and Malese to move to the far side of the drive where they wouldn't be spotted by the security cameras or guard. Hector circled wide, moving stealthily toward the guard house, hopefully out of view of the cameras.

David sauntered toward the gate. He pulled what appeared to be an early twenty-first century camera from the leather bag and started snapping pictures.

"No pictures allowed," the guard spoke through a loudspeaker. David waved at the man and continued taking pictures. Hector crouched behind the guard shack now. The guard stepped out of the small building, still shouting for David to leave.

A series of grunts filled the air followed by an eerie silence. The guard crumpled to the ground. Hector wiped the bloody knife on his jeans before putting it back in its sheath.

Matthew swayed on his feet while the serene trill of a bobwhite filled the air. Beauty surrounded by death. Brianna better be inside that house. If she wasn't here, Hector had killed an innocent man.

He buried these ominous thoughts as David used one of the gadgets in his camera case to open the security gate. He signaled for Matthew and Malese, then pulled a small disk-like object from his bag of tricks and aimed it at the security cameras. A piercing green light emanated out of the silver disk. In seconds, each camera disintegrated, leaving behind a puff of black smoke.

"Keep it moving!" David yelled as he and Hector ran across the driveway.

Matthew and Malese followed. Matthew glanced left and right as he ran, his rifle pointing ahead, ready for danger. He could barely hear Malese's footfalls behind him.

The sprawling house was built around a large open courtyard. The intense smell of a myriad of blooming flowers sickened Matthew's stomach. Bullets sounded the moment David and Hector stepped on the stone courtyard floor.

Matthew dove to the ground, pulling Malese with him, while David jumped to the side, firing his pistol. Two men barreled in their direction. Sparks flew when bullets struck the brick walls. Hector groaned. Blood gushed from Hector's arm, but he managed to level his gun and shoot one of the guards. David shot the other one.

Acrid smoke stung Matthew's nostrils as they all waited in silence. Had more guards been left to protect the house or was this it? Malese shivered in Matthew's arms.

"Clear!" David shouted.

Matthew jumped up and ran to Hector. The man sat on the hard floor, leaning against the brick wall. Blood dripped down his bicep.

Hector pulled the blue tie, which was barely dangling from his neck, and shook it out. "He winged me."

With some assistance from Malese, he wrapped the tie around his injury. The sweaty, germ-ridden fabric would probably bring infection, but what choice did they have? When this was all over, Timberlyn could treat Hector's wounds. Hopefully, her patient list wouldn't continue to grow.

David glanced at them, assessed Hector's condition, then moved cautiously toward the house.

"You two go help David," Hector ordered. "I'll be right behind you."

Matthew nodded. He helped Malese to her feet; then they dashed after David. They crept down one long hallway with several rooms branching out in different directions. At each one, David stopped and waited for approaching guards. No one came to confront them. As David had predicted, this particular prison was lightly guarded.

The house spread out before them in a colorful maze. They passed one empty room after the other. Orange, green, purple. Matthew squinted at the bright colors. One room contained a cluttered library with rows and rows of wooden shelves. An elegant parlor with delicate furniture and red walls stood beside the library. David's DNA sensor led them to the end of a long hallway.

They turned to the left. Matthew jerked and grabbed the wall for balance. Were his eyes playing tricks on him? He touched his brow, his heart surging. Dawson Montgomery stood in front of a stone wall, a deer head hanging above him. He held a pistol. A young woman with long red hair sat in an armchair a few feet away.

Matthew glanced around. This scene didn't make any sense. The long hall ended at this room. If it was a room at all. What kind of space contained a sofa and two chairs but didn't have any walls? Had they entered a strange mirage?

CHAPTER 35

"*B*rianna." Matthew spoke the name in awe. She existed, and she was here and alive.

Matthew's gaze traveled from Brianna to the bound and bloodied figure tied to a chair behind Dawson. Paul met Matthew's gaze, a mixture of relief and fear in his swollen eyes. Blood flowed from his split lip and smeared across his chin.

"Welcome to the party, Matthew." A maniacal smile twisted Dawson's face. "I was hoping you'd come. After the rescue Team Seven managed to pull off last night, I'm not surprised you were able to find us today." Dawson waved his pistol to indicate Brianna and Paul.

Brianna whimpered.

Paul hung his head.

"I believe I've figured out how Team Seven managed to breach our safe house last night. Victor must have removed the tunnel cover. No one else could have." Dawson raised his bushy eyebrows. "And those dogs. I only know one person who could handle them. I tried to tell my father that GCU was underestimating Team Seven." He chuckled. "The best of the best. They had no idea they were creating the Global Council's worst nightmare."

Sweat covered Matthew's brow and trickled down his spine. Had

Dawson's fanatical support of the Global Collective and his compulsion to please his father driven him completely crazy?

Matthew looked at Malese, who stood beside him, then glanced at David. David's brow furrowed as he studied Dawson, obviously sizing up their newest enemy. From the corner of his eye, Matthew spotted Hector crouched in the hallway, his arm bandaged, and gun held at the ready.

"Come in and join us, Hector," Dawson called. "There are monitors above me, and I can pretty much see all over this house."

Matthew wanted to knock that smug look right off Dawson's face.

"I saw your entrance in the courtyard," Dawson said as Hector entered. "I must say that the rebel leader Hector Alvarado" —Dawson shifted his gaze from Hector to David— "and the ex-Mossad agent have been a bit disappointing." He tossed his head back and laughed, his face turning red. "I really expected more out of you guys."

"Big talk from a little boy who's surrounded." Hector circled to the left, his rifle leveled at Dawson. Hector could easily strike the boy without endangering Brianna or Paul.

Dawson grinned and rocked back and forth on his heels. No doubt he was dangerously unstable, but surely, even in his current mental state, he had to realize that he had run out of options.

"Dawson, we don't want to shoot you, so put the gun down, and we'll take Brianna and Paul and leave." Matthew had to convince Dawson to release his captives soon so they could get Brianna back to the hotel.

David shot Matthew a look, and something in his expression cried, *keep Dawson talking*. Matthew took a deep breath and searched for the right words as David moved slowly to the right.

"You can't shoot me, Matthew," Dawson said. How could he sound so confident when he was surrounded and outgunned? "None of you can shoot me. I'll prove it." Dawson pointed his pistol directly at Matthew.

Matthew flinched and dove for the floor an instant before a flash of vivid fire burst from Dawson's gun.

Malese crouched beside Matthew as the sound of a muffled blast circled the room. A strong boom followed. The noise reverberated in

Matthew's ears, striking his skull like a hammer. He squeezed his eyes shut and waited for the bullet's fiery pain to invade his senses. Nothing. He opened his eyes, expecting to see a red streak across Malese's shirt or find a pool of blood on the floor. Nothing. What had happened?

There was no way Dawson could have missed both him and Malese at point blank range. The deafening noise told Matthew that Hector had returned fire. Hector wouldn't have missed his target, yet Dawson's wild laughter filled the room. Matthew looked up. A small caliber bullet hung in the air as if suspended on an invisible rope. The larger bullet that had flown from Hector's rifle was also lodged in midair.

"It's a force field." David ground out the words.

Like the mountain prison camp. No wonder only a few men had stayed to guard the house. Even alone, Dawson was invincible behind the protective barrier.

An ugly grin spread across Dawson's lips. "The Israeli has brains, I'll give him that, but not even the legendary Mossad can help you now."

Matthew climbed to his feet, pulling Malese up with him. David continued to scan the area. He pulled a device from that very helpful camera case and aimed it in the direction of the force field. Every force field had a flaw, a chink in the armor. Matthew prayed David had more force field savvy than he did because they'd never reach Paul and Brianna while that thing stood between them. At this moment, time was more precious than any jewel.

Matthew glanced over his shoulder at Hector. His jaw was locked so hard he feared the man's teeth would crack. Sweat covered his brow, and he kept his gaze trained on Dawson. If David managed to bring down the force field, Hector would bring down Dawson.

Malese walked slowly in front of the barrier, her feline grace accentuated with every move. She pressed her palms against the invisible structure then stepped back and studied it.

"Dawson, you don't have to do this," Matthew said. "You don't have to follow the orders of GCU, the Global Council, or your father. You can make your own decisions."

"I am making my own decision," Dawson shouted. "Sierra Stone is trying to destroy the Global Council. If she succeeds, my father and the Council lose their power, and I lose my future."

"That's not true. You're very intelligent. You could do so much to make the world better by working with Sierra Stone, instead of against her."

Dawson snickered. "Yeah, I can make a lot of money going around and saving the world. I'm not a do-gooder like you, Matthew."

"You aren't going to win, Dawson." The sour scents of blood and sweat tugged at Matthew. Anger raged in the pit of his stomach. "We aren't going to let your friends kill Councilor Stone, and we're going to expose the truth about GCU."

Dawson shifted his weight from one foot to the other. He caressed the gun barrel with his left hand but never took his gaze from Matthew.

"Sierra Stone is going to die in a little over an hour. She won't expose GCU, or the Council, in her speech as long as I have her sister."

Brianna bowed her head, hugging herself and rocking back and forth in her chair. Hector kept his rifle aimed at Dawson, not that it would do them any good. David and Malese still walked the perimeter, searching for cracks in the force field.

"The GC police will be here soon." Dawson's voice sounded flat and calm. "They're going to find Brianna Stone dead at the hands of a crazed Christian fanatic." He waved his pistol in Paul's direction. "This poor student was so overwrought by the violence he caused, he turned the gun on himself."

Paul struggled against his ropes, his face turning red as he choked on his gag.

A silent howl of frustration rose in Matthew. He now understood the mindless growls of the wild dogs last night. He held a rifle, yet he was powerless to help his friend who was soon to be blamed for a murder/suicide.

"As for the four of you." Dawson waved the pistol in front of him. "The police will scatter your bodies all over the city. It would look strange if all of you were found dead in the same spot."

Matthew shook his head. The people they were up against had

planned every detail and weren't concerned with the body count. "Dawson, please give up this crazy scheme. I don't want to hurt you."

David probed a certain spot, and the force field flickered. Matthew held his breath. Dawson flinched, but the field maintained its strength.

"Give up, Marah agent. You're never going to bring this force field down with that little toy. But if you happen to get lucky, I'll kill Brianna before any of you can get off a shot."

Brianna rocked to and fro, her dark auburn hair swinging against her waist, her complexion as clear and pale as a pearl. Brianna appeared haunted. One look at those emerald eyes and Matthew realized she lived in another world.

"Why do you want to hurt Brianna?" he asked. "She's innocent. So is Paul. They've never done anything to you."

"You're right. They are innocent." Dawson stared at the floor. He cleared his throat and wiped sweat from his face. "But they're tools." He lifted his head. "Expendable tools to take down Sierra Stone and all the crazy Christians who share her political beliefs. And that includes your girlfriend."

Dawson spat on the floor inches from Brianna's shoes. "Yes, sweet little Jordan Scott, good Christian girl. They all make me sick."

"You have no reason to hate Christians," Matthew said, desperate to give David more time to sweep the area with the strange tool. "Christians want to make things better. They want to share love, not spread violence or hatred."

"You sound like your friend here." Dawson pointed his chin at Paul. "That's the kind of nonsense he's been preaching to me. Trying to save my soul. I guess you can tell by looking at him what I think about his preaching."

Paul shook his head then stared down at his feet. He no longer tugged at the ropes that bound him. Was he at peace with his fate or defeated by all he'd endured?

"Matthew, I bet you're a Christian, too. Aren't you?" Dawson asked.

Matthew swallowed, his dry throat aching with the effort. "Yes, I am." Pride sounded in his voice. For months he'd hidden in a cellar, afraid to admit his faith. Now, God had given him the opportunity to openly speak the truth.

"What a waste." Dawson wagged his head, his rumpled blond hair falling across his brow. "With all of your abilities you could've risen high in the Global Collective. Not all the way to the top because of your birth in an inferior collective, but you could've gone far. Instead, you threw your future away."

"My future is bright and secure." The confidence of his salvation surrounded Matthew like a protective blanket. He'd always believed in Jesus, but he'd never needed Jesus more than he did right now. He'd never felt His presence more.

"I've wasted enough time with you." Dawson turned to face Brianna. "It's time to get this over with." He lifted his weapon and pointed it at her face.

Brianna whimpered again but didn't try to run. She sat motionless, staring at her executioner. Her sister would be facing her own assassin soon. Paul bowed his head. Praying, no doubt.

Hector stood with his rifle leveled at Dawson's back, Malese stood near Matthew. David continued probing the force field.

"Dawson, please don't make me shoot you," Matthew begged. *Lord, we need a miracle. Right now, please.*

That force field was coming down. If not, he'd be forced to watch an innocent young woman and one of his best friends die. Matthew had shared the last six months of his life with Dawson. Love him or hate him, he wasn't a stranger. He didn't want to kill Dawson, but he would to save the innocent.

"You can't shoot me, Matthew. It's impossible," Dawson bragged. "Even your God can't bring down this force field."

Matthew's heart pounded and sweat dripped into his eyes. David's arm jerked back from the force field. He grunted as the tool he'd held clattered to the floor. A high pierced squeal filled the room. The shrill noise attacked Matthew's eardrums. He wanted to cover his ears to stop the pain, but he didn't move. The force field glowed with an eerie blue light, flickered, and died.

CHAPTER 36

*D*awson's eyes opened wide. He looked up and down, seemingly unable to believe he'd lost his greatest defense. Matthew felt like he'd stepped into an old movie at the point where the video tape stuck, and the scene froze. Dawson turned toward Brianna and raised his gun.

Hector's rifle growled then choked. Hector swore and slapped the gun barrel. Matthew pointed his rifle at Dawson. Would his bullet strike Dawson before he managed to shoot Brianna? His hands shook, but he had to hit his target.

"Kiai!" The shout ruptured the tension. Malese soared across the room. Her legs struck Dawson, sending the pistol flying. He crumpled to his knees. Malese twirled, then leveled a roundhouse kick at her stunned victim. Dawson fell unconscious at Brianna's feet.

"Mercy!" Hector yelled.

Matthew lowered his rifle, sweat running down his face. Malese had spared him from shooting his former teammate.

Thank You, God, for this mighty creature.

"Grab Brianna and Paul," David said. "We've got to move."

Matthew ran to Paul, removed his gag, then untied the ropes.

"I'm so glad to see you." Paul rubbed his rope-burned wrists. "Thank God, you came."

"I've never been so happy to see anyone in my life," Matthew said. "We knew you didn't get sick and leave GCU voluntarily."

"I guess you know about the list now. I wanted to tell you about it the night I found it, but I didn't want to put you in any danger. The GCU computer system caught the intrusion and traced it back to me. In the middle of the night, they dragged me out of the room I shared with Dawson." He glanced over to where Dawson lay. "Now I know why he didn't try to help me."

A vivid bruise covered one of Paul's cheeks, and his busted brow would need stitches. Matthew's anger churned. Dawson often picked fights at GCU. Of course, he'd never been a match for Rafael, but Paul was a gentle genius, not a fighter. He never stood a chance against Dawson, especially with his hands tied.

Matthew choked back a chuckle. Malese deserved a medal. Dawson would never outlive the shame of being beaten up by a fifteen-year-old girl.

"Let's keep it moving," David yelled, motioning for Hector to lead the way.

Malese held Briana close and led her from the room. Matthew grabbed Paul's arm. David followed behind.

They reached the courtyard, and the sound of sirens blared in the distance. The GC police would be here soon. Matthew glanced at Paul then Malese. She chewed her bottom lip.

"Split up," David said with calm authority. "Hector and Matthew, take the boy to the jeep, fast. The girls will walk down the street with me. Pick us up at the end of the block."

Matthew and Hector led Paul through the courtyard then sprinted down the street. Older people sat on their front porches, a few children played in the yards, and a hound ran beside them, barking incessantly. A couple of teenagers sat in the back of a pickup truck. They glanced in the direction of the screeching sirens but never moved to investigate.

Paul panted, grimacing from the pain of his injuries. They hurried past filthy children digging through trashcans, apparently in search of valuable garbage. The aggravating hound appeared to be the only one paying any attention to the two fake security guards hurrying down the street.

They reached the jeep as the first GC police car careened by, its siren piercing the dense air. David and the two girls strolled casually down the street. They stepped to the side and turned to watch the police cars pull into the Juarezes' driveway. The neighbors moved toward the commotion now while David and the girls hurried to the waiting jeep. Matthew opened the back door and helped Brianna and Malese climb in. David jumped up front by Paul. As soon as the door clicked shut, Hector pulled away from the curb.

"What time is it?" Matthew asked, bouncing into Malese. The jeep sped over the huge potholes, then swayed abruptly to miss oncoming traffic.

"12:30," David said.

Matthew pulled his cap off and brushed his hand through his hair. "We've got one hour and fifteen minutes to get there, produce Brianna, stop the assassination, and rescue the girls."

"With Hector Alvarado behind the wheel, you have no need to worry. We'll be there with much time to spare."

Matthew grinned at Malese despite his fear. She smiled back. There was no doubt Hector was Rafael's brother. The bandanna around Hector's arm was deep red, and blood obscured several of his tattoos.

"Your arm needs treatment," David said. "Drop us at the hotel, get the boy to the safe house, and get your arm sewed up. I'll notify you when it's time to pick up the kids."

Pick up the kids? Matthew shot a look at Malese. She shook her head and wrinkled her brow, obviously as confused as he was. If this mission was successful, wouldn't they be standing at Sierra Stone's side explaining everything to the authorities and eventually heading home to family and friends? David's words didn't make sense. Maybe he was talking about a contingency plan. Matthew opened his mouth to ask, but Hector's protest about missing the action at the hotel stopped him.

David wouldn't relent, and Hector eventually agreed to the plan. Matthew breathed a little easier. He wanted Paul to be taken to safety as soon as possible. The boy had been living a nightmare for over four months. Plus, a security guard dripping blood on the hotel's marble floor was bound to draw attention, even in Old Venezuela.

* * *

HANNIE MOVED through the tightly packed crowd seated in the banquet room, her gaze scanning the area. The mayor of Old Venezuela stood at the podium. The air conditioning blew full blast, but Hannie's shirt clung to her chest in the muggy room.

Men with round bellies and women with multicolored hair, all members of the Global Council, sat in the front row. Principal Reed, Sierra Stone's assistant, Grayson, and Sierra Stone sat in chairs on the stage behind the speaker's podium. Reporters and camera crews covered the back wall and sides of the room, masked in clouds of cigar and cigarette smoke. A few crafty reporters had managed to work their way closer to the stage.

She elbowed her way through this small contingent of press, searching for any protrusion in their clothing that might indicate a gun. A dignitary grunted from his seat as she stepped on his foot and stumbled past him.

"*Perdone*," she said, glancing at the electronic clock suspended beside the large snow leopard banner emblazoned with the words Global Collective— 1:30 p.m. blinked at her.

Polite applause sounded when the mayor sat down and Principal Reed came to the podium to introduce Councilor Stone. Amidst claps and cheers, Ms. Stone walked to the podium. She thanked Principal Reed for the warm introduction.

Hannie shook her head, her sweaty curls hitting her cheeks. She wanted to throw up. Ms. Stone faced the audience and raised her hands to quiet the crowd.

Where was David? She glanced over her shoulder. He had to show up with Brianna soon.

A couple of Hector's men were positioned in the balcony with Rafael, also scanning the crowd for would-be assassins.

Hannie spoke into the mouthpiece. "Anything to report?"

"Negative."

Brushing her unruly hair back from her face, she walked to the arch on the far side of the room. Only last night, she and Rafael had shared a kiss in this spot. In only fifteen minutes, Sierra Stone would be dead.

What's wrong with me? I should be able to pick out the assassin. She'd been trained to recognize suspicious people and neutralize threats. Was her radar out of whack, or had her senses become numb with friendships and possible romance?

Security guards ringed the room. Of course, she couldn't trust any of them. The hotel staff filled the entrance area between the lobby and the banquet room. An assassin wouldn't stand that far back. A waiter stood to the left of the stage, an empty silver tray dangling from his hand. Why was the waiter still here? Refreshments had been served to the privileged elite earlier but had been cleared away before the speeches began.

"Check out the waiter below the stage to the left," Hannie whispered into her mouthpiece. Juan, dressed as a hotel staff member, headed toward the waiter then purposefully bumped the man. The man stepped toward Juan, his shoulders back, fists clenched. Juan tipped his cap, and the supposed waiter stepped back to let Juan pass.

"He's armed," Juan spoke into his mouthpiece.

"Rafael, did you hear that?" Hannie asked.

"I've got him in my sights." Rafael's voice was low and steady.

"Keep a good eye on him. He's our only suspect."

"I've got him, my little *tigresa*. Never fear."

Sierra Stone's life depended on this clown. *Unbelievable.*

Councilor Stone continued speaking to the audience, but her usual magnetism had vanished. What was wrong with these people? Couldn't they hear the terror in the woman's voice?

Hannie's ear tingled. She jerked to attention and pushed the earpiece tighter to her head, straining to hear above the creaky chairs, coughs, and whispers of the crowd.

"I can't believe we're standing backstage watching Ms. Stone give her last speech."

Jordan's voice. She must have managed to reactivate the transmitter. Hannie pressed her hand over her other ear. She had to hear every word.

"Laurel, last night you stood in this exact spot, waiting to perform and now—"

"Shut-up, little girl," a gruff voice ordered.

Hannie drew in a deep breath. They're backstage. Which side of the stage did Laurel come out on last night? Right—left—no, right. Why hadn't she paid better attention? She slammed her fist against her palm. She never gave Laurel much notice or credit.

Think, Hannie, think. Victor sat across from her last night, and he'd blocked her view so Laurel must have stepped out on the right side.

She headed toward the backstage area. She needed a gun. She stopped and looked around. Juan lingered close to the suspected assassin, but she couldn't pull him away from his post. If Rafael missed his shot, Juan would be Ms. Stone's last possible defense.

Slinking past security guards, she moved closer to the stage. If only she could grab one of their guns. She had to rescue Jordan and Laurel before the assassin took his shot. Could she pull off a rescue alone and unarmed? What choice did she have? An empty champagne bottle leaned against the wall. It would have to do. She grabbed it as the digits on her watch slipped to 1:37 p.m.

Behind her, women gasped, cameramen cursed, and a loud, familiar voice yelled from the entrance door. Hannie spun around as David, Matthew, Malese, and a woman with long red hair stepped into the banquet room.

"She's here, Councilor Stone!" David yelled. "Brianna is safe."

Murmurs and curses in both English and Spanish filled the thick air. Council members jumped to their feet, shouting in multiple languages. Cimarron sprang from her front row seat. She rushed toward Principal Reed, who now stood at the edge of the stage. David pushed Brianna toward Matthew then ran down the aisle, Matthew and the woman following.

"Malese!" Hannie hollered. "You're with me. Let's move it."

Thankfully, Malese didn't pause or question. Hannie shouted that they had to rescue Jordan and Laurel as they ran toward the backstage entrance.

CHAPTER 37

*J*ordan tugged on the precious jewel dangling against her chest. Had her message gotten through? Was anyone listening on the other end of this transmitter?

The thick, balding guard standing beside her rubbed his palm over the barrel of the pistol holstered by his side. The other guard smiled and slapped him on the back. They seemed to like this killing business way too much. Jordan had no way of knowing if Hector had received her transmission. Even if he had, he might not be able to rescue Brianna. She and Laurel were on their own, and they had to save themselves.

Malese had taught them some simple defensive techniques back at GCU. Jordan took a deep breath. *Please God, let this work.*

While the guard still ogled Laurel, Jordan stomped on his foot, grinding her booted heel into his instep. He cursed and grabbed her throat. His meaty fingers encircled her neck. Her windpipe ached from the pressure, but she grabbed his pinky finger and twisted with all her strength. He roared and pulled back his fist to strike her.

Jordan's vision blurred. She squeezed her eyes shut. Would he knock her out, break her jaw, flatten her nose? She might faint and deny him his brutal pleasure altogether. The sharp sound of shattering glass rang in her ears. The guard clutched his scalp. Blood oozed through his fingers as it gushed from a deep wound on the top of his skull. His eyes rolled back, and he crumpled to the ground. Hannie stood behind his prostrate body, the jagged neck of a champagne bottle dangling from her hand.

What... where...? Hannie had materialized out of thin air.

The second guard pulled his gun from its holster, but Malese kicked him in the chest. He fell to his knees, sending the pistol clattering across the floor. He was out of breath but still conscious. Malese knelt and elbowed him across the jaw, while Hannie gathered both guards' weapons. She passed Jordan one of the pistols and shoved the other one into her own pocket. For a frozen moment, the four girls stared at each other, unsure of their next move.

"Marah sent David to help us." Hannie struggled to catch her breath as she updated Laurel and Jordan. "They've rescued Brianna, so Councilor Stone can finally tell the truth about GCU and—"

A thunderous blast shook the floor. Jordan covered her ears and swayed to the side. Hannie ducked. Screams, shouts, and groans drifted backstage. The all too familiar smell of gun smoke clung to the tropical air. Jordan grabbed the curtain and yanked it back. Hannie and Laurel stood beside her.

A man dressed like a waiter lay unconscious at the foot of the stage. A small amount of blood pooled beside his head. Obviously, Rafael had succeeded in implanting the transmitter. A menacing European Collective pistol lay several feet from the man's still form. Shattered boards framed the edge of the stage where the assassin's bullet had lodged—the bullet intended for Ms. Stone.

"Rafael actually did it," Hannie whispered, shaking her head and brushing bouncy curls away from her face.

Jordan clutched the curtain tighter. The rough linen against her fingers proved this wasn't an awful dream. People ran and shoved their way toward the exit, stumbling over chairs and sending them crashing to the floor. A few reporters rushed toward the stage, brandishing their cameras in front of them. Principal Reed jumped down and grabbed Cimarron.

Councilor Stone shouted into the microphone. "Global Council tried to kill... GCU students kidnapped..." The words floated through the chaos, but could anyone possibly hear them?

Grayson lunged toward Ms. Stone. "I'll kill you myself, Sierra!" He grabbed the councilor's arm and pulled her away from the podium.

She kicked his shins and jerked and twisted her arm, trying to break free of his hold. Grayson pulled a pistol from his jacket then shoved the deadly metal against the councilor's head.

Laurel screamed. Hannie swore. Jordan clutched her throat, her rapid pulse pounding against her hand. *No! Sierra Stone can't die now. Not after all we've been through.*

A well-built man brandishing a pistol charged toward Ms. Stone.

"David," Hannie whispered.

Grayson moaned, wobbled on his feet, then crumpled to the floor. Blood gushed from his stomach wound.

David shoved his smoldering weapon into the holster at his waist. He grabbed Ms. Stone's arm and dragged her backstage, pushing Jordan and the other girls out of the way. Ms. Stone stumbled over the two bleeding guards sprawled on the floor, but David caught her before she fell.

"Jordan." Matthew's voice sounded from behind her.

Jordan spun around as Matthew ran toward her. His rumpled brown hair hung lank over his sweaty brow, and he had a rifle slung over one shoulder. She was used to seeing him cleaner and neater, but he'd never looked better than he did right now. She ran to him, and he wrapped her in his arms. His heartbeat pounding against her chest told her how worried he'd been.

"Are you girls all right?" Matthew asked.

A woman stood beside Matthew. She must be Brianna. She held her arms out like a small child needing her mother.

Ms. Stone rushed to her sister then pulled her close, tears pouring down her cheeks. "I'm so grateful they didn't hurt you."

David stepped up beside Ms. Stone, his arm wrapped around Hannie's shoulders. "Councilor Stone, it appears you need a new assistant and head of security. I'm applying for the job."

Ms. Stone released a deep breath. "I've no idea who you are, but you're hired."

David nodded. "We have to move quickly before the GC police overrun this place."

"We can't go back to my suite." Ms. Stone frowned. "That's the first place they'll look."

"What about the Montgomery suite?" Laurel suggested. "Hannie, do you still have the key."

"We don't need a key. Follow me." Hannie ran down the backstage ramp then headed to Laurel's small dressing room. They all followed.

Hannie opened the closet door, stepped inside, and removed a wooden wall panel to reveal a ladder. "It's a secret passageway to the Montgomery penthouse." A strange blue light illuminated the cramped space. "I'll lead."

David grabbed Laurel's elbow. "Laurel, you're next. When we reach the top, you go in first and make sure the place is deserted. No one would be surprised to find you in the Montgomery suite."

Laurel agreed then started up the ladder after Hannie. Malese followed. David placed his hand on Jordan's back to push her forward. She took a step forward then stopped and stared up into David's rugged face.

"Why are we running? We're the victims. I thought once Ms. Stone revealed the assassination plot, we'd all be safe."

David wrinkled his brow. He and Ms. Stone exchanged quick, worried glances.

David's fingers hovered inches above his pistol, and tense energy radiated from him. "It's a mob scene right now. The assassin is injured, and Grayson is probably dead. People are scared and confused. Most of the Global Council members out there are Ms. Stone's enemies, and I'm in no mood to try and explain all of this to the GC police." He motioned for Jordan to start up the ladder. "Let's keep it moving."

What kind of explanation was that? She wanted the entire truth. Who did he think he was that he could show up at the last minute and start making the rules? No wonder Hannie was such an arrogant handful. She'd grown up with this man as a surrogate brother.

Jordan glanced at Matthew. His blue eyes echoed her confusion. Surely he wanted answers, too, but he shrugged. Obviously, he wanted her to follow orders. Spanish voices rose and fell, and police whistles cried in the distance. What choice did they have? She sighed and moved to the ladder.

David reached for Brianna. "Brianna, you go after Jordan." The woman pushed him away and refused to move. Her body shook, and her eyes were wild, as if she might have a seizure.

Matthew pulled her to his side. "Come with me, Brianna. I'll be right behind you. You'll be cradled in my arms the whole way." He spoke softly.

Brianna's posture relaxed. She took his arm and followed him to the ladder. Jordan scurried on up to provide more space for Matthew and the frightened woman. Matthew held the ladder with one hand and kept his other arm around Brianna.

Matthew, you are amazing. You always share your strength with me, and now you're helping Brianna, too. A woman you barely know.

As they inched to the sixth floor, Jordan gained a new appreciation for Matthew's rock-climbing classes back at GCU. She was definitely in better shape than she used to be. Matthew's rifle banged against the side of the ladder, and the sounds of heavy breathing echoed in the cramped chamber. Surely, no one could hear their noisy escape over the pandemonium in the hotel.

"Dawson was the one holding Brianna hostage," Matthew shouted to Jordan. "Paul was there, too. He's safe now."

Thank God.

"Do you think anyone heard Ms. Stone before Grayson pulled her away from the microphone?" Jordan shouted over her shoulder.

"I don't know," Matthew said.

Jordan remembered the mass chaos. No one was paying attention, but hopefully, the reporters' microphones had recorded her words. The whole frenzied scene would be broadcast around the globe, and people would finally hear the truth about the Global Collective Council and GCU. Wouldn't they?

Jordan paused to catch her breath and rested her cheek against the cold metal ladder. What were the odds that the Global Council would allow any of this to be broadcast? Her head swam. *Now I understand why David and Ms. Stone insisted that we run.*

No doubt, at this very moment, the Global Council spin room was in high gear, shaping today's events to fit their agenda. Naïvely, she and Matthew had believed that all their problems would be solved if they stopped the assassination. They'd already made plans for Matthew to go to Old Hollywood, get Chloe and his father, then join Jordan's family in Old Memphis. Her grip tightened on the rusty ladder. They wouldn't get their fairytale ending today. She shivered. Only God knew what the rest of the day would bring or how it would end.

CHAPTER 38

*A*fter their long climb, Jordan stepped from the ladder into a large walk-in closet. How many hotels had rooms with secret passages? To her knowledge, none of the hotels in Old Memphis did. At least, not the few that were still in business.

Laurel checked the suite and determined it was empty; then they all headed into the parlor. Two nights ago, Jordan had sat on that green velvet sofa. Then, she'd been nervous and impressed by the room's grandeur. Now, she wasn't sure if this room was a needed refuge or a beautiful trap.

Ms. Stone collapsed onto the sofa. "I'm not in good shape like you kids." She took great gulps of air and struggled to catch her breath.

Jordan bent over, placed her hands on her quads and breathed deeply. "You did great, Ms. Stone."

Matthew leaned his rifle against a wall before sprawling out on the floor. Brianna sat by Ms. Stone and rocked back and forth, softly crooning to herself.

"I'll get you some water, Ms. Stone." Laurel hurried to the kitchen.

She soon returned, balancing a silver tray with eight glasses of water. Leave it to Laurel to become the ideal hostess, even when the world was falling apart. Jordan grabbed a glass and downed the water. It tasted like sweet nectar.

"One of the hotel staff is bound to tell the police about the secret passage to this suite," David spoke between swallows.

"And Dawson will be returning to the penthouse at some point." Laurel's words pierced the air like one of those aggravating warning sirens.

Dawson. Jordan had forgotten all about him. She glanced at Matthew. He leaned back on his elbows and stretched his long legs across the floral throw rug. She dropped to her knees beside him. Matthew hadn't said what happened to Dawson. Did he escape? Did Hector or David kill him?

Lord forgive me, but I'd be relieved if that vicious boy was dead.

Matthew looked down, his face partially hidden by a lock of hair. "Malese knocked Dawson out, but he can't be far behind us."

David set his empty glass on the end table beside the couch. "We don't want to deal with Dawson or the police. The first thing we have to do is get Councilor Stone and Brianna out of here."

He pulled a small computer phone from his camera case then made a few keystrokes while they all waited in silence. Were they all too tired to speak or scared to death? Jordan would bet money on the latter.

David closed the phone and put it away. He stared at Ms. Stone. "Our ride should be here in five minutes."

Ms. Stone's brow wrinkled. "Ride?"

Jordan studied David. He appeared sane, but surely, he had lost his mind. They were on the eighth floor. Unless Councilor Stone grew wings and flew out the window, she couldn't escape from this penthouse.

David shifted his camera bag on his shoulder. "My friends have recently gained access to a European Collective Leopard Translifter."

"Wow," Matthew said, like a little boy impressed with a new toy.

Ms. Stone tilted her head. "I don't know where you came from, young man, or who your friends are, but you're a godsend."

"I still don't understand any of this." Jordan pushed the words from her tight throat. "Why is Ms. Stone running away? Why isn't she holding a press conference and telling the world that River Wallis and GCU tried to kill her?"

David folded his arms across his chest "It's not that easy. Ms. Stone has some very powerful enemies. I need to get her away from here so we can regroup and gather our forces, so to speak." He walked toward the glass door that led to the balcony, then examined the sky.

"You make it sound like you're waging war," Laurel said.

David turned to Laurel. His stiff posture relaxed, and his eyes softened. Even this tough Israeli spy seemed captivated by Laurel's perfect beauty. "I'm afraid we are fighting a war. There are powerful forces on each side. River Wallis is determined to get rid of Ms. Stone. It won't be easy to stop her."

Jordan bit her cheeks, trying not to cry. This whole nightmare should have ended today. Instead, they were going to war.

Ms. Stone scooted to the edge of the sofa then reached out and clasped Jordan's hand. "It's true that I have powerful enemies, but I also have a lot of influential friends and supporters. We will win this battle, Jordan."

"We should all be going home now," Jordan whispered. If only she could hold her mother's hand, see her face, and hear her soothing voice. That was not going to happen today or anytime soon.

"Well, you can't go home yet," David said.

"What about the students we rescued?" Matthew asked. "What's going to happen to them? Was all of this for nothing?"

Leave it to Matthew to think about other people. He wasn't the type to indulge in a pity party. So unlike her at this moment. Had fear turned her into a selfish soul?

"The students have been transferred out of Old Venezuela," David said. "They're going home to their families, but Team Seven has participated in illegal activities. You've been involved in gunfights, attacked security guards, broken into homes, and hung out with Hector Alvarado. To some people, you're heroes. To the GC police, you're criminals."

"What are we supposed to do? Stay here and wait to be arrested?"

Hannie's normally sedate tone now thickened with emotion. No doubt, she had expected David to take her home with him today. Jordan's own pain and disappointment was reflected in Hannie's expression.

David stroked Hannie's cheek. His brow was furrowed and jaw set, but the tenderness of a big brother shone in his eyes. "We made contingency plans for today. Hector and I arranged for him to meet you guys in the park where Carlos picked up Jordan and Rafael on your first day here. He'll take you to his base camp in the mountains. You'll be safe there."

Jordan's pulse raced as the room seemed to tilt. David expected her to go live in the jungles with a bunch of freedom fighters.

She jumped to her feet. "What about our families? If we're fugitives, won't our families be in danger? Surely, the Global Council will go after them to get to us."

Matthew stood, then stepped closer to David. "What about my sisters, my father?"

Ms. Stone stood. "I'll protect your families." She pushed her shoulders back and stared directly at Jordan. "I have friends in each collective who can guard your families. Without Team Seven, Brianna and I would be dead. You can count on me to keep your families safe."

Jordan stepped into the woman's outstretched arms. "Thank you."

A sense of peace danced down Jordan's spine as Ms. Stone rubbed her back the way her mother used to do. "As soon as everything has settled down, we'll get all of you safely home to your families." The councilor stepped back. "You have my word on it."

Could she trust this woman? How much was her word worth? Jordan's idealistic opinion about Ms. Stone had been diminished somewhat, but she had no right to blame Ms. Stone for the things she'd done in the past. Perhaps she'd misled her friends and possibly had a fling with Hunter Wallis, but her motives had been noble. Even if she was far from perfect, Councilor Stone was the best hope they had.

"How long will it be before it's safe to go home?" Jordan asked.

Ms. Stone glanced at David, seemingly unable to answer this simple question.

David brushed his hand across his close-cropped hair. "That's unpredictable. Things are very tumultuous in the Global Council right now. Plus, each collective has its own internal problems and loyalties to specific councilors. This could all be settled in a few weeks, maybe a few months. It might take longer."

Jordan wanted to crumple to the floor and yell that she was "tired of fighting and would take her chances with the Global police." Perhaps they'd have mercy on a gullible teen and send her back to her family in Old Memphis. More likely, she'd die in a Latin Collective prison.

She studied her friends. Laurel stood like an ice sculpture, face ashen and jaw rigid. Malese stared straight ahead. Hannie leaned against David's arm, her head resting near his shoulder. When Jordan's gaze fell on Matthew, he smiled slightly, as if to say, *it's going to be okay.*

The strange sound of giant wings beating the air broke the tension. David flung open the glass door leading to the balcony, and a blast of wind rushed into the room driven by the propellers of a Leopard Translifter. David's shirt rumpled and flowed across his chest. Matthew fought against the roaring wind to get a better view. Jordan clung to his arm for support, clutching her blowing hair in one hand.

The dun-colored monstrosity hovered above the eighth floor. *So much for keeping our location secret.*

Laurel moved closer to the balcony, followed by Hannie and Malese. Everyone knew about the legendary Leopard Translifters, but very few people ever saw one. The leopard spots that covered its body concealed powerful weapons. This practically indestructible machine was capable of the latest technological feats and far superior to any craft owned by the other collectives.

David moved back to the sofa where Brianna sat huddled among the pillows. "Ladies, we have to move now." He directed them to the balcony.

Surely, the alley below was packed with spectators and local police gaping at the Translifter. The beast was safe though. Even if the local police had weapons capable of wounding it, they wouldn't dare shoot at it and risk the wrath of the European Collective, who no doubt planned to recapture this expensive prize one day.

"We're going to win this battle, Jordan," Ms. Stone shouted above the deafening noise. "You will be reunited with your family. I promise."

Jordan nodded, unable to speak.

Brianna paused when she reached the balcony door and threw her arms around Matthew. "Thank you," she said. "You saved my life."

Matthew blushed. Ms. Stone patted him on the back, then took Brianna's arm and led her out onto the balcony.

The two women stepped into a square, clear object dangling from the Translifter. Silver beams marked the four corners of the invisible structure. When its passengers were secure, the sleek contraption moved upwards until it was swallowed by the Translifter, disappearing into its round belly.

David stood with one foot on the balcony and the other foot inside the suite. "The police will be searching this side of the hotel now, so you kids hurry back down the passageway and head to the park." He pulled Hannie into his arms. "I wish the Translifter could carry more than three passengers, but unfortunately, it was built to be a fighting machine not a transport."

Hannie stepped back. David's mouth twisted as he looked at each of them in turn.

"You kids do what Hector says. He'll keep you safe." He kissed Hannie on the forehead then stepped outside.

The clear object returned and lifted him into the creature's waiting shelter. The Translifter growled like a mighty leopard before piercing the murky clouds and vanishing.

They were on their own once again.

"I can't believe we've become fugitives overnight. I'm tired of running. I want to go home," Jordan said.

Is that my voice? How can I sound so calm when I'm screaming on the inside?

Hannie swiped at her nose with her fist and took a few deep breaths. "This is only a temporary situation."

"Hannie's right—only temporary." Matthew wrapped his arm around Jordan's shoulders, pulling her away from the open door. "We'll vacation in the mountains for a few weeks. It'll be fun."

"We're going to vacation with Venezuelan rebels in their jungle hideout," Jordan said. "Oh, what joy."

"We really need to get out of here, guys," Malese spoke from the back of the room, already in mid-stride. "You heard David."

"She's right." Matthew walked to the corner and grabbed his rifle. Hannie made sure the pistol clipped to her belt was secure. "Let's keep it moving."

They followed Malese toward the bedroom.

Laurel sat on the sofa as still as someone who'd fallen into a trance, her face void of emotion.

Jordan stopped beside the sofa and patted the pistol tucked inside her own pocket. She hoped she'd never get used to carrying a gun. "Come on, Laurel, we have to hurry."

"I'm not going with you, Jordan." Laurel's abrupt announcement halted everyone's escape. "I'm staying right here."

"What're you talking about? Of course, you're coming with us," Jordan said. "You're part of the team now."

What had gotten into Laurel? No doubt she was frightened about life in the jungle. Who wasn't?

"I'm staying here, Jordan." Laurel's voice sounded firm, jaw clenched. "Dawson will be here any minute. He'll want to catch all of you and throw you in prison. I can stop him."

"That's crazy talk." Jordan waved her arm to brush away Laurel's foolish words. "If you stay here, Dawson will kill you."

Laurel laughed. A strange sound—a combination of confidence and fear. "Dawson would never hurt me. And I can stop him from hurting the rest of you."

Matthew stepped close to Jordan. "Laurel, are you sure about this? Dawson was willing to kill Brianna and Paul. If he finds out you helped us... there's no telling what he'll do."

"I can handle Dawson." Laurel glanced from Matthew to Jordan, her pale green eyes intent and determined. "I know Dawson's temperamental, but he's obsessed with me. He won't hurt me."

Jordan gripped Matthew's arm. Their eyes met and held. She would drag Laurel out of here if she had to, but she couldn't subdue her alone.

Matthew released a pent-up breath, then nodded at Laurel and stepped back. Jordan's spine stiffened. He might be willing to let Laurel take on a suicide mission, but she wasn't.

She tugged Laurel to her feet. "You're coming with us."

Laurel shook free of her hold.

Jordan glared at Matthew. He had to help. "Make her come with us."

Mathew ran his hand through his rumpled hair and shuffled his feet. "I can't make Laurel do anything. It's her decision."

"Blondie, come with us or stay here," Hannie spoke from the middle of the room. "But make up your mind quick. We're running out of time."

Laurel folded her arms across her chest. "I've made my decision." She eyed Matthew. "Make Jordan leave. Now."

Matthew grabbed Jordan's shoulders, spun her around, and propelled her toward the bedroom. She wriggled and twisted, but Matthew's fingers gripped like a steel wrench. Hannie ran ahead of them. Malese disappeared into the bedroom.

What was wrong with them? How could they abandon a friend? Didn't they know that a good soldier never left a buddy behind?

"Laurel is old enough to make her own decision," Matthew whispered, his breath blowing the tendrils of hair around her face and tickling her ear. His words made sense, but they broke her heart.

She stopped struggling. "You can let go of me, Matthew. I'll go with you, but please let me tell Laurel goodbye."

Matthew released her. "Hurry," he said.

Hannie groaned.

Jordan rushed to Laurel, then pulled her close. "Laurel, I'll always be your friend."

She couldn't cling to Laurel, and she couldn't force her to come with them, but she could make certain that Laurel understood how much she cared. Jordan brushed stinging tears from her cheeks and stepped back.

Laurel's bottom lip trembled. "You were my first... well, my only female friend. You introduced me to Jesus and changed my life completely."

Jordan glanced around the trashed room. The Translifter's intense wind had knocked over vases and scattered sweet smelling flowers all over the floor.

"You risked everything for us when you stole Dawson's computer book. Now you're willing to face Dawson and the Montgomerys all alone. You don't have to do this."

"I'm not alone. Jesus is with me," Laurel said. "We all know I'd never survive in the jungle. No beauty enhancers." She cocked her head and posed.

Matthew ran his hand up and down Jordan's arm. "We have to go."

Laurel nodded and motioned for Jordan to leave. "This is only a temporary goodbye. I'll see you again. I might even come to Old Memphis and hangout with you for a while, once this mess is over."

"You better," Jordan said, as Matthew tugged her across the room. "They'd love you in Old Memphis. They've never seen anyone like you."

Laurel wiped tears from her cheeks. Jordan whispered *goodbye* right before Matthew spun her around and propelled her into the bedroom.

He pulled her into the closet then shoved her down into the dark passageway behind Hannie and Malese. The eerie blue glow shimmered through the light of her tears. She struggled to find the next rung, her shoe slipping on the smooth metal.

Lord, please protect Laurel. I'm afraid she just made the biggest mistake of her life.

CHAPTER 39

*J*ordan jumped from the last rung of the ladder and stood by Hannie and Malese in the dark dressing room closet. They waited for Matthew to join them, then cracked the door and peeked outside. Surely, the GC police wouldn't expect to find the notorious Team Seven cowering in a backstage dressing room. Her breath quickened as they stepped out of the closet.

Hannie tossed a brown scarf to Malese. "Why let a room full of props go to waste?"

Malese draped the scarf around her head and shoulders. Hannie covered her brown curls with a straw hat.

Jordan stepped into a maid costume and pulled it over her clothes. She twisted her hair into a knot and positioned the small black and white cap on her head. Her blazing mop would point her out to every GC police officer in the area.

"I'll go out first and make sure the hall is clear," Matthew said. "Might as well put this security guard get-up to good use." He stepped out then motioned for the girls to join him.

"This morning, I spotted a rear exit leading from the kitchen to the garden," he whispered. "It's the best way I can think of to get out of here."

Jordan, Hannie, and Malese followed Matthew down the hall then down several concrete steps leading to the kitchen. Jordan glanced around the cavernous room. It appeared to be empty. Apparently, an assassination attempt and a menacing Leopard Translifter blocking the sun had caused the kitchen employees to abandon their posts.

They hurried through the kitchen. Large metal pans dangled from hooks, and an assortment of knives protruded from a solid butcher block. The aroma of baked bread, spicy fish, and pungent bananas filled the air.

In front of her, Matthew jerked to a stop. Jordan slammed into his back.

In the corner of the room, a tall, thin man scrubbed dishes in a deep sink, his back to them, and his arms hidden in the silver depths. Soap bubbles and steam floated around him. Jordan held her breath as the man pulled his hand from the water, wiped it on a towel, then turned on a radio. He brushed sweat from his forehead and started singing along with the Latin song.

Matthew pressed his finger to his lips and edged a few feet ahead. He reached an industrial-size freezer about a foot from the door. Two refrigerators stood on either side of the freezer. The man didn't turn around. Matthew waved for the girls to follow.

Jordan tiptoed toward the freezer, her eyes trained on the man. Hopefully, the loud music hid her footsteps. Matthew pulled her beside him. She released a silent sigh as they waited for Malese and Hannie to join them.

Once they were all hidden behind the metal barricade, Matthew inched forward and opened the back door. It squeaked. The music stopped. Jordan's heartbeat sounded like a drum in her ears. Surely, the man would spin around in search of the odd sound. No one moved. The man batted at a fly.

Matthew held the door open and motioned for them to step out as an emergency bulletin blasted from the radio.

"The group of young rebels known as Team Seven are on the run in our city," a female reporter's high-pitched voice stated. "They are considered armed and dangerous. All citizens are ordered to call the GC police if they see these criminals. River Wallis herself is offering a substantial reward."

Jordan shivered as she stepped through the door. River Wallis wouldn't rest until they were imprisoned or dead. Their pictures would be broadcast all over the Latin Collective, maybe even the entire planet.

Her parents would be worried to death. No one in Old Venezuela would help them. Everyone would want the reward. If they failed to reach Hector, Team Seven would become nothing more than foxes surrounded by a pack of hounds.

Jordan struggled against these fears while they hurried down the narrow passageway winding between the kitchen and the west side of the hotel. The eerie silence surprised her. The area seemed deserted. Not even one curious guest stood on the balconies towering above them. Apparently, the police and bystanders had been drawn to the opposite side of the hotel.

A large, vibrant garden separated the hotel from rows of dingy shacks and crumbling apartment buildings. An abundance of green and golden hues promised the way to freedom. Matthew let out a deep breath. The skin around his eyes crinkled in the sunlight, and his jaw was set. *He's as scared as I am.*

A tin can clattered across the cement in front of them, and a shadow covered the area. Mr. Flynt stepped into the alley. He stood a few feet away, blocking their escape. Matthew pointed his rifle at him, and Hannie reached for the pistol at her side.

"I spotted you kids coming through the kitchen." Mr. Flynt motioned to the small door behind him. "Guess you didn't know about the door where they throw out the trash."

"Don't try to stop us, Mr. Flynt." Matthew's voice trembled. "We won't give in without a fight, and I really don't want to hurt you." The rifle shook in Matthew's hands.

Why did Flynt have to confront them now? Sleep and food were the only things he'd ever shown any interest in so, of course, he'd be haunting the kitchen in search of an abandoned feast.

"I don't want to stop you, boy." Mr. Flynt rubbed his round stomach. "I'm proud of my team. I wanted to say goodbye and good luck."

Jordan glanced at Hannie. Her brow wrinkled. Confusion painted Malese's round face. They were cornered. If they retreated through the kitchen, the GC police would nab them. If they barreled past Mr. Flynt, he'd yell for the cops, if he hadn't called the police already. He couldn't possibly be proud of them. What was he up to?

"Aren't you worried about the damage this will do to GCU?" Jordan asked. "If the school goes under, you're out of a job."

"GCU will survive," Mr. Flynt said. "Can't say the same for Principal Reed and Cimarron. I'm going to enjoy watching those two squirm. They always believed they were better than me. I'd bet money that Hunter and River Wallis are behind all of this, but they need a scapegoat. Cimarron and Reed will be lucky if they escape with their lives."

Jordan swallowed the disdain flooding her system. Mr. Flynt didn't care about Sierra Stone's noble ideas or the fact that Cimarron and Principal Reed had tried to kill her. Mr. Flynt enjoyed watching his perceived enemies fall. What a pitiful little man.

"So, I thought I'd congratulate you kids on bringing down the mighty GCU schemers." He stepped out of their way and motioned for them to pass. "Go with my blessing."

Matthew took a few cautious steps. He never looked away from the man or lowered his rifle. Jordan followed close behind. Mr. Flynt could still alert the authorities. But what could they do? They had to trust him. They couldn't shoot an unarmed man, especially not one they'd shared the last six months of their lives with. Mr. Flynt beamed like a proud father as they crept by.

They stepped into the picturesque garden. Harsh, ragged voices danced on the wind that swirled around them. Police officers formed a line in front of a curious crowd at the far end of the garden. The front parking lot had been barricaded, and the cops shouted for the citizens to go home and the guests to return to their rooms.

Malese sought out the tree lined border, and Hannie wound her way through a path of sculpted bushes. Matthew draped his arm around

Jordan's shoulders as they strode past the tall coconut palms and mango trees. *Clever boy.* Surely, no one would be surprised to see a security guard and a hotel maid slipping off for a stroll in the romantic gardens. Jordan jumped at the flutter of wings above her head. A pair of vultures settled on the treetop, sending leaves cascading to the ground.

"I can't believe there aren't more police out here," Matthew whispered. "It's miraculous."

"This has been a week of miracles." Jordan rested her head on Matthew's shoulder as an electric blue butterfly danced in front of them. "I pray God will grant us a few more."

She took a deep breath when she and Matthew stepped from the garden into the alley leading to the park, their journey halfway complete. The stench of trash overflowing its buckets turned her stomach. Plastic cords crisscrossed above them, stretching from one tin roof to the other. Tattered clothes blew in the breeze. Sirens and screeching whistles blared in the distance.

Matthew nodded at several teenage boys working on a muddy car. One of the boys glanced up from the hood long enough to shout a suggestive innuendo at them. Matthew laughed and hugged Jordan close.

Malese limped a few feet in front of them. With the scarf wrapped tightly around her small frame, she looked like an old woman hobbling along.

Jordan twisted her neck to make certain Hannie followed. She didn't like the large expanse between them, but Hannie was an excellent strategist. Hannie's shoulders were back, her stride determined. Soon, they'd all be safely hidden away in the welcoming jungle.

HANNIE WRINKLED her nose at the collection of odors thickened by the damp air. She stepped over a large crack in the blacktop, filled with rancid water. A couple of children played outside a shack on the other side of the alley, and a woman removed clothing from one of the plastic lines.

Hannie peered into the shadows of every connecting alley she passed. The paths crisscrossed like a giant, haphazard puzzle. A dog barked in one alley, and a cat sunbathed on top of a dumpster in another. So far so good. Matthew and Jordan moved at a steady pace ahead of her. Malese should reach the park before any of them. Hannie sighed. Soon, they would be safe. A little girl skipped down the alley with a puppy nipping at her ankles. No threat there.

A heavy weight fell against her, driving her face-first to the blacktop and sending her hat flying. Her nose and cheeks stung. Blood slithered down her throat. Someone grabbed her shoulders and flipped her onto her back. She groaned and looked up into the hard face of a GC police officer. She reached for her pistol, but the man grabbed her wrist and pulled her arm over her head. His knee crushed her left hand into the pavement, making her fingers scream with pain. How could she have been so stupid? She'd let her guard down for only a moment, and now she was trapped.

She squirmed beneath the muscular man, but his weight immobilized her, while gravel and bits of blacktop tore into her fingers. Electrical shocks climbed her spine. The policeman tore the pistol from her belt and flashed a wicked smile, one gold tooth sparkling in the sunlight. He pointed the gun at her face. Hannie closed her eyes.

Why, God, why? One of the chosen people? What a joke.

CHAPTER 40

*H*annie waited for death. Would it hurt? Would she know the moment her soul left her body, if it left at all? Suddenly, the bone-crushing pressure disappeared. Had her soul been whisked away? No gun blast. Perhaps, she was still alive.

She opened her eyes. The police officer lay sprawled about three feet away. Rafael stood beside him. Where had he come from? The officer jumped to his feet, and the men eyed one another, obviously weighing their next moves.

Hannie rose up on her elbows and winced from the pain. Was any of this real? She should be dead now. Her pistol lay on the ground on the other side of the struggling men, way out of her reach.

Rafael punched the officer in the stomach. The officer groaned but soon righted himself and pulled his gun from his holster. Rafael leveled a roundhouse kick, causing the pistol to dislodge and clatter to the pavement. The man staggered then regained his balance and punched wildly. Rafael evaded him. Even though the man was strong and stocky, Rafael's speed and precision gave him a distinct advantage. After landing a couple weak blows, Rafael followed with a knock-out punch to the officer's jaw. The man crumpled to the alley floor, banging his head on the cement.

Hannie couldn't move. Every muscle screamed. She gulped air and struggled to capture her breath in the humid air.

Rafael knelt beside her. He helped her to a sitting position while glancing around the area. "Are you all right, baby? Anything broken?" He'd called her baby. No one ever called her baby. She should object to the demeaning name, but it sounded so nice.

The thud of sneakers struck the pavement. Jordan and Matthew stood above her, panting for air. Malese stepped around the officer's prone body and retrieved both fallen pistols. Crows yelled as they flew over the alley, and a light breeze cooled Hannie's scraped cheeks.

"Are you all right, Hannie?" Jordan's voice cracked.

Hannie managed to nod, still emitting shaky breaths, as Rafael's fingers moved across her arms and ribs. The sun reflected off his raven hair. A romantic young girl might think of him as her knight in shining armor. She blinked and swallowed hard. Thankfully, she was *not* a silly girl.

"She's okay," Rafael said. "Just had the wind knocked out of her. Going to have some nasty scrapes and bruises though." He bent her arm at the elbow. She cringed. Rafael manipulated each of her fingers to make sure they weren't broken, seemingly oblivious to his own bloody knuckles.

"Where've you guys been anyway?" Rafael asked, his brows drawn and annoyance thick in his voice.

"We've been lounging by the swimming pool all day," Jordan said. "Where do you think we've been?"

Hannie grinned. *That should have been my line.*

"Why aren't you waiting for us in the park with Hector?" Matthew asked.

"I couldn't leave my team behind." Rafael winked at Hannie. "I thought you might need me."

Hannie bowed her head. What should she say? *Thanks for saving my life.* Probably the polite thing to say, but this was Rafael, and he'd make a joke out of it or call her a lousy soldier for getting tackled by the enemy.

Rafael stood and motioned to a couple of curious teens on the other side of the alley. "We gotta get out of here. The park isn't far."

He helped her stand then held her while she steadied herself. Her heart rate had slowed, and she no longer gasped for air. No doubt she'd breathe much better when Rafael took his hands off her.

"Where's Laurel?" Rafael asked.

Matthew frowned. "She stayed behind to deal with Dawson."

"What a lousy break." Concern darkened his eyes for a moment, but their rakish sparkle soon returned. "Hector's men would've enjoyed meeting her."

Hannie shook her head. He'd never change.

Rafael wrapped his arm around her waist and pulled her close. Their hips collided, and she tried to move away but he held her tight. "No one will think twice about a couple of security guards helping some frightened girls find their way to the park."

Matthew pulled Jordan close, then grabbed Malese by the arm and moved through the alley.

Rafael propelled Hannie onward. "Come on, baby, let's move."

There he goes with that baby stuff again. I will put a stop to that. Later.

Adults, shaking their heads and murmuring, filled the park while curious, dirty children scurried around, shouting and playing. Food vendors sold their goodies to the people scanning the sky or watching the procession of limos clogging the streets as dignitaries fled the chaos. Team Seven meandered through the crowd without difficulty.

Hector and Juan waited beside a fly infested fruit stand. As soon as Hector spotted them, he waved them to the back of a muddy pickup. Matthew climbed into the truck bed then reached down and helped Jordan and Malese climb in.

"Your chariot awaits." Rafael lifted Hannie into the truck then jumped in behind her. Several large bushels of mangoes, papayas, beans, and rice were stacked on one side of the pickup, leaving only a small hiding space for the fugitives.

"Lie down." Rafael pulled back a black tarp.

Matthew stretched out on his back and pulled Jordan down beside him. Malese obediently sprawled out next to Jordan. Rafael removed his security guard shirt. The sweaty white T-shirt he wore clung to his chest, accentuating every sleek muscle. After donning a baseball cap, he seemed like a typical Venezuelan youth delivering bushels of produce to family and friends. Hannie lay down beside Malese, then Rafael covered them with the dirty tarp.

The scent of rotting produce and human sweat turned her stomach. She flung the thick tarp away. "Get this filthy thing off me."

Rafael smiled at her from his perch on the side of the truck. "Welcome back my little *tigresa*. Now be still and shut up." He tossed the tarp over her face and shouted for Hector to move out.

Hannie bit her tongue to keep from screaming obscenities at Rafael. No doubt, he was enjoying this. He didn't have to lie under some stinky tarp while every bone in his body screamed in pain.

"Go with Hector, and do what he says." David's words haunted her.

So, here she was, heading off to the jungle to live under the control of a rebel leader and his aggravating little brother.

Of course, the little brother did have dreamy dark eyes, ebony hair, and a cocky grin that tore at her heart. His fingers had been gentle when he checked her for broken bones, and she loved it when he held her and called her baby. Hannie cringed at her foolishness. She wasn't a high school girl running away with her buddies for a wild weekend. The Global Collective was spinning out of control, soon to be irrevocably divided over Sierra Stone and her vision for the planet. Hector and his men would eventually be pulled into the fight. They couldn't hide in the mountains forever. She couldn't let her guard down for one minute.

And she certainly couldn't let herself be taken in by Rafael's dubious charms. Yes, he'd been kind to her. He came to her rescue when she needed him, but he'd have done the same for Jordan or Malese. She wasn't special—even if he did call her baby.

Jordan sniffled, and Hannie groaned. She loved Jordan, but the girl was so emotional. She would not allow herself to turn into a crybaby, and she would never allow Rafael to make a fool of her.

Hannie rubbed her bloodied hand and winced at the pain. Hot tears stung her eyes.

"Stop crying, Jordan, before you make me cry." She and Jordan weren't that different after all.

* * *

JORDAN SNIFFED. Hannie was right to yell at her. She shouldn't be weeping in Matthew's arms. Enough was enough. So, things didn't work out quite the way she planned. She wouldn't be reunited with her family today, but Zoe and Paul and the other students were safe. Sierra Stone was alive, and her vision for a liberated Global Collective was still a possibility. God had answered their prayers. Miraculously, they had all survived this crazy adventure. She should be grateful instead of lying here crying.

Oh, Lord, please help me to accept Your will for my life instead of fighting it.

As Matthew said, they'd vacation in the mountains for a while. This would give her more opportunity to minister to Malese and continue to point her toward Jesus. She might pick up some martial arts tricks along the way. Timberlyn was a rare treasure, and she'd enjoy getting to know her better. Her heart swelled when she thought of Victor, her gentle giant, so anxious to learn about Jesus. No doubt, Rafael would keep them all laughing, and maybe she'd finally crack through Hannie's tough exterior and deepen their friendship.

Best of all, Matthew would be by her side. Jordan snuggled closer to him. She reached up and twirled a lock of his hair around her finger. Hopefully, Rafael would remove the smelly tarp when they left the city. Sweat covered her body, and she longed for some cool breeze and the ability to stretch her legs. She bit her lip, determined not to complain. Without Hector, she'd be sweating in a Global Collective prison or dead. She could endure an uncomfortable truck ride.

Matthew's chest rose and fell beneath her cheek. Slow and steady. He'd fallen asleep. Malese lay as still as a corpse. She probably slept, too. Jordan's mind screamed for sleep. Why fight it? God had brought them this far. He would carry them to safety. Jordan closed her eyes and surrendered to the rhythm of the bouncing truck. Soon, she drifted into oblivion.

CHAPTER 41

*J*ordan brushed her hair away from her face as the cool mountain breeze lifted her curls. Matthew stood beside her, lush, green mountain tops surrounding them. Trees swayed. Red, purple, and yellow blossoms covered the bushes and danced on the wind. This was nothing like Old Memphis or the flat delta where cotton grew, and the muddy river flowed by. The mountains surrounding GCU were beautiful in their snowcapped glory, but these mountains sizzled with warmth and life. Jordan took a deep breath and squeezed Matthew's hand while an amusing parrot serenaded them.

"This place is beautiful," she said. "A real Garden of Eden."

"The Pacific coast is awesome, and the western mountains are beautiful, but I've never seen anything like this."

A week had passed since their frantic getaway. Two days of hard travel brought them to Hector's hidden camp. Unlike the sweltering city below, the days in the mountain hideaway were pleasantly warm and humid. At night, the temperatures dipped enough to make everyone appreciate their blankets or sleeping bag.

This jungle camp consisted of tents that could be picked up and moved at a moment's notice, and a few wooden buildings. One stucco structure held modern computer equipment. At least seventy-five men of various ages and several women and children inhabited the camp.

Rafael had assured them they'd be safe here. Hector had warned his men they'd answer to him if they laid a finger on one of the girls. Jordan couldn't imagine anyone wanting to answer to Hector, so she wasn't worried about her safety or the safety of her friends. Of course, any man foolish enough to touch Malese would be thrown across the room by the girl or crushed in Victor's grasp.

Matthew slapped a gnat feasting on his arm. "This certainly isn't the worst place in the world to hide. Although, I could do with fewer biting gnats and mosquitoes."

Jordan nodded. She wanted to claw the back of her legs to stop the incessant itch. Thankfully, Timberlyn had recently discovered a leaf which she'd made into a salve to keep mosquitos away. It wasn't one hundred percent effective, but it helped.

Malese's soft laughter floated on the air. She and Victor sat cross-legged on the ground near Victor's tent. He tickled her face with a pink flower. His bandaged arm hung in a sling that Timberlyn had fashioned to give him extra support while his shoulder wound healed.

"Timberlyn did a great job on Victor's shoulder," Jordan said. "I don't know what we'd do without her."

"She's had a lot of patients since we got up here." Matthew laughed. "She could open her own medical clinic."

Timberlyn knelt at the edge of a dirt path, gathering leaves and roots to make more medicine. The abundance of therapeutic plants growing in this jungle thrilled her. Jordan had teased her about her excitement, but every day Timberlyn dug up something useful.

Paul stood beside Timberlyn, holding a straw basket full of leaves. There hadn't been enough time to sneak Paul out of Old Venezuela after his rescue, so Hector's men had brought him up the mountain. Paul was sad that he wouldn't be returning home right now, but grateful to God and Team Seven to be alive and safe.

"What are you lovebirds up to?" Hannie shouted as she walked down the path toward them, dust flying around her sneakers. Not bothering to acknowledge Timberlyn or Paul, she came to stand beside Jordan and Matthew. With each fading bruise and healing cut, Hannie's feistiness returned.

"We were saying that this is a pretty nice place to hide away for a while," Matthew said.

"Well, I'm not going to get used to this place. I plan to get out of here and join the fight in the real world as soon as possible."

Jordan folded her arms across her chest. "You can't do that. David told us to wait here with Hector, and that's what we're going to do." Hannie might be impulsive, but she wasn't stupid. "You wouldn't know where to go or what to do anyway. You'd probably get arrested."

Hannie frowned and scratched the mosquito bites dotting her arms. "I'll wait for a little while, because David said to, but this place drives me crazy."

"It's beautiful here," Matthew said. "Try to relax and enjoy it."

Rafael sauntered up to them, a smile covering his tanned face. Dressed in fatigue pants and an olive-green T-shirt, he looked at home in the jungle. "Relax and enjoy yourself a little, baby doll."

Hannie put her hands on her hips and glared at Rafael. "I've told you to stop calling me baby. And forgive me if I don't enjoy being stranded in the middle of nowhere with a bunch of misfit, wanna-be soldiers."

Jordan grabbed Hannie's arm and glanced around to see if anyone had overheard. A couple of men stood in the distance, sharing a cigarette, seemingly oblivious to Hannie's harsh words.

"Hannie, these people saved our lives."

Hector had given them this secluded space encircled by thick trees and protective brush so the group could stay together and maintain some privacy.

"You should be grateful to Hector and his men," she said.

Hannie opened her mouth to respond, but Rafael poked her in the ribs. "My little *tigresa*, you should be happy in the jungle. It's your natural habitat."

Hannie slapped Rafael's hand. "How many times do I have to tell you to stop calling me names?"

A spark raced up Jordan's spine. Hannie was in a foul mood today. Was she trying to start a fight with Rafael or just blowing off steam? Thankfully, Rafael ignored her childishness. "When I was younger, I wanted to live up here in these mountains with Hector and his rebels."

"And now here you are. I guess God was listening," Matthew said.

"It is beautiful," Jordan said. "I just hope our time here is limited."

Hannie grunted. "Very limited."

Rafael turned to Hannie. "Come on, baby, let's go play in the jungle and enjoy ourselves while we can."

Hannie's camouflage headband kept her wild curls out of her face as she shook her head and groaned. "You're certifiably *loco*. This whole place is crazy." She moved past Rafael, but he reached out and grabbed her.

In an instant, he'd scooped her up in his arms like a groom carrying his bride over the threshold. He let out a wild yell and started down the dirt path. Jordan's mouth popped open, amazed at Rafael's brazen action and Hannie's calm composure. The calm didn't last long.

"Put me down, you idiot," Hannie yelled, twisting in Rafael's arms.

Rafael ignored her protests and walked straight ahead like a soldier following orders and completely oblivious to the danger he'd stepped into.

Jordan glanced at Matthew. Was he going to interfere? A crooked grin covered his face. Victor and Malese sat on the ground, holding hands and staring wide-eyed at the commotion. Rafael nodded at them as he walked by.

"Matthew, should we stop him?" Jordan asked.

Matthew shook his head. "Rafael would never hurt Hannie. But if he ever puts her down, he'd better run, because she's going to kill him."

What had Hannie said about Rafael months ago at GCU? *"Rafael is scorching hot."* The memory tickled Jordan.

Of course, a lot had happened since then, but the two had kissed last week at the banquet. Matthew had told Jordan about the kiss, since Hannie hadn't bothered to share this big news with her. Jordan had overlooked the rules of best friend etiquette and let it pass considering they were trapped in the middle of a life and death struggle. But Matthew had said Rafael enjoyed the kiss and was attracted to Hannie.

"Oh, Hannie will be mad, and she'll want to kill him, but..." Jordan leaned her head against Matthew's shoulder. "Somehow, I think he'll win her over."

* * *

HANNIE BOBBED up and down in Rafael's arms as he strode down the bumpy path. She took a deep breath. If rage could kill, Rafael would hit the dirt any minute. He had no idea how much trouble he was in.

Just wait until I'm back on my feet, buddy.

"Put me down, right now," she said. "I'm getting sick." She wasn't lying. Her stomach sloshed, and her head ached.

Rafael came to a sudden stop. The sound of rushing water caught her attention. The dirt path blended with a green blanket-like expanse that led down to a bubbling stream. Sunshine sparkled on the water as it flowed over slick rocks. Rafael wouldn't dare throw her in that cold stream. What was she thinking? This was Rafael Alvarado. He'd dare anything.

"You've had your fun, Rafael. Put me down, now." Her teeth chattered, anticipating that he would soon toss her in the water. "I may throw up or faint."

"Ha, you're too mean to faint. But my arms are tired."

"Then put me down you simple-minded, conceited, louse."

"I get the picture, and I'll do anything for you, my lovely *tigressa*." He placed her on her feet and offered a chivalrous bow.

Hannie staggered. Her hand itched with the desire to slap that mischievous smile off his face, but she wanted answers first.

"Why did you drag me out here?" She folded her arms over her chest. "Have you gone completely crazy?"

"I wanted you and me to have a chance to talk about... things."

Hannie's cheeks burned. She took a step back. He wanted to talk about that blasted kiss at the banquet. Why did he have to bring that up?

"We don't have anything to talk about."

"Well, this is a jungle paradise." He motioned toward the vine-laden trees that stretched for miles in every direction then seemingly climbed to the top of the mountain to be kissed by the waiting sun. "I know you hate being stuck up here, but you might enjoy it more if we spent some time together. We could swing from the trees, baby."

Hannie sparked at his arrogance. Did he really expect her to be happy in the middle of nowhere just because she could be with him? She was not a member of his teenage fan club.

She straightened her shoulders. "Rafael, you're not my dream man, and I'm certainly not your girl." She moved farther back, needing to distance herself from the aggravating boy before she slapped him or kissed him. She wasn't sure which was more likely.

Rafael's eyes grew wide. Was he angry? Hurt? Embarrassed? He reached out to her. "Don't take another step back."

"Stop telling me what to do." Hannie's shoe slipped, and she wobbled side to side. She grabbed for Rafael, hoping to keep her balance. No such luck. The mush beneath her feet disintegrated. The ledge she stood on disappeared, taking both of them to the muddy floor below.

"Ugh," she yelled. Thankfully, the soft mud had cushioned her fall. She had enough bruises already. Rafael lay sprawled on his stomach across from her. She flung a fistful of mud at his already filthy face.

He laughed. "Do you want to mud wrestle?"

She slapped the muck that encased her. Mud flew in all directions. "I want to drown you."

"Let's clean up first." Rafael slowly extracted himself from the oozing mud then plunged into the stream. He swam under the glistening water and emerged on the other side. Spotless.

She groaned. Could life get much worse? Here she was stuck in these mountains far away from the action. It wasn't fair. She had a lot to contribute to the cause. After all, if she hadn't convinced Jordan to hack Cimarron's computer back at GCU, Sierra Stone would be dead now. She and Team Seven had foiled River Wallis's scheme, and David sent them away to hide like children who needed protection. Hannie didn't believe

David's optimistic prediction that this political struggle would soon end. He might have fooled the others, but not her.

She sighed. She didn't care for long baths, and she'd never been a beach girl. A quick shower every morning was enough for her. But slime covered every inch of her body. What choice did she have? She pulled her feet out of the goo and staggered toward the stream. The cold penetrated her sneakers as she put her foot in the water. She waded out to waist level then splashed her arms, neck, and face.

Rafael sat, laughing, on the other side of the stream. Hannie held her breath and ducked her head under the surface. Her thick curls fanned out in the water since she'd lost her head band in the muck. Her sneakers would never be the same. Shivering, she tossed her soaked hair over one shoulder and started for the shore.

"Rafael, if you had any sense, you'd run while you still can."

"You're beautiful when you're wet and angry," he said.

She stopped. Had Rafael really uttered those words? No. She must be hallucinating. "I'm not beautiful. Angry or otherwise." She continued trudging through the cold water.

A toucan screeched from an overhanging tree. Was he complaining because she'd destroyed his solitude or chiding her for her foolishness? If she believed Rafael's dubious compliments, she'd deserve the toucan's rebuke.

She reached the shore, and Rafael stretched out his hand. Against her better judgment, she took it and let him pull her down beside him. All her angry, hateful words had vanished. She couldn't speak. She certainly couldn't think straight.

He brushed wet strands of hair away from her face "You're beautiful to me. I've never understood why you try so hard to make people dislike you. What are you afraid of?"

"I guess I'm afraid of crazy apes like you." She punched his shoulder hard. Too hard. She wanted to do much more. She wanted to strangle him. But when she stared into his chocolate eyes, her heart flipped.

Rafael bent his head and brought his lips to hers. The touch was gentle, as if he was trying to read her mind before he went too far.

Push him away, Hannie. You're too smart to fall for this.
She pressed her lips closer to his and deepened the kiss. She shivered. He pulled away from her. "You're cold. I need to get you back to camp so you can get in some dry clothes."

"I'm not shivering because of the cold water." She slapped her palms against her burning cheeks. *Shut up, shut up, Hannie.* She'd just admitted that Rafael's kisses made her shiver. Had she lost her mind? She clasped her trembling hands in front of her. "So, exactly what do you like about me?" What was she doing? She must have jungle fever. But she couldn't stop now. "Are you interested in me because I'm here and available?"

"You're brave, strong, and terrific in a fire-fight. I like that combination in a girl." He wrapped his arm around her and pulled her close. "I've always thought you were pretty, but I've always been afraid of you."

"And I've always been afraid of you because you're a Latin playboy."

"No, I'm not," Rafael said. "I'm just a boy."

"A boy who has girls flirting with him all of the time."

"Is it my fault I'm irresistible?"

She jerked away from him. A smart retort rested on her lips, but Rafael winked, and she relaxed. "What about Jordan? Have you gotten over her? She broke your heart, didn't she?"

Rafael slapped his hand across his chest and grinned. "You sure expect a lot from an eighteen-year-old guy. Sure, I was attracted to Jordan, but it's over now. I never loved her or anything, not the way Matthew does. She was a challenge."

Hannie twirled a soggy curl around her finger. "Like I am? Just a challenge."

He grinned. "Baby, no one is more challenging than you."

She stared hard at Rafael, hoping to find the truth somewhere in his dark eyes.

"Could you really be interested in a girl like me?"

"You're the only girl I want to run through the jungle with." He gripped her chin and brought his lips to hers once again. The kiss was stronger this time and full of warmth.

After the kiss, Hannie rested her head on Rafael's shoulder. They silently watched the sparkling brook meander through the jungle. Maybe she should relax and act like a girl for a little while. She'd played many roles in life. Orphan, stepchild, student, soldier. Never teenager on the verge of love. She sighed. A few months in these mountains wouldn't be so bad after all.

CHAPTER 42

*J*ordan watched the large condor soaring over the mountaintops. What did he see from his vantage point, free to fly overhead and watch the human chaos below? If only she had the condor's insight.

"I wonder what's happened in the real world since the last update Hector received," she said, never looking away from the giant bird. She was afraid to look at Matthew. Afraid of the fear and concern she might see on his face.

"Everything is probably a big mess right now. When David sent the last update from Israel, he said Ms. Stone would soon be going to Paris to confront Hunter and River Wallis." Matthew took her hand in his. "Ms. Stone is a smart politician, and David is there to help her. They'll know the right things to do."

Jordan wanted to believe Matthew's prediction. She wanted to share his confidence, but she didn't. Sierra Stone would be fighting Hunter and River Wallis once again. She'd lost the first time. How much of this battle would be political, and how much would be vicious and bloody? Hunter and River Wallis would never relinquish one drop of power. Not without a fight.

"Do you think our families will be safe?" Jordan asked the question that haunted her dreams. She pictured the fear in Abby's eyes as the GC police dragged her family from their beds and put them in some awful prison. The idea that her family might be suffering while she lived in relative safety tortured her.

Matthew squeezed her hand. "Ms. Stone said she'd protect them, and I believe her. Plus, the Global Collective Council is plenty busy trying to survive the publicity of a failed assassination attempt and dealing with Ms. Stone's supporters. Harming our families wouldn't help them."

Jordan nodded. "That makes sense." Their families weren't important to the great Global Collective Council. Obscurity could be a blessing.

A spider monkey screeched overhead, tree limbs swaying as he flew through the branches. Jordan jumped and stepped closer to Matthew.

"Do you think Laurel's safe?" she asked. "We both know how crazy Dawson is."

"There's no doubt he's crazy." Matthew shook his head. "But I don't believe he'd harm Laurel. I'm sure he was furious, but in his own twisted way, he loves her. And a man will do anything in his power to protect the woman he loves." He flashed his wonderful, crooked smile, then wrapped his arm around her shoulders and pulled her close. She snuggled against his chest, a perfect fit.

"Ms. Stone and her supporters will be victorious," Jordan said. If only her heart believed her confident words. She glanced up at Matthew when he didn't respond. "You believe that, don't you?"

He bent his head and kissed her forehead. "I know Ms. Stone will be victorious because God is on her side. He sent us to stop her assassination. It wasn't dumb luck. He has a plan."

"I wish that plan hadn't made us criminals. It was never my girlhood dream to grow up and become a fugitive."

"We're criminals to some, but heroes to others."

"What a strange bunch of heroes." Jordan giggled. She was the least heroic of all. Heroes weren't afraid of spiders, they didn't jump at the sound of a jungle jaguar, and they didn't cry. Did they?

"God's strength is made perfect in weakness." Matthew reminded her of one of her favorite Bible verses.

Jordan had never been strong. She depended on God to be her strength. "Maybe that's why he decided to use this bunch of hesitant heroes," she said. "It's been a wild, miraculous ride."

"And now here we are on a beautiful mountaintop in the Latin Collective." Matthew gestured toward the thick jungle surrounding them. "Pretty romantic, huh." He winked and squeezed her shoulders.

"Considering we're living with dozens of dirty rebel fighters, we sleep on the ground, and use outdoor toilets, I'm not sure I'd call it romantic." A tarantula crawled up the side of a tree, and Jordan shuddered.

"Consider it an extended camping trip, like people used to take for fun years ago."

"I can rough it for a while, as long as it's temporary."

"You heard David. A few weeks, maybe a few months, but temporary."

She'd endured life at GCU for almost a year. She could survive a few months in the jungle. "And then you and your dad and Chloe will move to Old Memphis. We can attend the local university and do typical teenage things."

A comically shocked expression covered Matthew's face. "What do you mean? Firefights, destroying force fields, and rescuing government leaders aren't typical teenage activities?"

"As much fun as all of that may be, I'd rather go for a walk in the park, play with my little sister and brothers, and go to our small, homey church on Sunday morning," she said.

"And sit on your favorite pew holding hands with your boyfriend?"

She bowed her head. Why did she still get shy at the thought of romance? Without warning, Matthew scooped her up in his arms. "Maybe I should take a cue from Rafael. This will be good practice for the day I carry you over the threshold."

Jordan laughed, but her cheeks burned. Threshold? Was he serious or cutting up like Rafael? She gently swung her legs and snuggled closer to Matthew.

"I'm serious, Jordan." Matthew's voice was hoarse. Had he read her mind? "I know that's our destiny."

She wanted to believe that they had a wonderful future ahead of them, but everything was so chaotic. Surely, God didn't bring them this far to abandon them now. She took a deep breath, and hope filled her lungs along with the floral-heavy mountain air.

"It's like the story of Esther in the Bible," she said. "God brought us to GCU for a certain mission at a certain time. GCU believed they put our team together, but Team Seven was crafted by God. Look how He's used every one of us to accomplish His purposes. He won't leave us now. He's leading us forward into a better future for our collectives."

Matthew set her on her feet then spun her around to face him. "And we'll have some great stories to tell our grandchildren." He grinned, and Jordan's heart plummeted the way it had the first day they met. Grandchildren? He was moving a little fast, but it sounded so good.

"For such a time as this." She smiled. "For such a time as this."

"…And who knows but that you have come to royal position for such a time as this."

ACKNOWLEDGMENTS

It's taken many years to write *Hesitant Heroes* and the other books in *The Divine Destiny Trilogy*. Many people have helped me along the way.

First, I'd like to thank my parents, who have always been supportive of my dreams. Even the foolish ones.

My family and friends have encouraged me in my writing endeavors.

As I wrote *Hesitant Heroes*, I submitted chapters to the ACFW Scribes online critique group. Many wonderful people chose to read my submissions and offer invaluable feedback.

A big thank you goes out to Scribes 209, the Storyteller Squad. I have learned so much from this talented group of writers. I couldn't have written *Relentless Rebels* and *Defying Destiny* without their feedback. They are great blog partners, too.

I can't begin to say how much my local ACFW Memphis chapter means to me. Our meetings are always fun and informative. They have guided and encouraged me in this writing adventure.

I'd like to thank Cyle Young for submitting my manuscripts to Anaiah Press. I'm very grateful that Anaiah Press was willing to take a chance on an unknown YA author.

Thank you, thank you, thank you to my wonderful editor Kara Leigh

Miller. She helped me craft *Hesitant Heroes* into a solid and well written manuscript.

Above all, I want to thank the Lord Jesus Christ. He is the source of my talent and my dreams.

ABOUT THE AUTHOR

Sharon Rene is a legal assistant who loves cats, and writing. She lives in Memphis, Tennessee where she has taught Sunday school in the children's and youth departments for over fifteen years. In 2018 her book of short stories for children entitled A Mixed Bag of God's Grace was published. She's also published numerous flash fiction stories.

As an only child, Sharon has always been very close to her parents. She spent a lot of time reading and developed a huge imagination which she now channels into writing.

Church has always been an important part of Sharon's life and she's participated in mission trips to Argentina, Venezuela and Nicaragua. Sharon could vividly picture the wild beauty of the country as she wrote the Venezuela scenes in Hesitant Heroes.

Sharon has lived in Mississippi, Texas, Louisiana, and Florida. She currently resides in Memphis Tennessee.

Sharon is grateful that God has given her the opportunity to reach young people with her words and hopes her writings will help them grow closer to God.

If you'd like to contact Sharon Rene, write her at sharonrene17@ gmail.com. She loves to hear from her readers.

Website
www.sharonreneauthor.com

The Storyteller Squad blog
https://storytellersquad.com/2021/04/22/

Made in the USA
Monee, IL
24 September 2021

78028851R00167